PEARL
OF THE SEA

by Anthony Silverston,
Raffaella Delle Donne
and Willem Samuel

Published by Catalyst Press
El Paso, Texas, USA

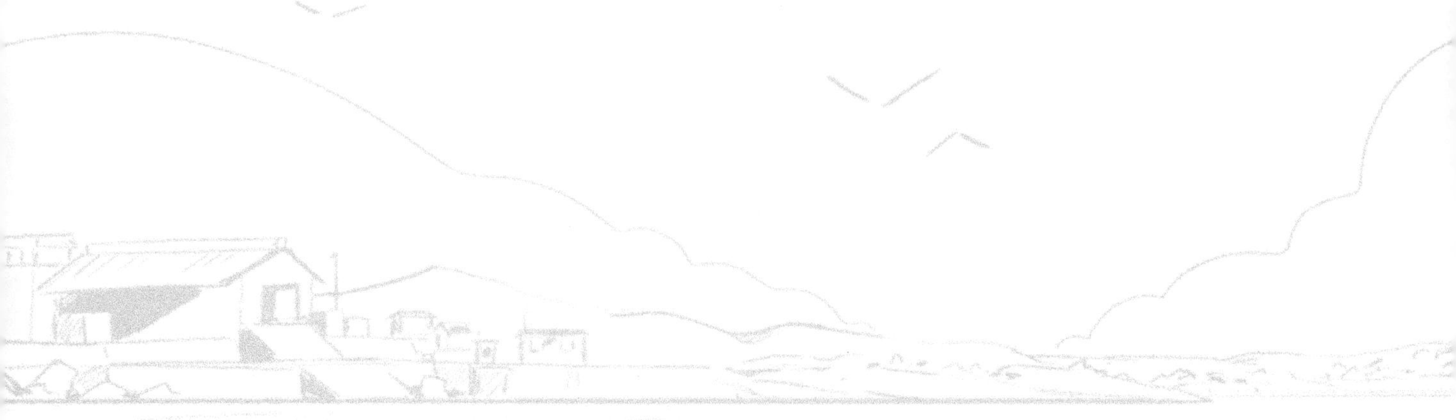

For further information, write info@catalystpress.org
In North America, this book is distributed by
Consortium Book Sales & Distribution, a division of Ingram.
Phone: 612/746-2600
cbsdinfo@ingramcontent.com
www.cbsd.com
In South Africa, Namibia, and Botswana,
this book is distributed by Protea Distribution.
For information, email orders@proteadistribution.co.za.
FIRST EDITION
10 9 8 7 6 5 4 3 2 1
ISBN 9781946395740
Library of Congress Control Number: 2022944731

STORY BY

Anthony Silverston and Raffaella Delle Donne

Willem Samuel

LAYOUT

Willem Samuel

ADDITIONAL LAYOUT

Gabriela Camarillo

Kay Carmichael

Jessi Ochse

INKING AND TEXT

Jessi Ochse

COLOUR

Clyde Beech

EDITS

Wayne Jones

THANKS

Bernice Purdham · Lara Goodman · Julia Smuts Louw

Stuart Forrest · Mike Buckland · Jean-Michel Koenig

James Middleton · Julie Hall · Aoife Lennon-Ritchie

Vanessa Sinden · Wayne Thornley

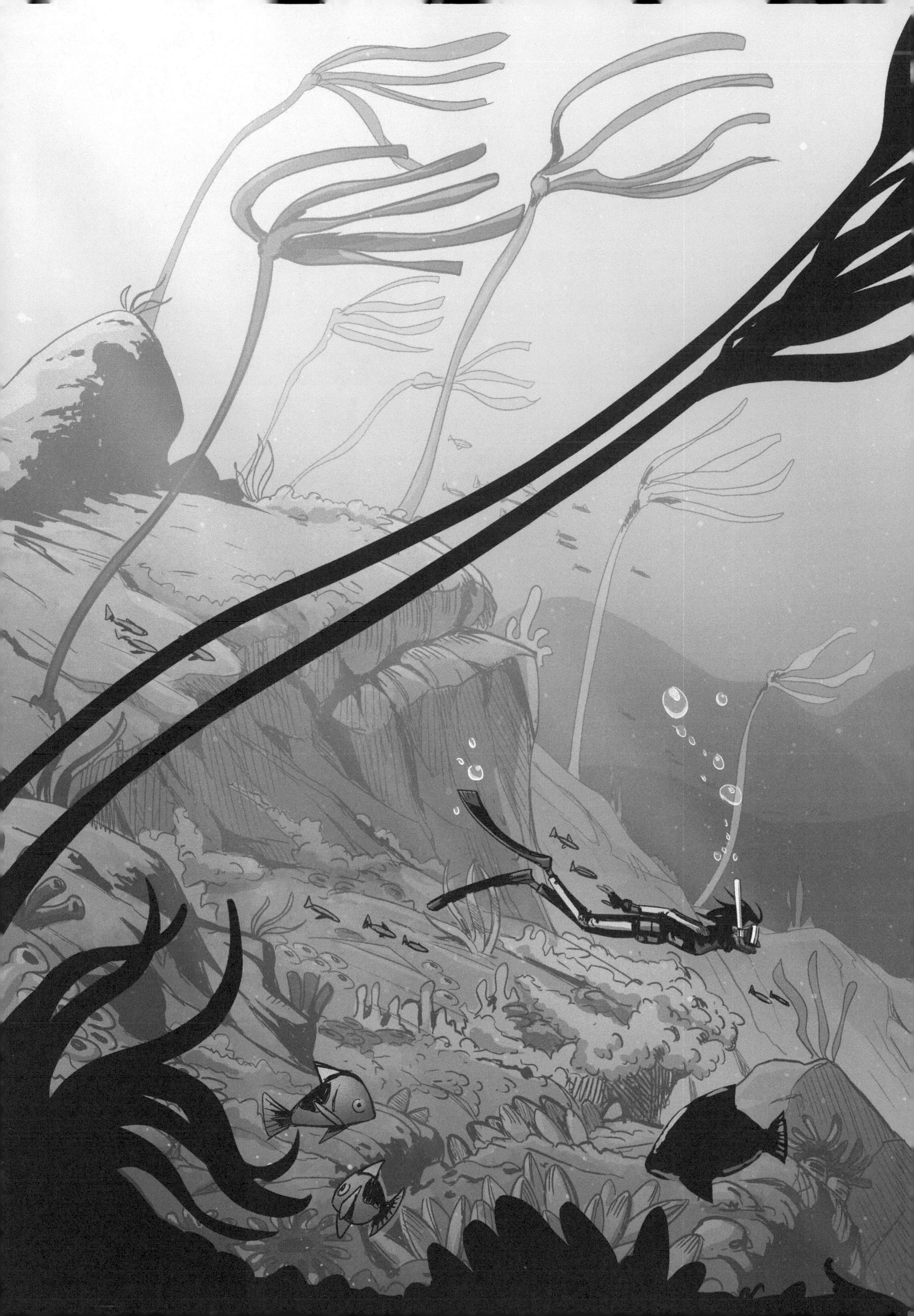

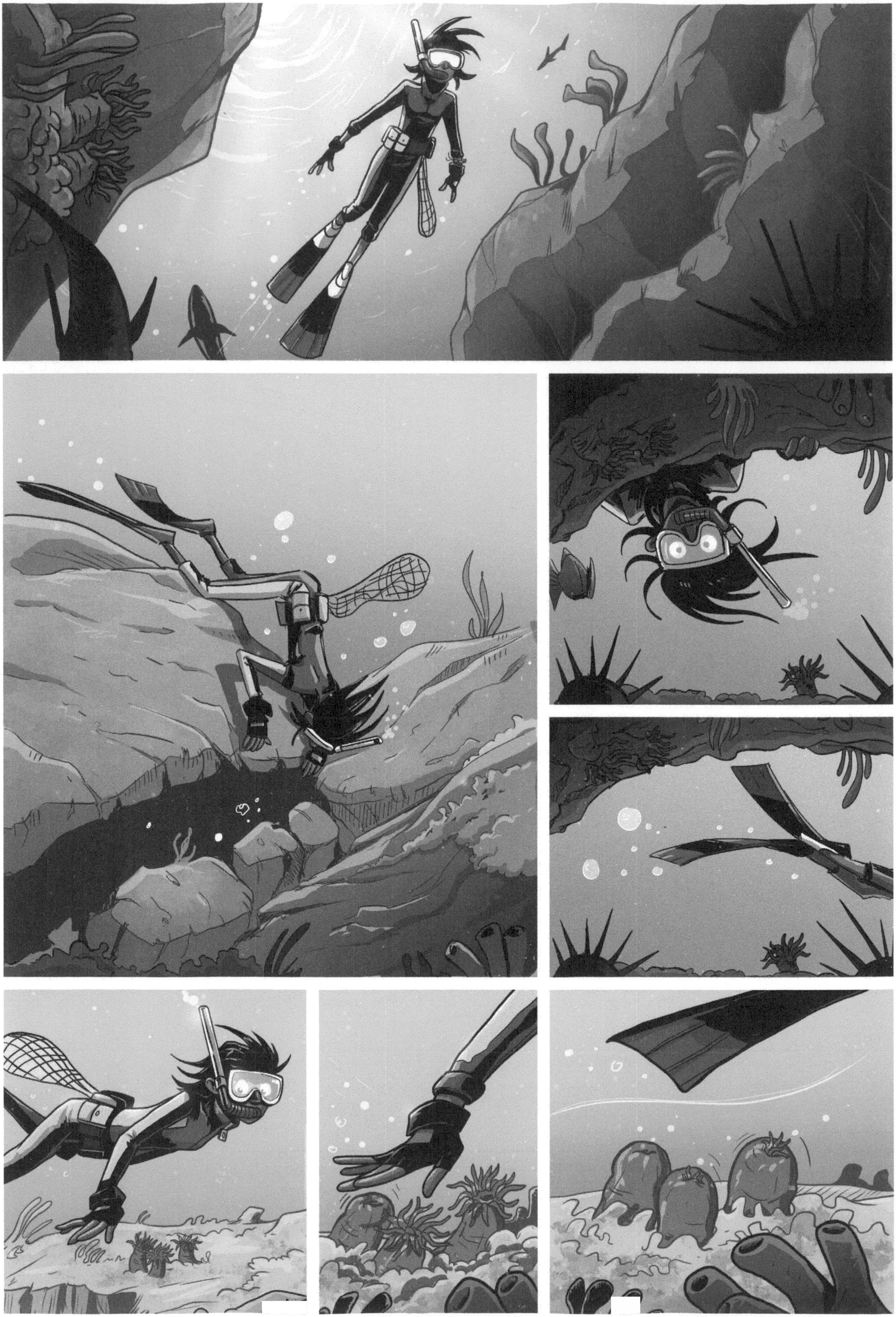

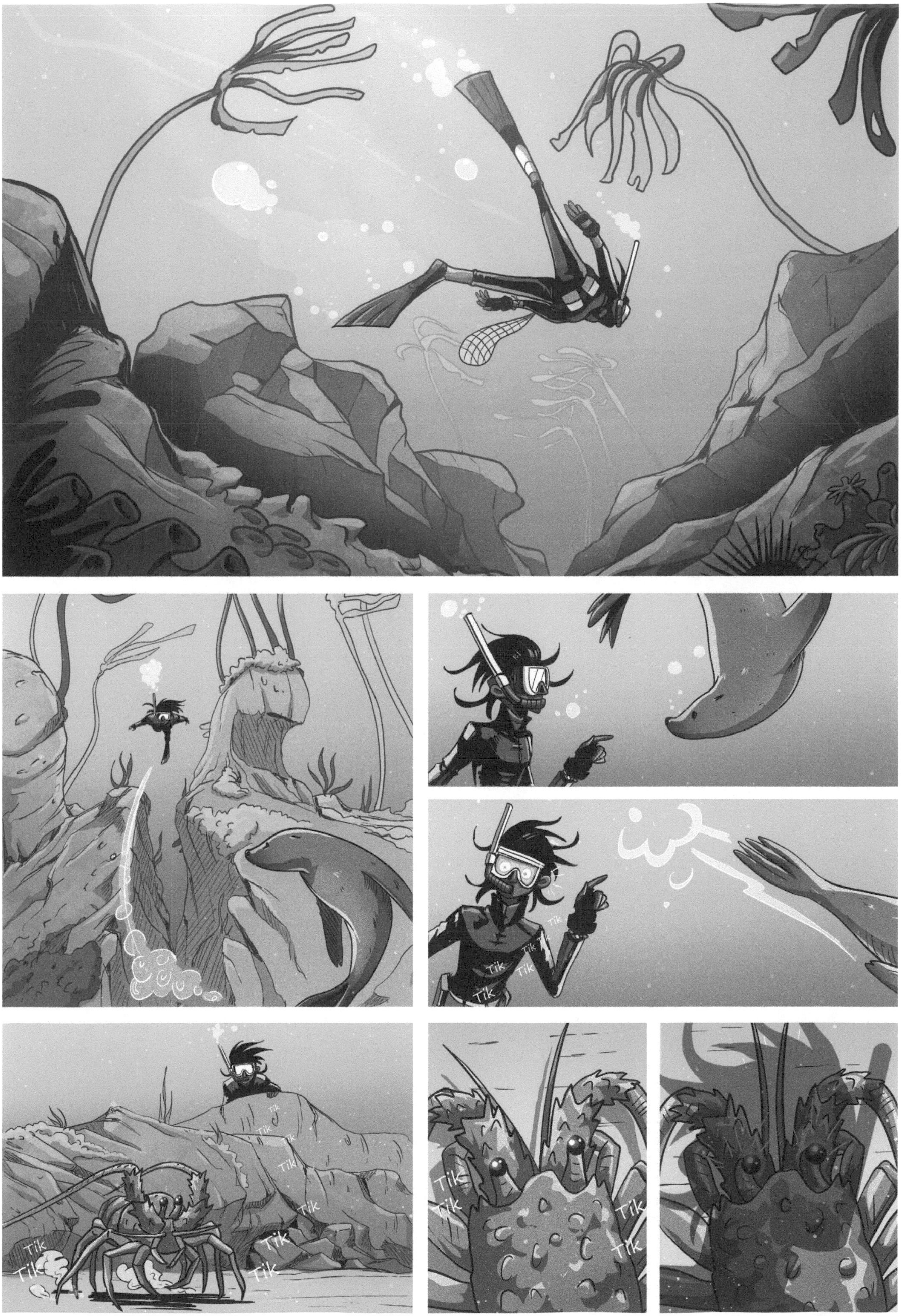
Tik
Tik
Tik
Tik
Tik
Tik
Tik
Tik
Tik
Tik
Tik
Tik
Tik
Tik
Tik
Tik
Tik
Tik

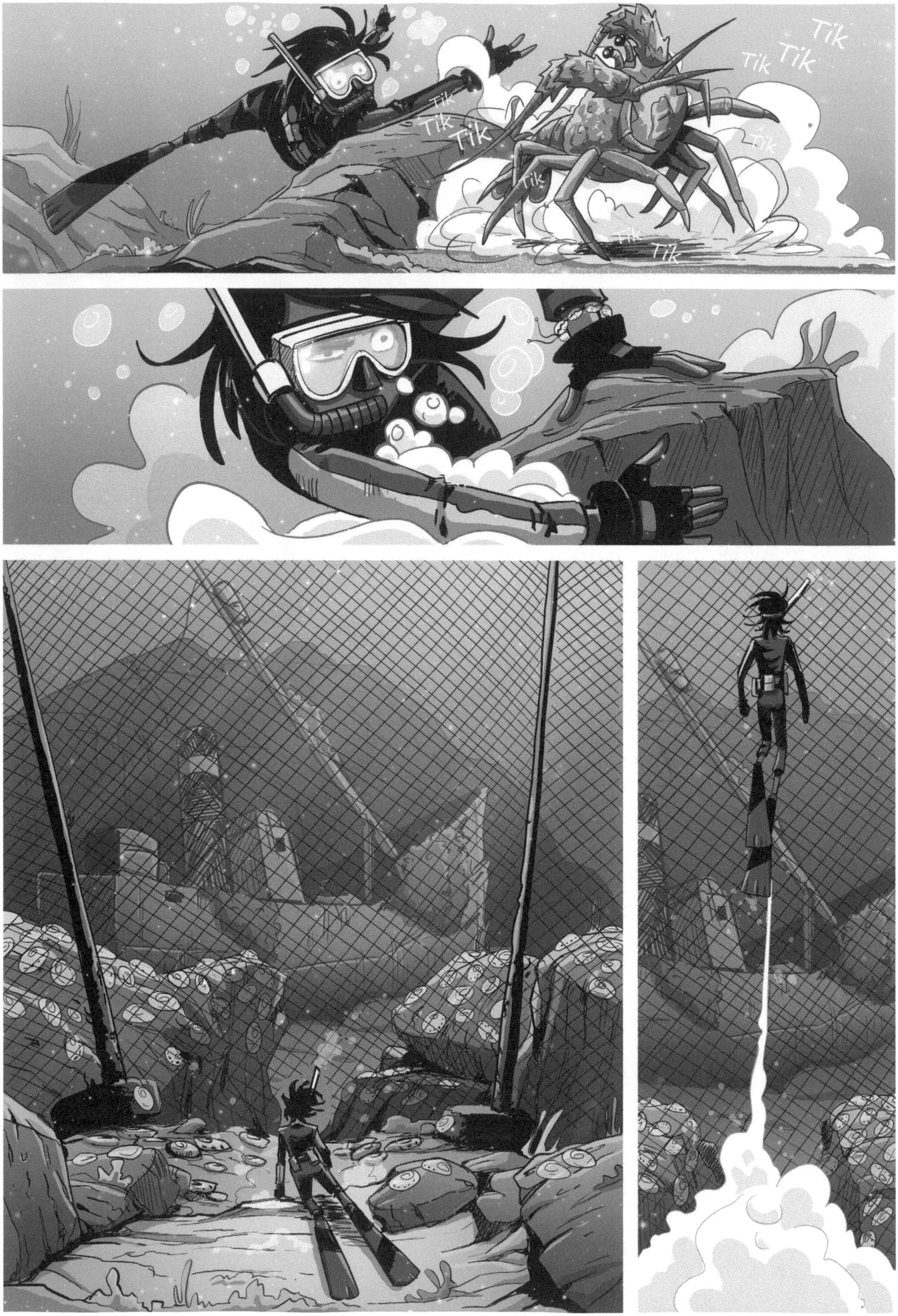
Tik
Tik
Tik
Tik
Tik
Tik
Tik
Tik
Tik
Tik

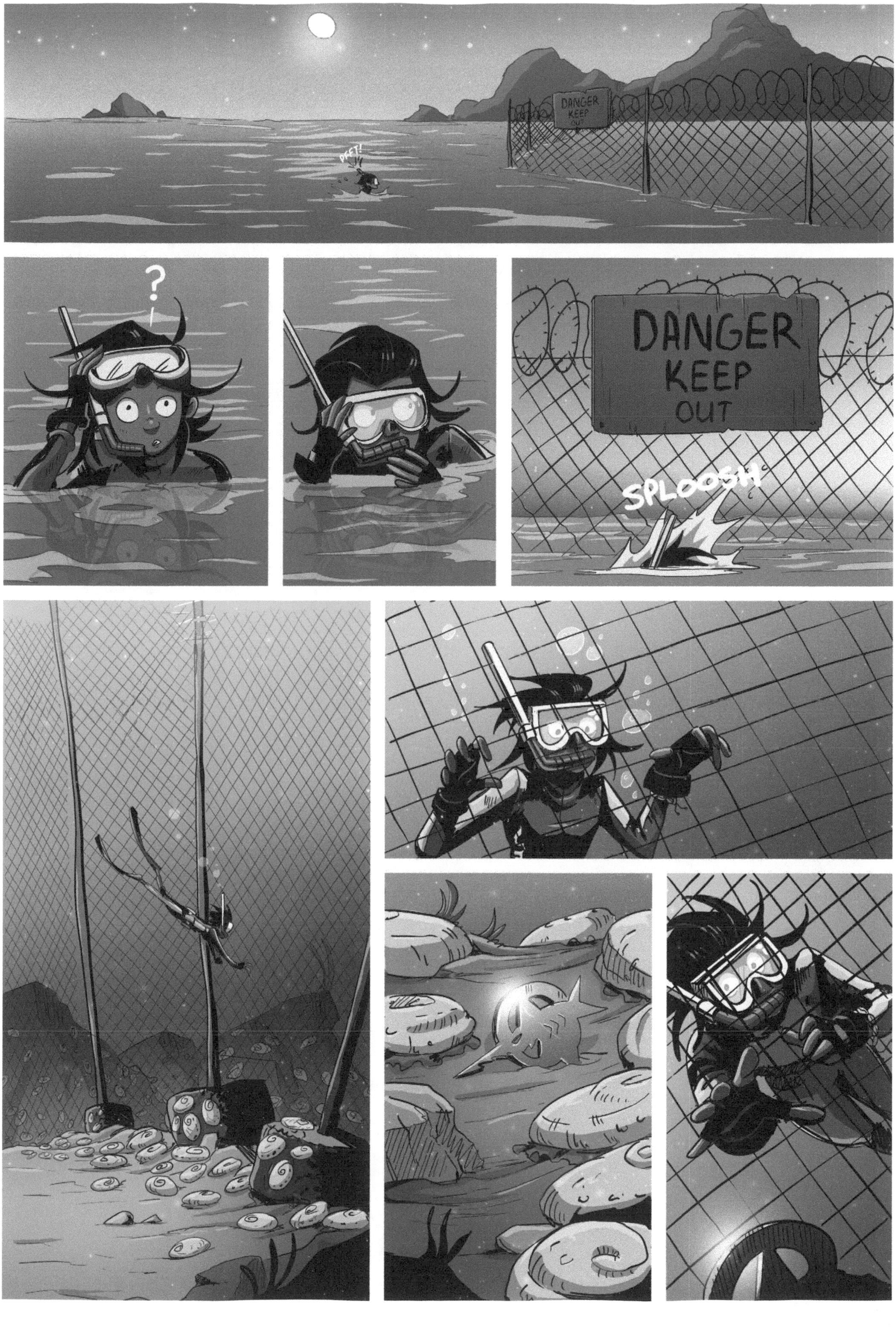
DANGER KEEP OUT
PFFT!
?
DANGER
KEEP
OUT
SPLOOSH

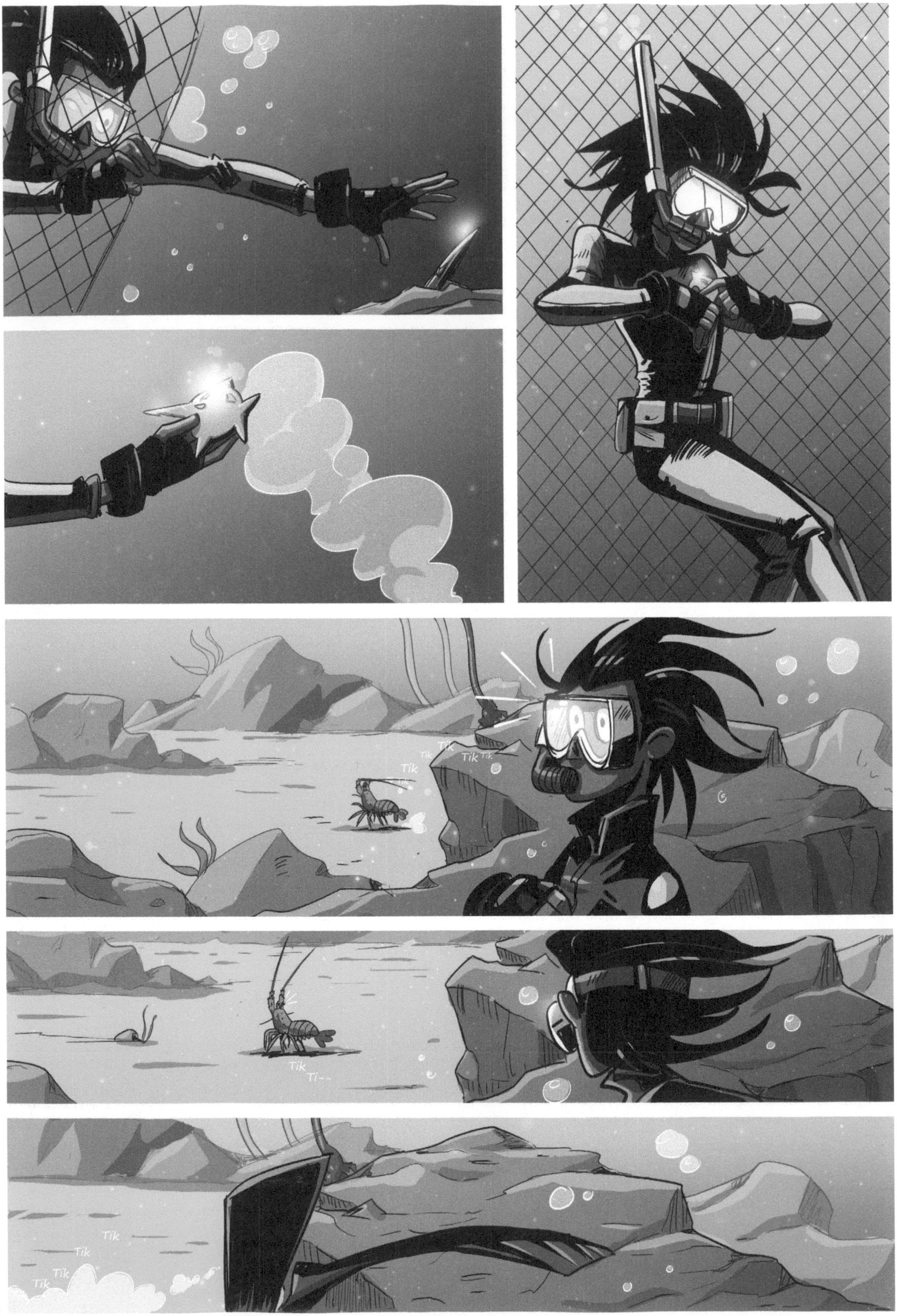
Tik Tik Tik Tik Tik
Tik
Tik
Tik
Ti--
Tik
Tik
Tik
Tik

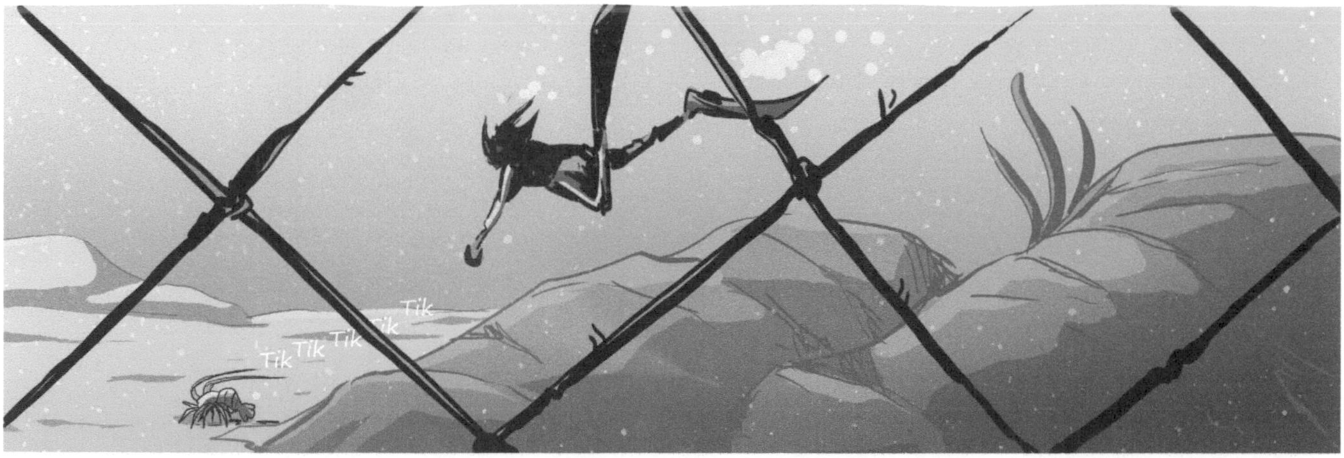
Tik Tik Tik Tik Tik

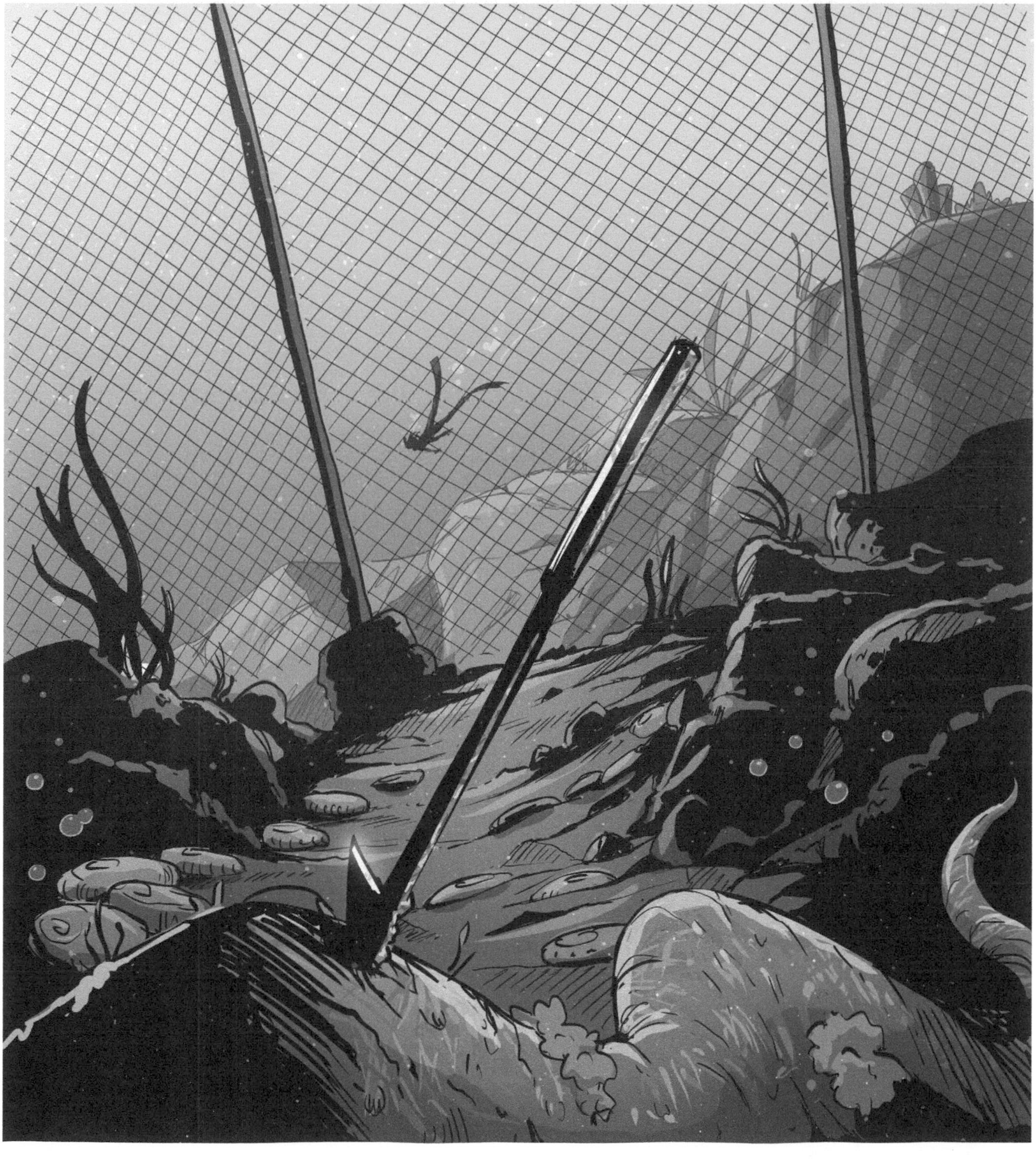

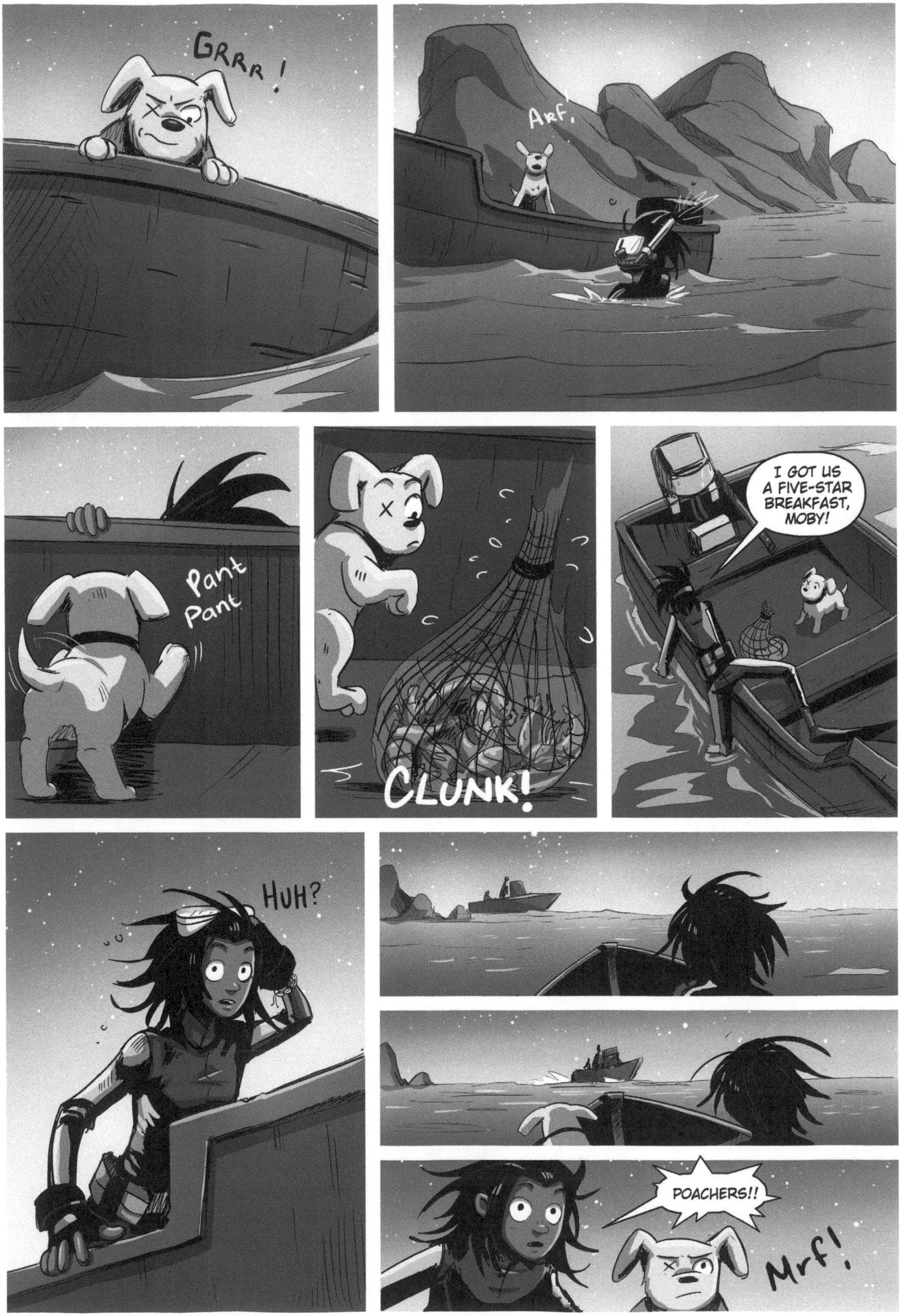
GRRR!
ARF!
Pant Pant
CLUNK!
I GOT US A FIVE-STAR BREAKFAST, MOBY!
HUH?
POACHERS!!
Mrf!

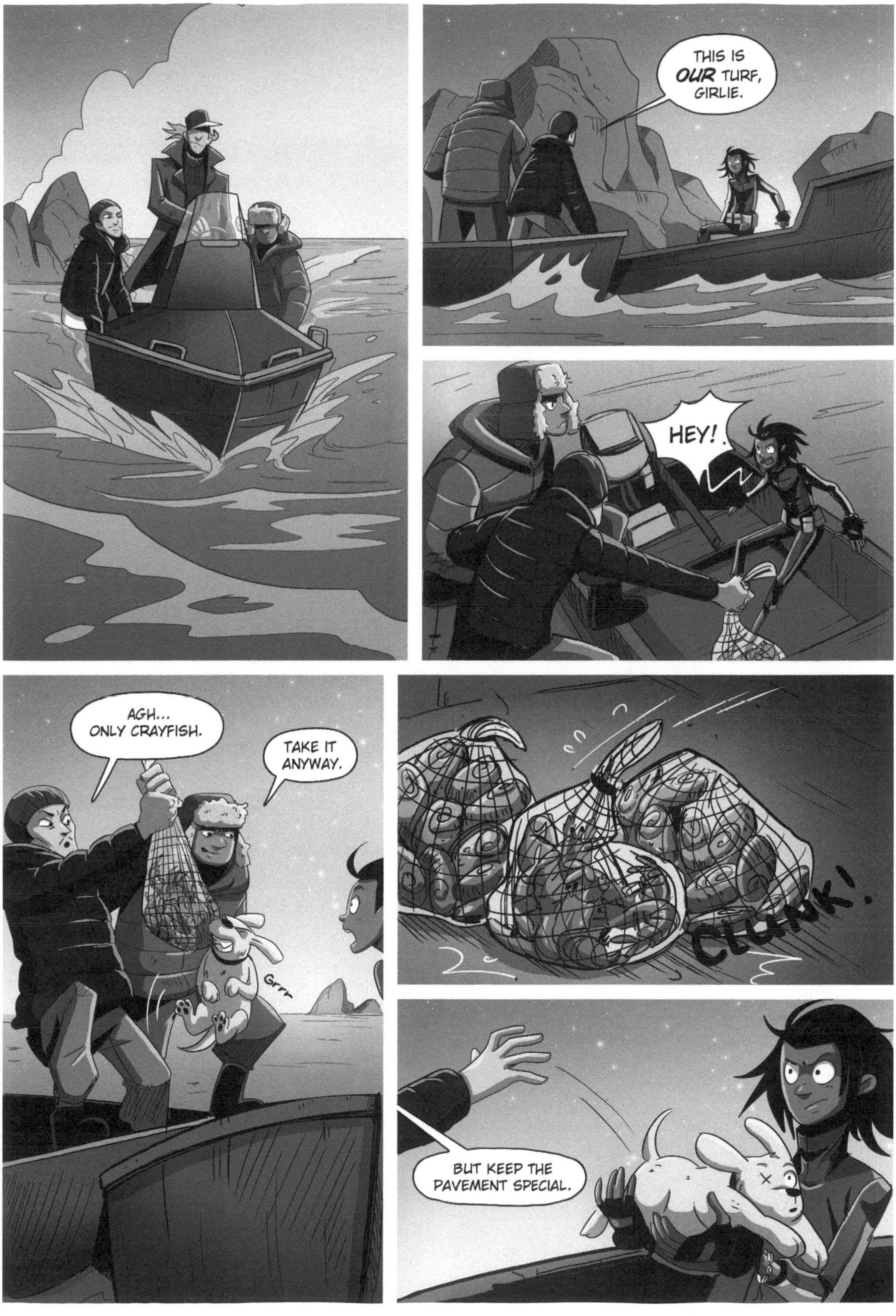
THIS IS OUR TURF, GIRLIE.
HEY!
AGH... ONLY CRAYFISH.
TAKE IT ANYWAY.
Grrr
CLUNK!
BUT KEEP THE PAVEMENT SPECIAL.

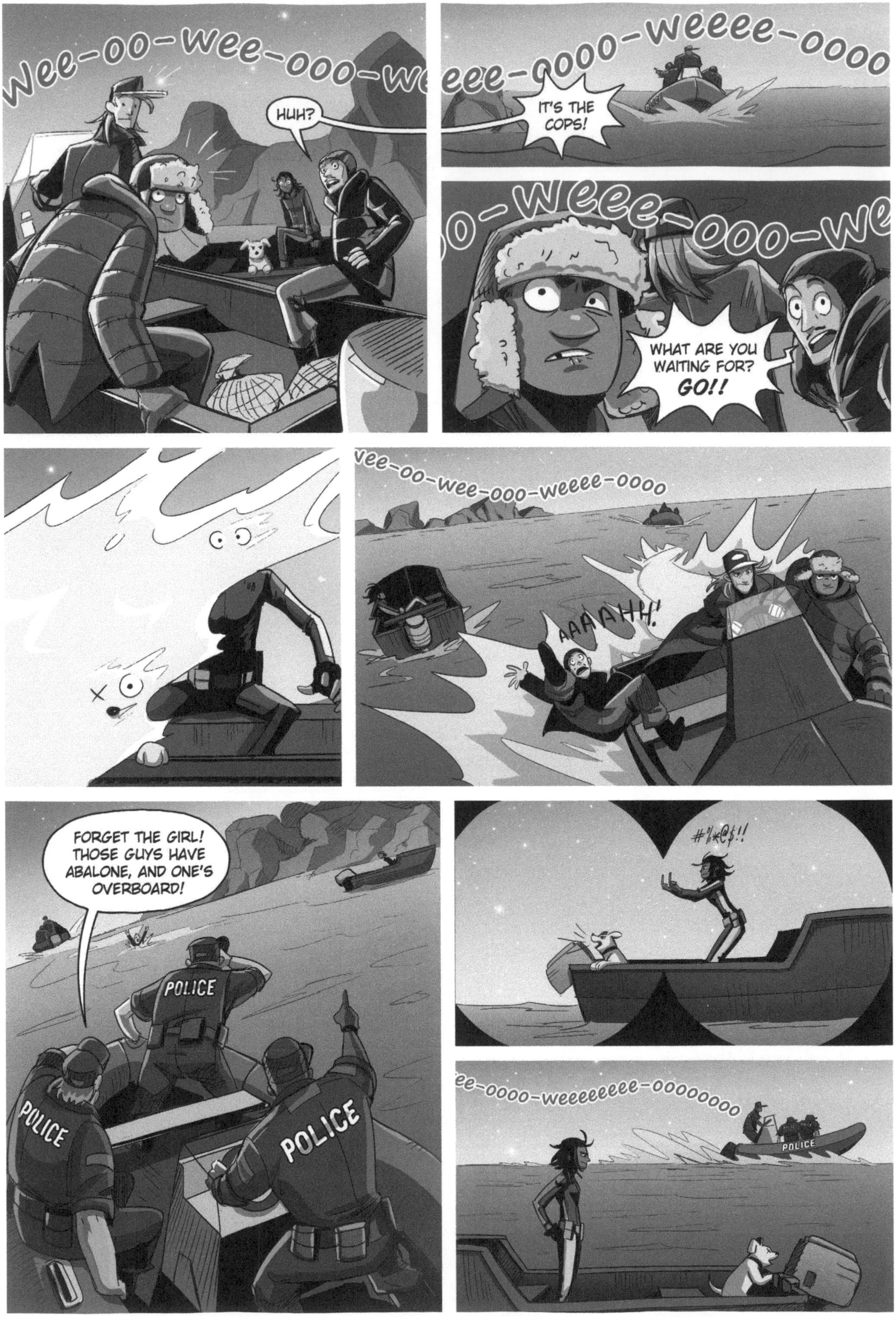
Wee-oo-wee-ooo-w
eee-oooo-weeee-oooo
HUH?
IT'S THE COPS!
o-weee-ooo-we
WHAT ARE YOU WAITING FOR? GO!!
wee-oo-wee-ooo-weeee-oooo
AAAAHH!
FORGET THE GIRL! THOSE GUYS HAVE ABALONE, AND ONE'S OVERBOARD!
POLICE
POLICE
POLICE
ee-oooo-weeeeeee-ooooooo
POLICE

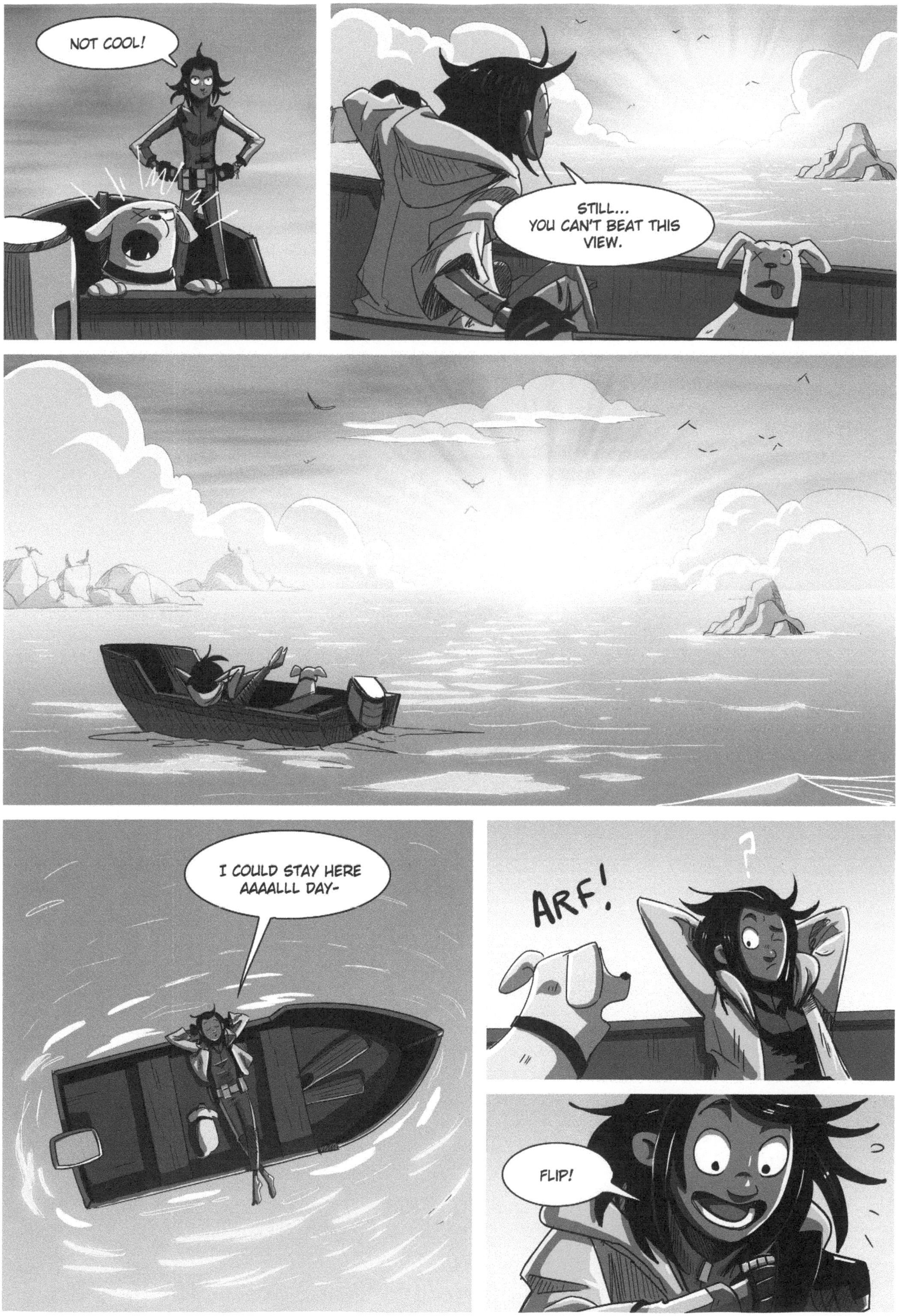
NOT COOL!
STILL... YOU CAN'T BEAT THIS VIEW.
I COULD STAY HERE AAAALLL DAY-
ARF!
?
FLIP!

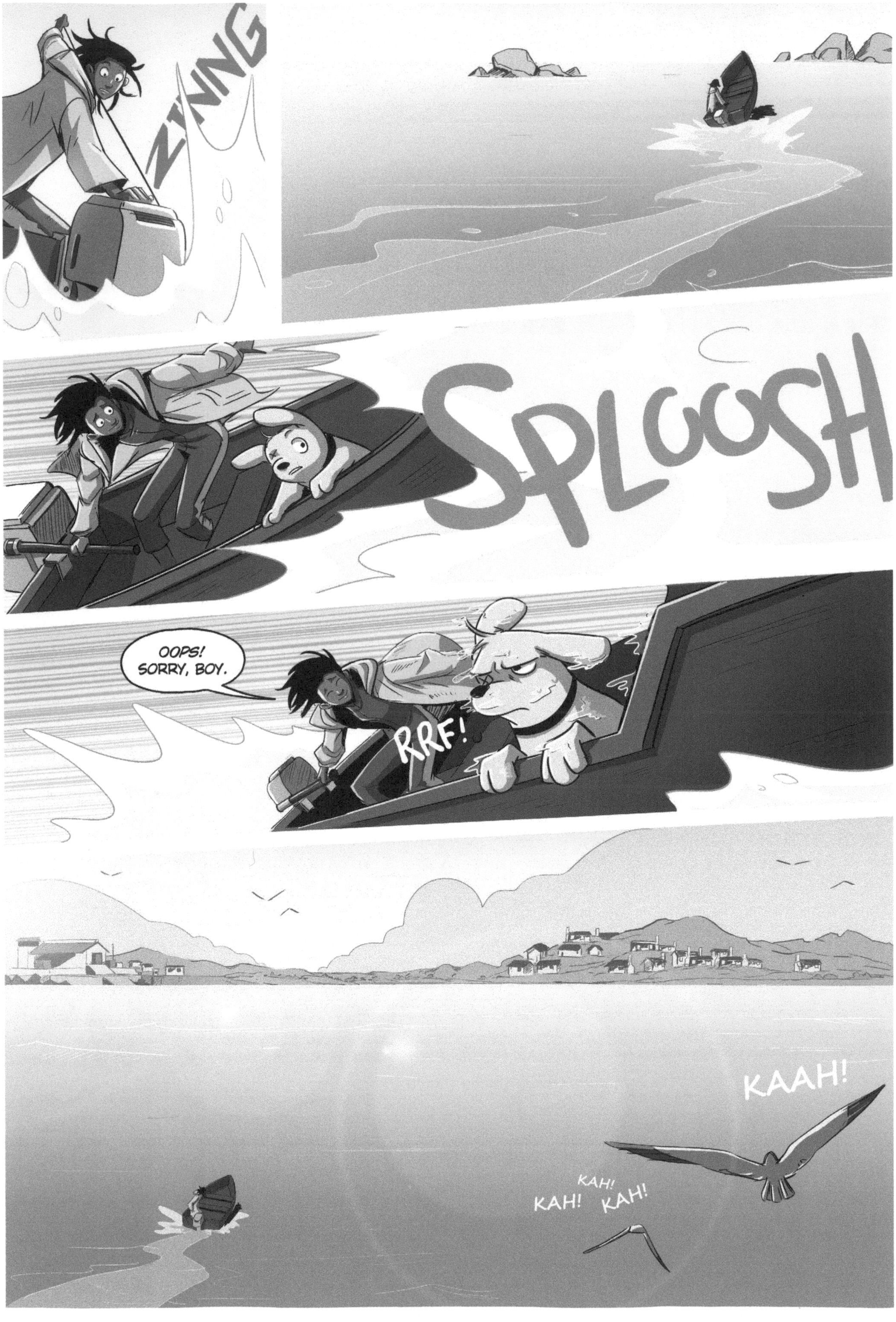
ZING
SPLOOSH
OOPS! SORRY, BOY.
RRF!
KAAH!
KAH! KAH! KAH!

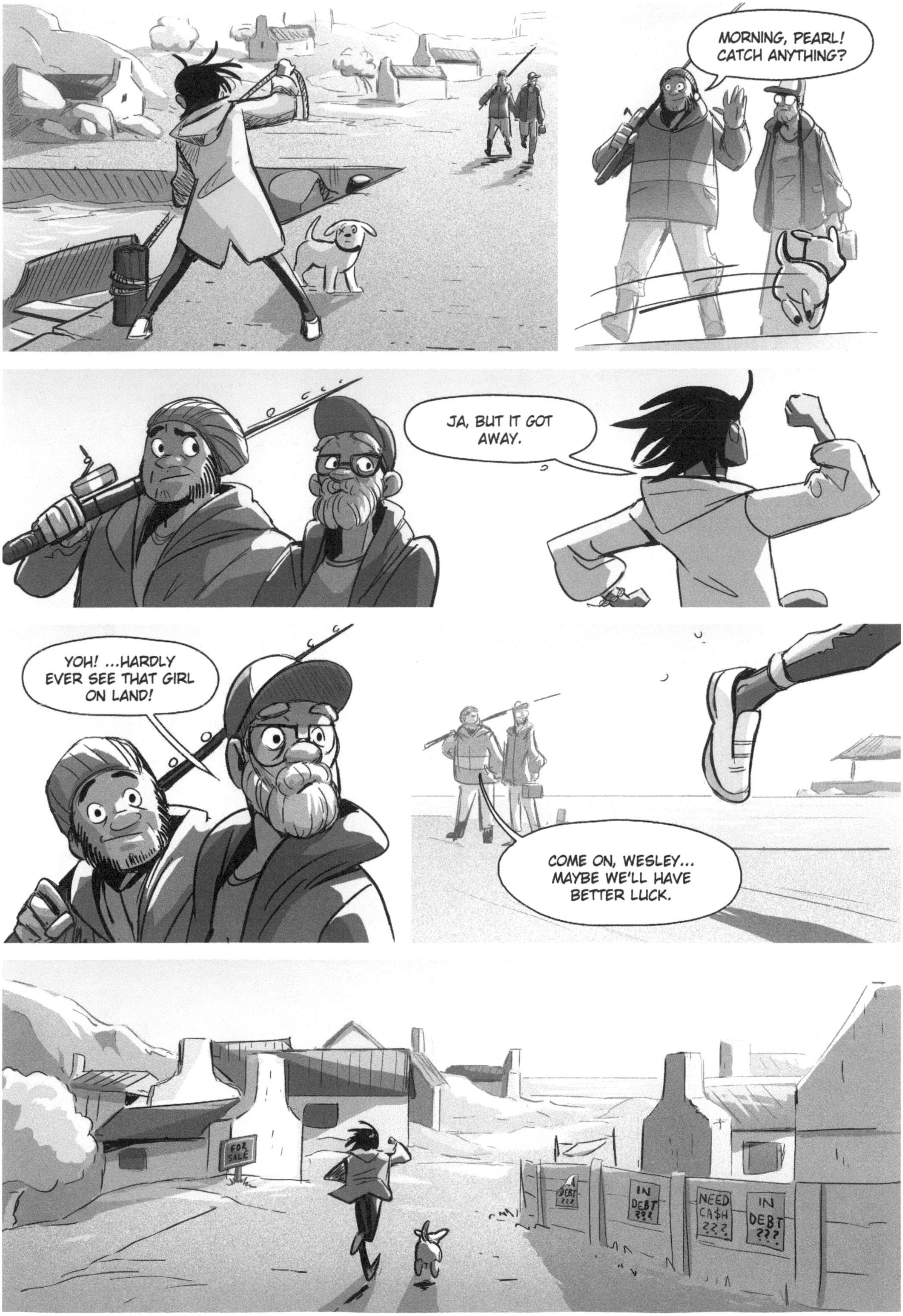
MORNING, PEARL! CATCH ANYTHING?
JA, BUT IT GOT AWAY.
YOH! ...HARDLY EVER SEE THAT GIRL ON LAND!
COME ON, WESLEY... MAYBE WE'LL HAVE BETTER LUCK.
FOR SALE
DEBT ???
IN DEBT ???
NEED CA$H ???
IN DEBT ???

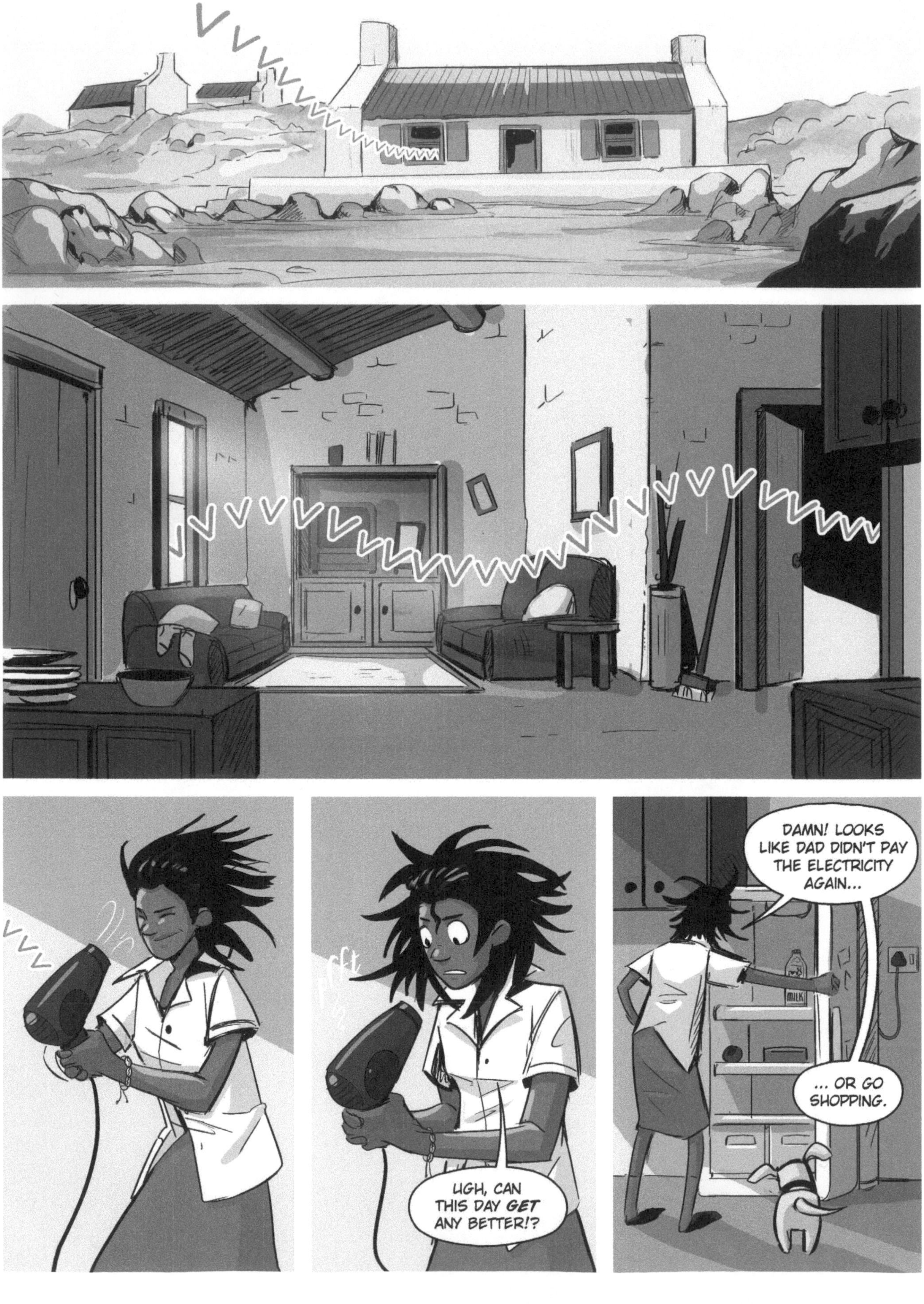
pfft
UGH, CAN THIS DAY GET ANY BETTER!?
DAMN! LOOKS LIKE DAD DIDN'T PAY THE ELECTRICITY AGAIN...
MILK
... OR GO SHOPPING.

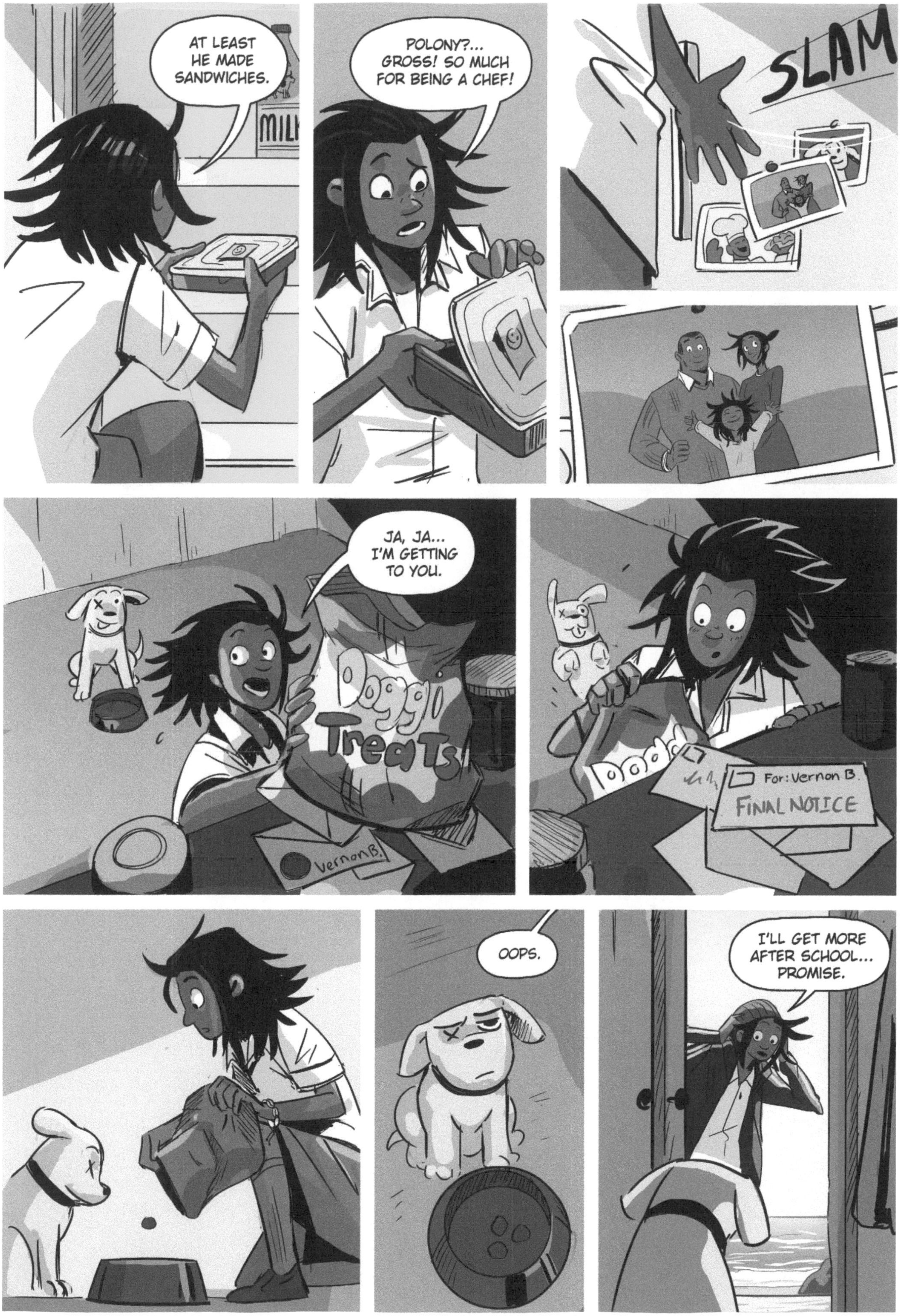

AT LEAST HE MADE SANDWICHES.
POLONY?... GROSS! SO MUCH FOR BEING A CHEF!
SLAM
JA, JA... I'M GETTING TO YOU.
Doggi Treats
VernonB.
For: Vernon B.
FINAL NOTICE
OOPS.
I'LL GET MORE AFTER SCHOOL... PROMISE.

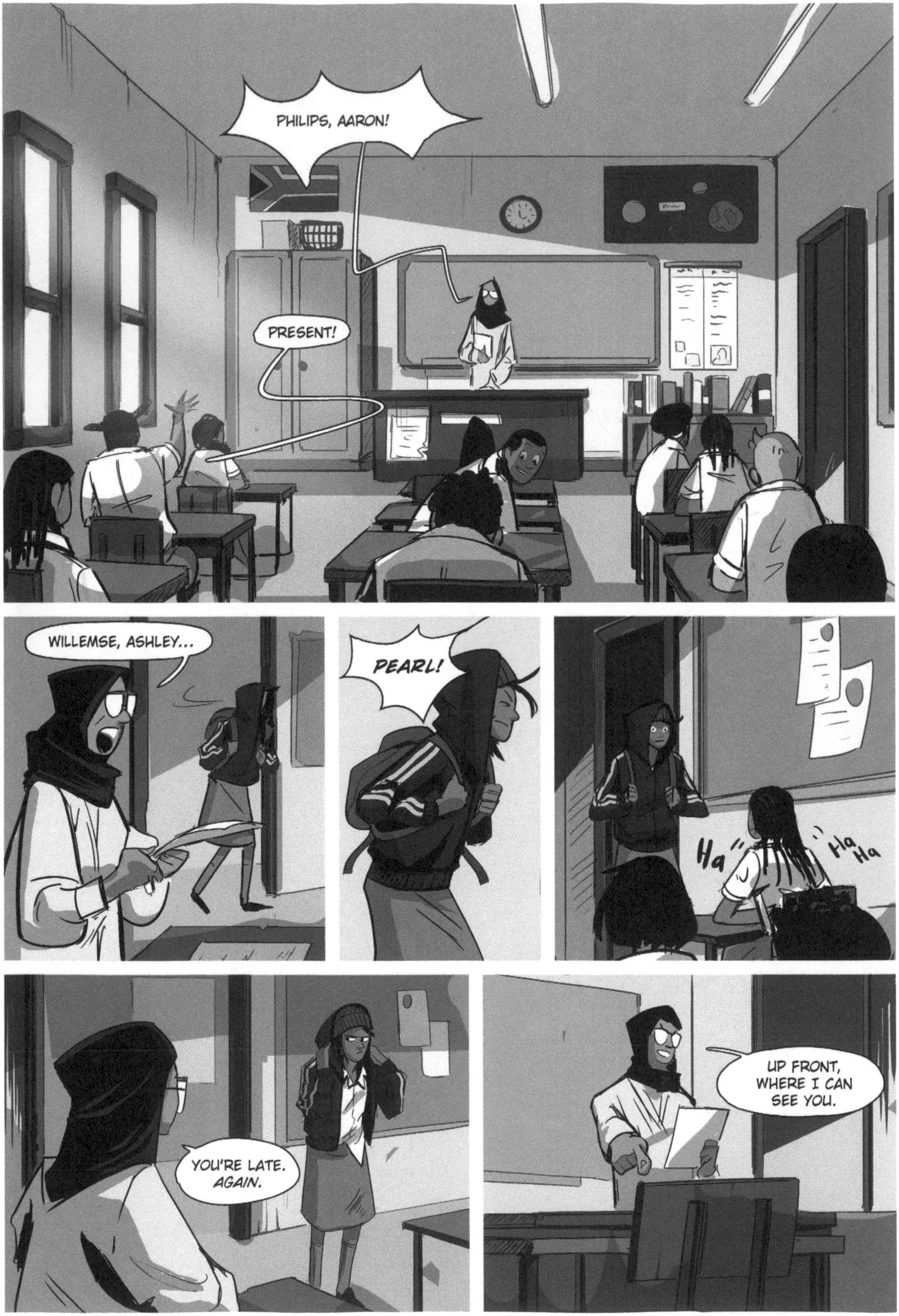
PHILIPS, AARON!
PRESENT!
WILLEMSE, ASHLEY...
PEARL!
Ha
Ha Ha
YOU'RE LATE. AGAIN.
UP FRONT, WHERE I CAN SEE YOU.

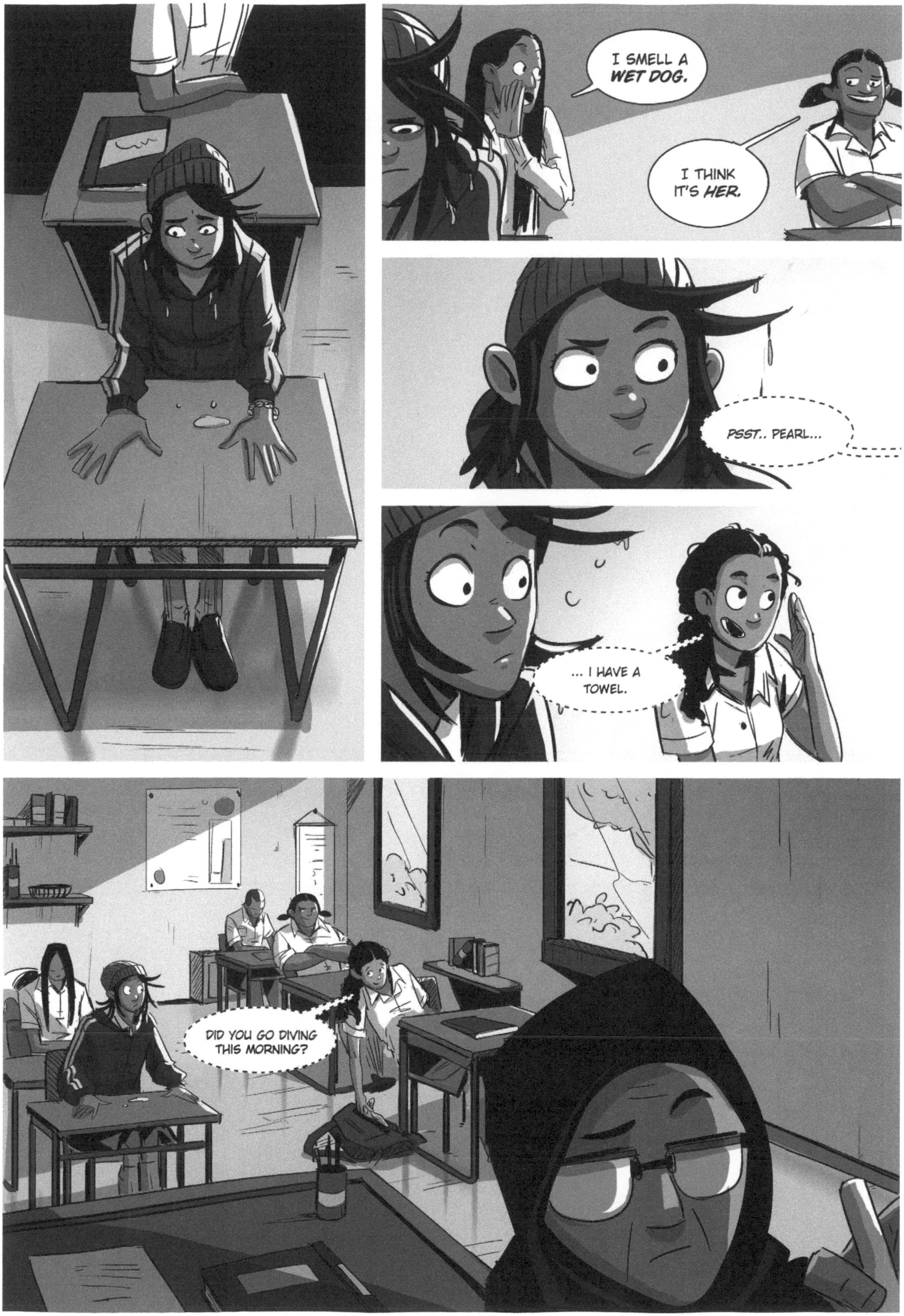
I SMELL A WET DOG.
I THINK IT'S HER.
PSST.. PEARL...
... I HAVE A TOWEL.
DID YOU GO DIVING THIS MORNING?

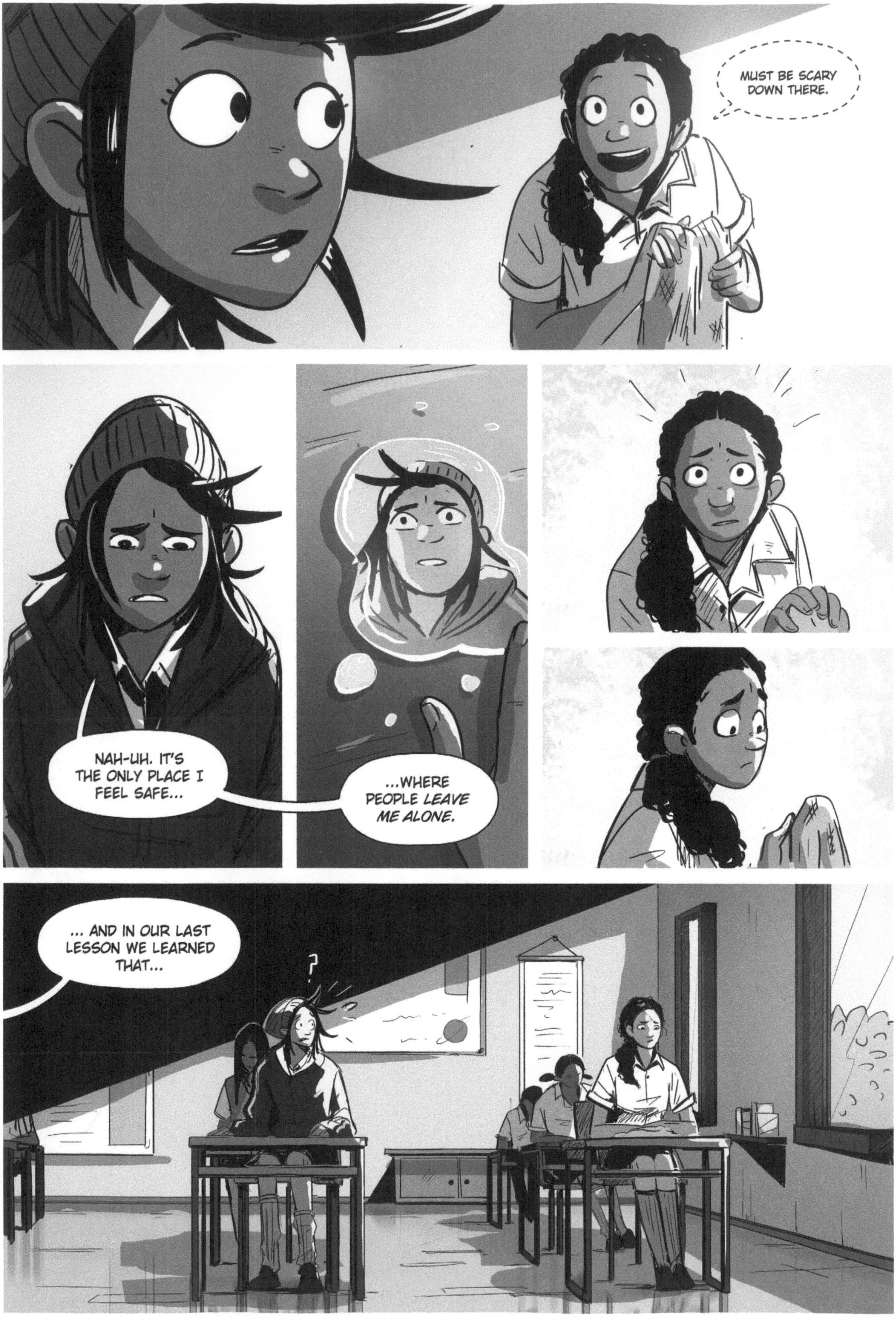
MUST BE SCARY DOWN THERE.
NAH-UH. IT'S THE ONLY PLACE I FEEL SAFE...
...WHERE PEOPLE *LEAVE* ME ALONE.
... AND IN OUR LAST LESSON WE LEARNED THAT...
?

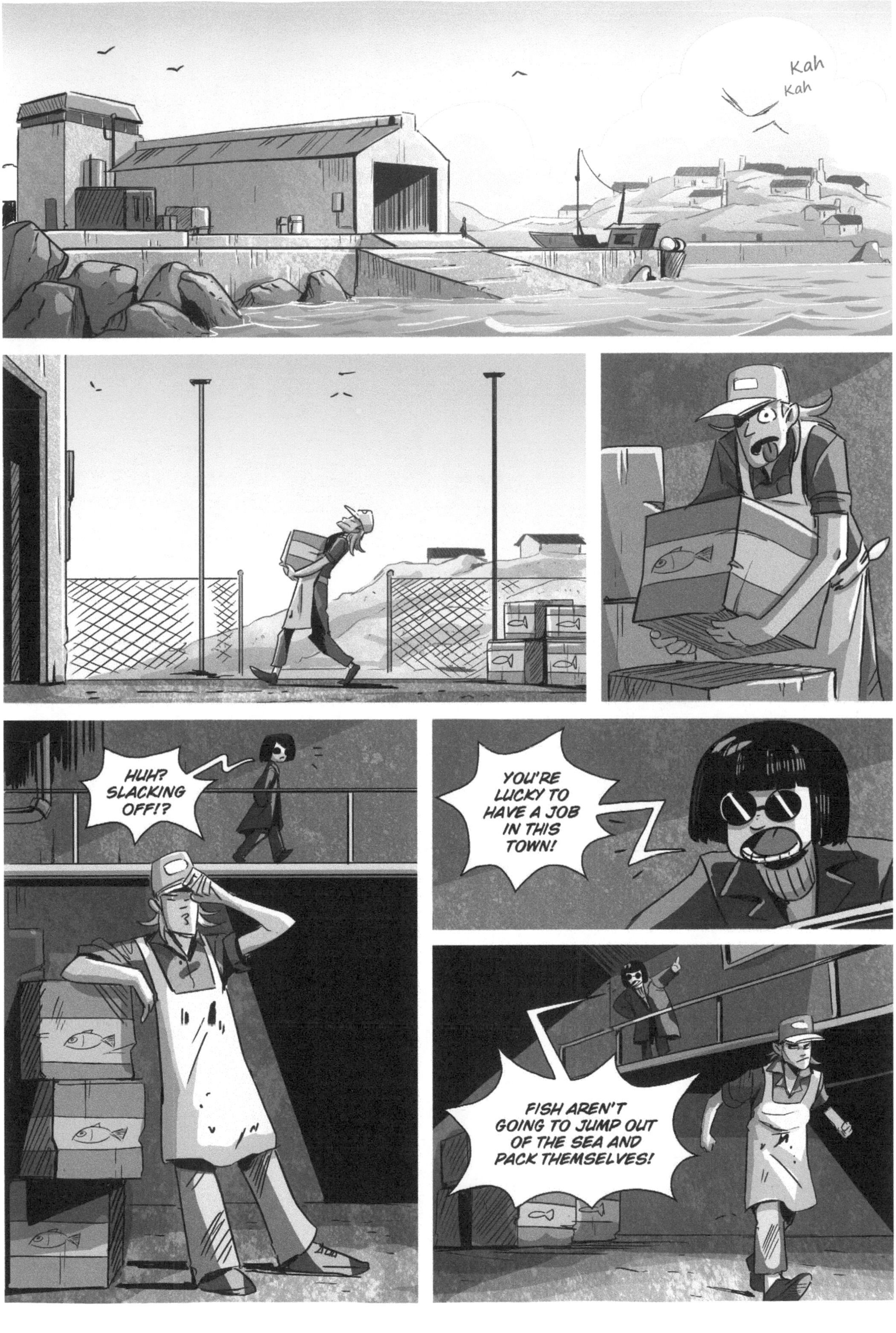
Kah
Kah
HUH? SLACKING OFF!?
YOU'RE LUCKY TO HAVE A JOB IN THIS TOWN!
FISH AREN'T GOING TO JUMP OUT OF THE SEA AND PACK THEMSELVES!

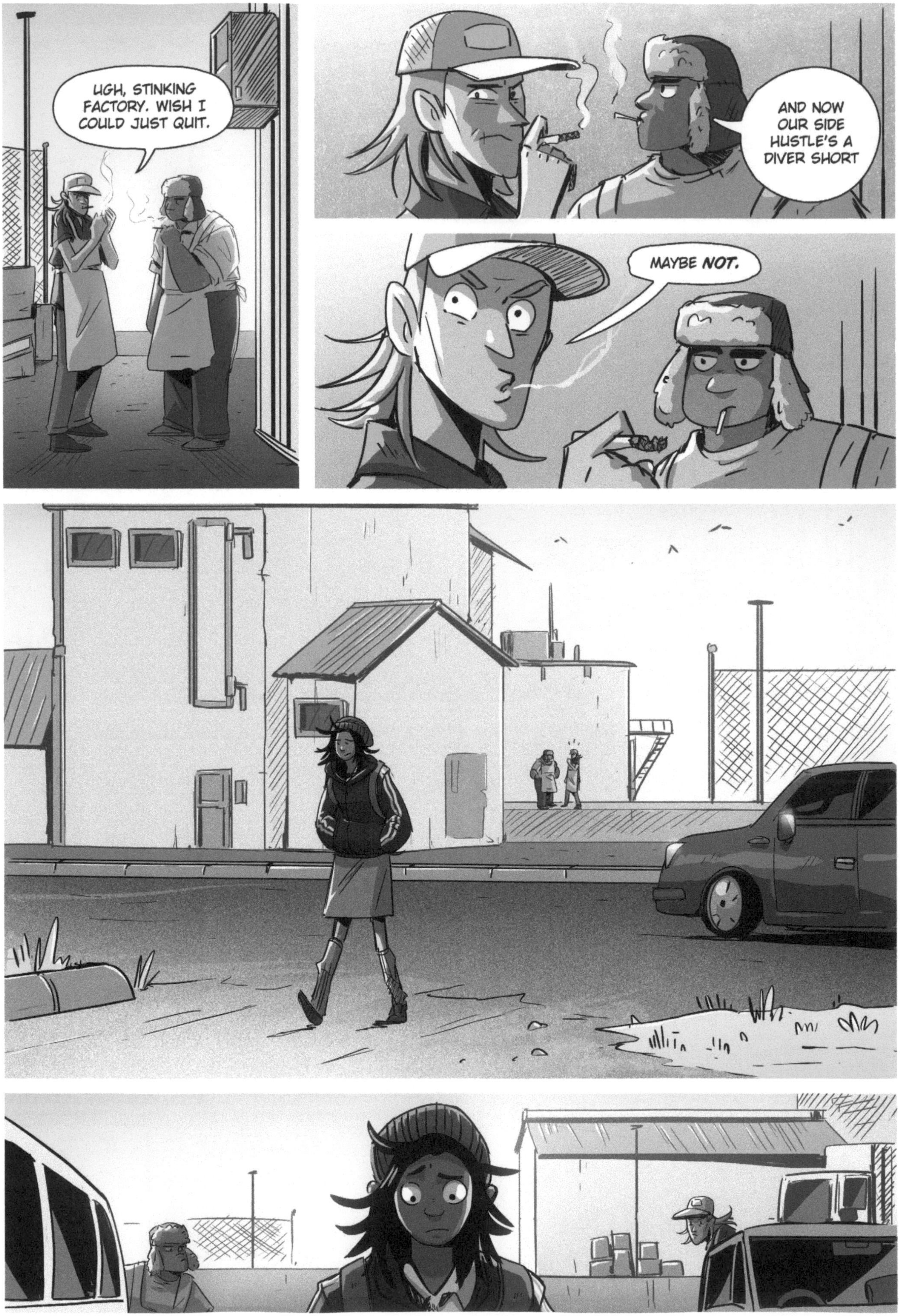
UGH, STINKING FACTORY. WISH I COULD JUST QUIT.
AND NOW OUR SIDE HUSTLE'S A DIVER SHORT
MAYBE NOT.

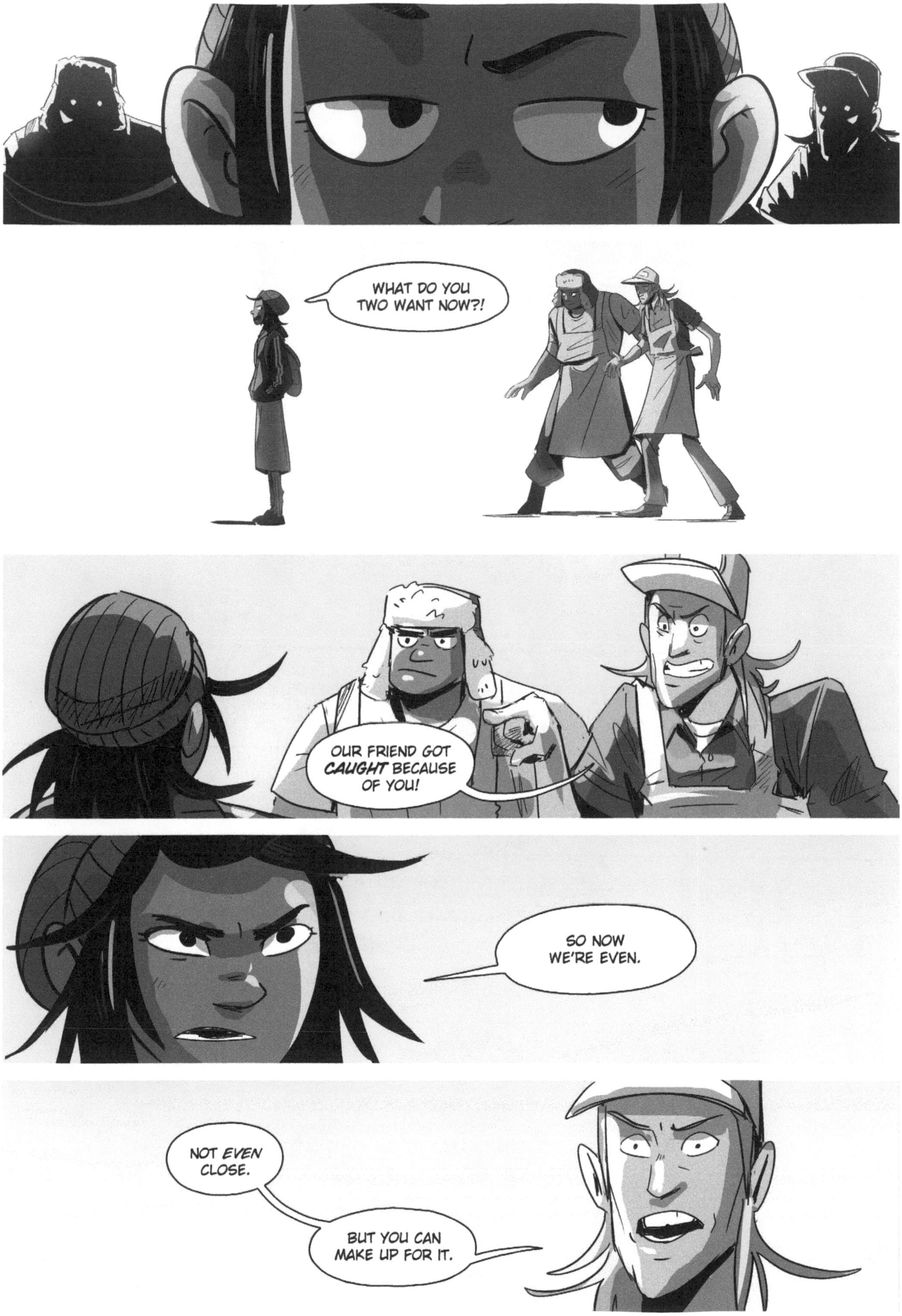
WHAT DO YOU TWO WANT NOW?!
OUR FRIEND GOT CAUGHT BECAUSE OF YOU!
SO NOW WE'RE EVEN.
NOT EVEN CLOSE.
BUT YOU CAN MAKE UP FOR IT.

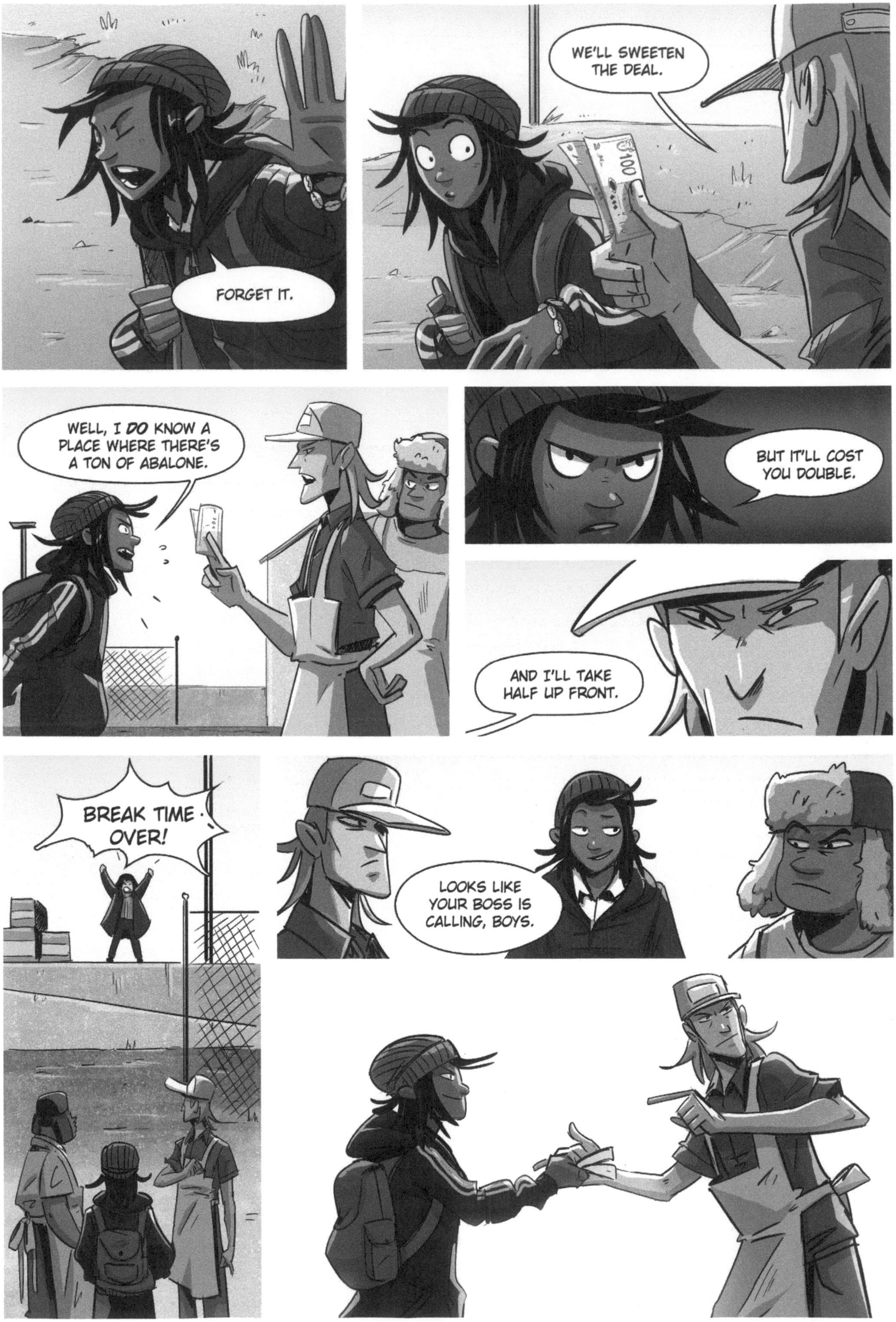
FORGET IT.
WE'LL SWEETEN THE DEAL.
WELL, I DO KNOW A PLACE WHERE THERE'S A TON OF ABALONE.
BUT IT'LL COST YOU DOUBLE.
AND I'LL TAKE HALF UP FRONT.
BREAK TIME OVER!
LOOKS LIKE YOUR BOSS IS CALLING, BOYS.

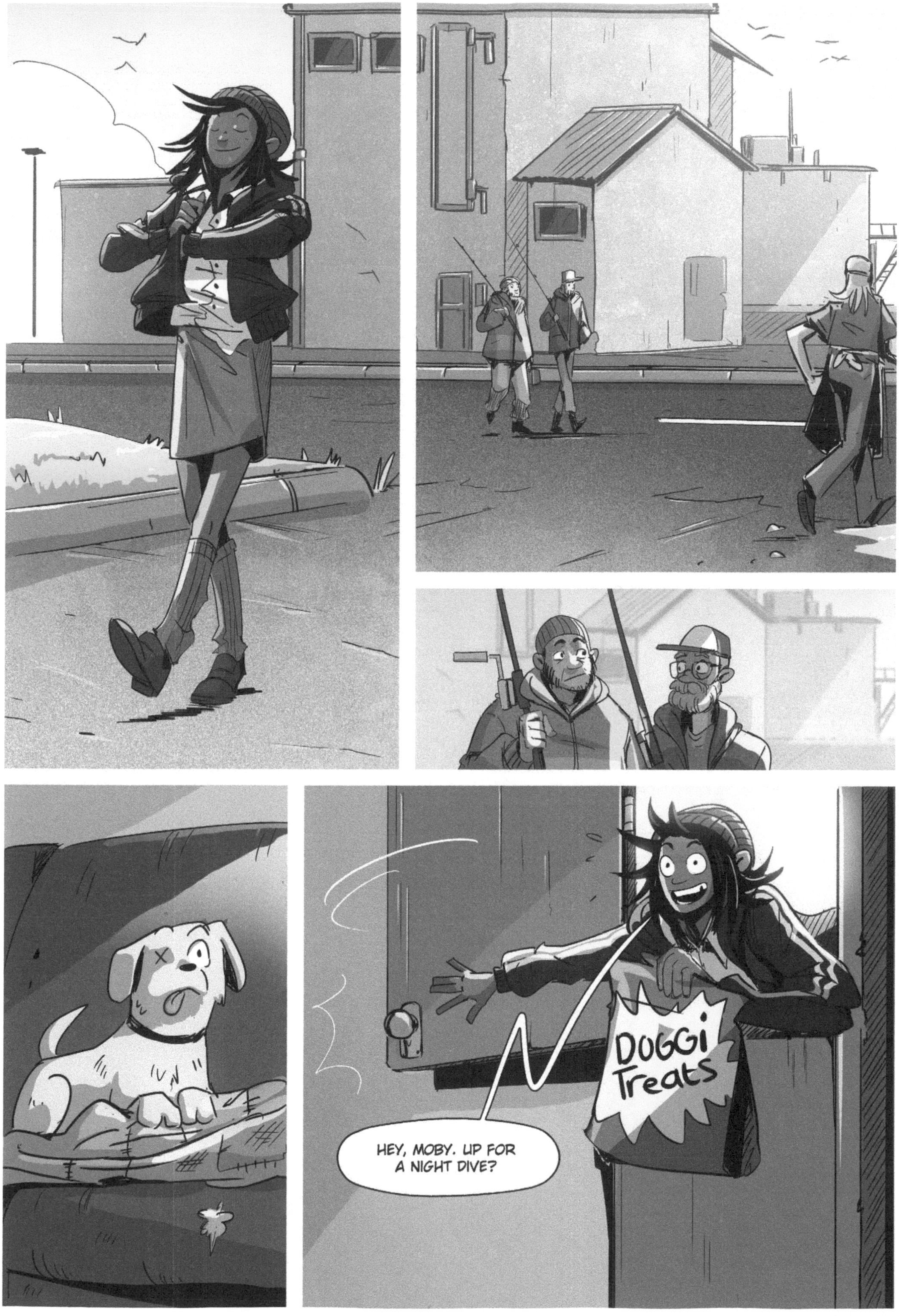
DOGGi Treats
HEY, MOBY. UP FOR A NIGHT DIVE?

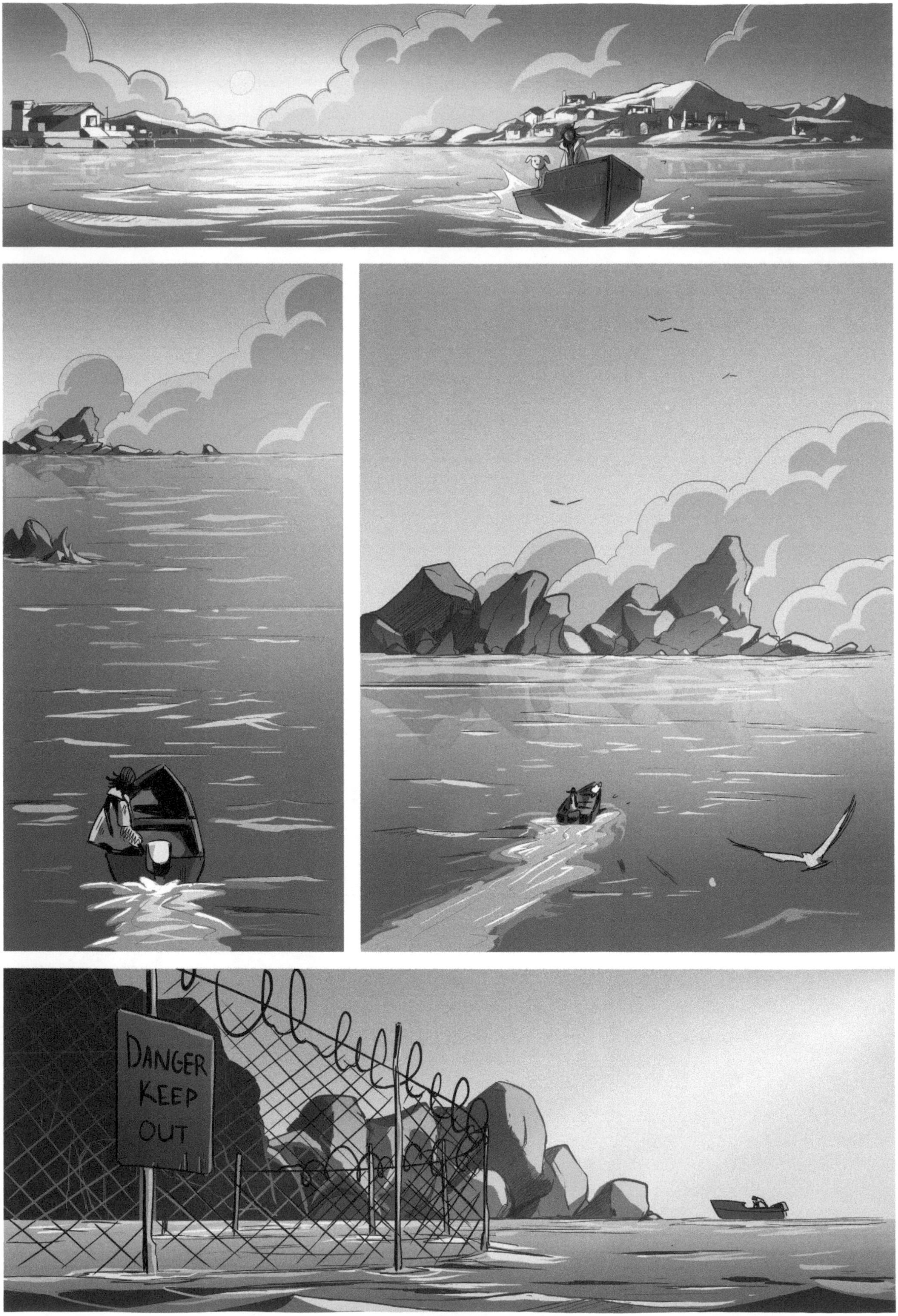
DANGER
KEEP
OUT

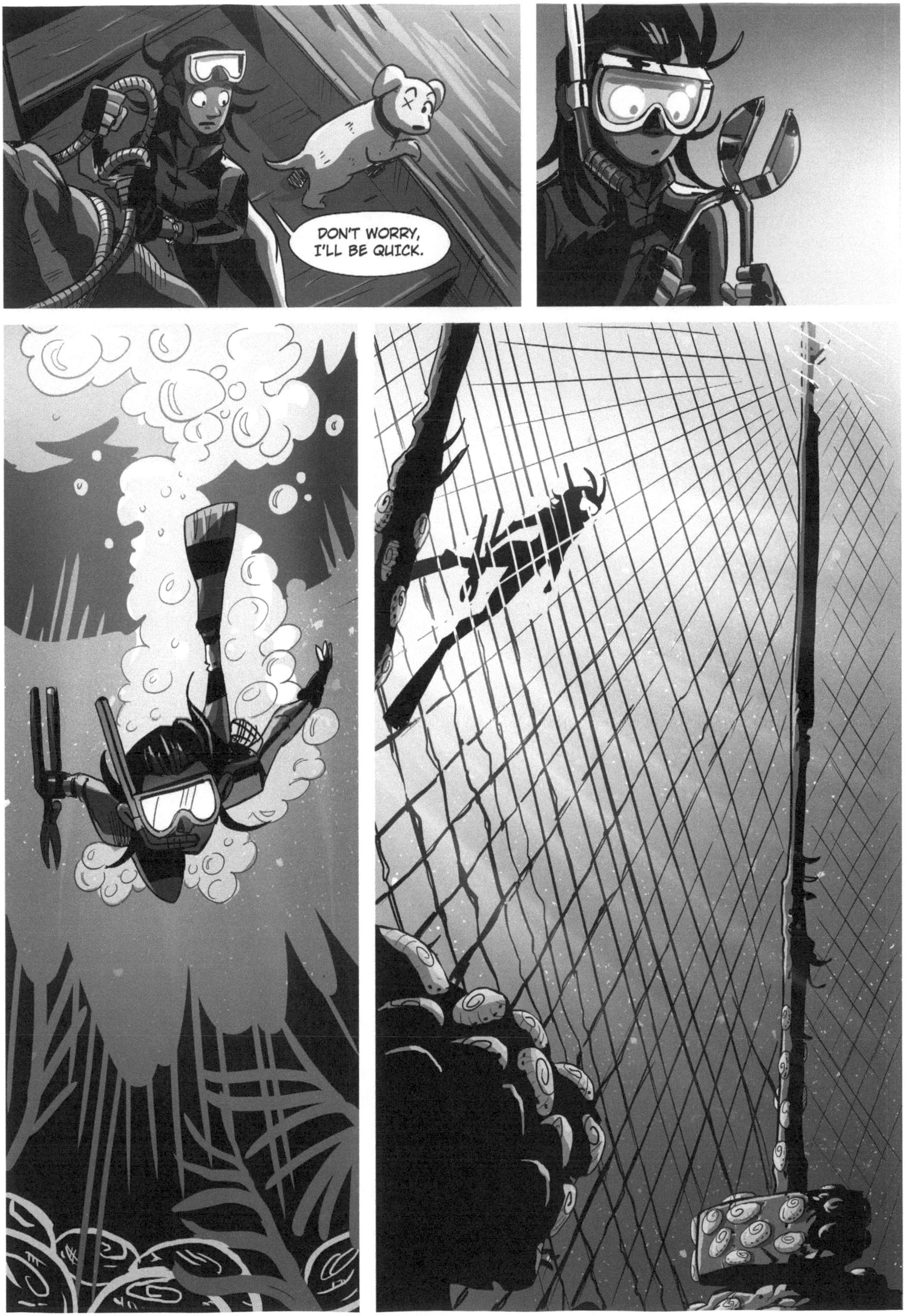
DON'T WORRY, I'LL BE QUICK.

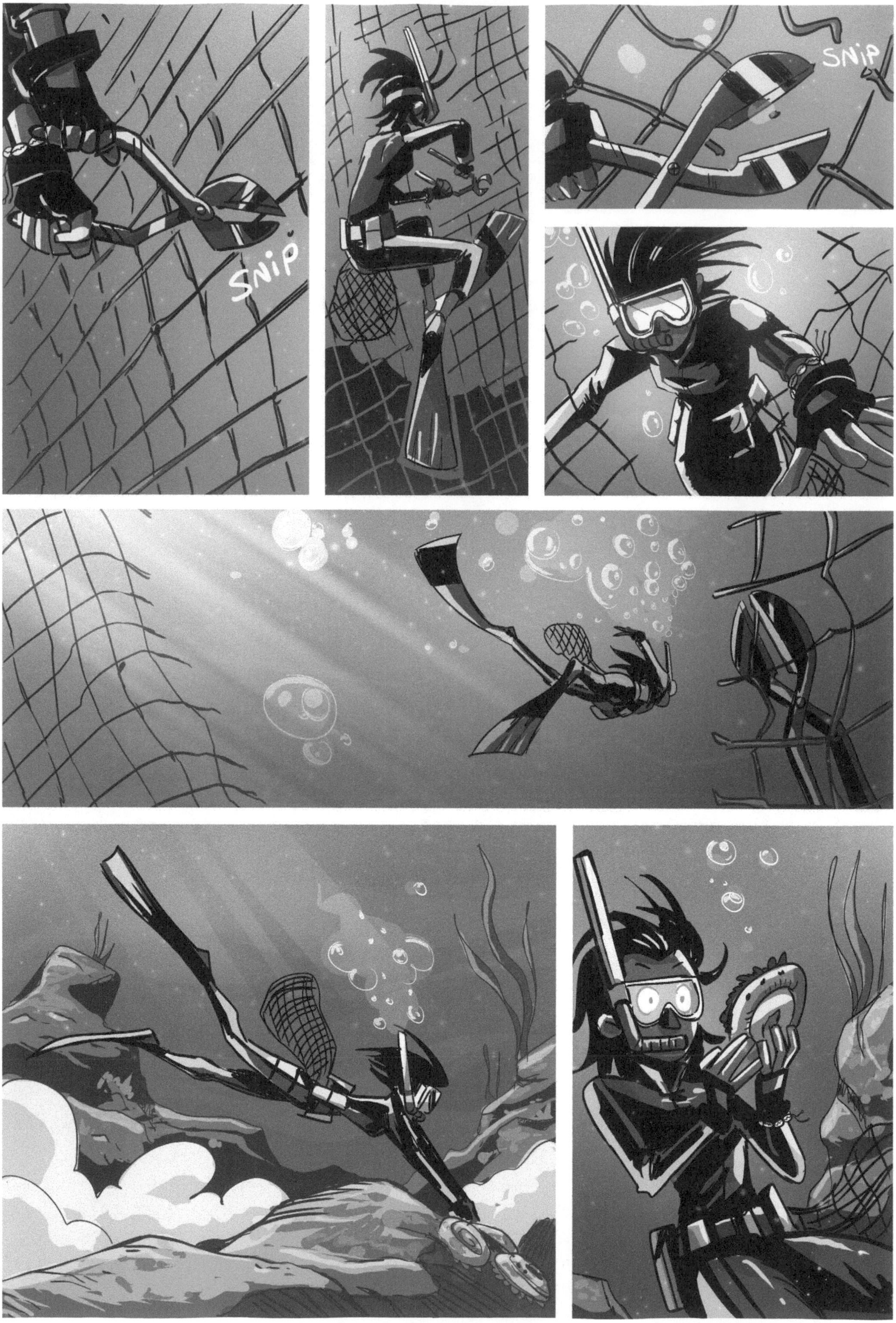
SNIP
SNIP

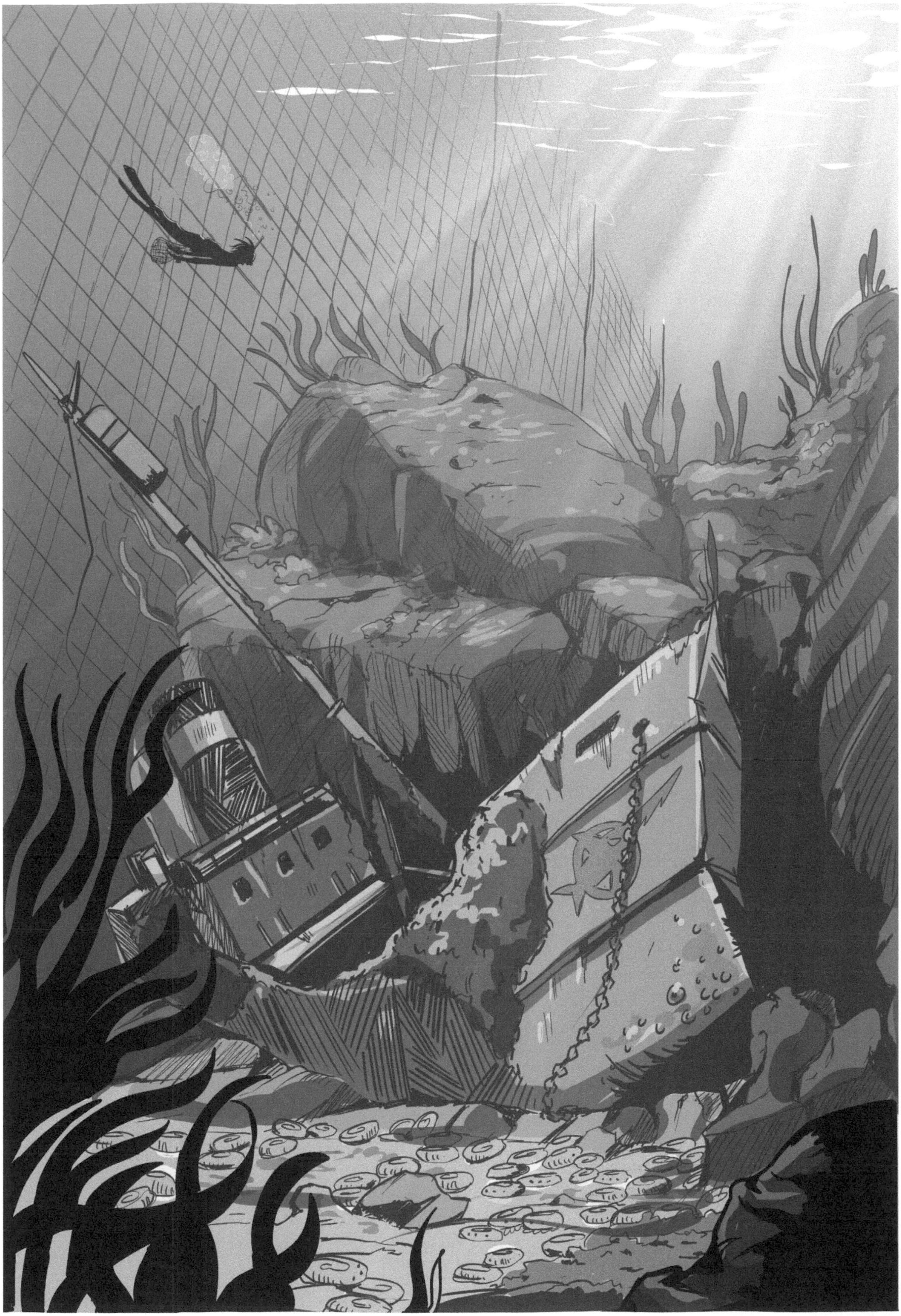

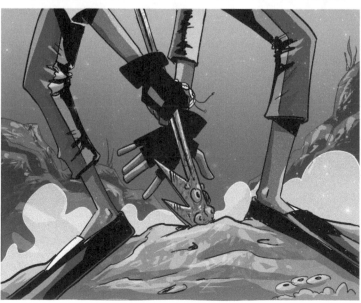

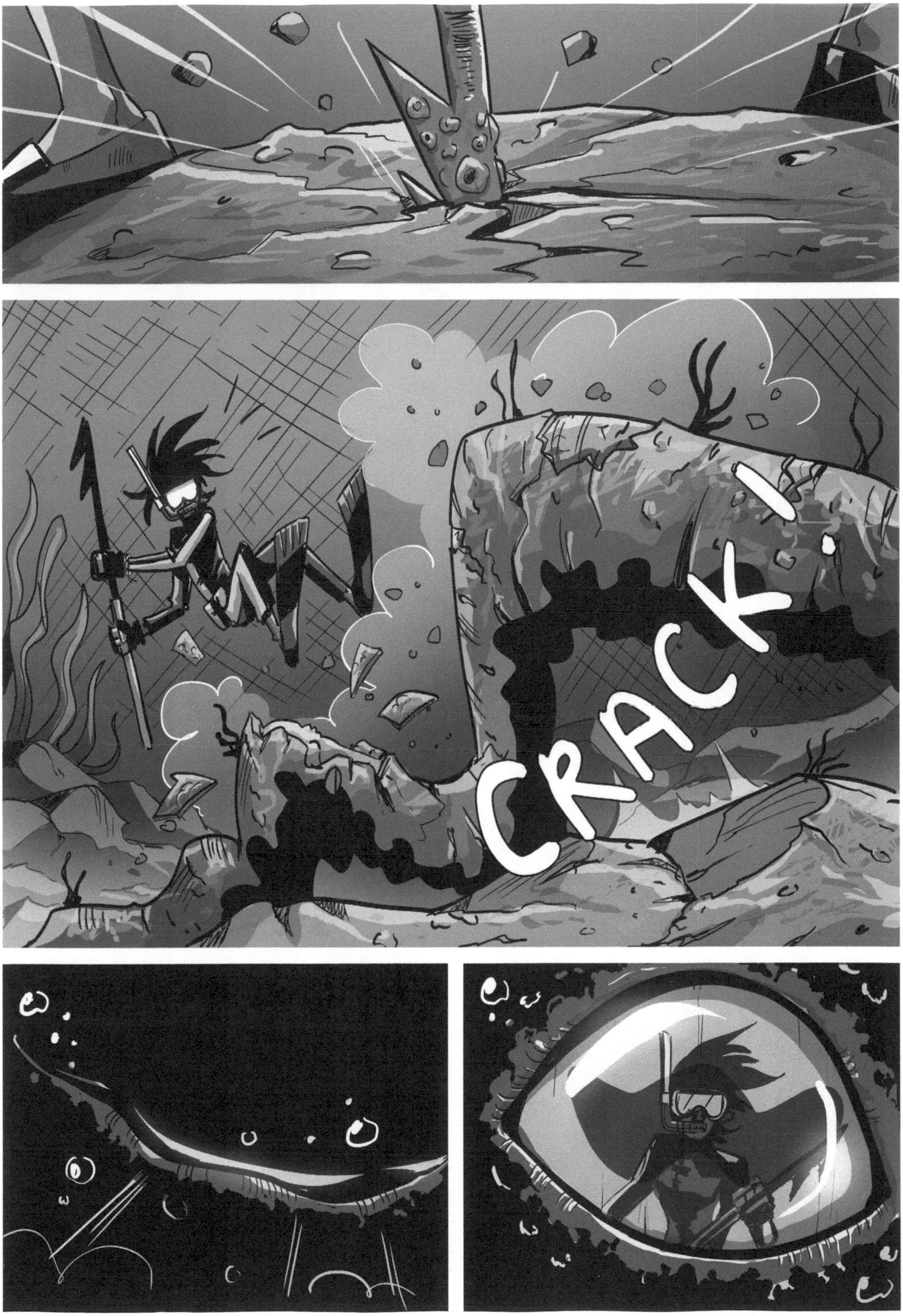
CRACK!

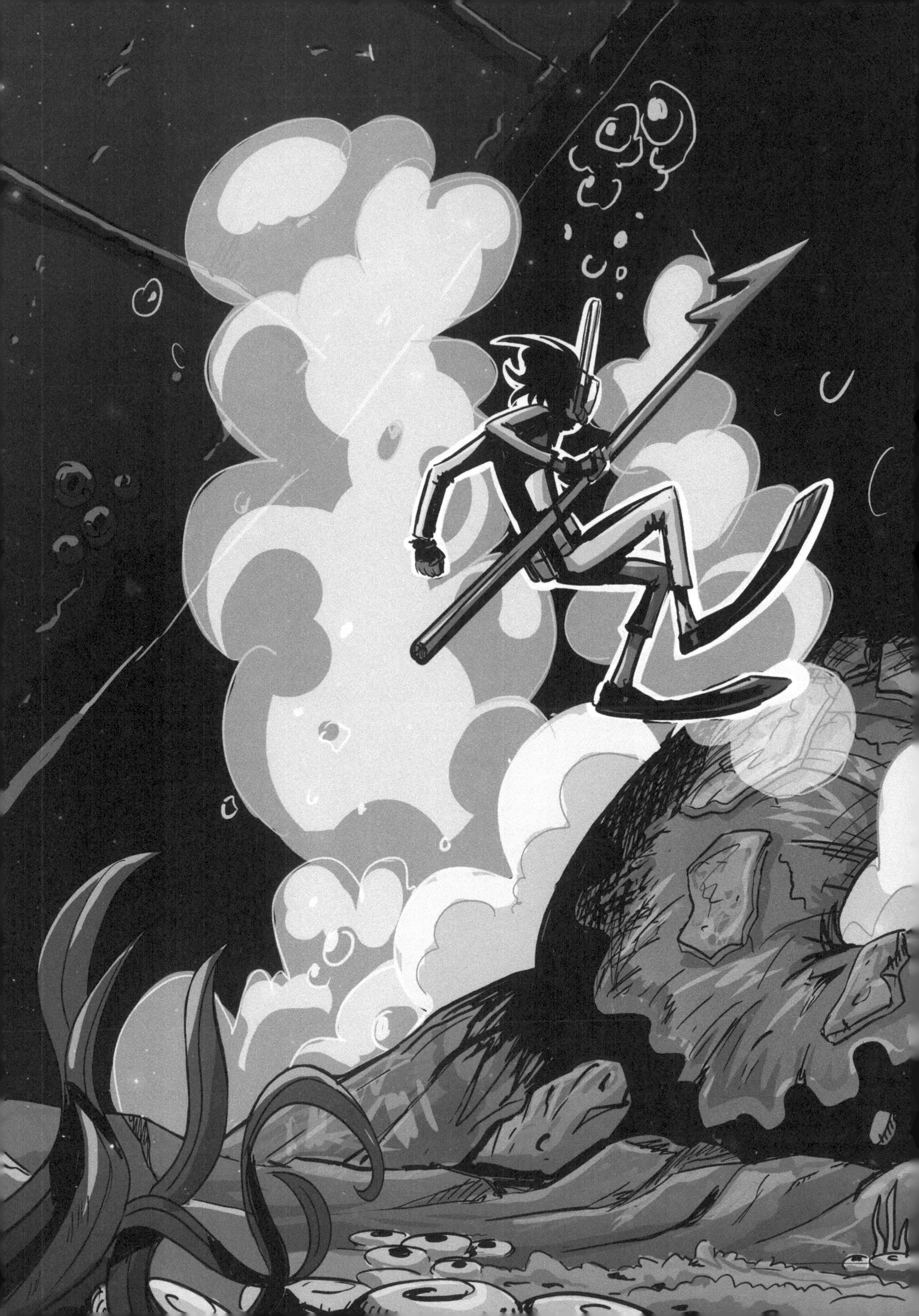

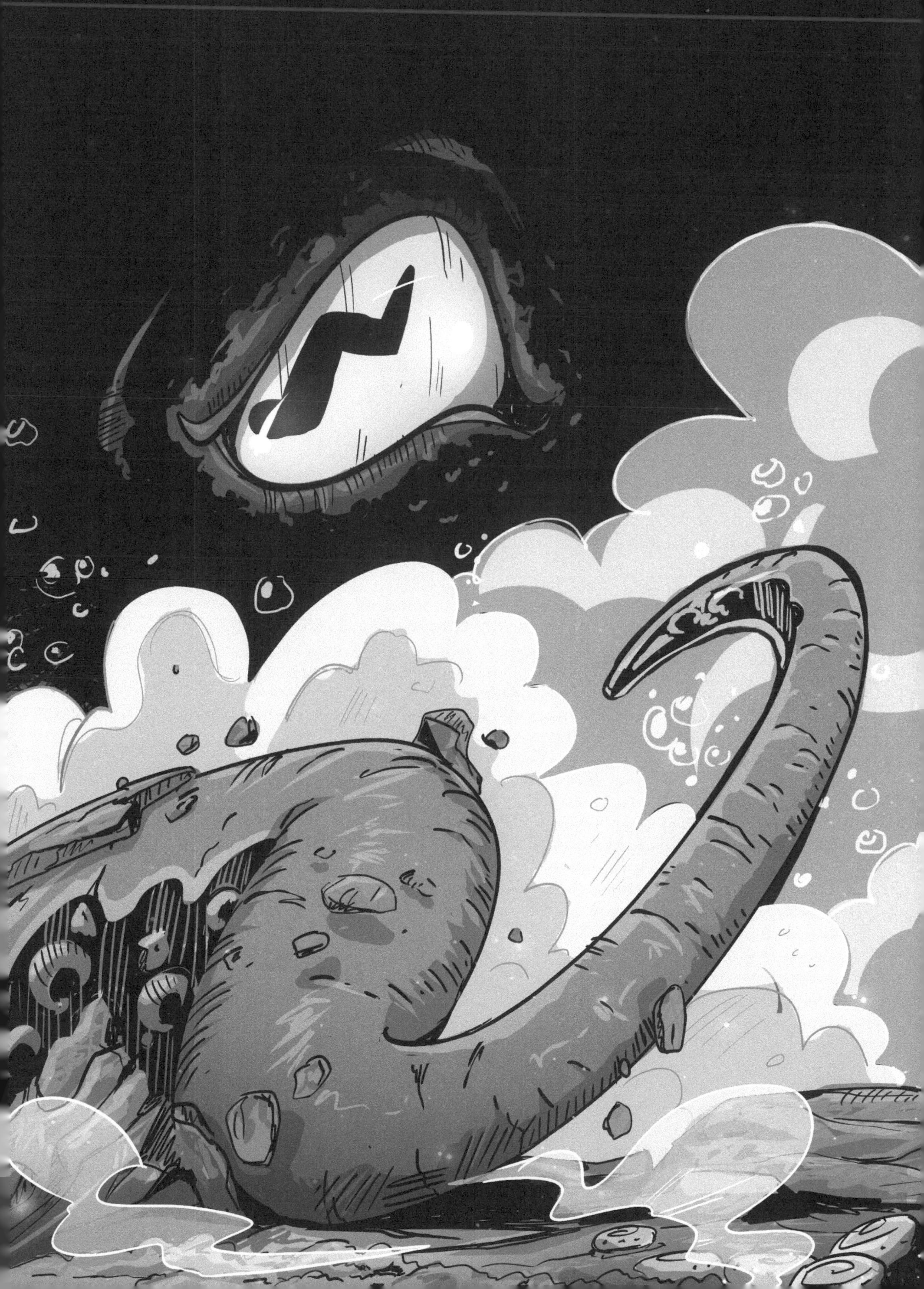

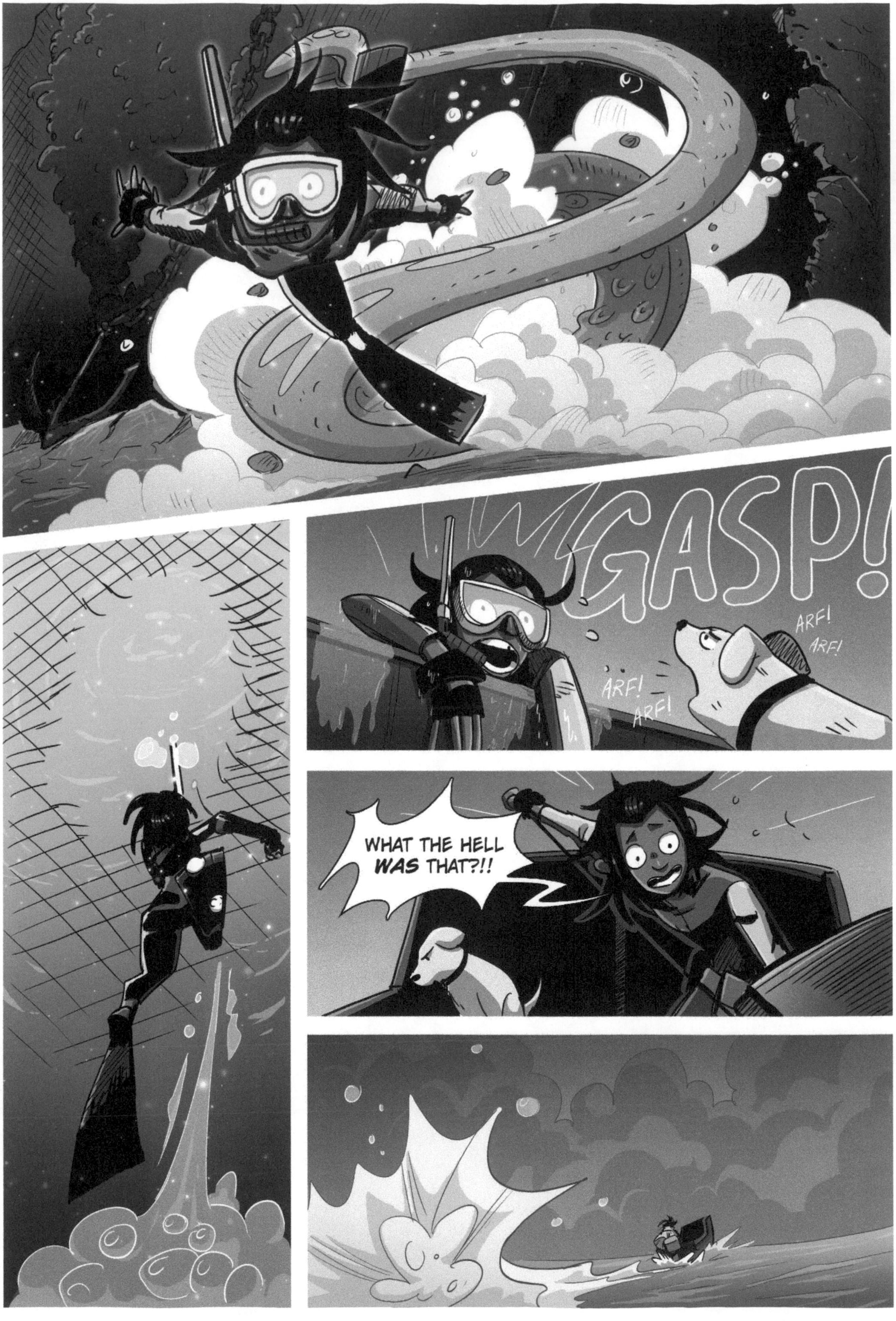
GASP!
ARF!
ARF!
ARF!
ARF!
WHAT THE HELL WAS THAT?!!

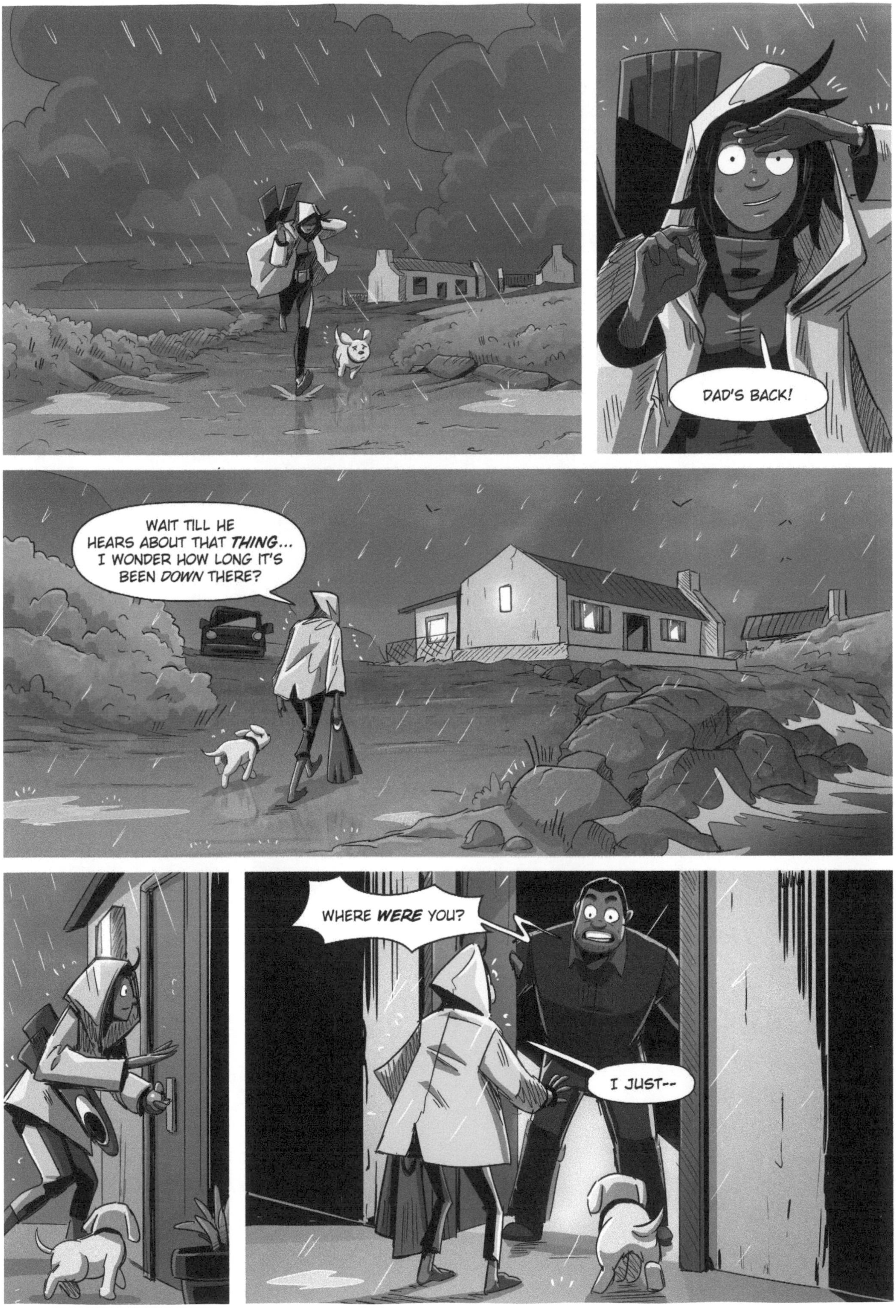
DAD'S BACK!
WAIT TILL HE HEARS ABOUT THAT THING... I WONDER HOW LONG IT'S BEEN DOWN THERE?
WHERE WERE YOU?
I JUST--

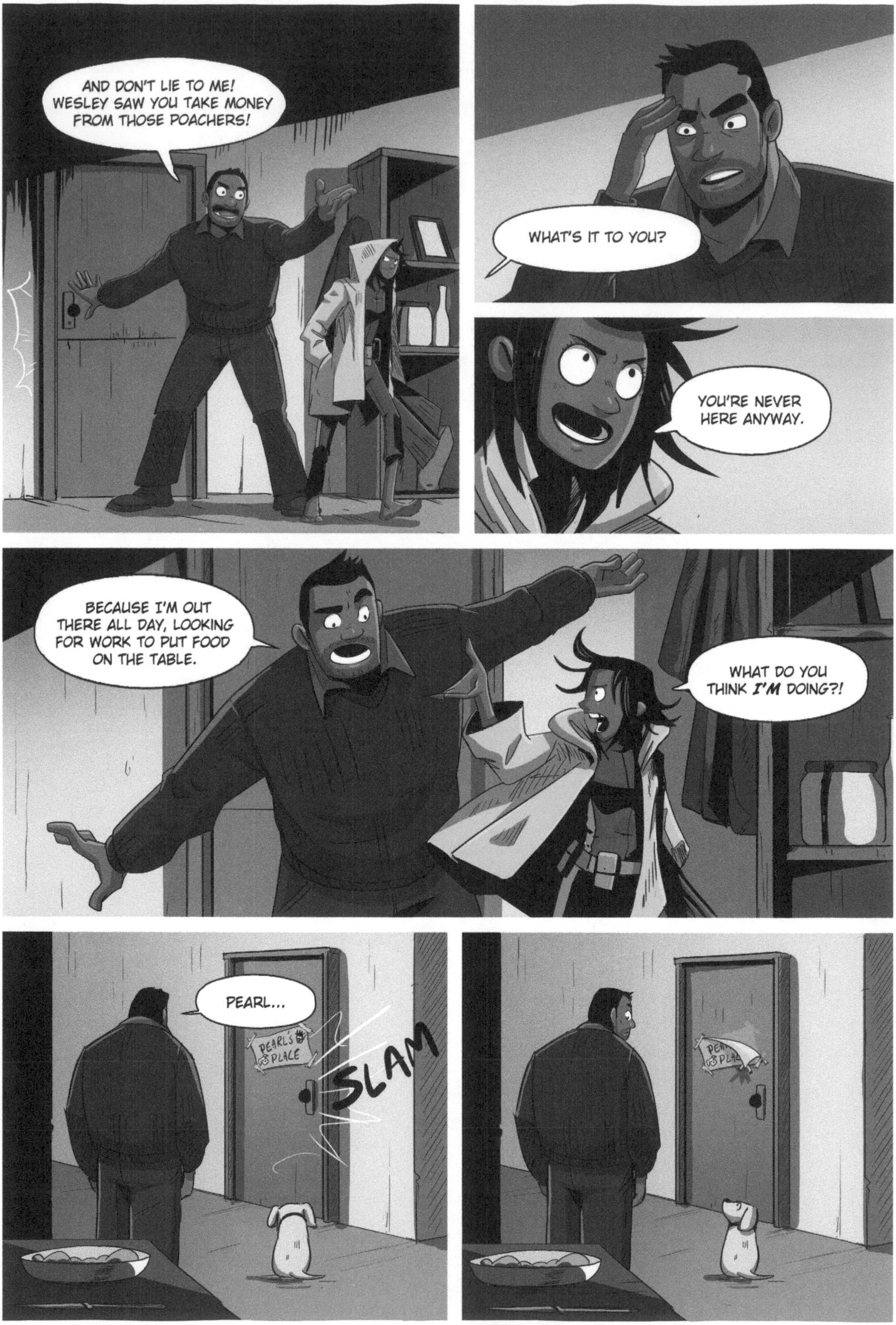
AND DON'T LIE TO ME! WESLEY SAW YOU TAKE MONEY FROM THOSE POACHERS!
WHAT'S IT TO YOU?
YOU'RE NEVER HERE ANYWAY.
BECAUSE I'M OUT THERE ALL DAY, LOOKING FOR WORK TO PUT FOOD ON THE TABLE.
WHAT DO YOU THINK ***I'M*** DOING?!
PEARL...
PEARL'S PLACE
SLAM

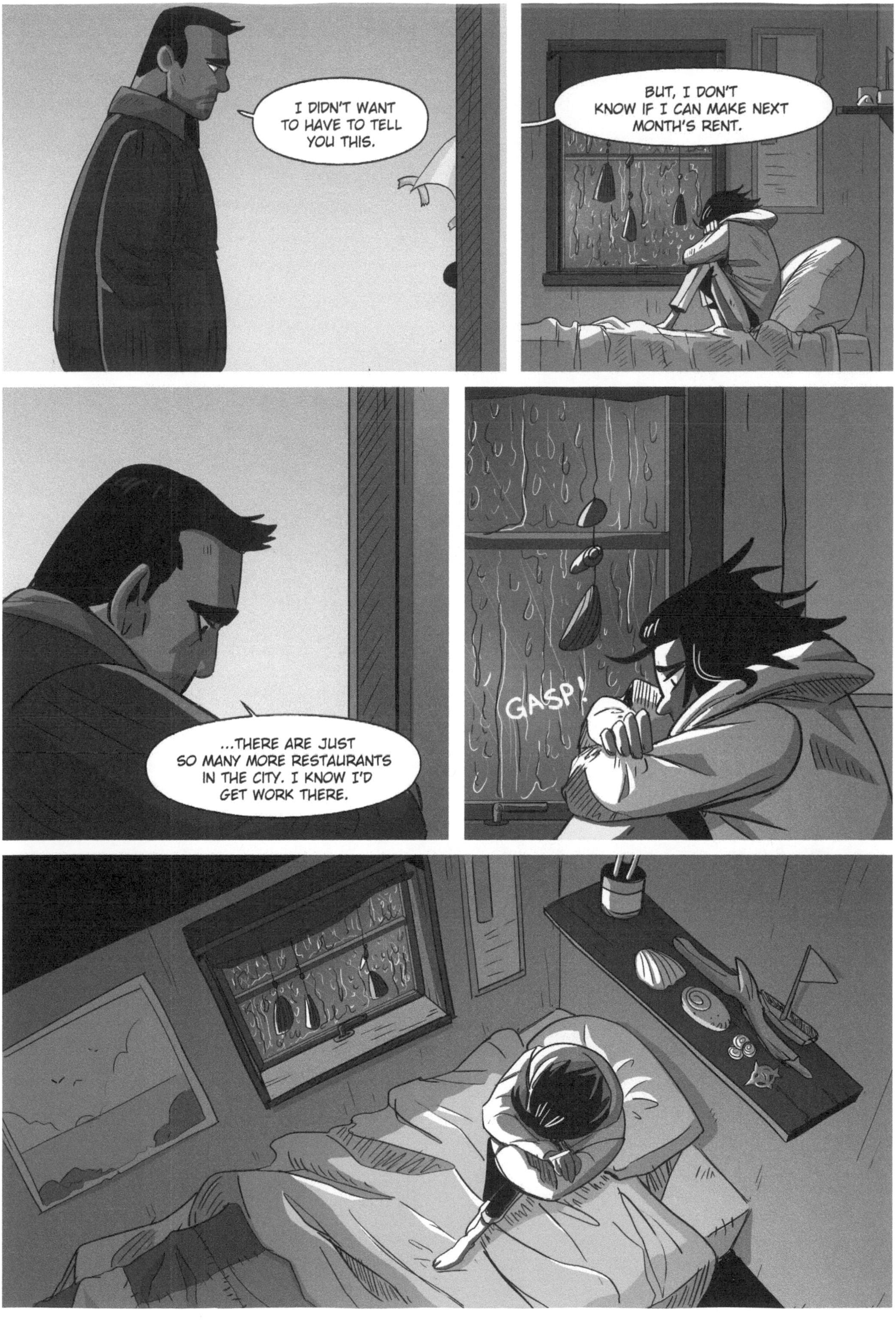
I DIDN'T WANT TO HAVE TO TELL YOU THIS.
BUT, I DON'T KNOW IF I CAN MAKE NEXT MONTH'S RENT.
...THERE ARE JUST SO MANY MORE RESTAURANTS IN THE CITY. I KNOW I'D GET WORK THERE.
GASP!

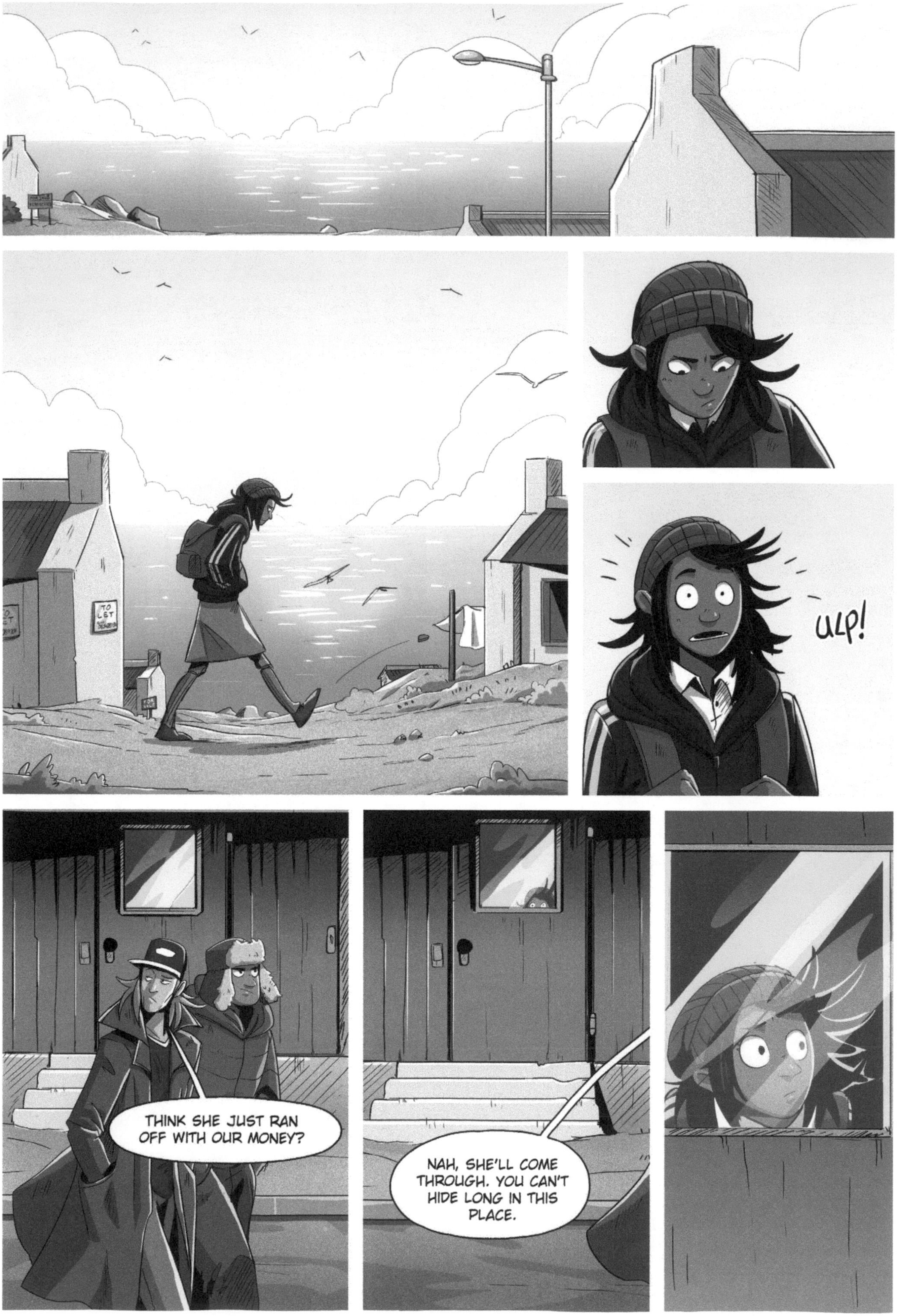

ULP!
THINK SHE JUST RAN OFF WITH OUR MONEY?
NAH, SHE'LL COME THROUGH. YOU CAN'T HIDE LONG IN THIS PLACE.

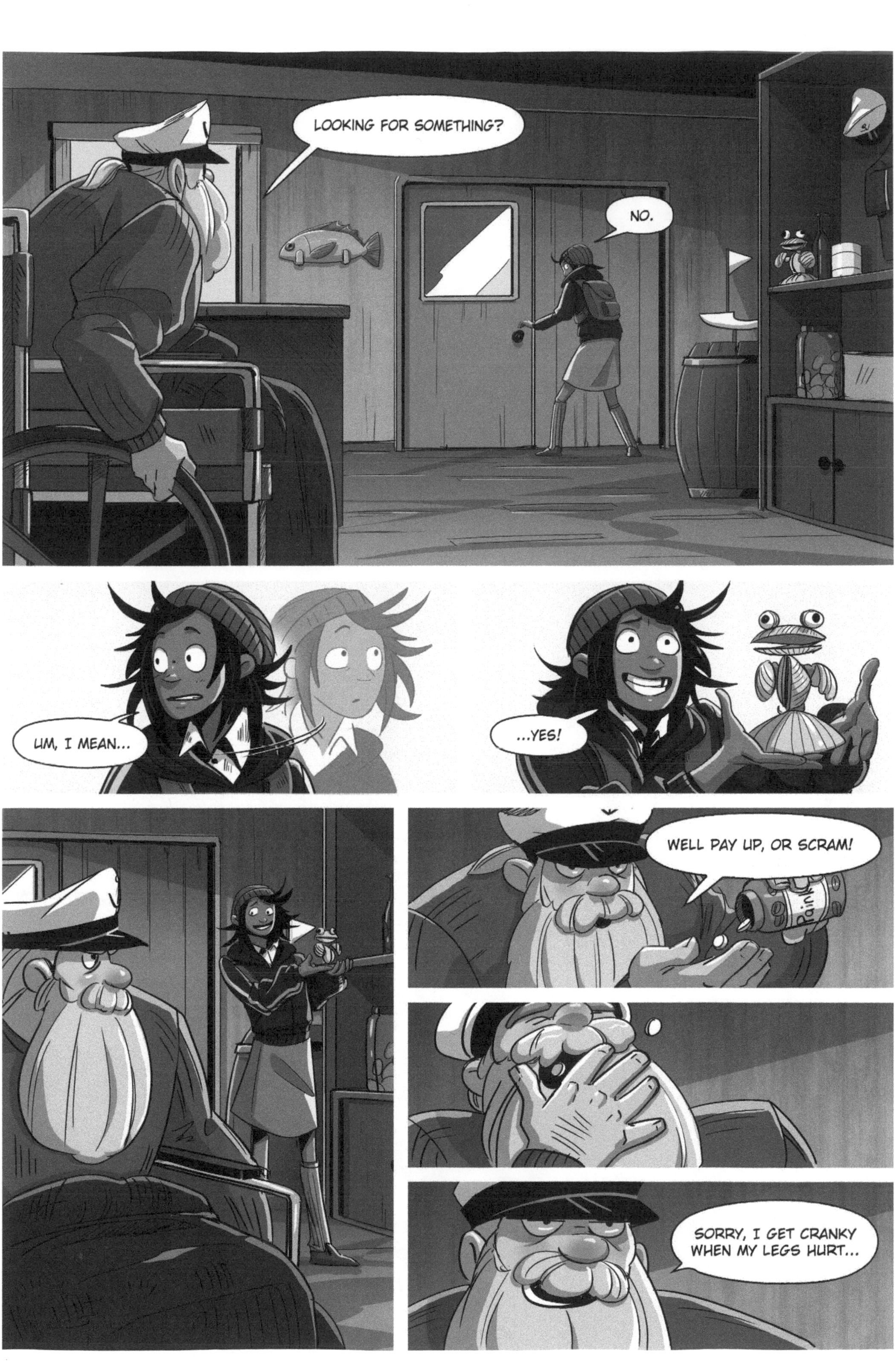
LOOKING FOR SOMETHING?
NO.
UM, I MEAN...
...YES!
WELL PAY UP, OR SCRAM!
SORRY, I GET CRANKY WHEN MY LEGS HURT...

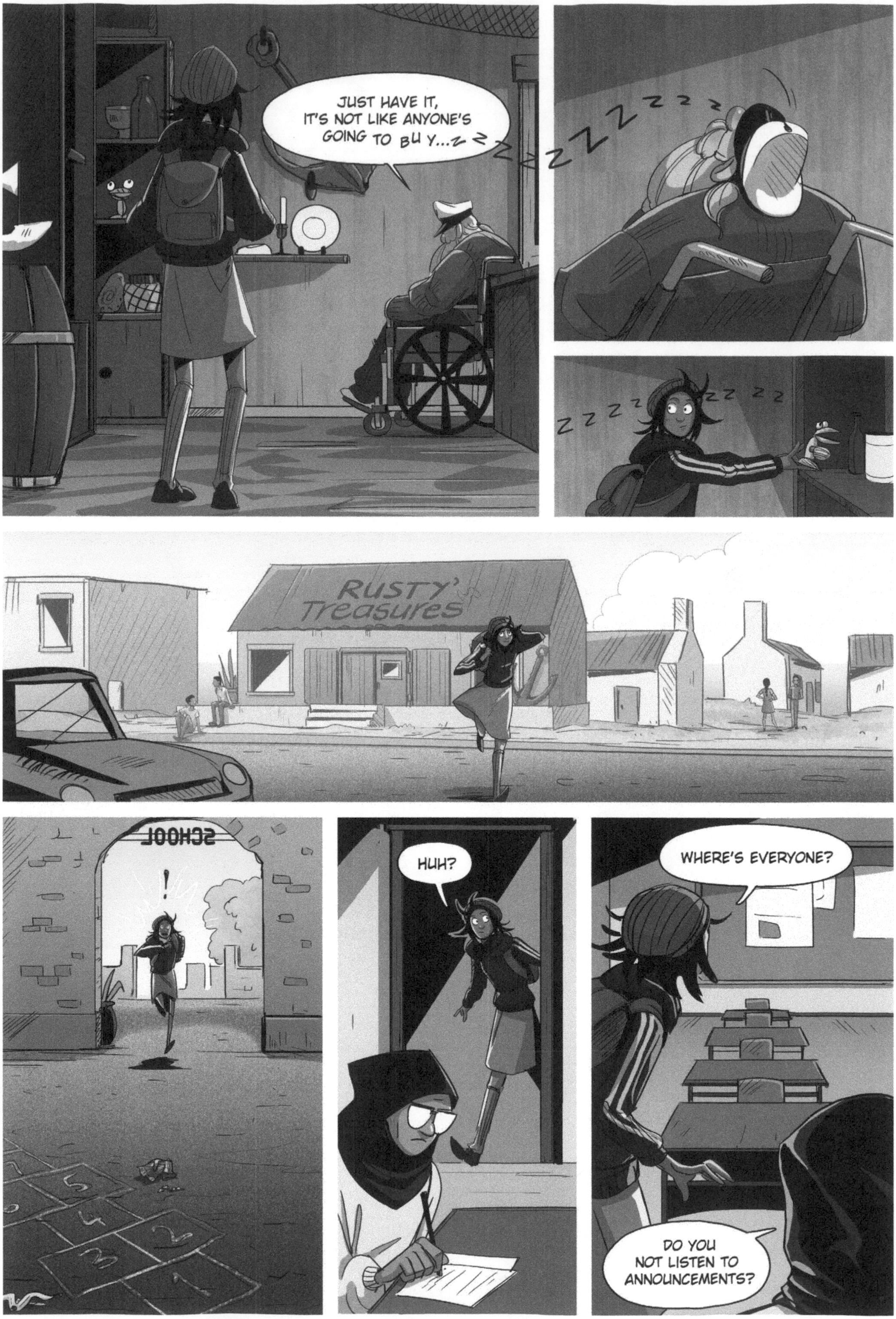
JUST HAVE IT, IT'S NOT LIKE ANYONE'S GOING TO BUY...Z Z
ZZZZZZZ Z Z Z
Z Z Z Z
Z Z Z Z Z
RUSTY' Treasures
SCHOOL
!
HUH?
WHERE'S EVERYONE?
DO YOU NOT LISTEN TO ANNOUNCEMENTS?

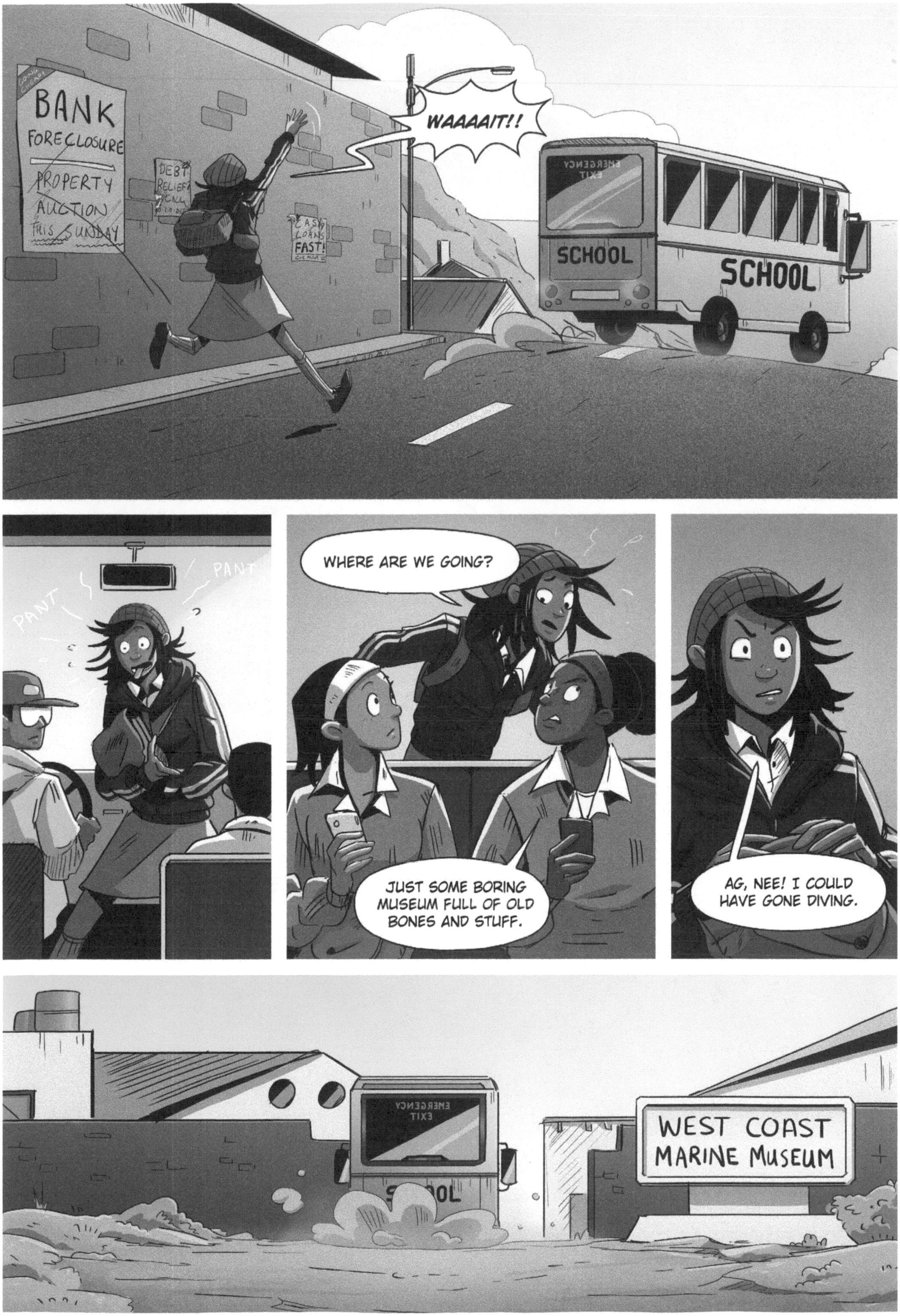
BANK
FORECLOSURE
PROPERTY
AUCTION
THIS SUNDAY
DEBT RELIEF CALL
CASH LOANS FAST!
WAAAAIT!!
SCHOOL
SCHOOL
PANT
PANT
WHERE ARE WE GOING?
JUST SOME BORING MUSEUM FULL OF OLD BONES AND STUFF.
AG, NEE! I COULD HAVE GONE DIVING.
WEST COAST MARINE MUSEUM

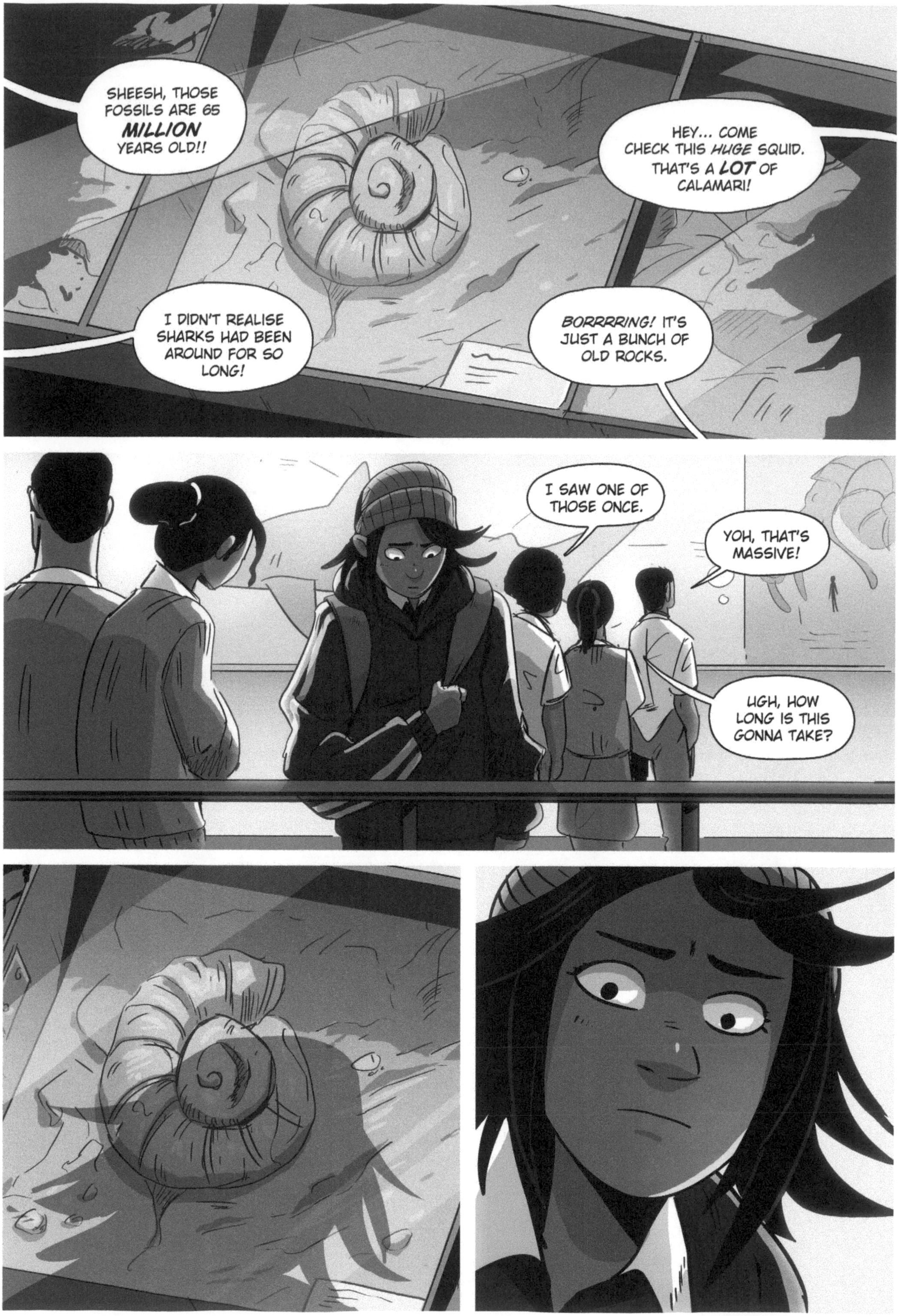
SHEESH, THOSE FOSSILS ARE 65 MILLION YEARS OLD!!
HEY... COME CHECK THIS HUGE SQUID. THAT'S A LOT OF CALAMARI!
I DIDN'T REALISE SHARKS HAD BEEN AROUND FOR SO LONG!
BORRRRING! IT'S JUST A BUNCH OF OLD ROCKS.
I SAW ONE OF THOSE ONCE.
YOH, THAT'S MASSIVE!
UGH, HOW LONG IS THIS GONNA TAKE?

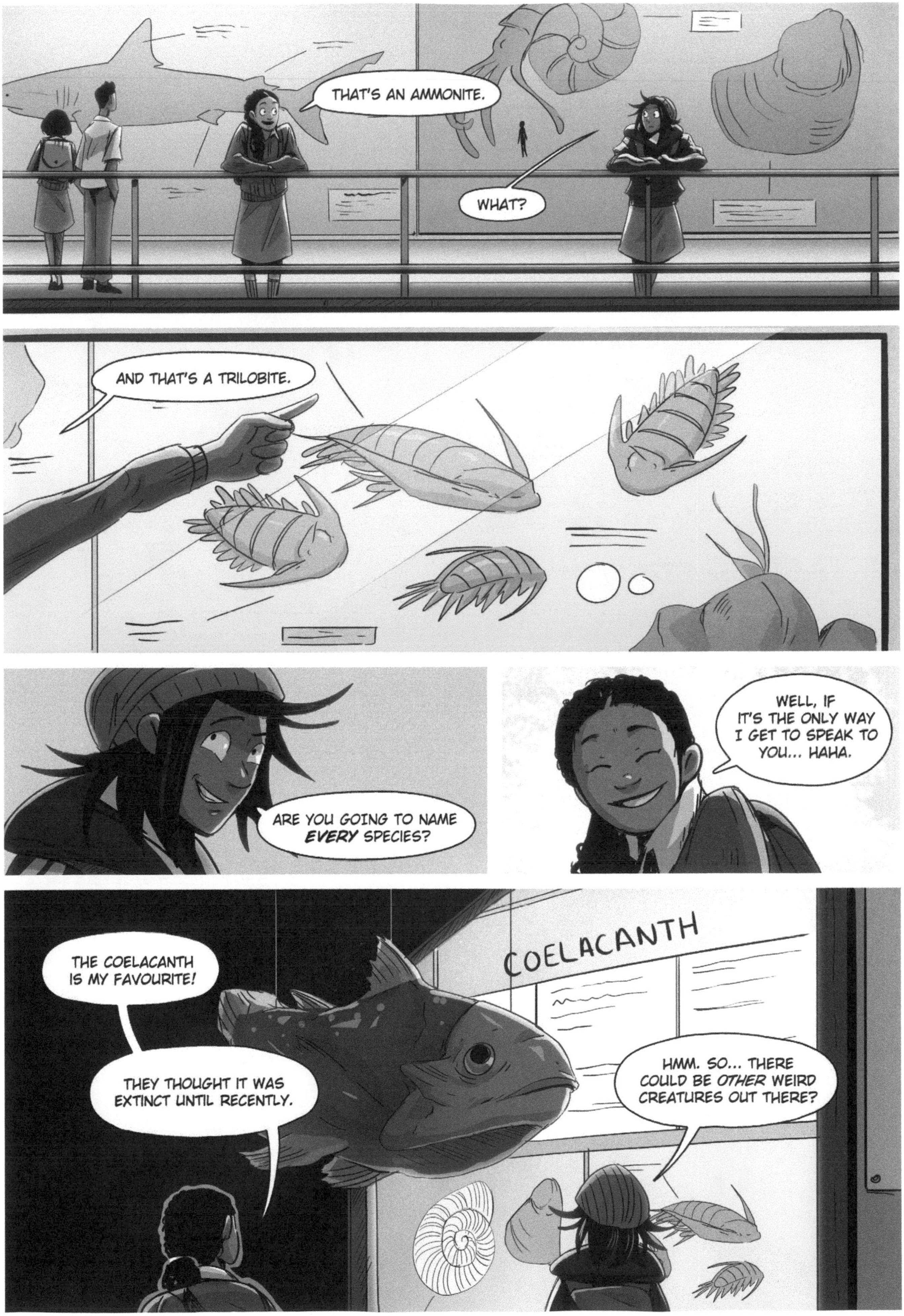
THAT'S AN AMMONITE.
WHAT?
AND THAT'S A TRILOBITE.
ARE YOU GOING TO NAME *EVERY* SPECIES?
WELL, IF IT'S THE ONLY WAY I GET TO SPEAK TO YOU... HAHA.
COELACANTH
THE COELACANTH IS MY FAVOURITE!
THEY THOUGHT IT WAS EXTINCT UNTIL RECENTLY.
HMM. SO... THERE COULD BE *OTHER* WEIRD CREATURES OUT THERE?

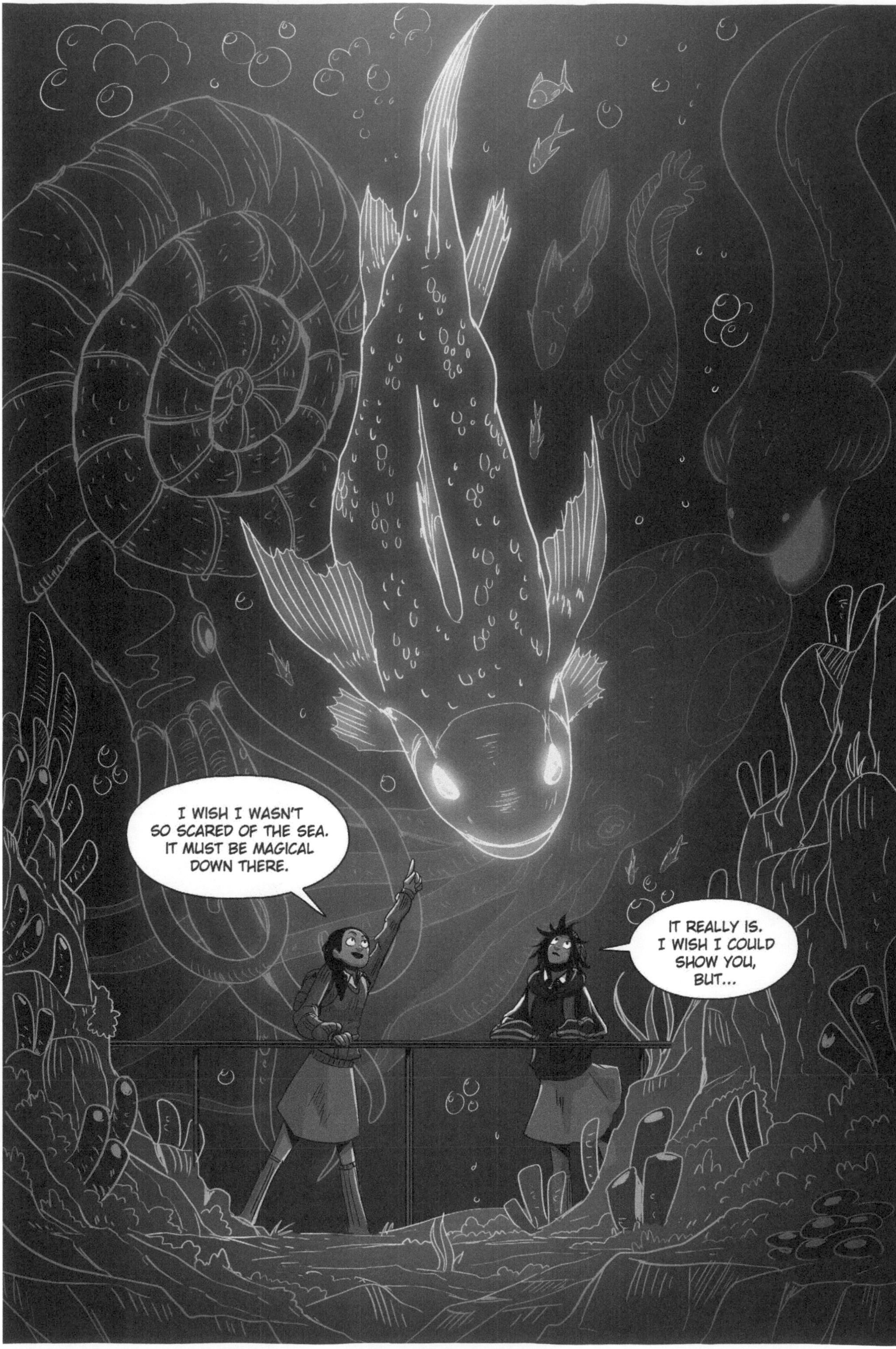
I WISH I WASN'T SO SCARED OF THE SEA. IT MUST BE MAGICAL DOWN THERE.
IT REALLY IS. I WISH I COULD SHOW YOU, BUT...

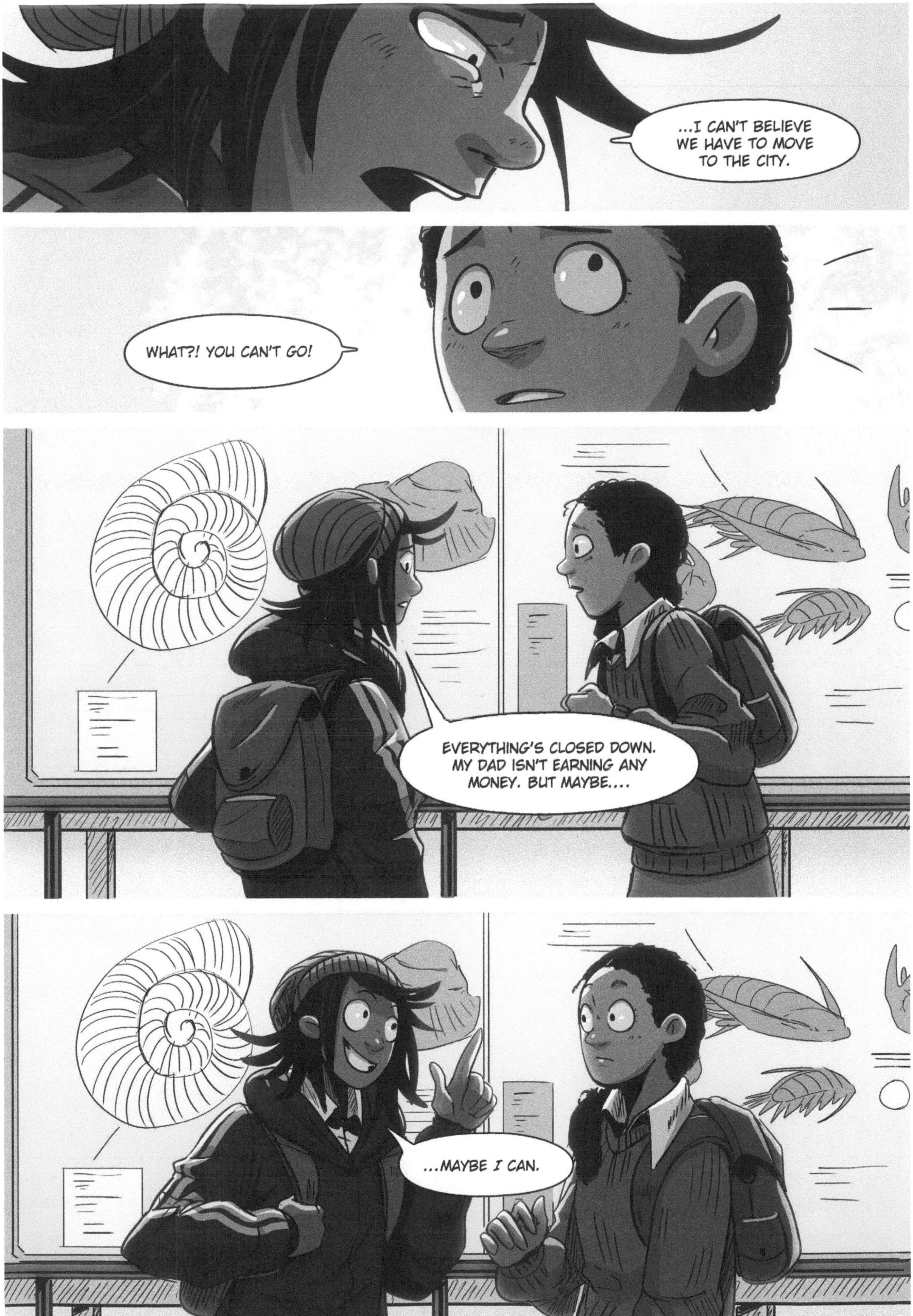
...I CAN'T BELIEVE WE HAVE TO MOVE TO THE CITY.
WHAT?! YOU CAN'T GO!
EVERYTHING'S CLOSED DOWN. MY DAD ISN'T EARNING ANY MONEY. BUT MAYBE....
...MAYBE I CAN.

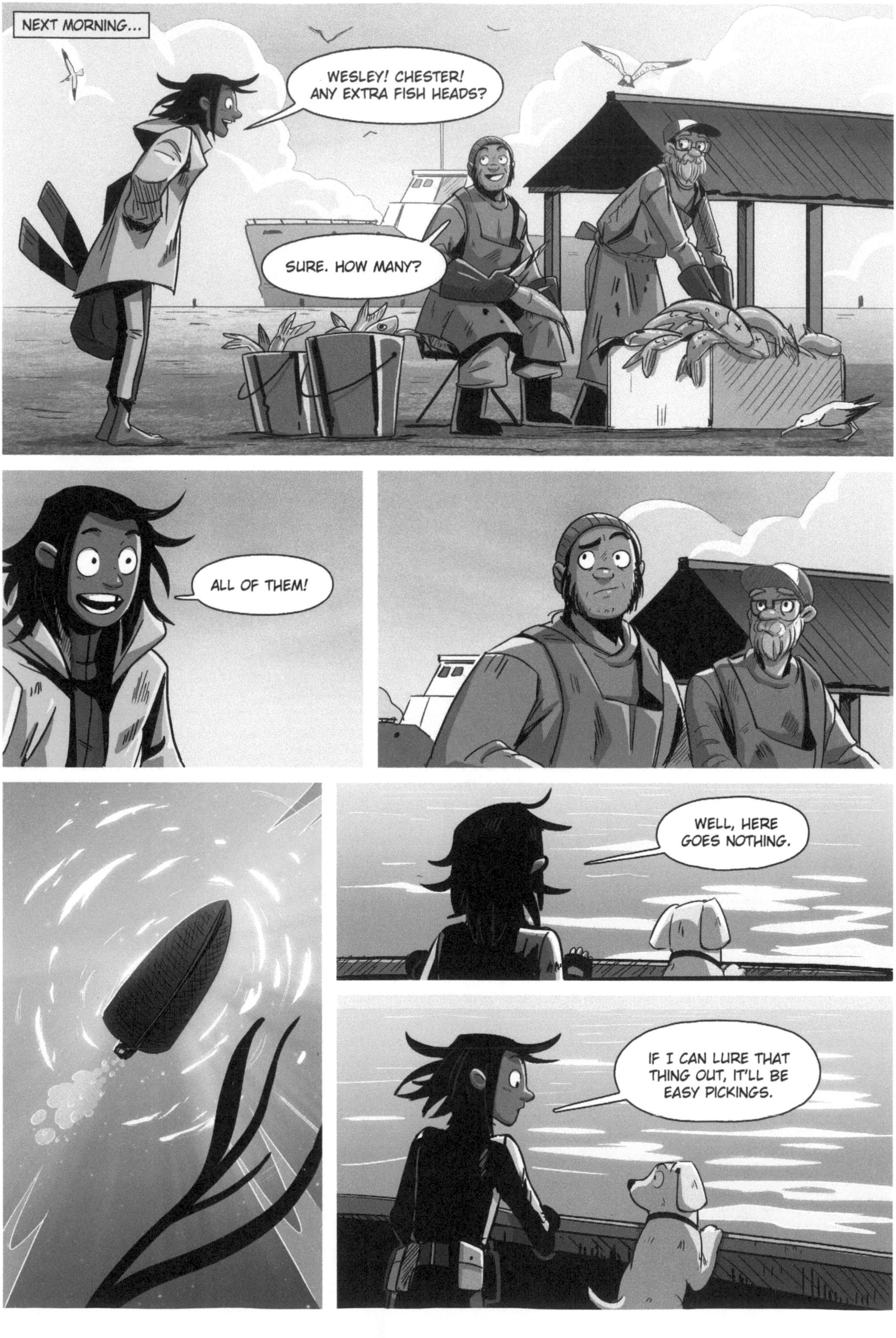
NEXT MORNING...
WESLEY! CHESTER! ANY EXTRA FISH HEADS?
SURE. HOW MANY?
ALL OF THEM!
WELL, HERE GOES NOTHING.
IF I CAN LURE THAT THING OUT, IT'LL BE EASY PICKINGS.

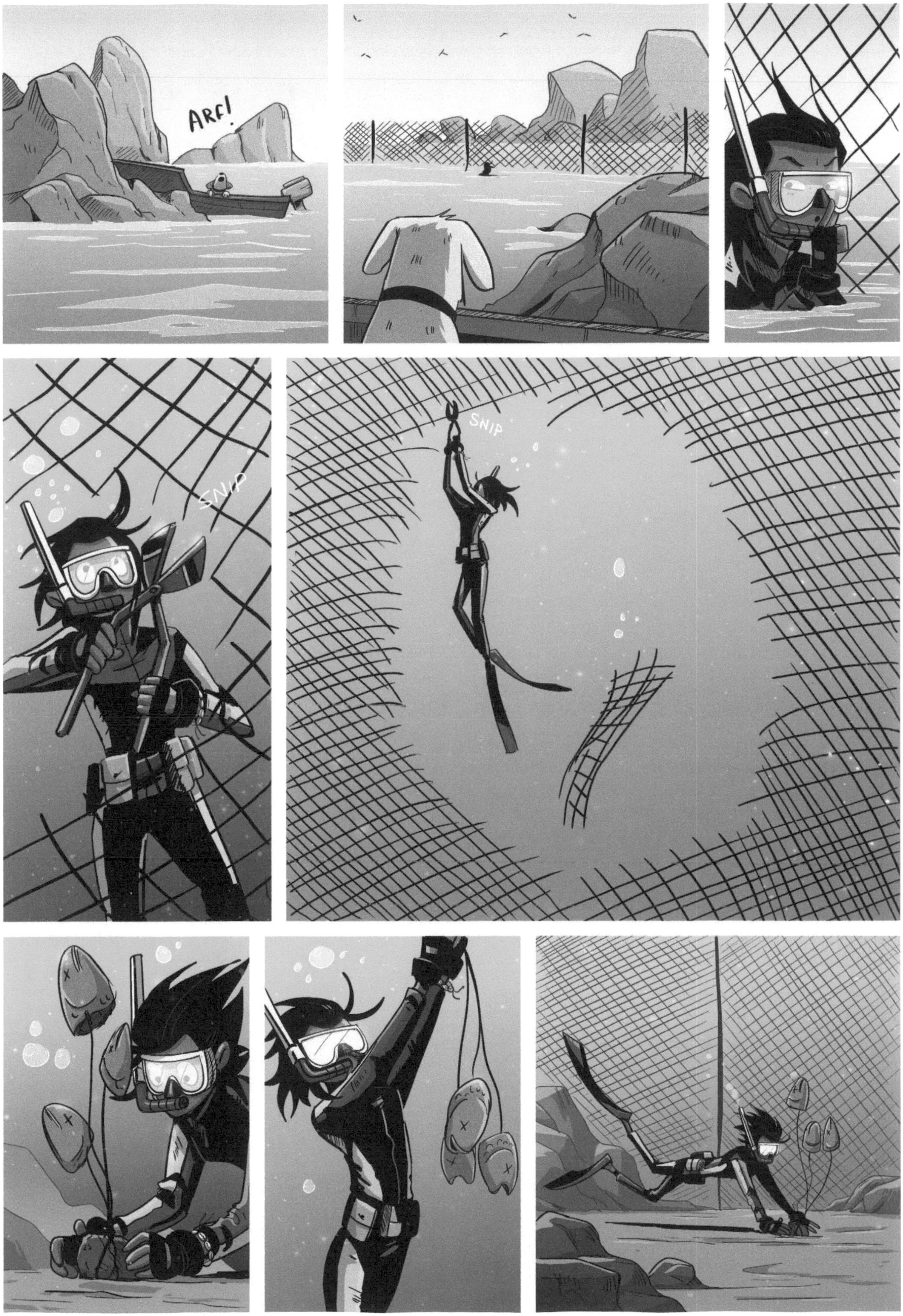
ARF!
SNIP
SNIP

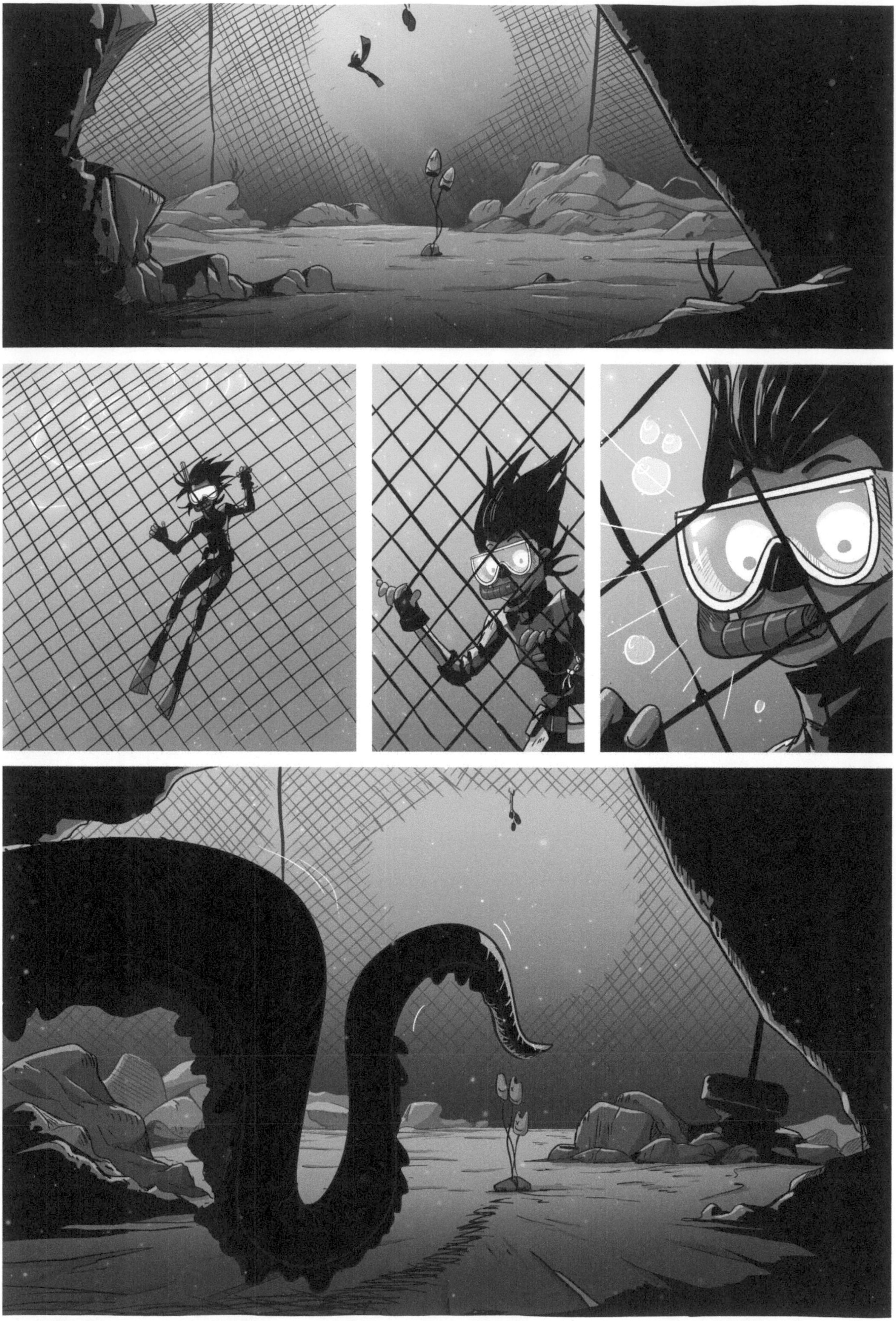

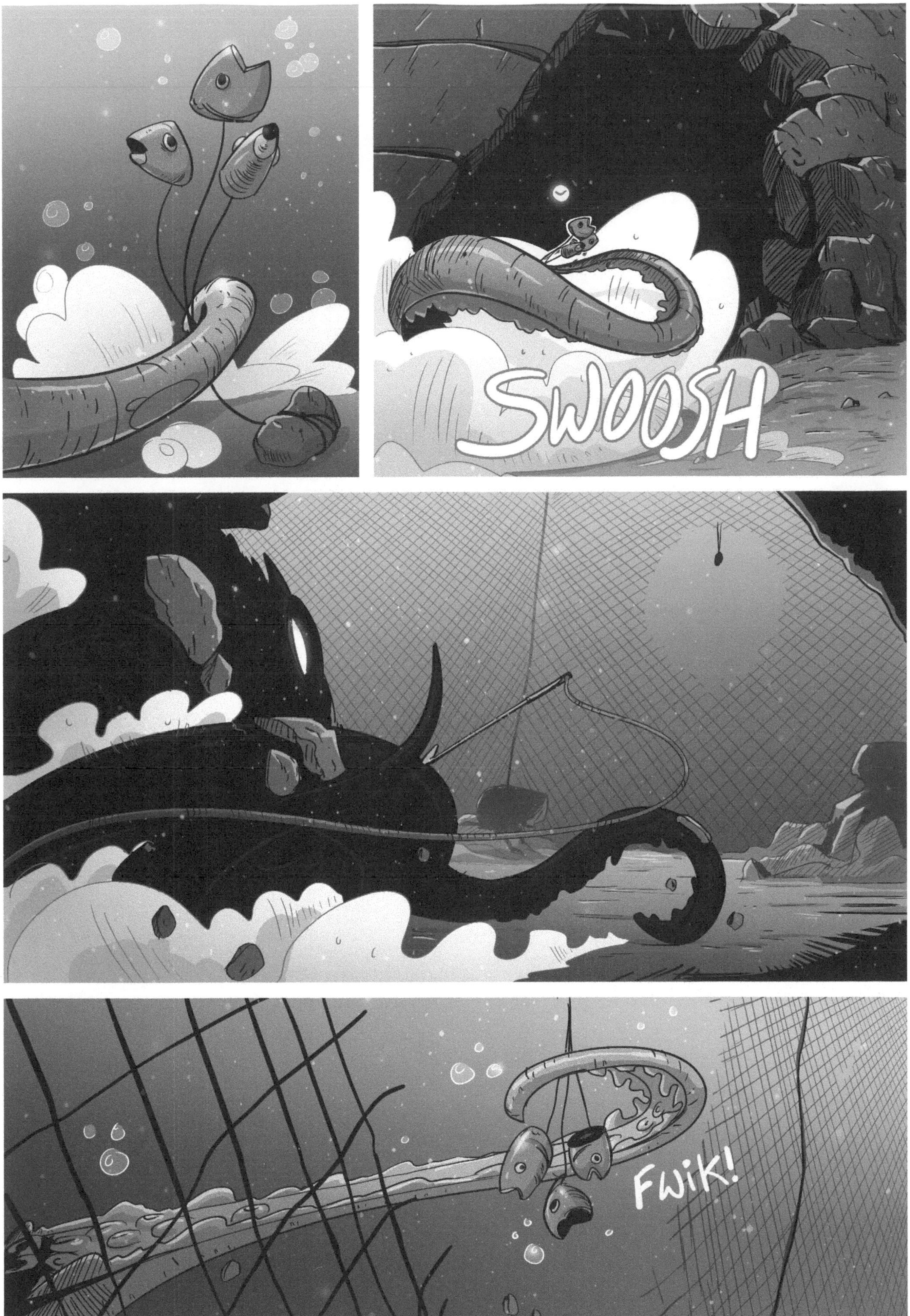
SWOOSH
FWIK!

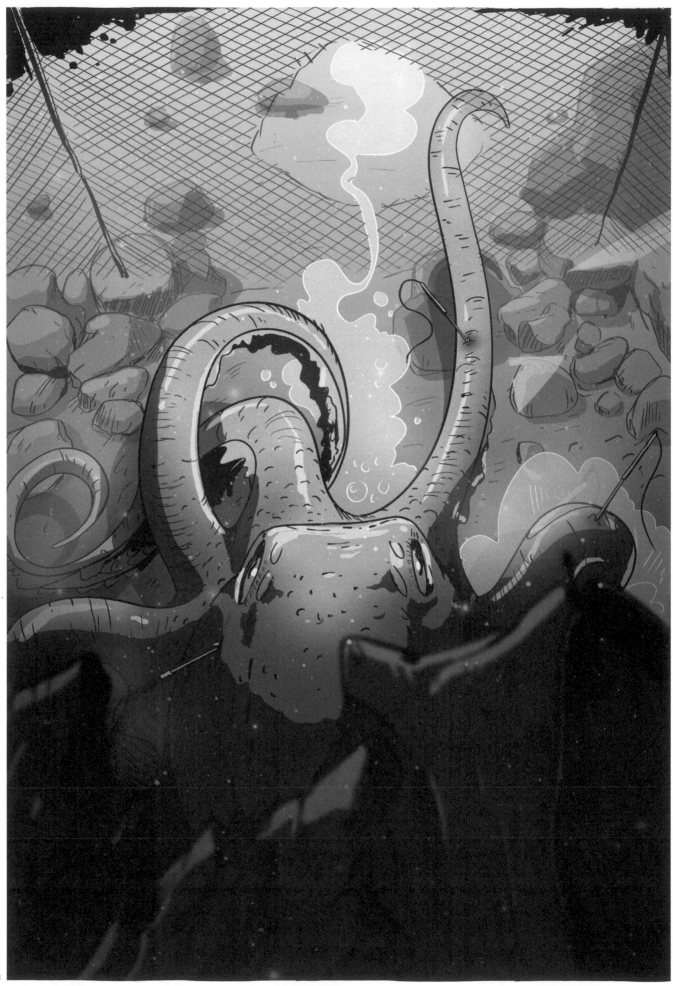

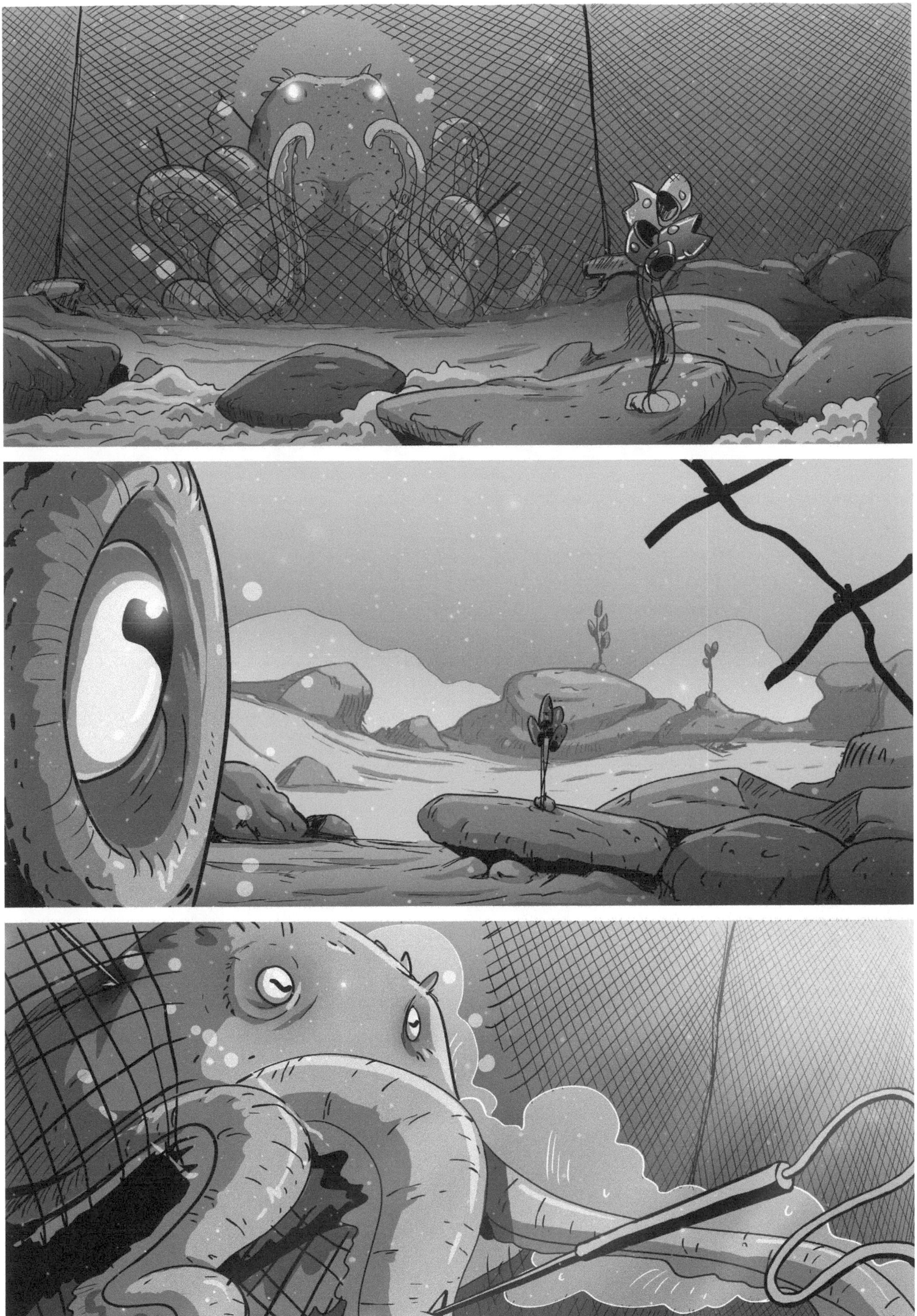

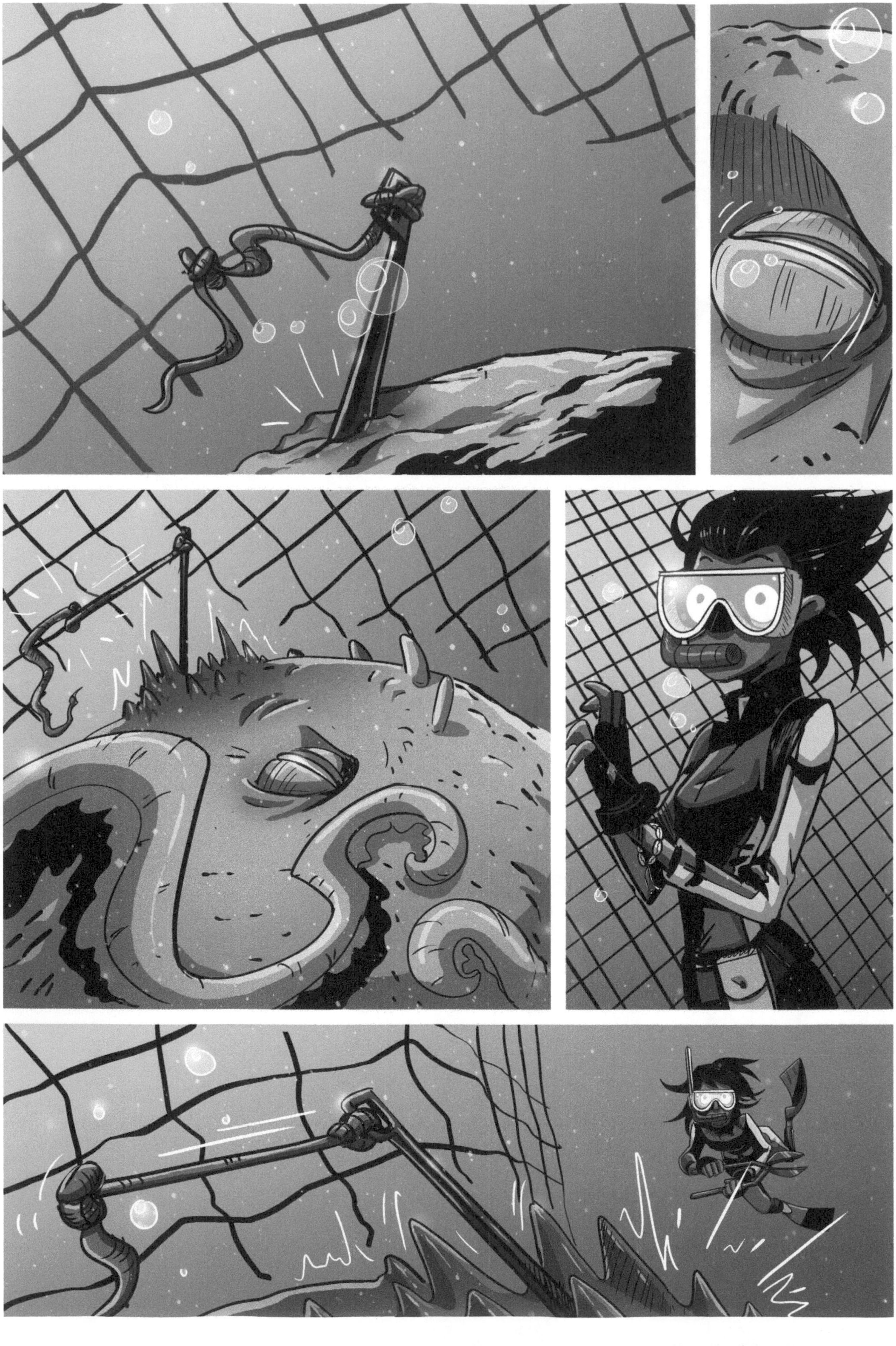

CLIP

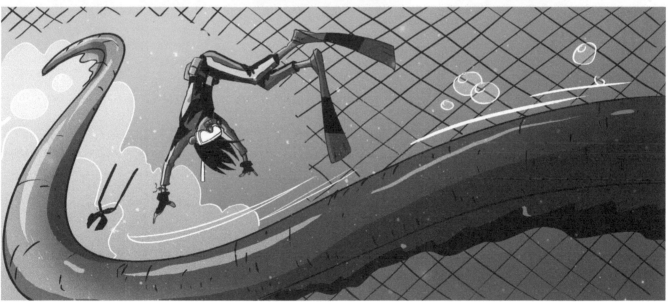

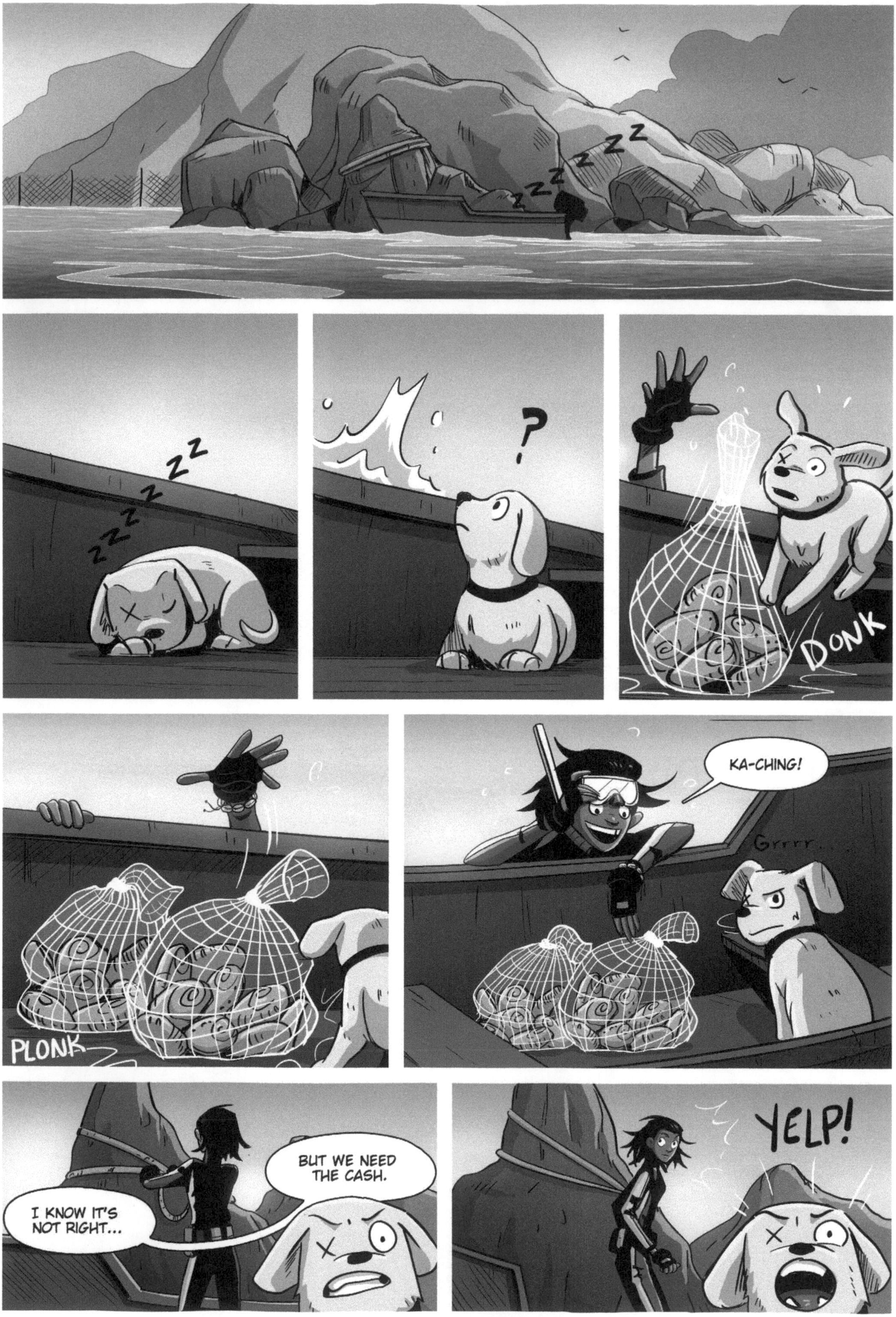
ZZZZZZZ
ZZZZZZ
?
DONK
PLONK
KA-CHING!
Grrrr...
I KNOW IT'S NOT RIGHT...
BUT WE NEED THE CASH.
YELP!

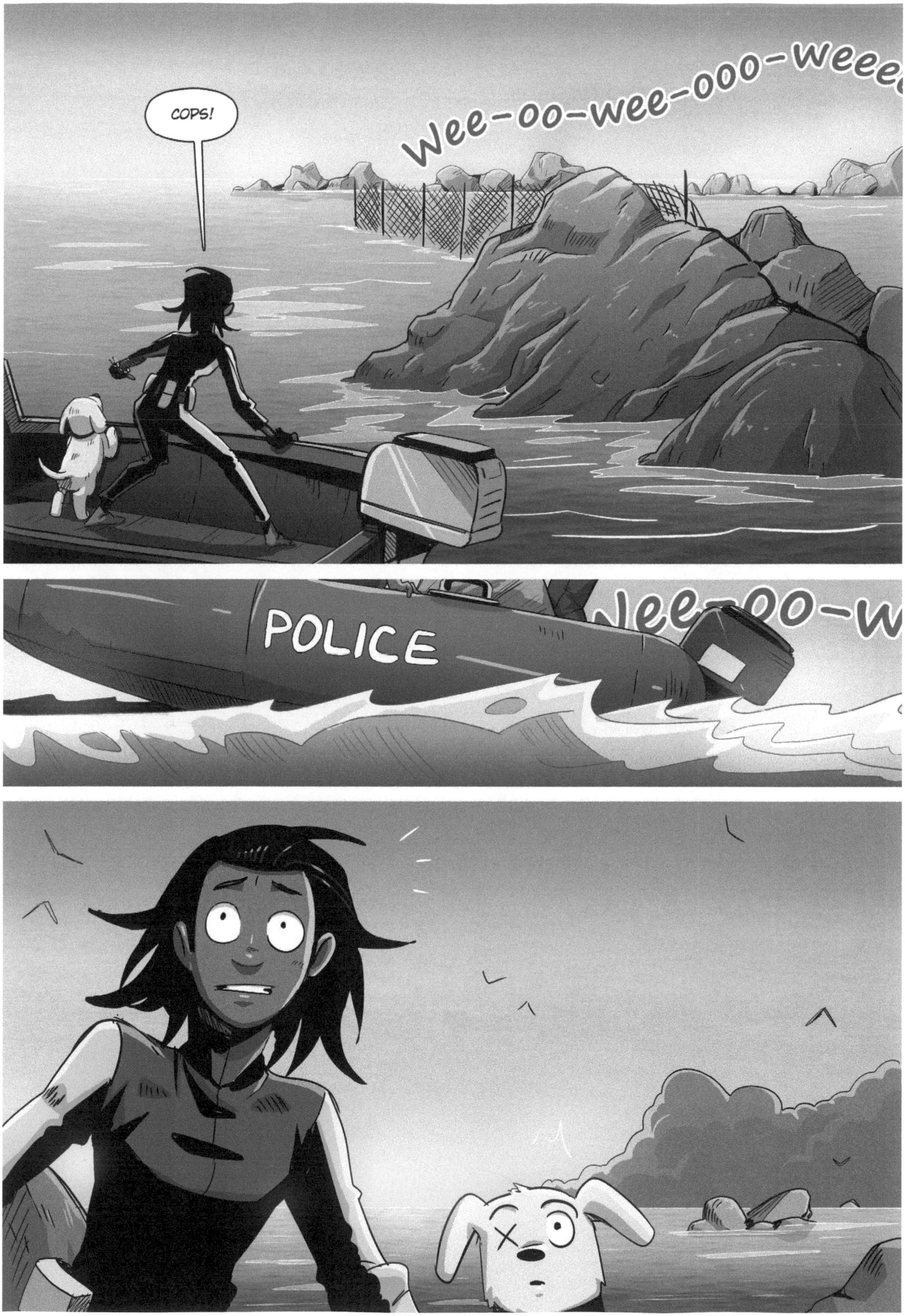
COPS!
Wee-oo-wee-ooo-weeee
POLICE
Wee-oo-w

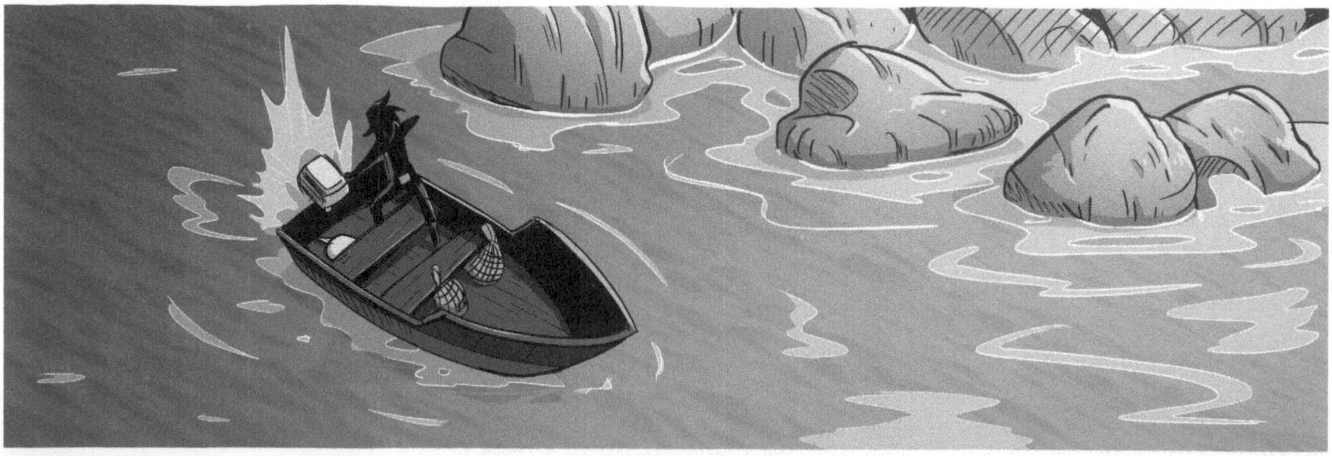
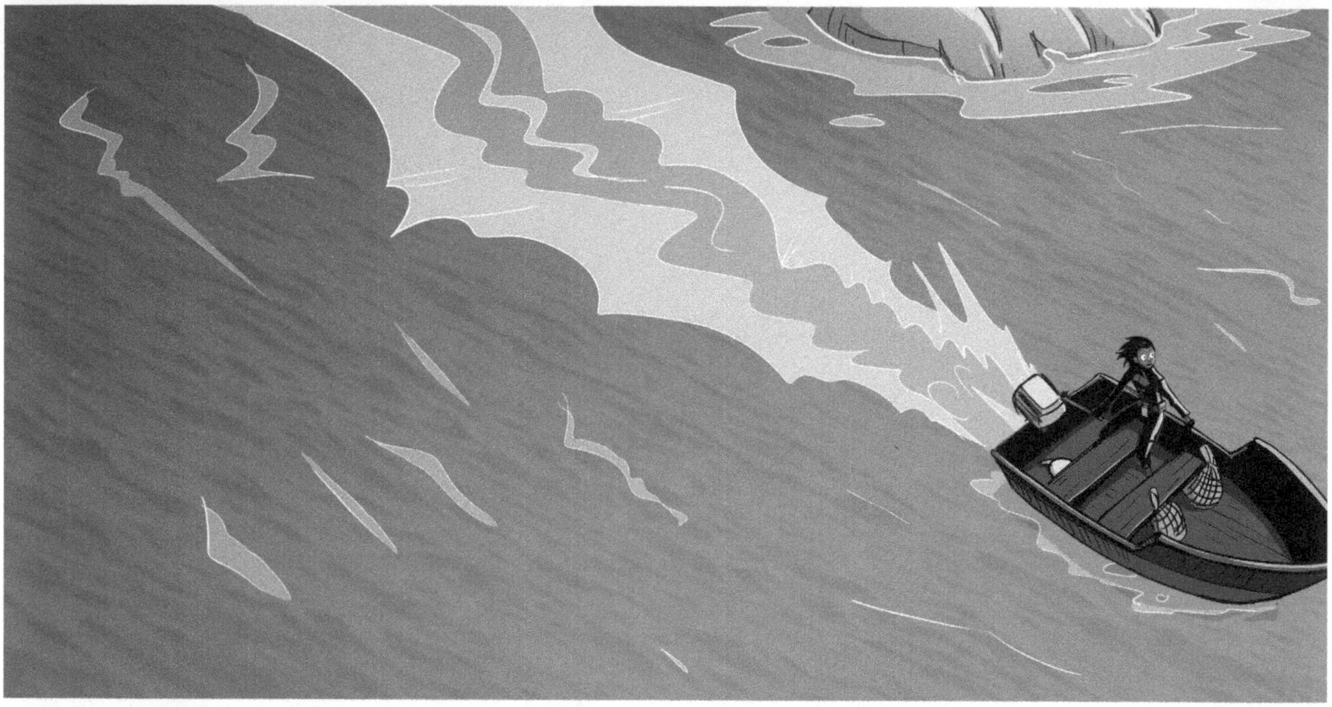
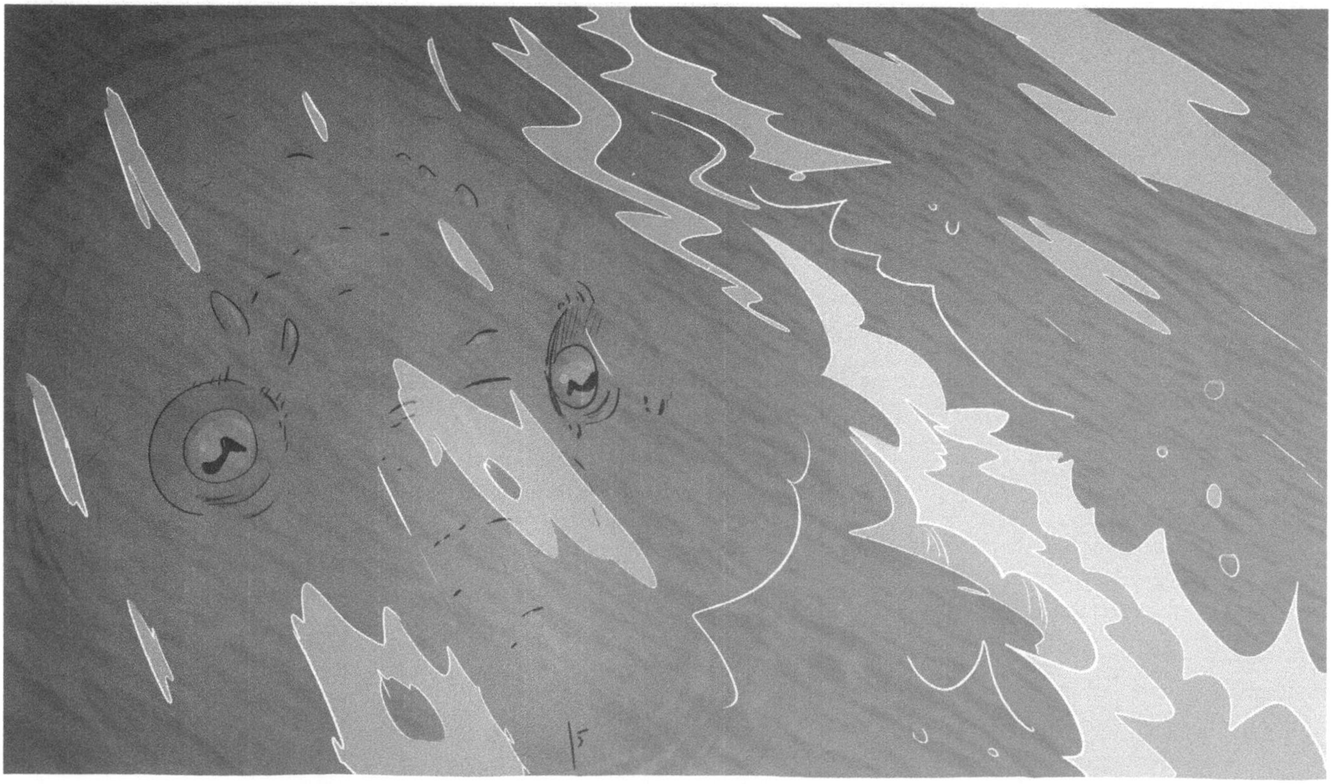

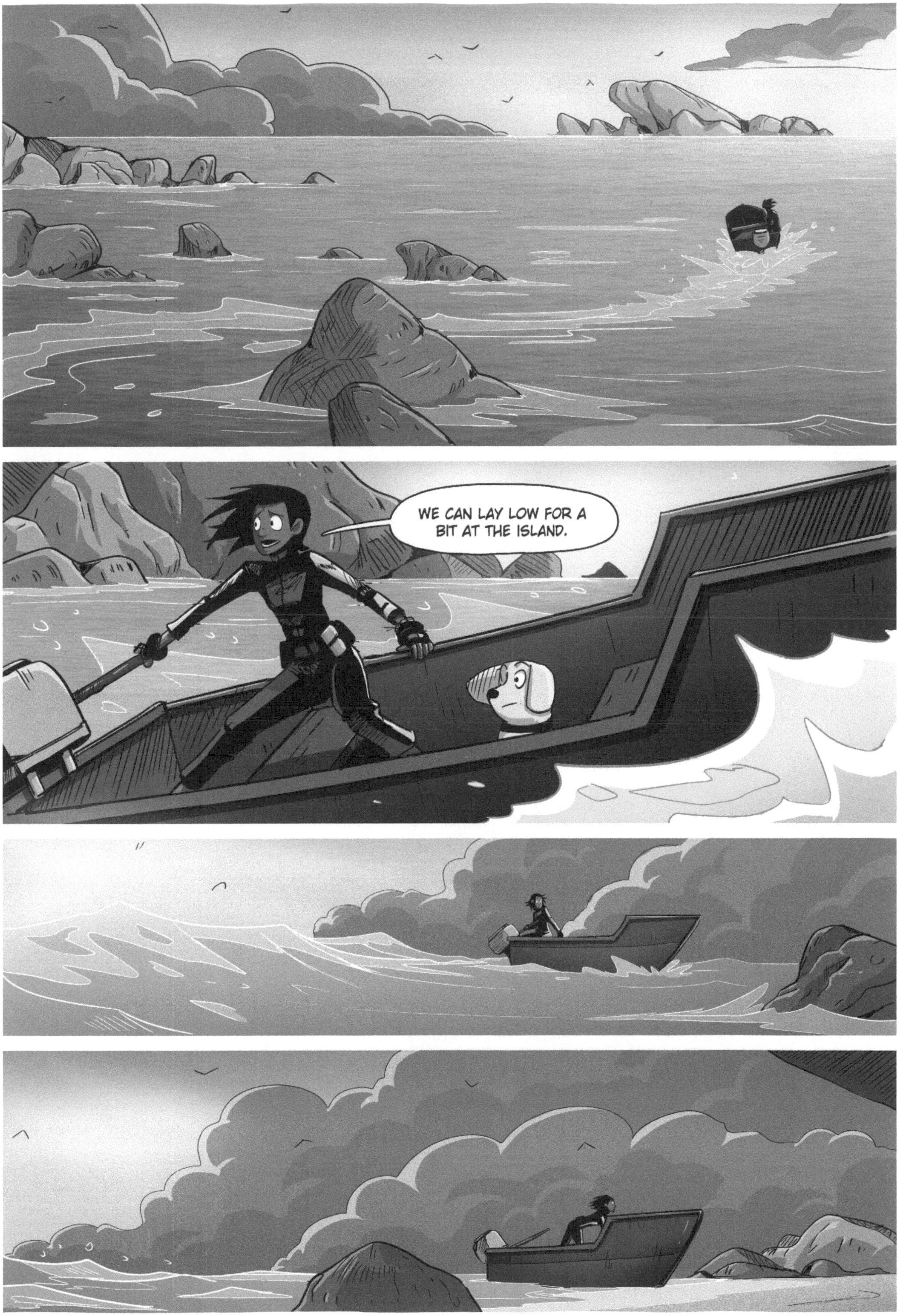
WE CAN LAY LOW FOR A BIT AT THE ISLAND.

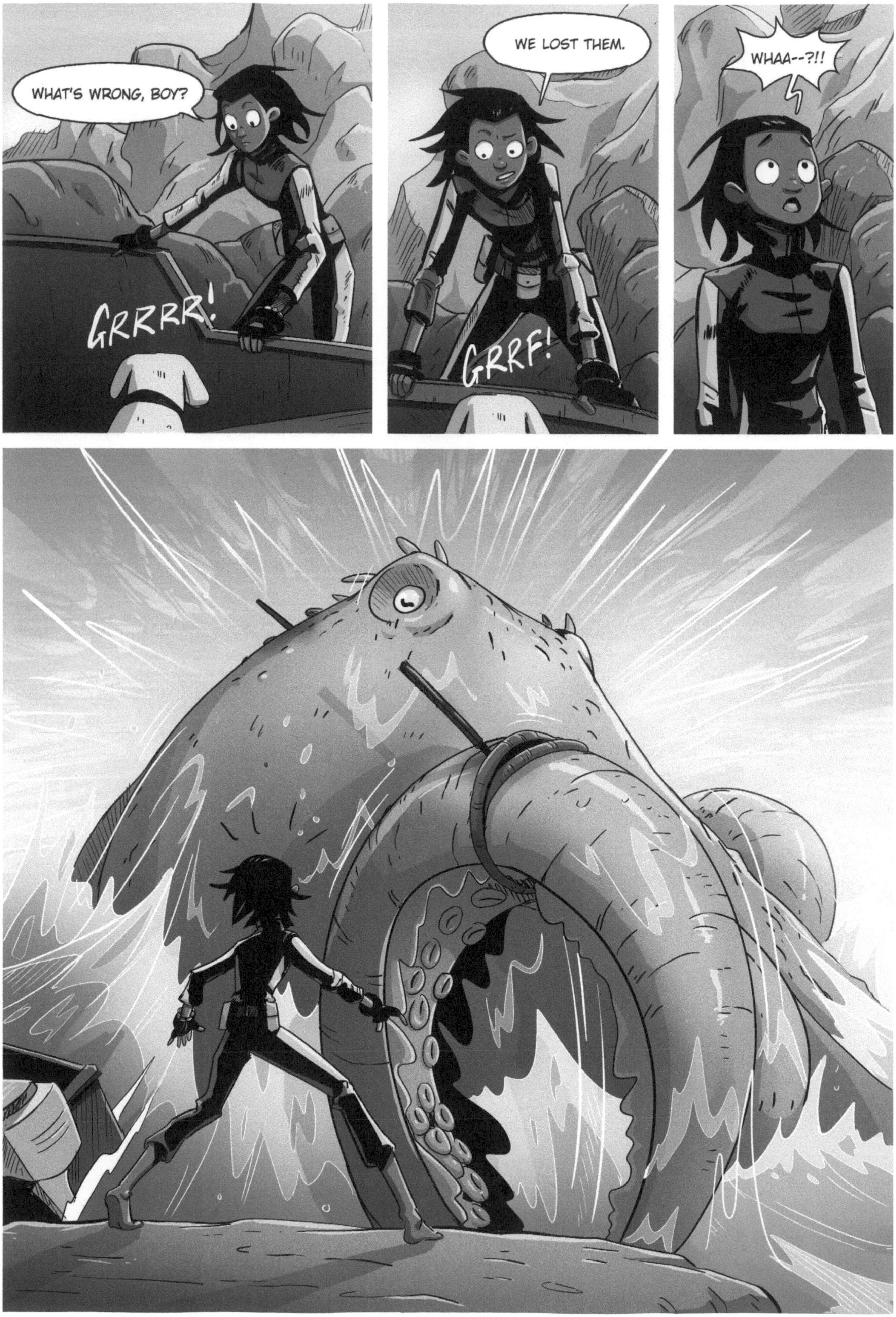
WHAT'S WRONG, BOY?
GRRRR!
WE LOST THEM.
GRRF!
WHAA--?!!

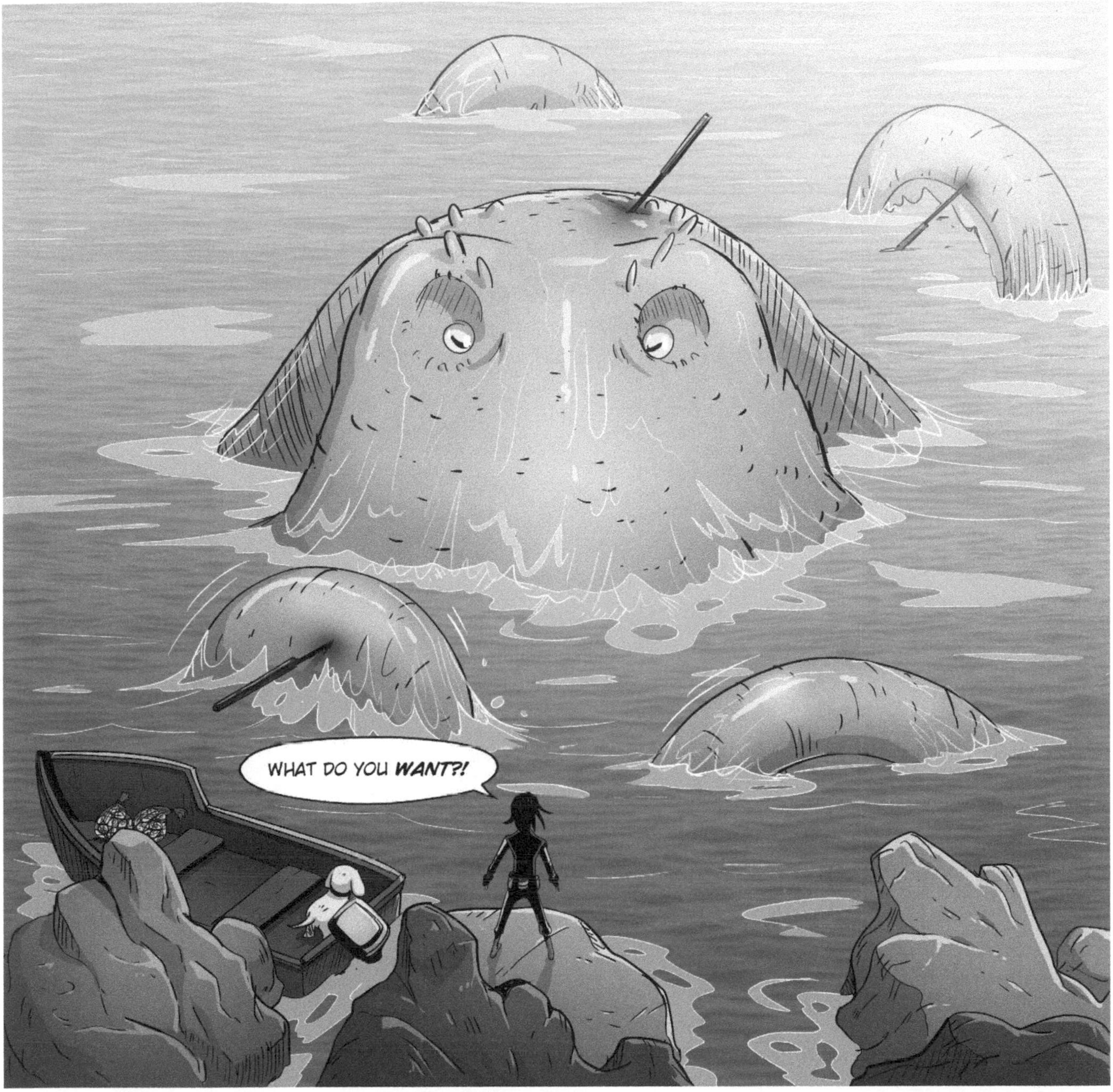
WHAT DO YOU WANT?!

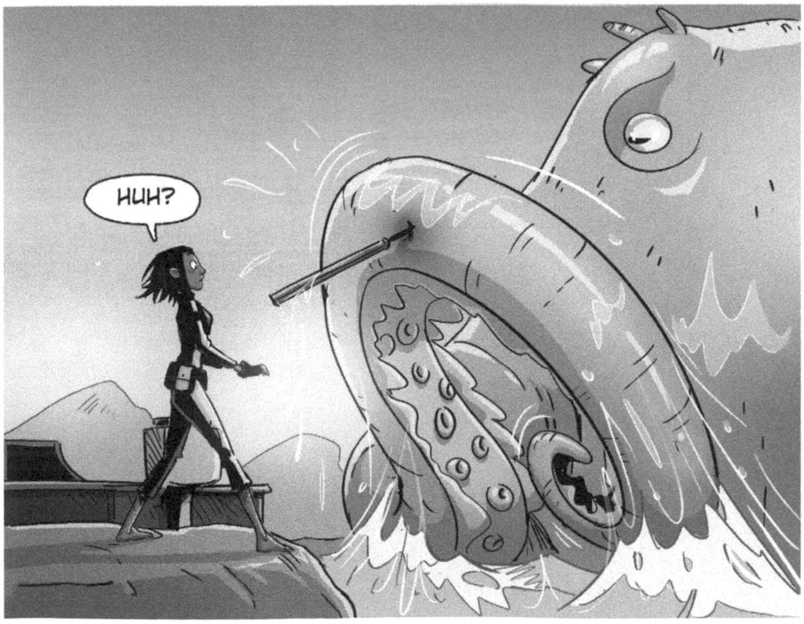
HUH?

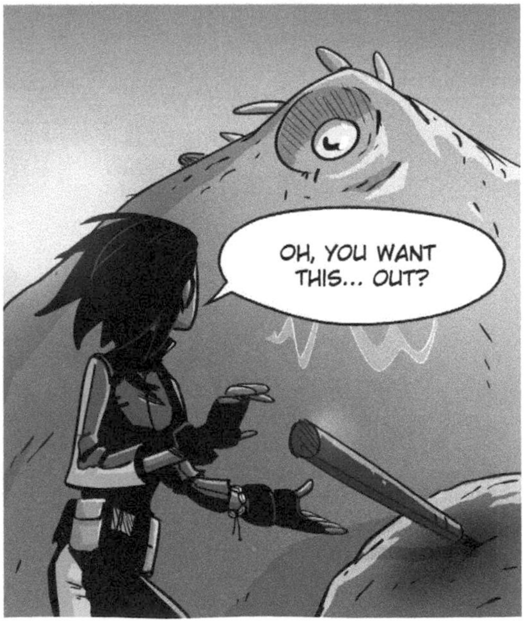
OH, YOU WANT THIS... OUT?

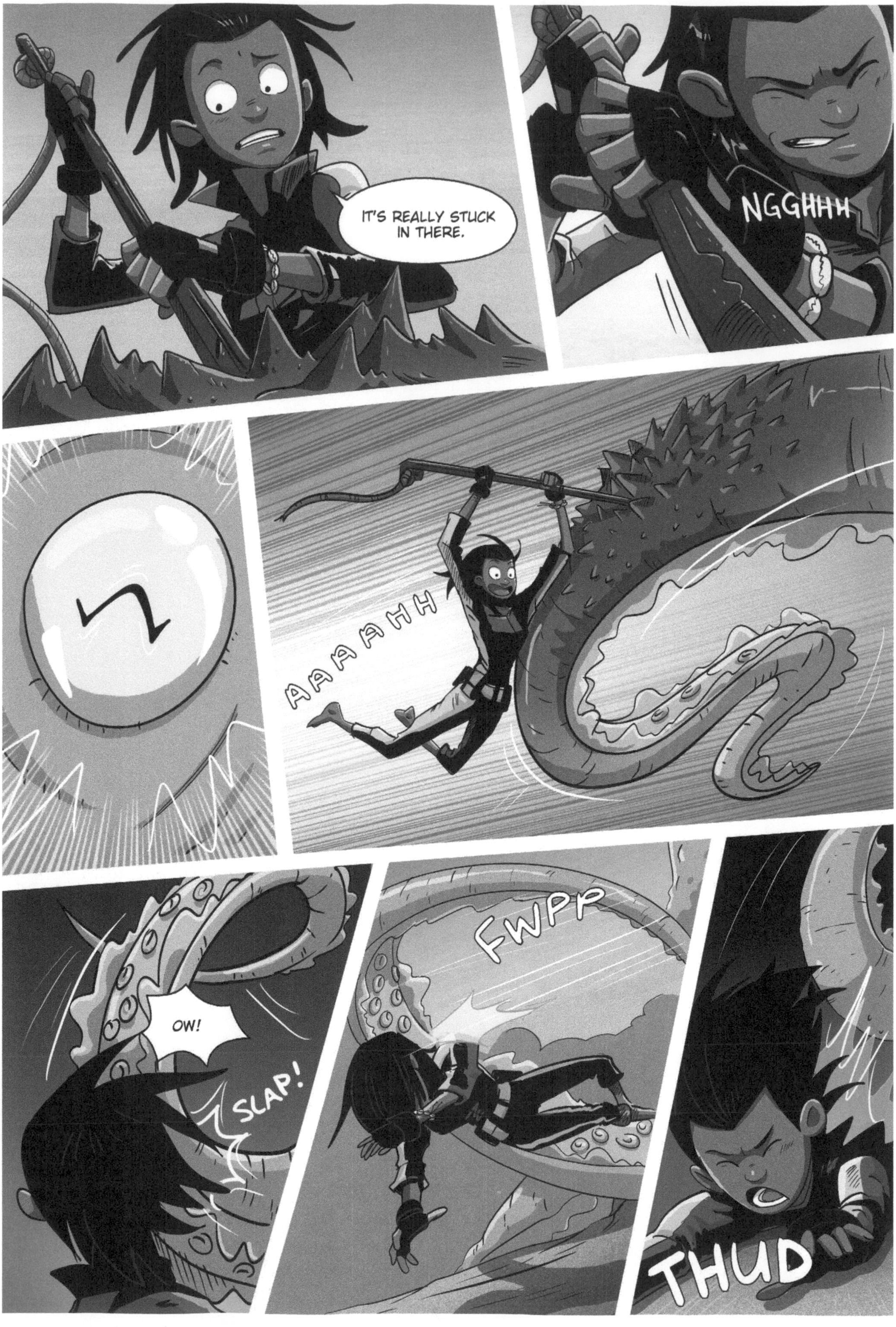

IT'S REALLY STUCK IN THERE.
NGGHHH
AAAAAHH
OW!
SLAP!
FWPP
THUD

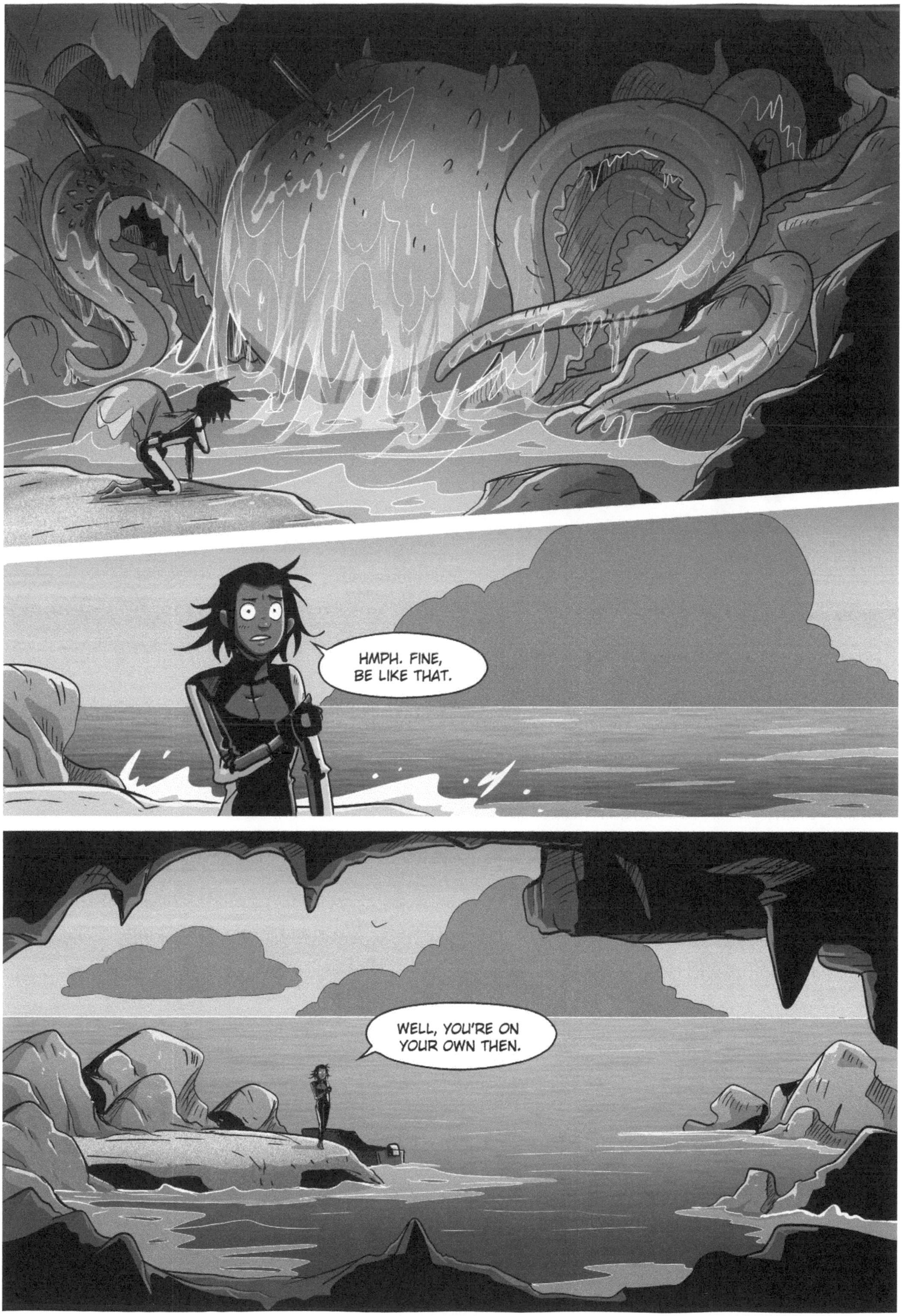
HMPH. FINE, BE LIKE THAT.
WELL, YOU'RE ON YOUR OWN THEN.

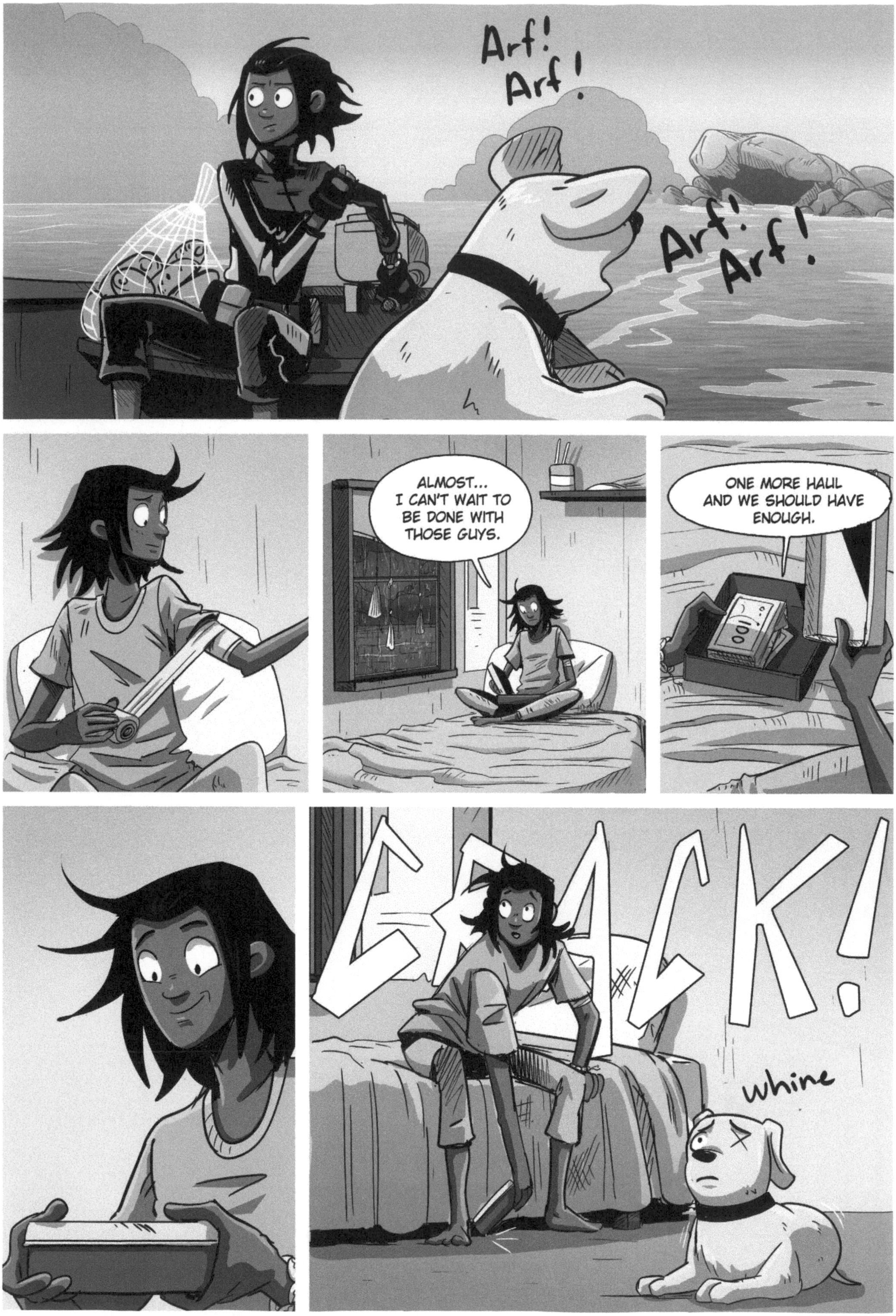
Arf! Arf!
Arf! Arf!
ALMOST... I CAN'T WAIT TO BE DONE WITH THOSE GUYS.
ONE MORE HAUL AND WE SHOULD HAVE ENOUGH.
CRACK!
whine

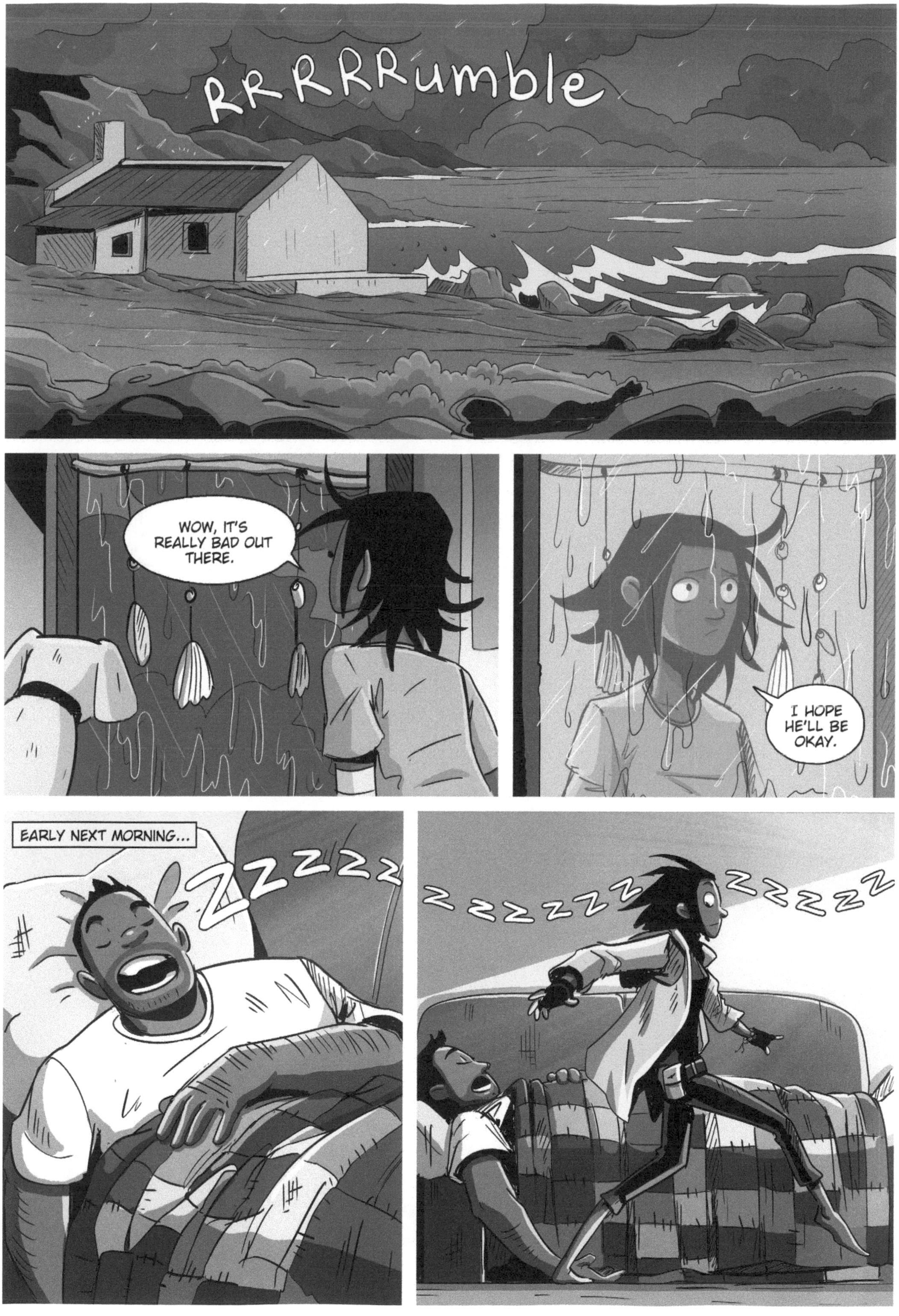
RRRRRumble
WOW, IT'S REALLY BAD OUT THERE.
I HOPE HE'LL BE OKAY.
EARLY NEXT MORNING...
ZZZZZ
ZZZZZZZ
ZZZZZZ

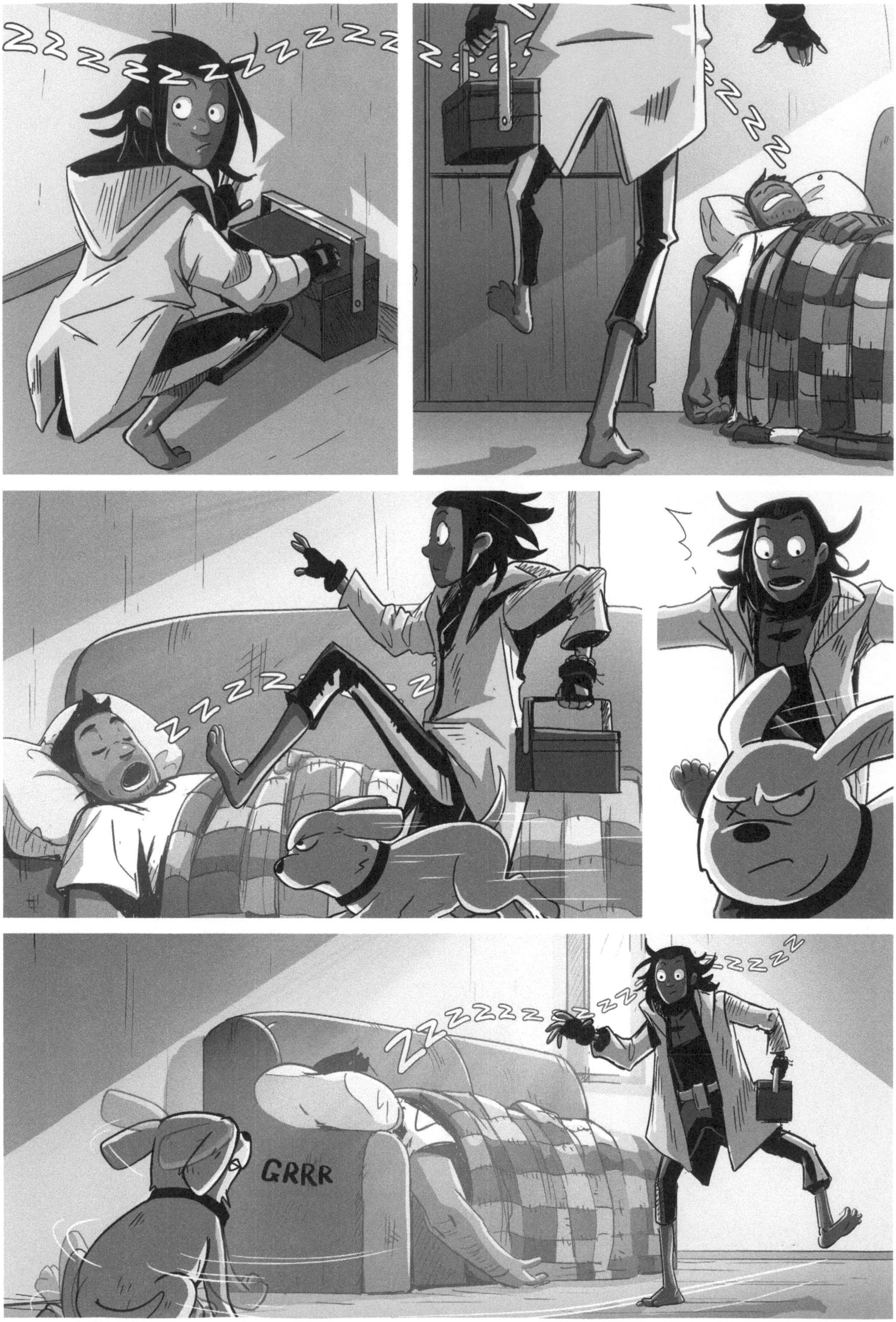
ZZZZZZZZZZZZZZ
ZZZZZZ
ZZZZZZZZZZZ
GRRR

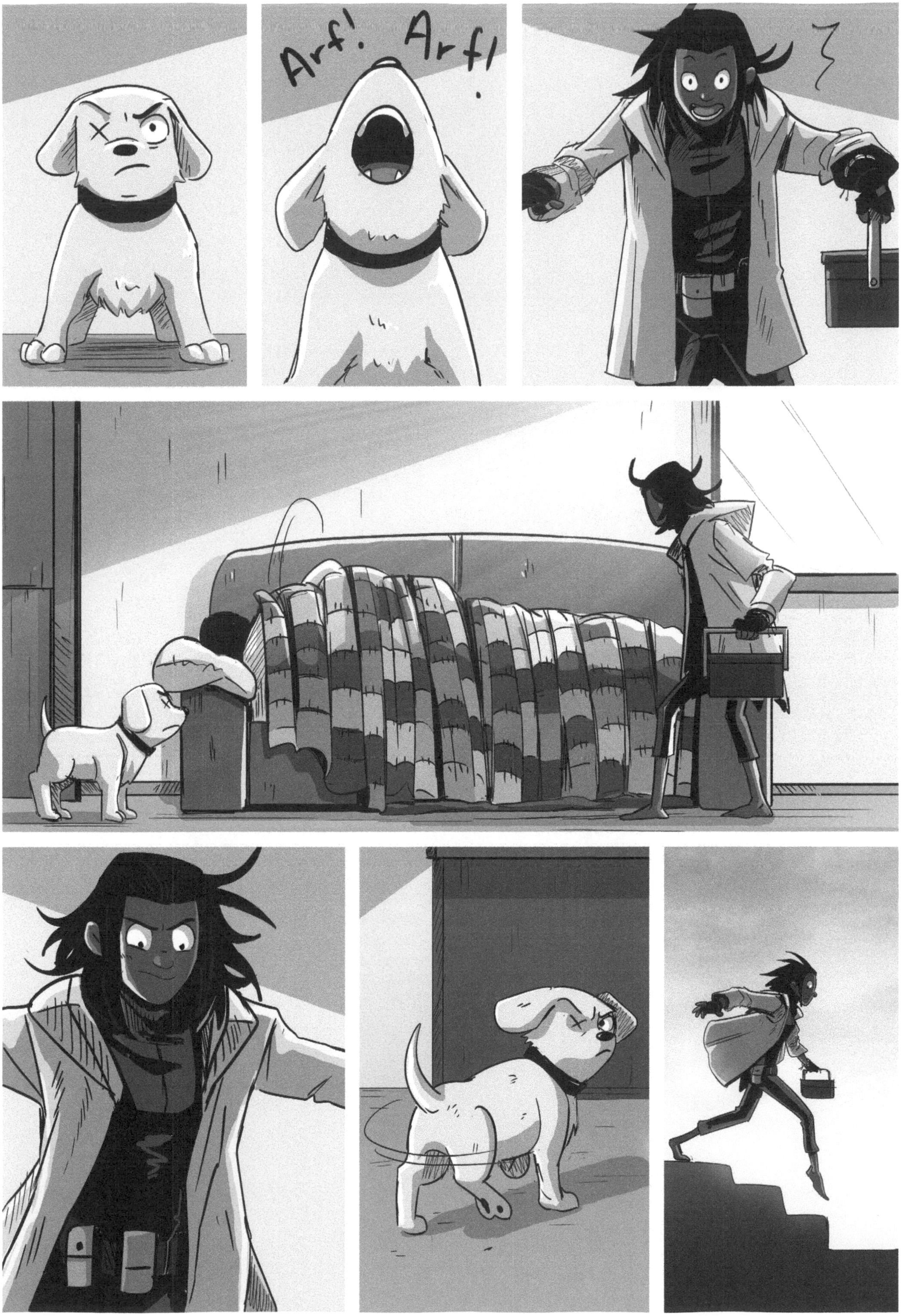
Arf! Arf!

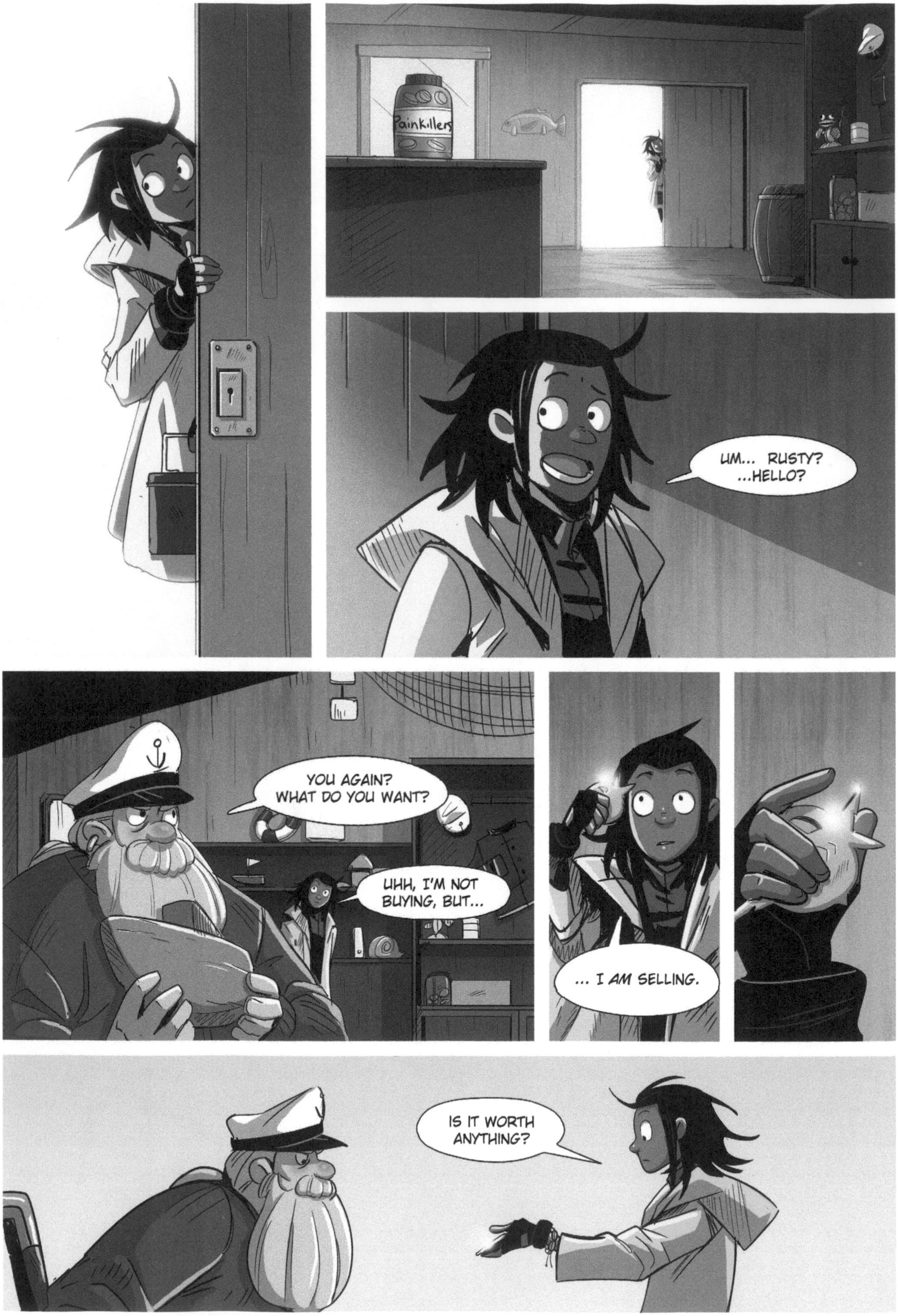
Painkillers
UM... RUSTY? ...HELLO?
YOU AGAIN? WHAT DO YOU WANT?
UHH, I'M NOT BUYING, BUT...
... I AM SELLING.
IS IT WORTH ANYTHING?

LET'S HAVE A LOOK-SEE.
Painkillers
Painkillers
20

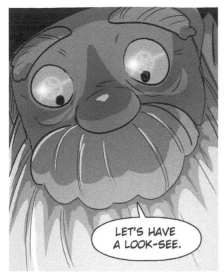

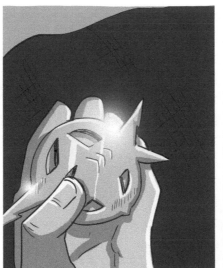

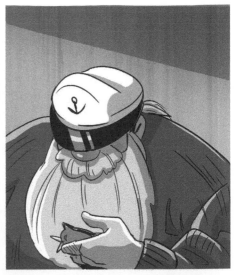

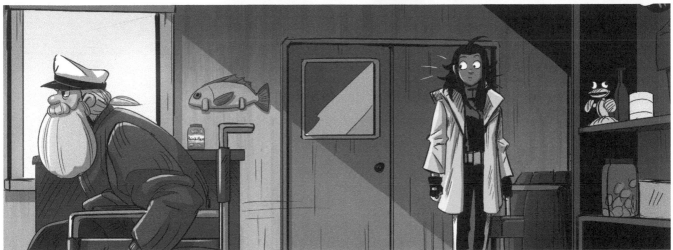

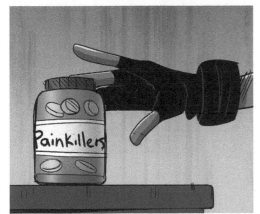

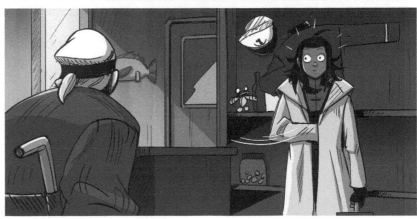

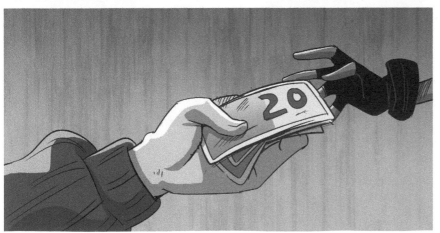

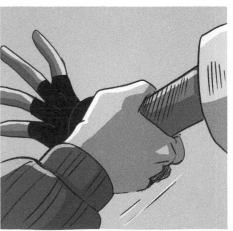

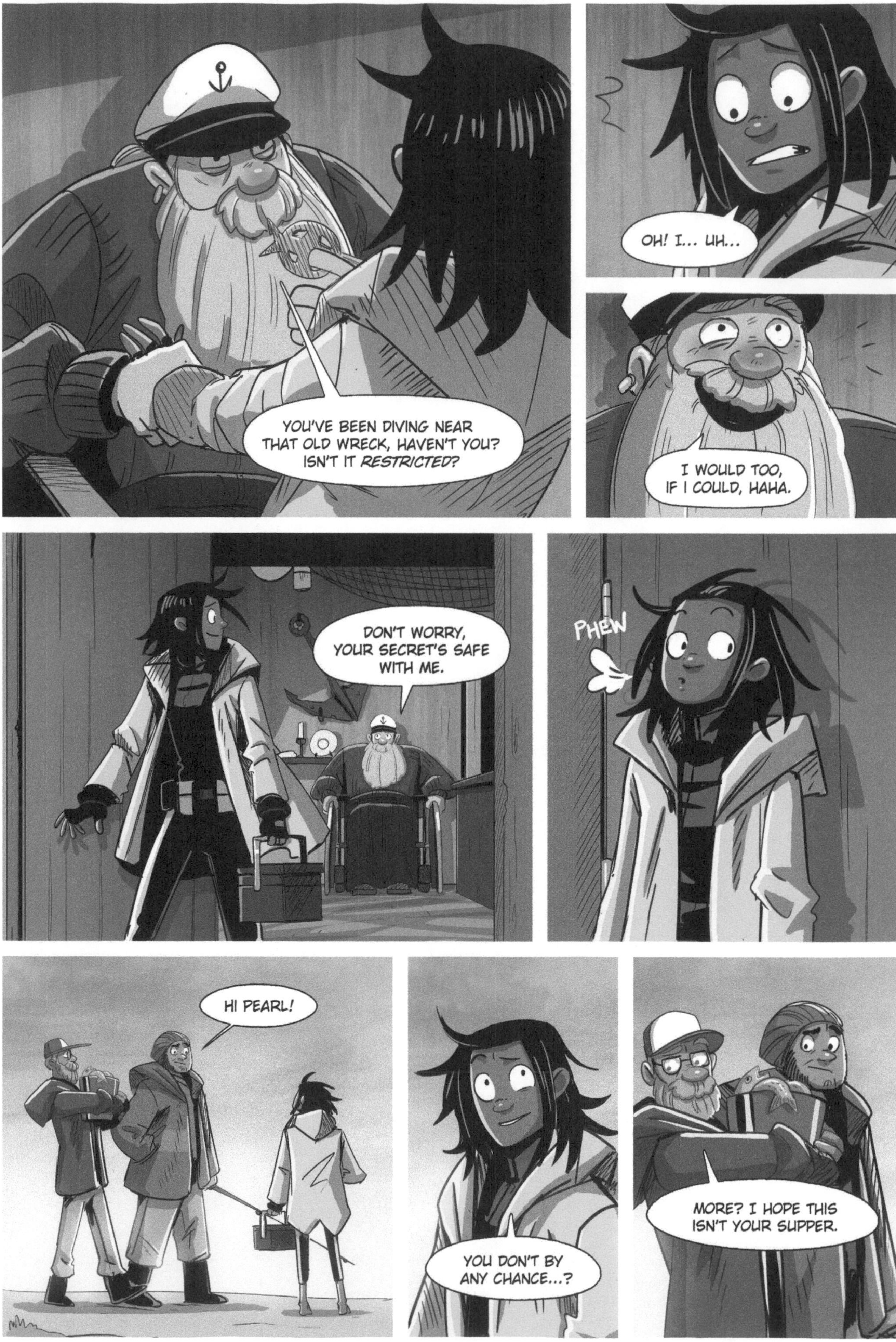
YOU'VE BEEN DIVING NEAR THAT OLD WRECK, HAVEN'T YOU? ISN'T IT *RESTRICTED*?
OH! I... UH...
I WOULD TOO, IF I COULD, HAHA.
DON'T WORRY, YOUR SECRET'S SAFE WITH ME.
PHEW
HI PEARL!
YOU DON'T BY ANY CHANCE...?
MORE? I HOPE THIS ISN'T YOUR SUPPER.

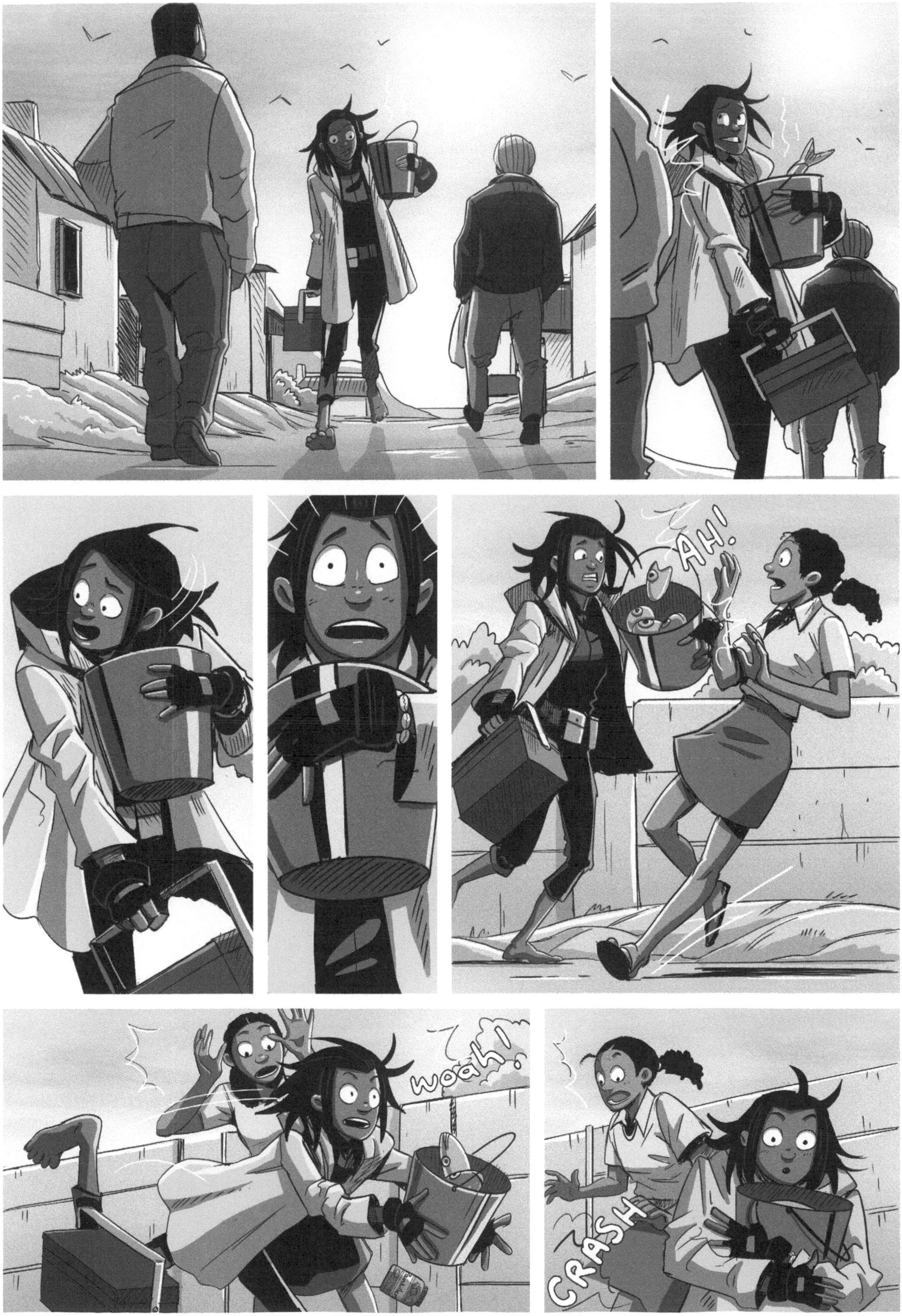
AH!
woah!
CRASH

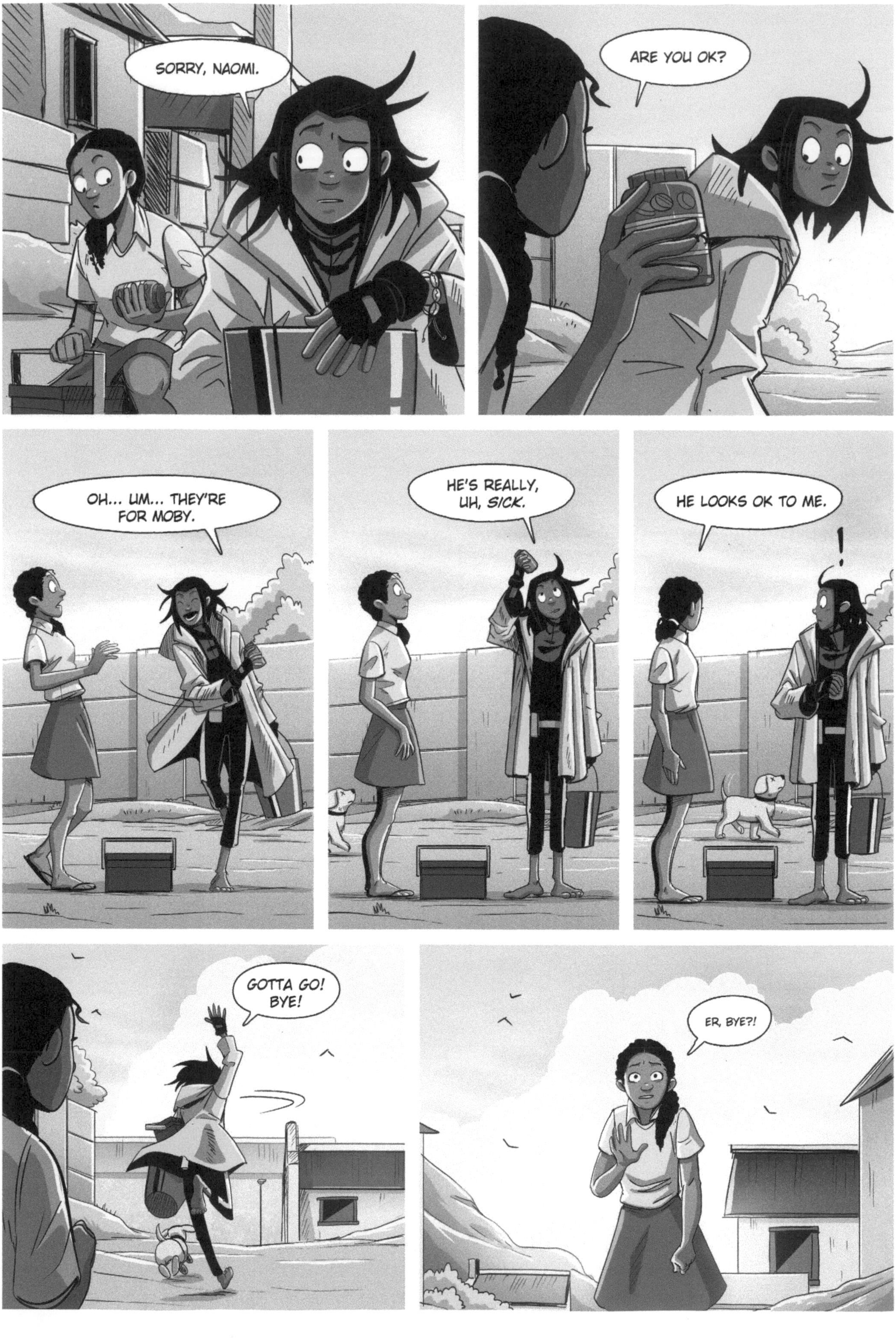
SORRY, NAOMI.
ARE YOU OK?
OH... UM... THEY'RE FOR MOBY.
HE'S REALLY, UH, *SICK*.
HE LOOKS OK TO ME.
!
GOTTA GO! BYE!
ER, BYE?!

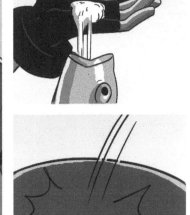

CRUNCH

NOT COMING?

HMPH

HELLO?
...STILL HERE?
...HUNGRY??

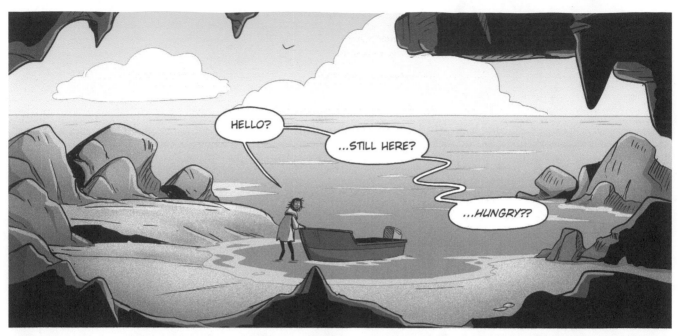

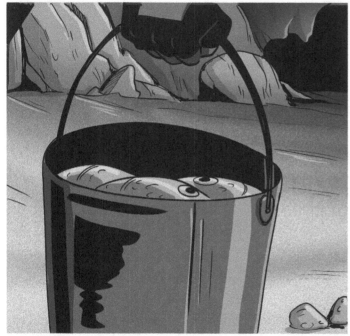

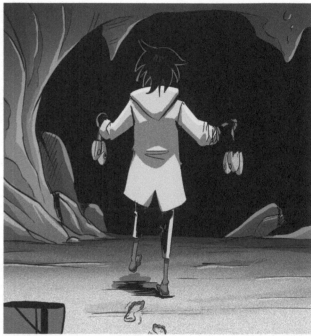

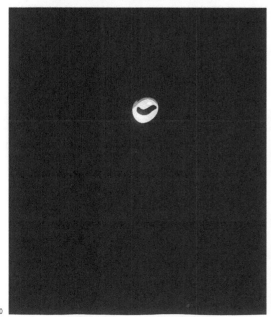

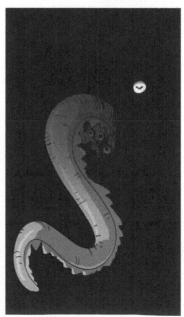

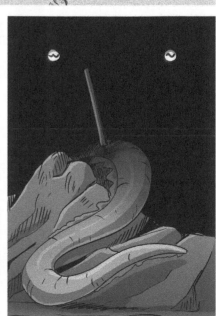

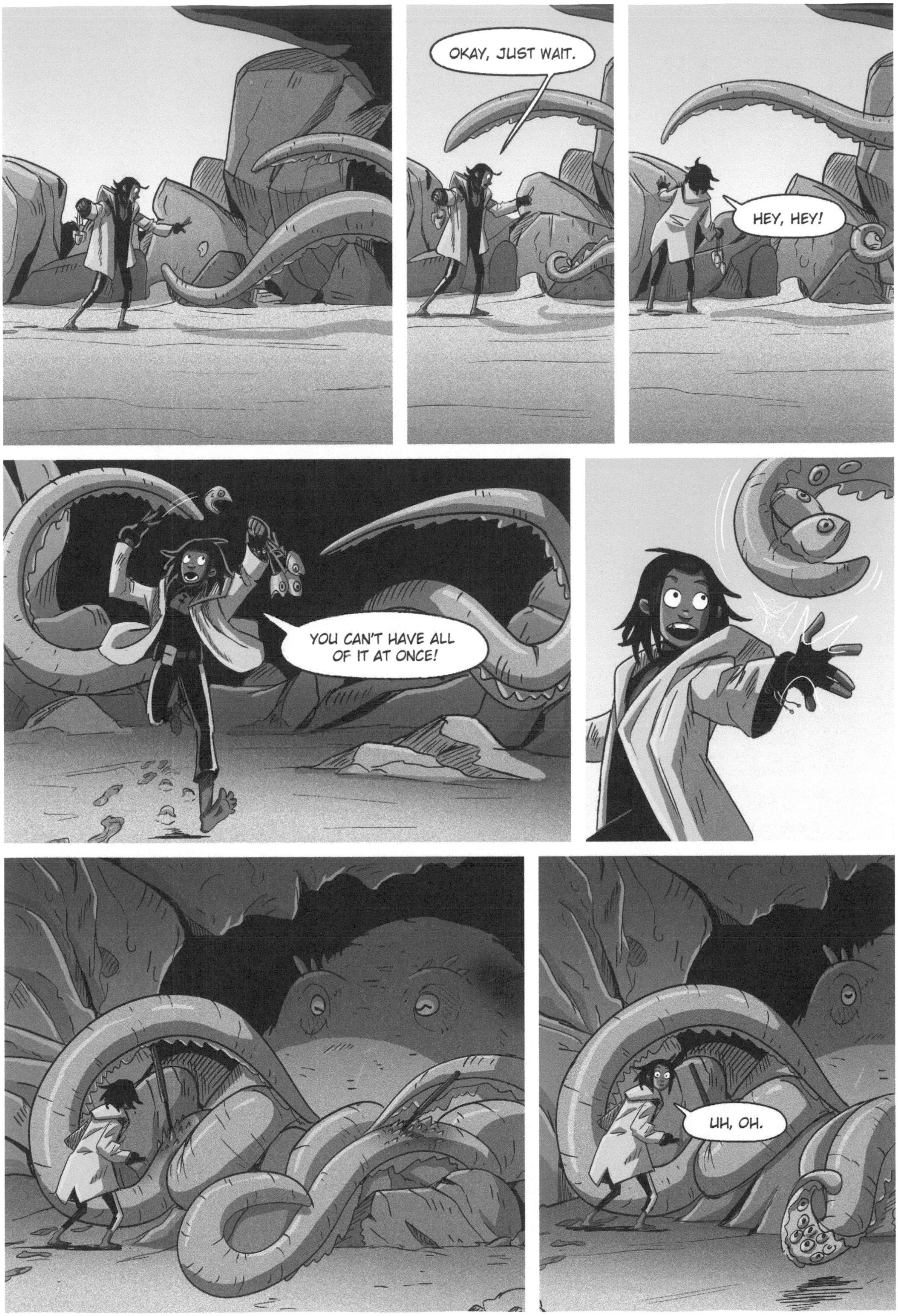
OKAY, JUST WAIT.
HEY, HEY!
YOU CAN'T HAVE ALL OF IT AT ONCE!
UH, OH.

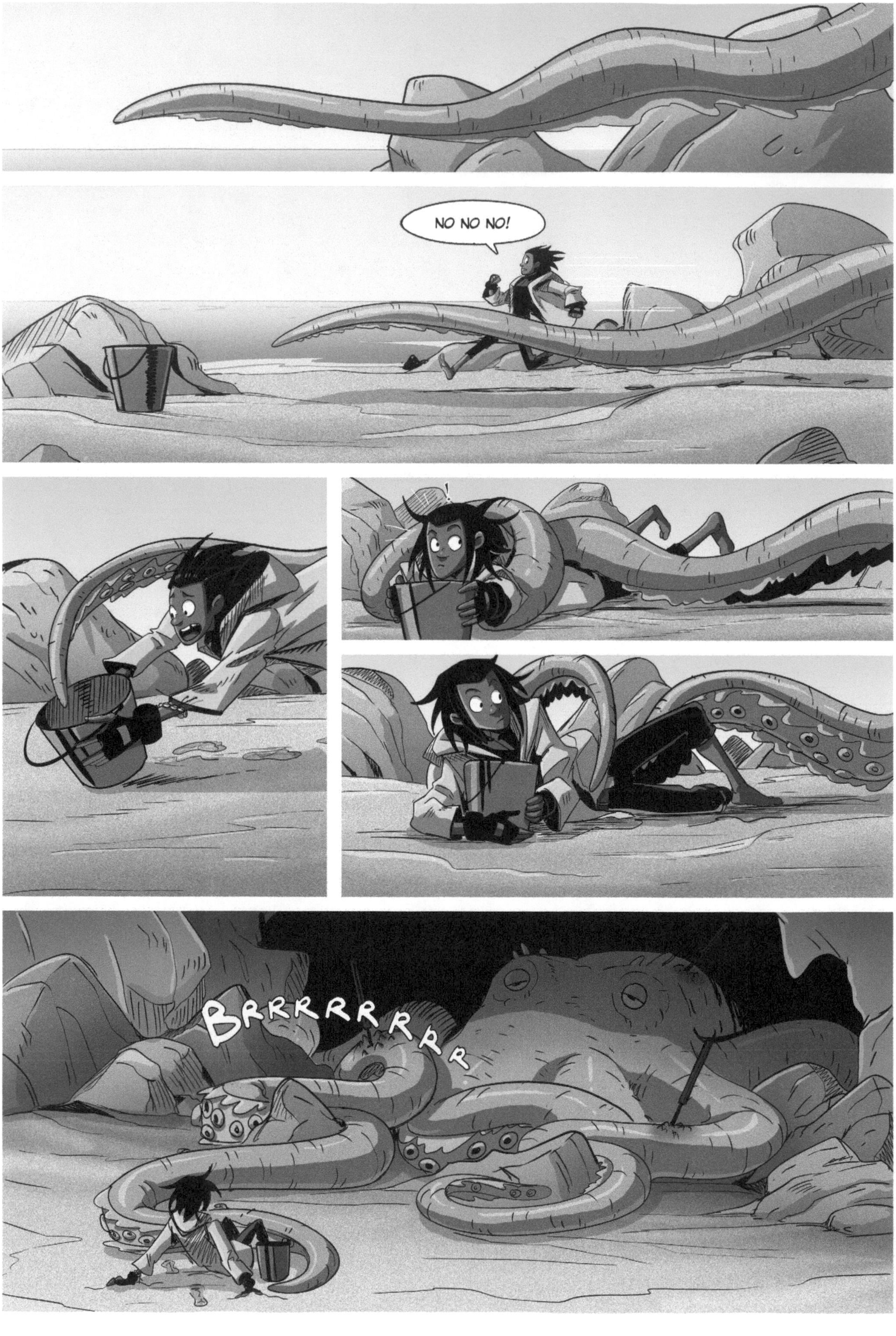
NO NO NO!
!
BRRRRRRRRR

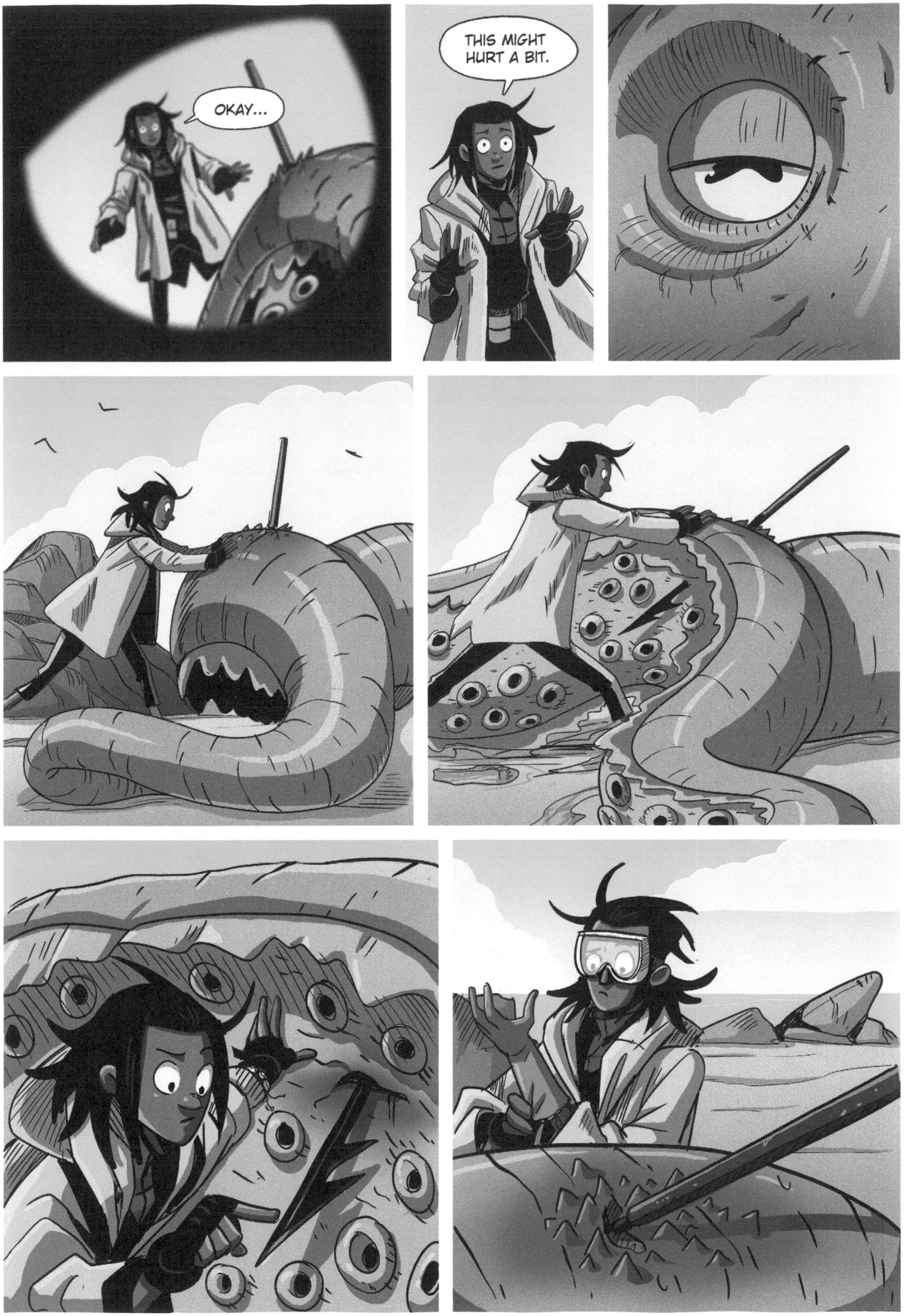
OKAY...
THIS MIGHT HURT A BIT.

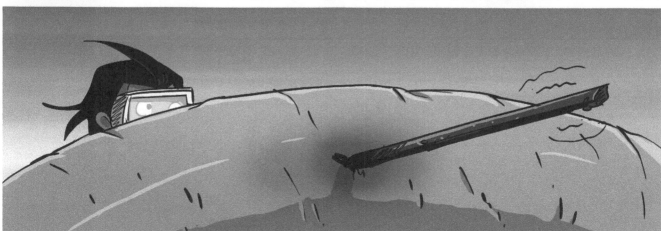

LATER...

SHIK

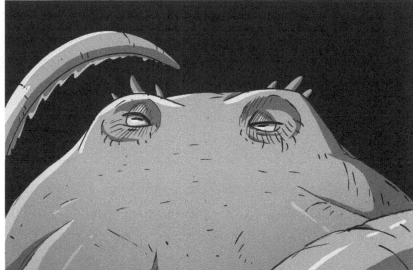

TA-DA! FEEL BETTER?

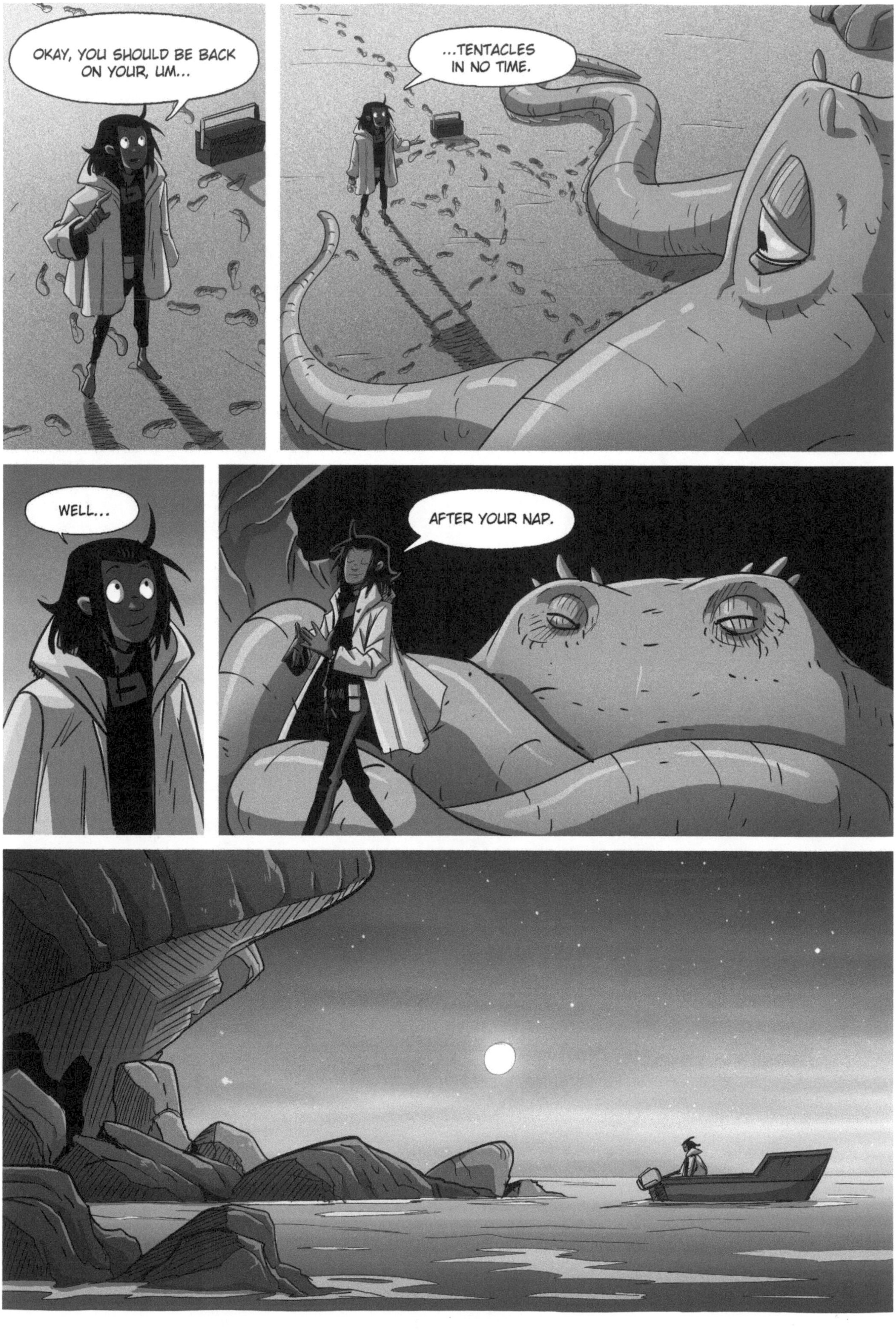
OKAY, YOU SHOULD BE BACK ON YOUR, UM...
...TENTACLES IN NO TIME.
WELL...
AFTER YOUR NAP.

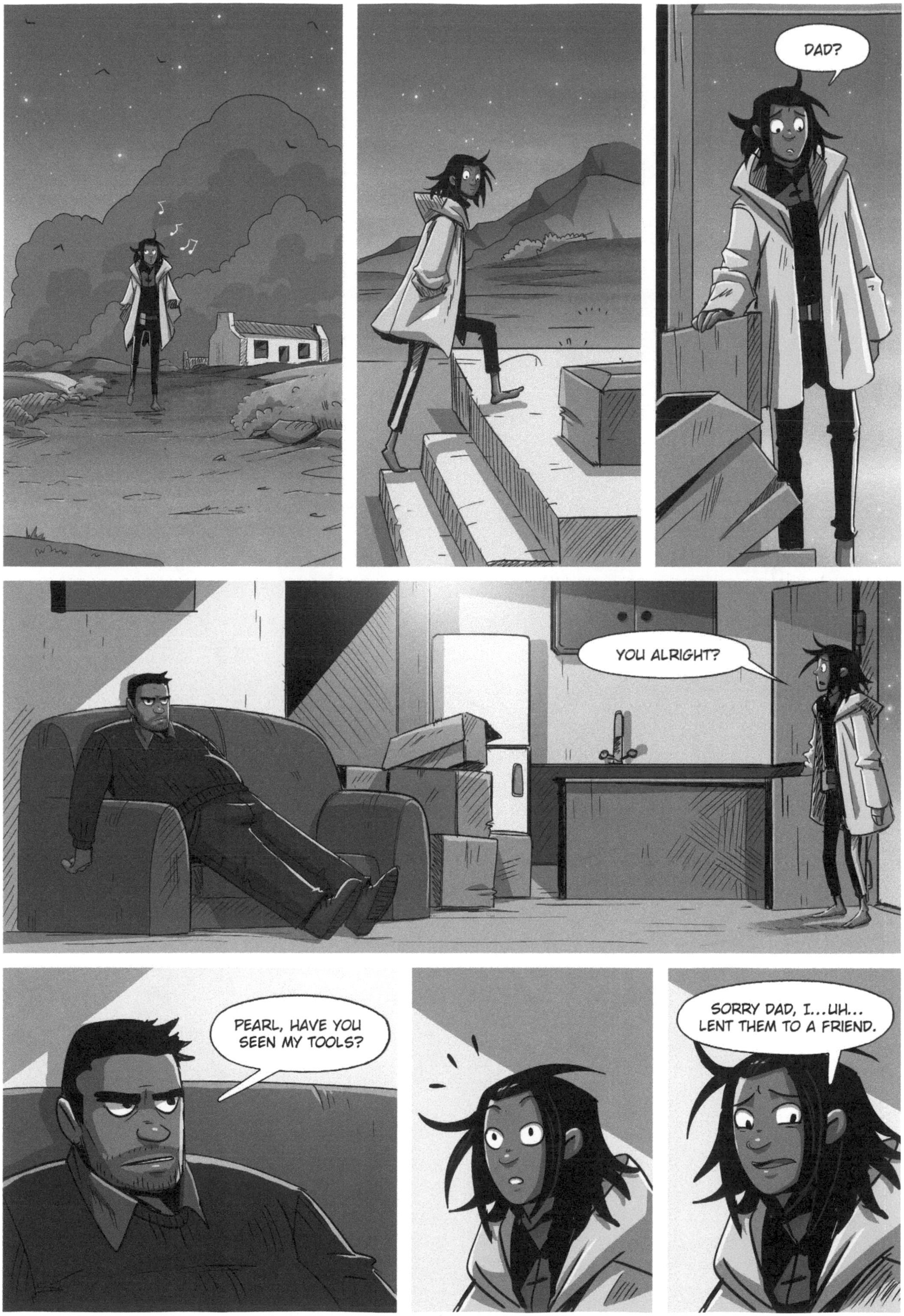
DAD?
YOU ALRIGHT?
PEARL, HAVE YOU SEEN MY TOOLS?
SORRY DAD, I...UH... LENT THEM TO A FRIEND.

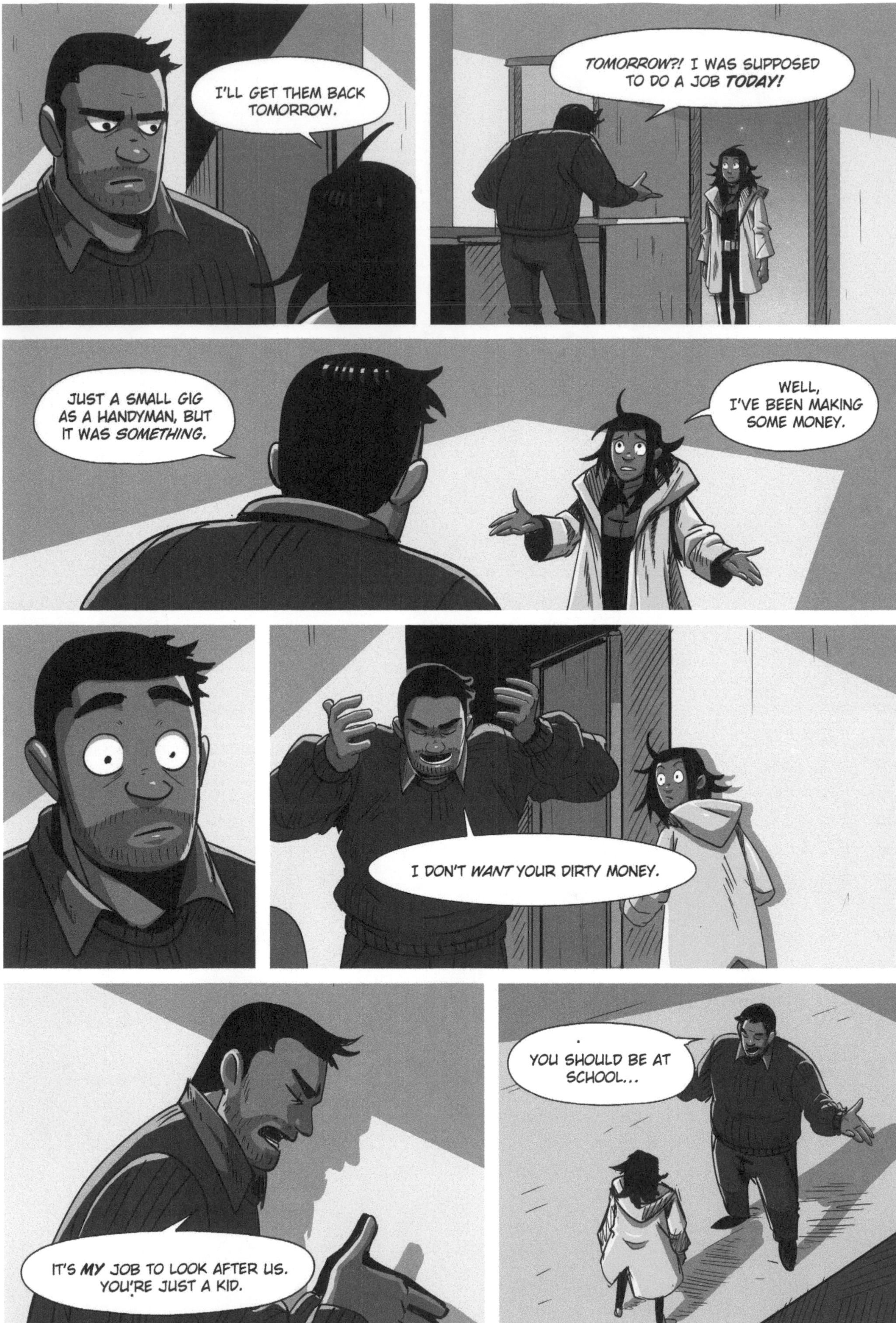
I'LL GET THEM BACK TOMORROW.
TOMORROW?! I WAS SUPPOSED TO DO A JOB ***TODAY!***
WELL, I'VE BEEN MAKING SOME MONEY.
JUST A SMALL GIG AS A HANDYMAN, BUT IT WAS *SOMETHING*.
I DON'T *WANT* YOUR DIRTY MONEY.
IT'S ***MY*** JOB TO LOOK AFTER US. YOU'RE JUST A KID.
YOU SHOULD BE AT SCHOOL...

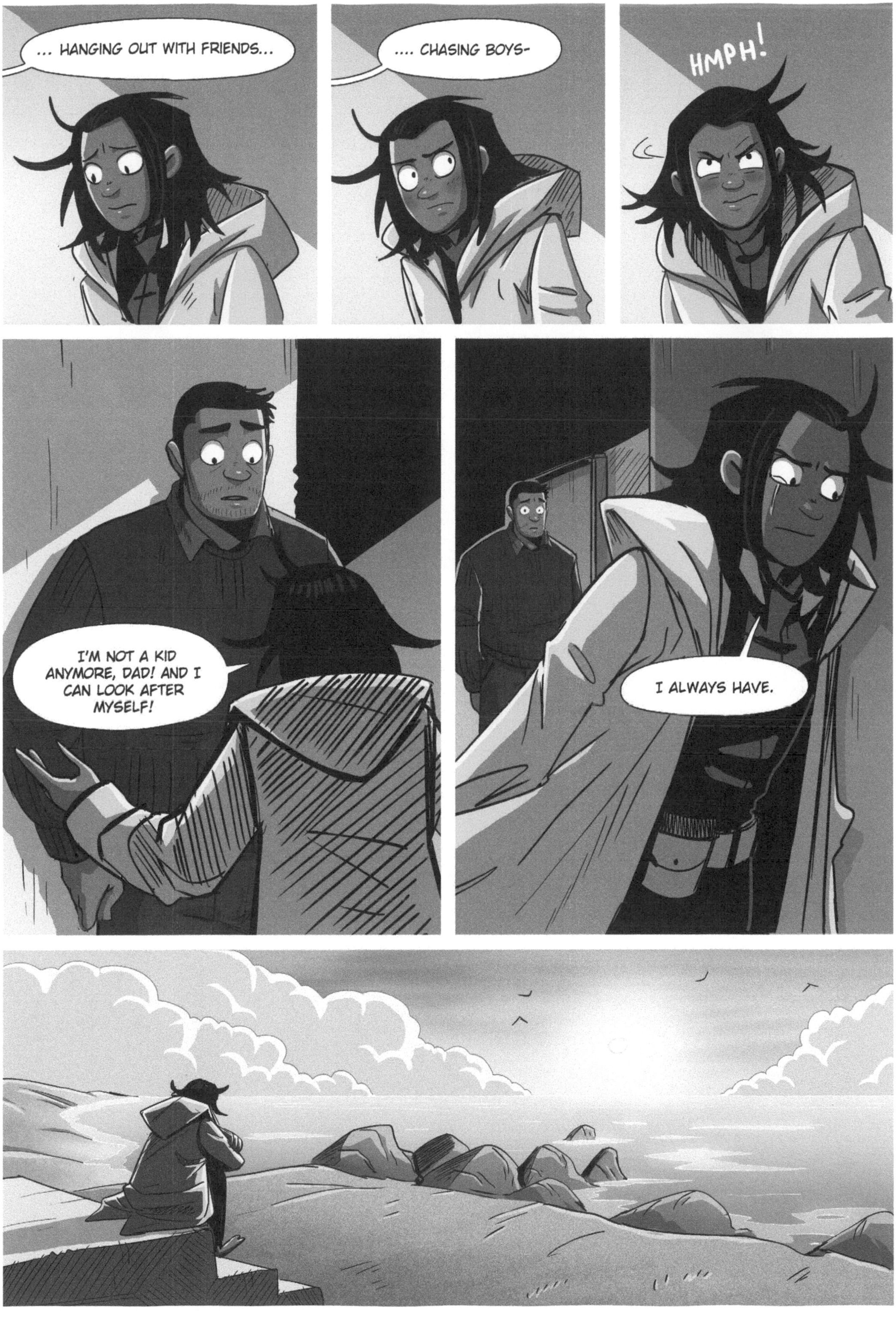
... HANGING OUT WITH FRIENDS...
.... CHASING BOYS-
HMPH!
I'M NOT A KID ANYMORE, DAD! AND I CAN LOOK AFTER MYSELF!
I ALWAYS HAVE.

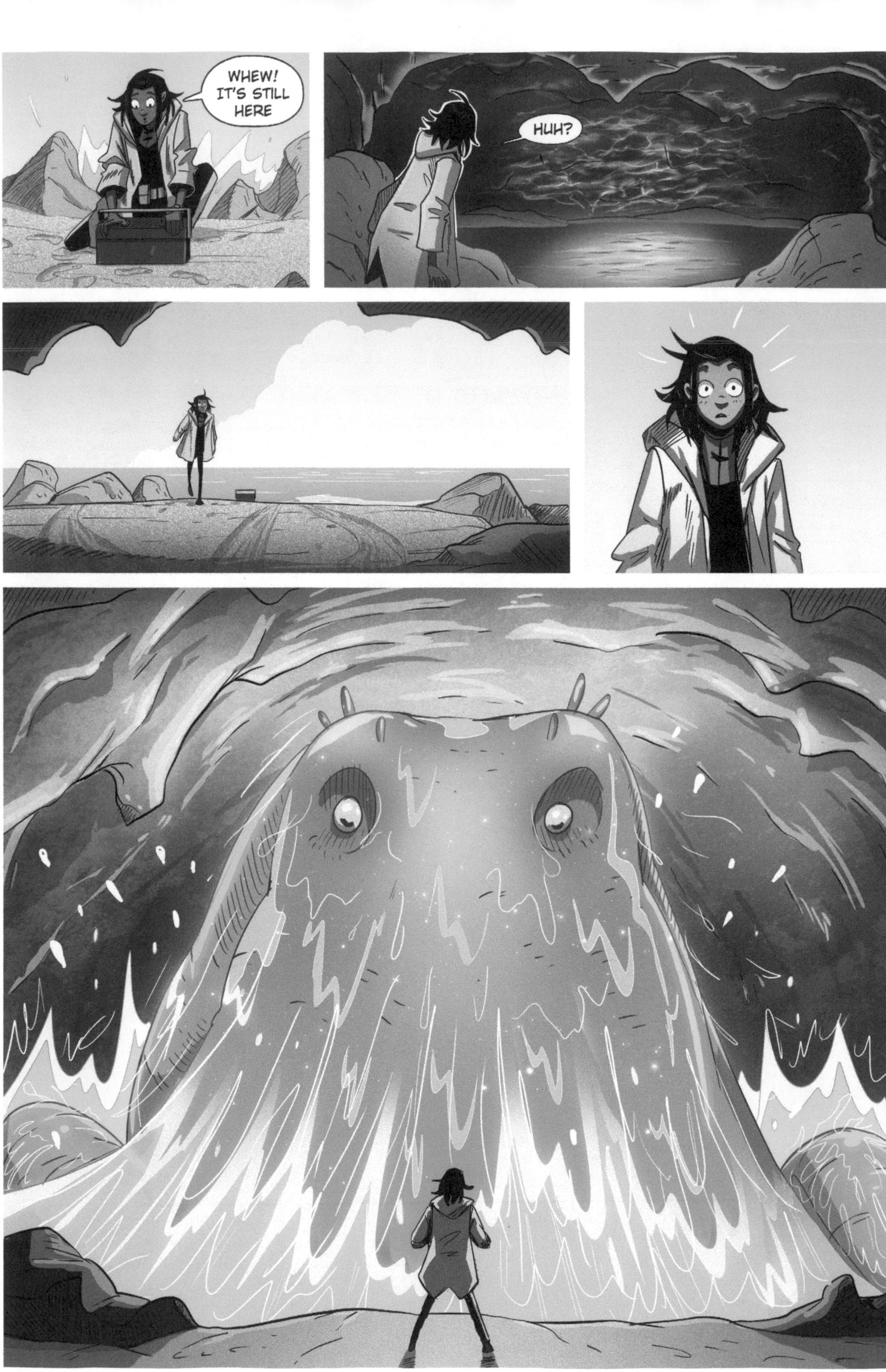
WHEW! IT'S STILL HERE
HUH?

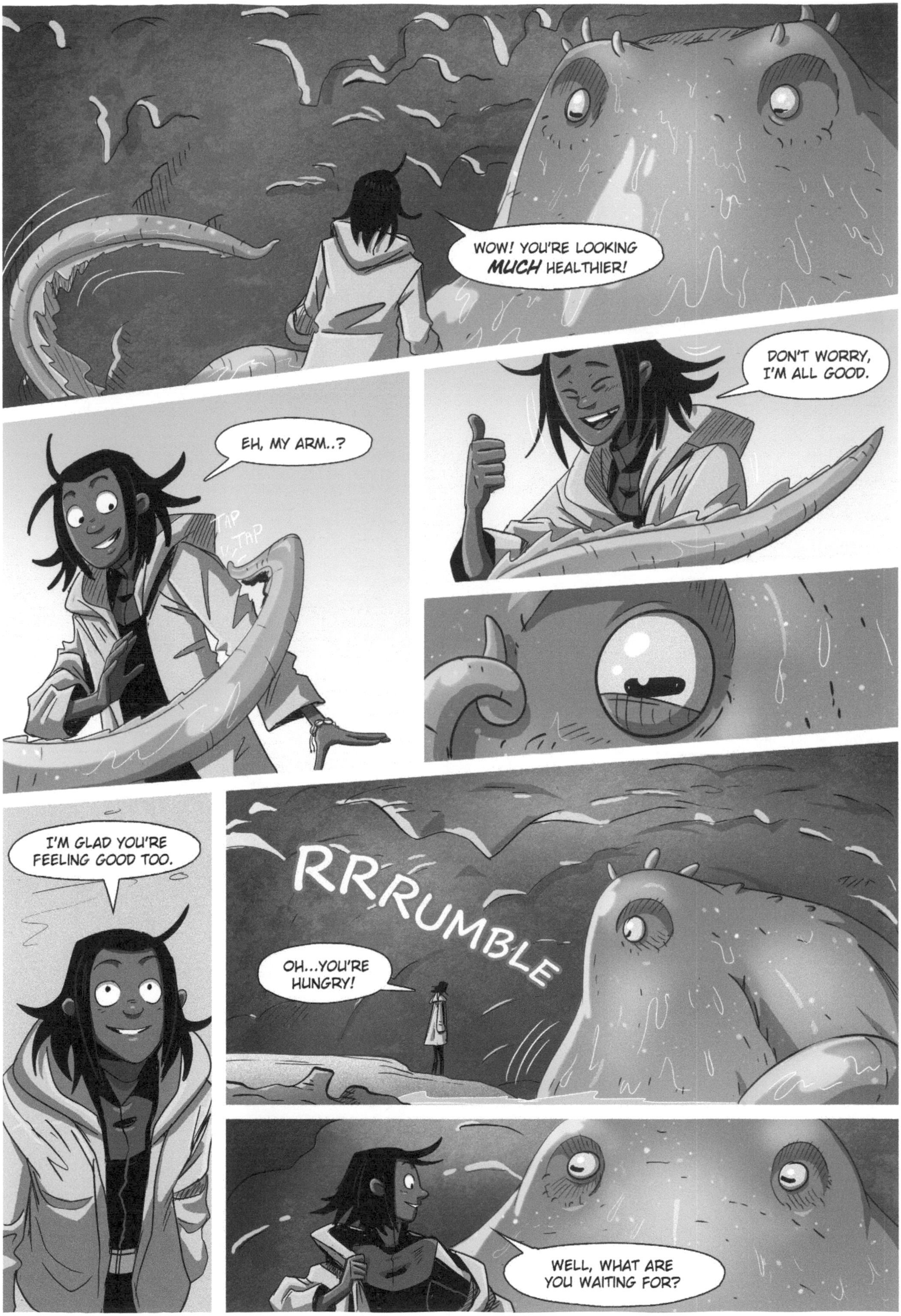
WOW! YOU'RE LOOKING *MUCH* HEALTHIER!
DON'T WORRY, I'M ALL GOOD.
EH, MY ARM..?
TAP TAP
I'M GLAD YOU'RE FEELING GOOD TOO.
RRRUMBLE
OH...YOU'RE HUNGRY!
WELL, WHAT ARE YOU WAITING FOR?

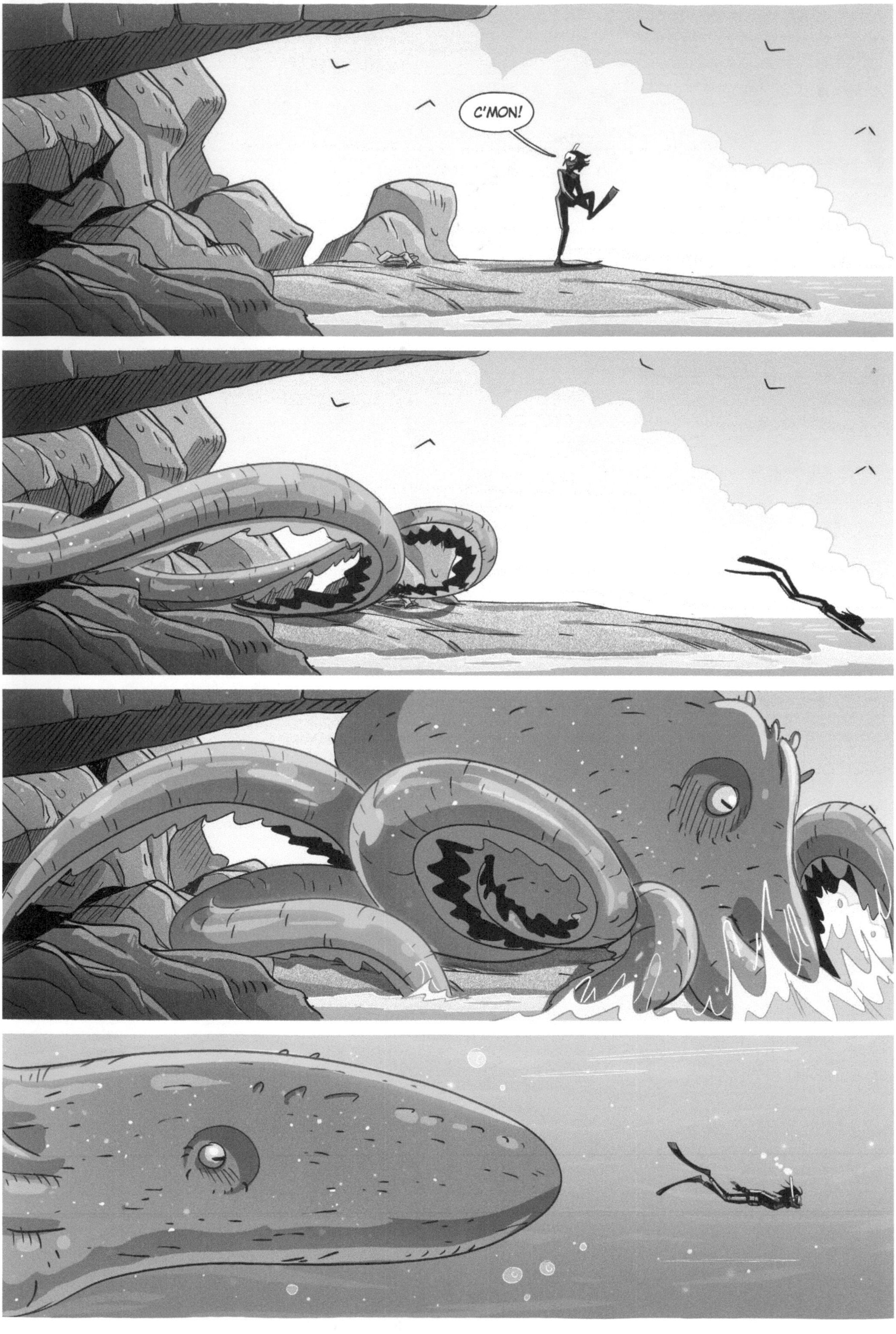
C'MON!

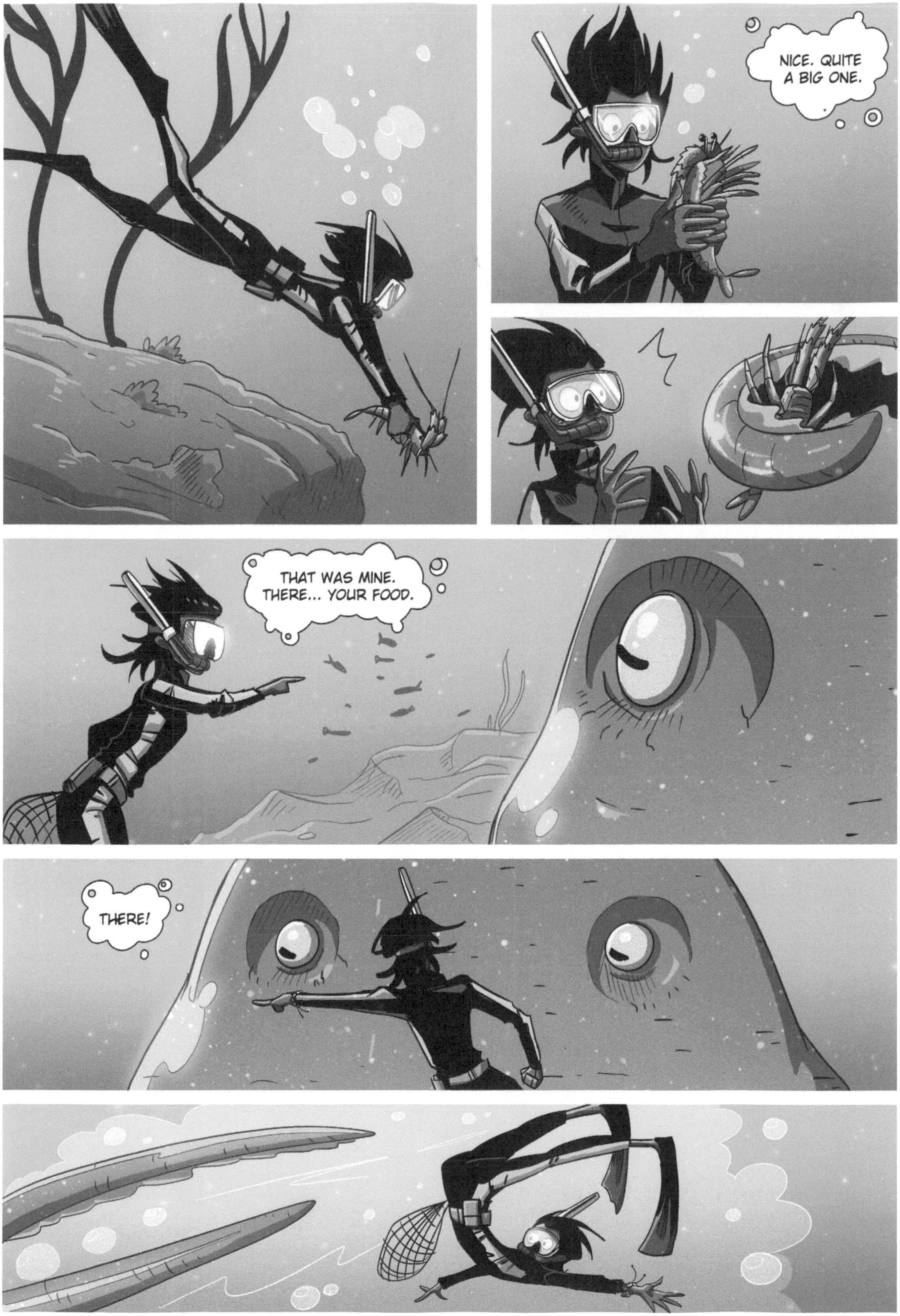
NICE. QUITE A BIG ONE.
THAT WAS MINE. THERE... YOUR FOOD.
THERE!

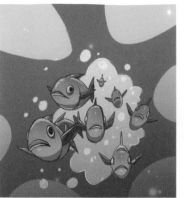

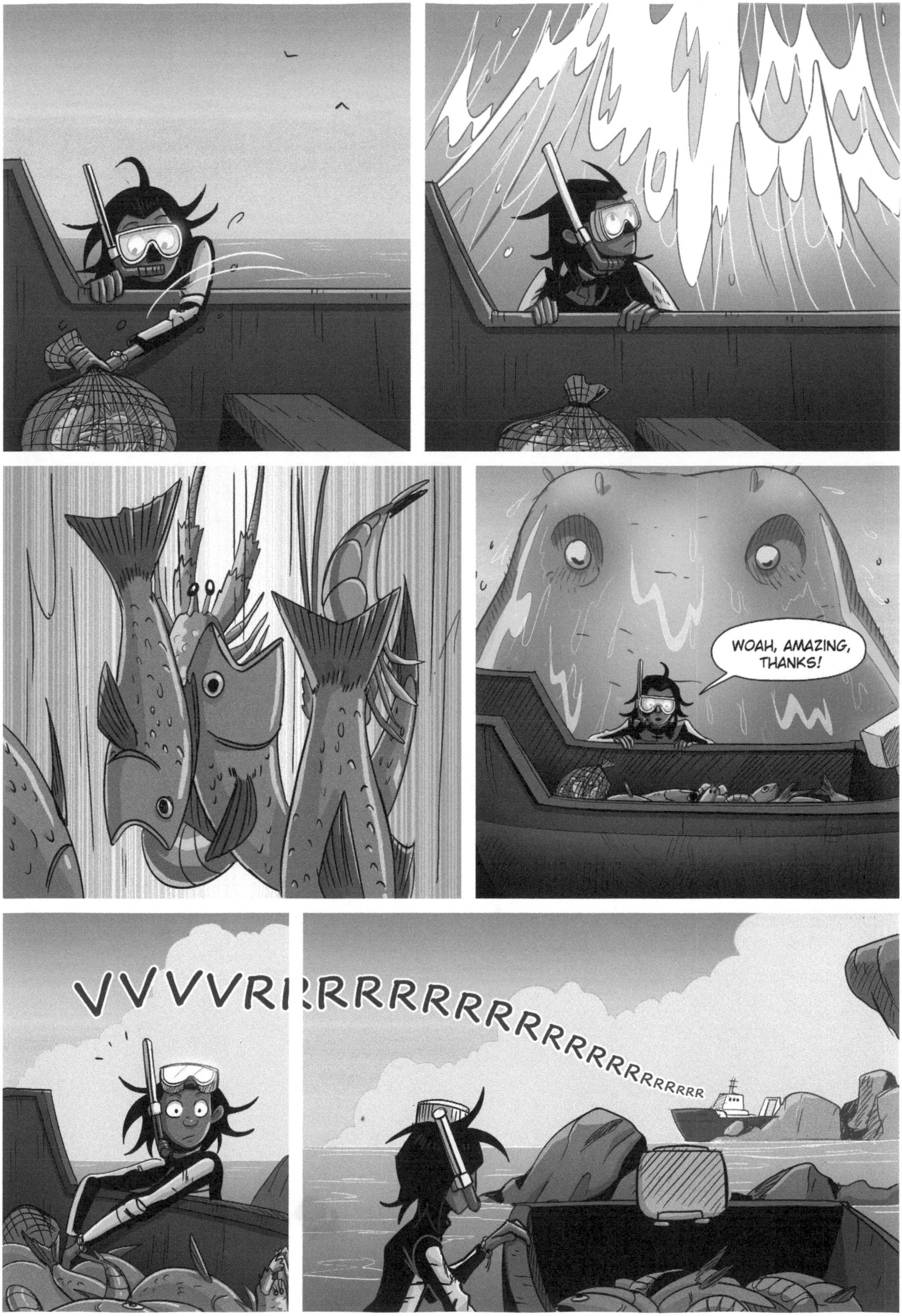
WOAH, AMAZING, THANKS!
VVVVRRRRRRRRRRRRRRRRRRrrrrrr

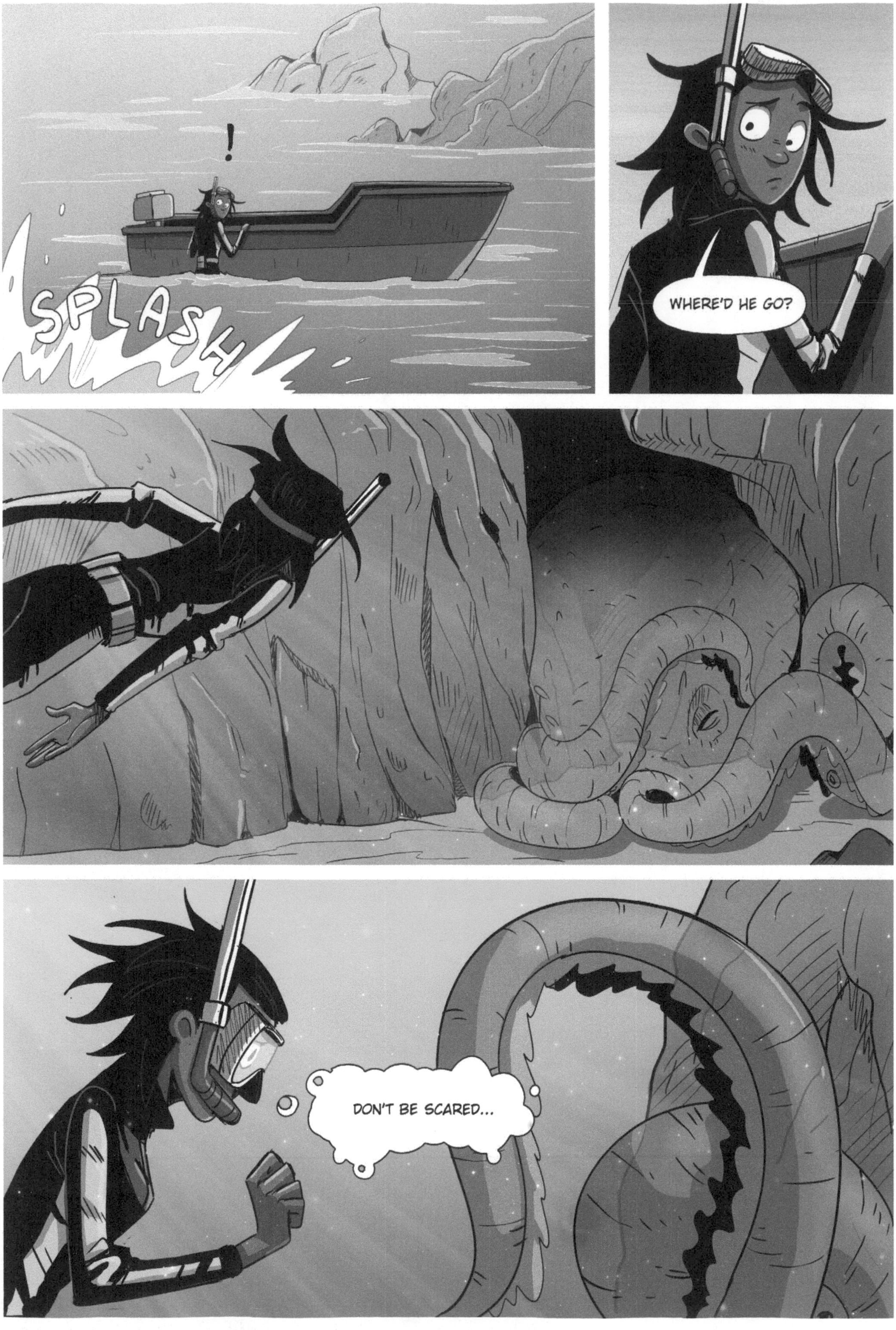
!
SPLASH
WHERE'D HE GO?
DON'T BE SCARED...

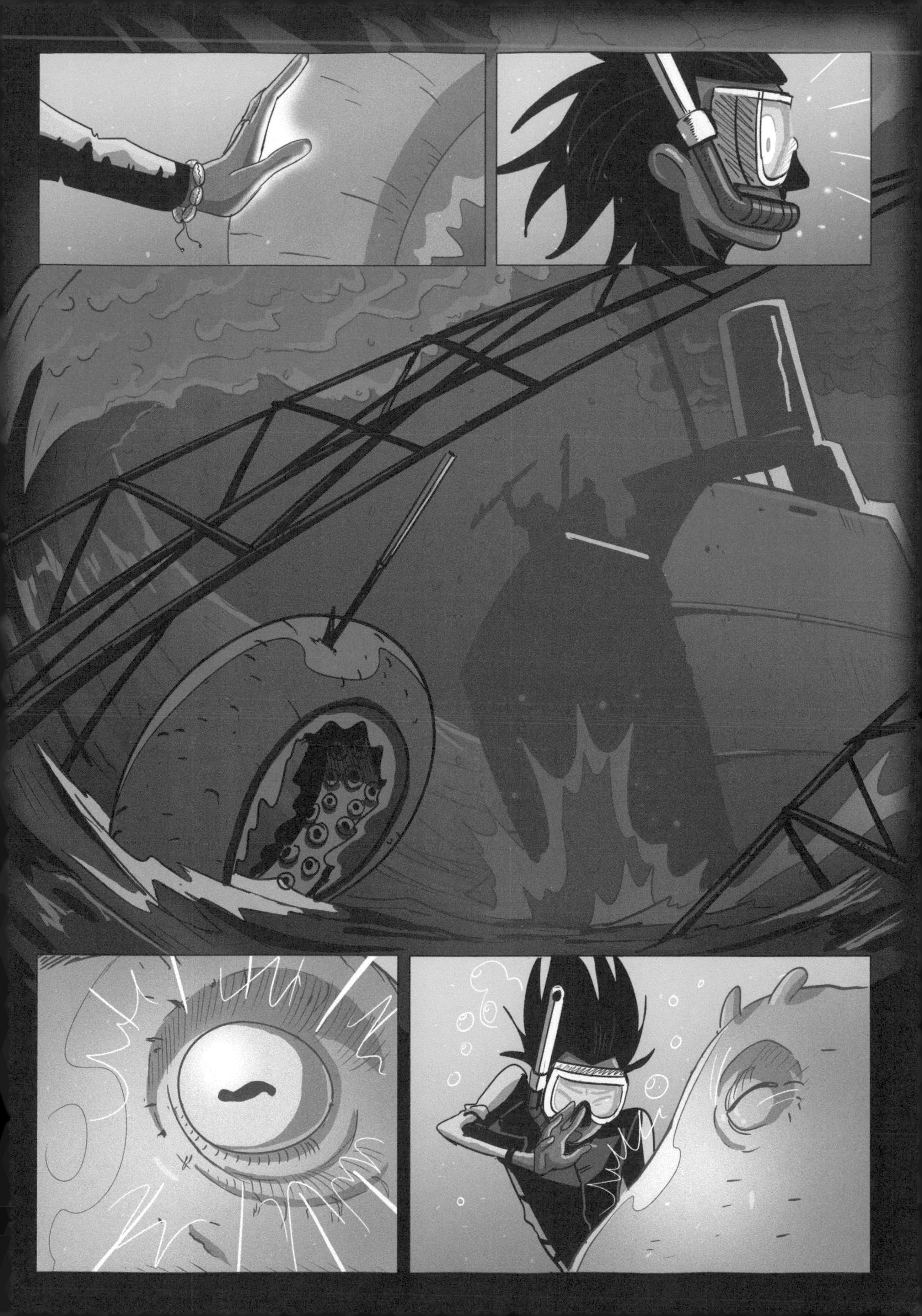

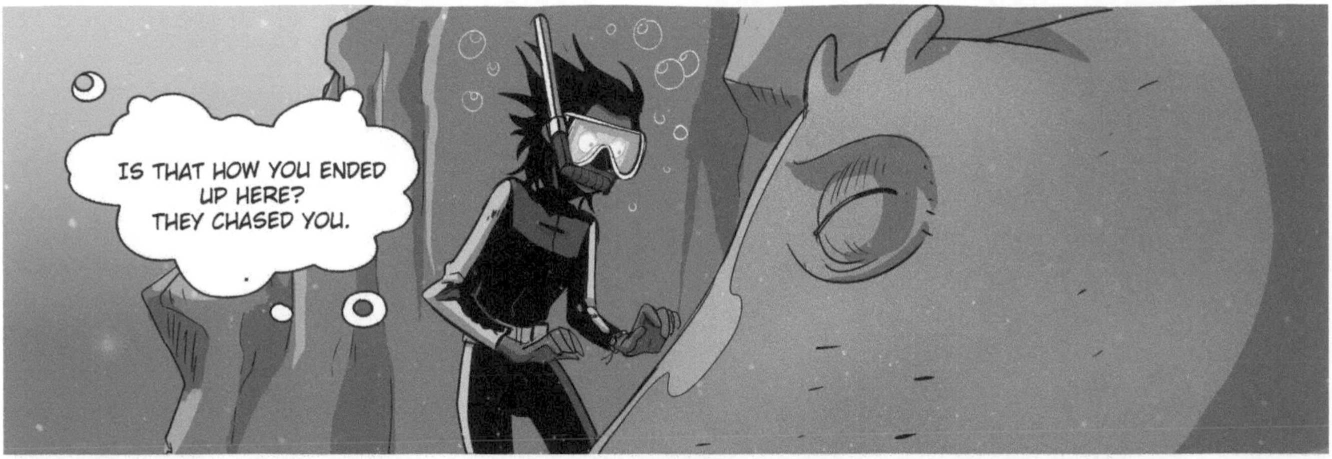
IS THAT HOW YOU ENDED UP HERE? THEY CHASED YOU.

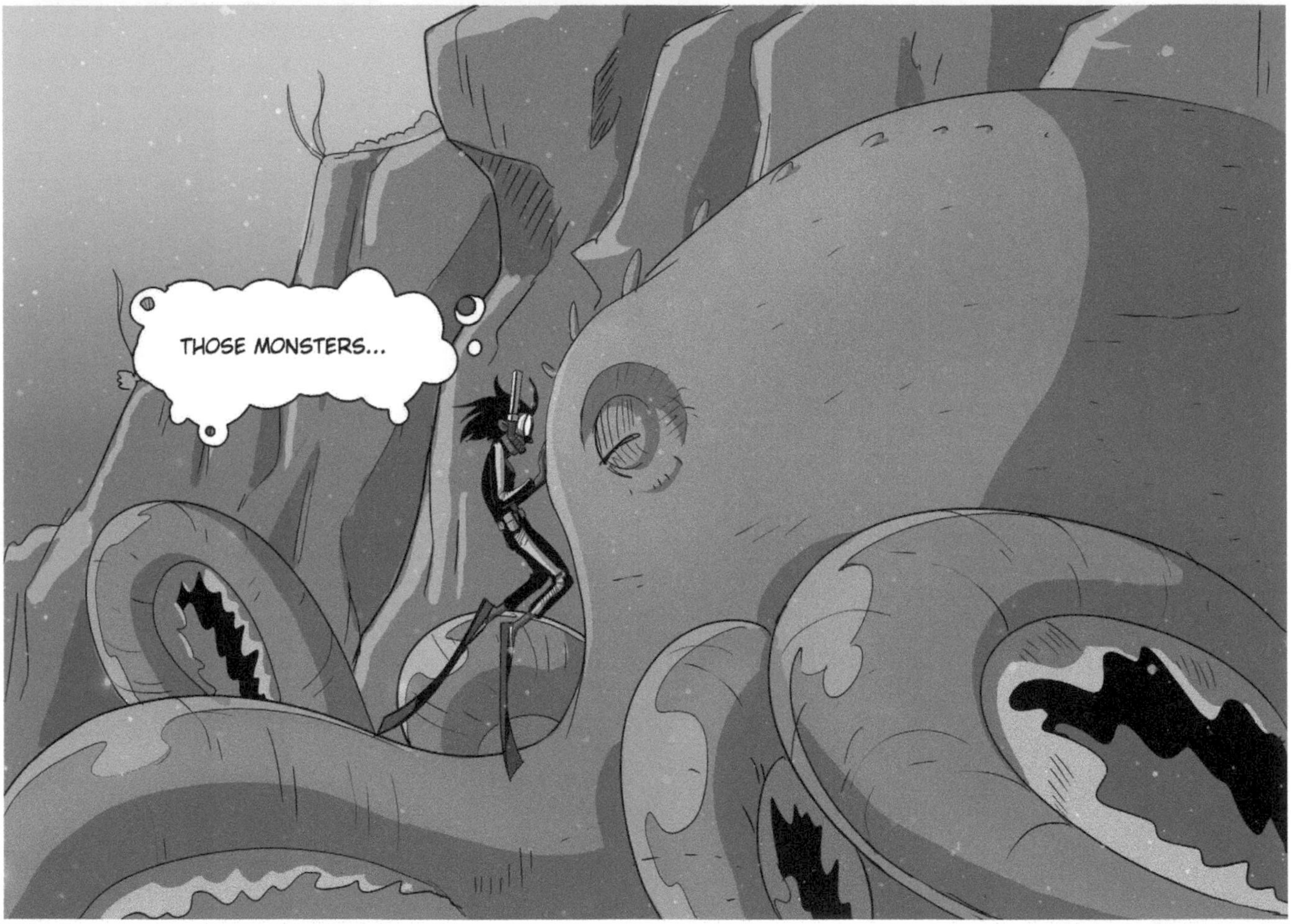
THOSE MONSTERS...

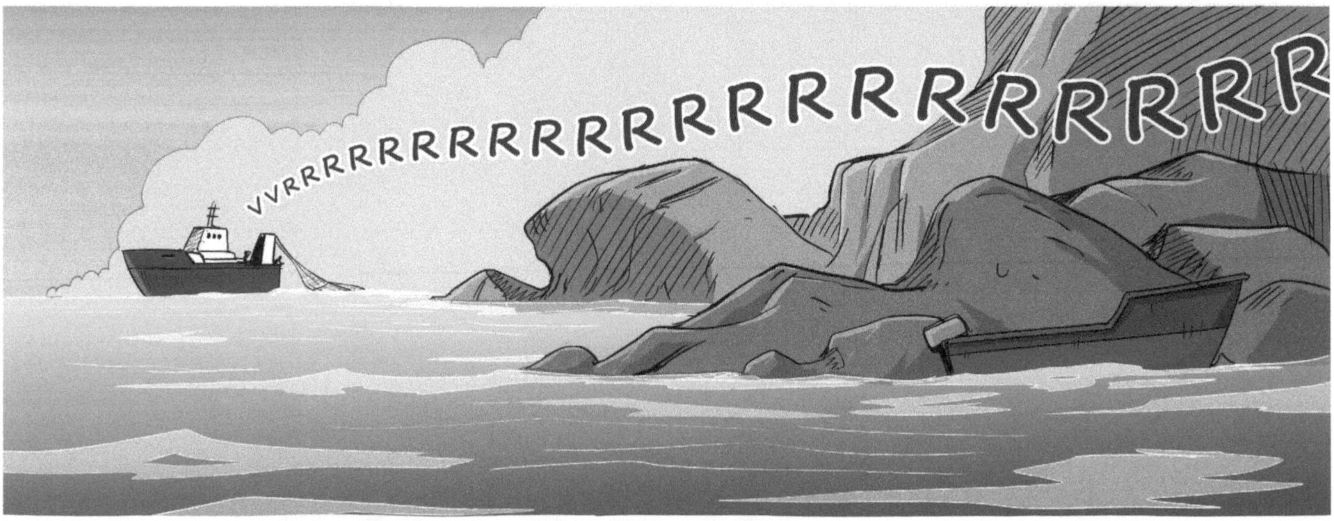
VVRRRRRRRRRRRRRRRRRRRRRR

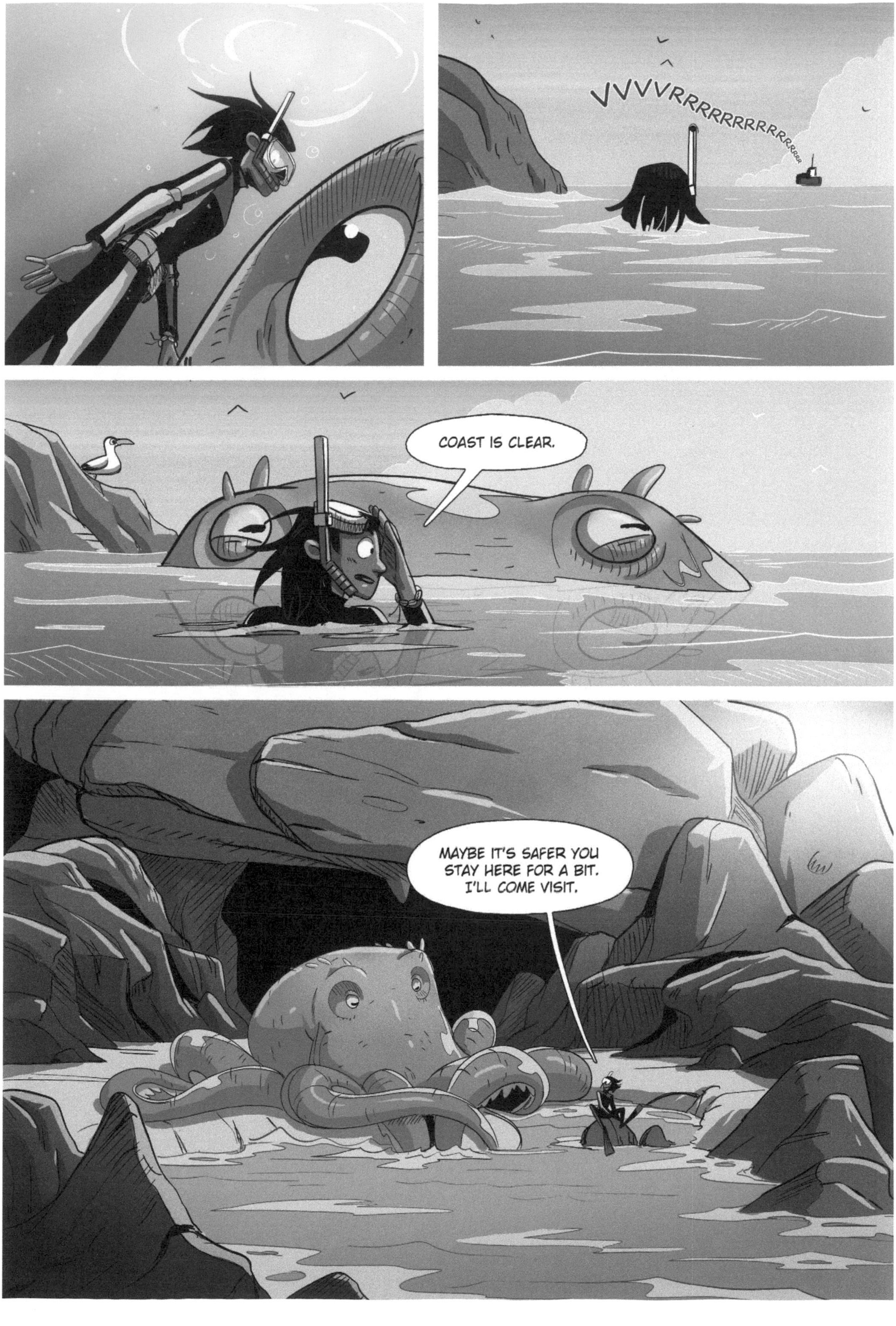
VVVVRRRRRRRRRRRRrrrr
COAST IS CLEAR.
MAYBE IT'S SAFER YOU STAY HERE FOR A BIT. I'LL COME VISIT.

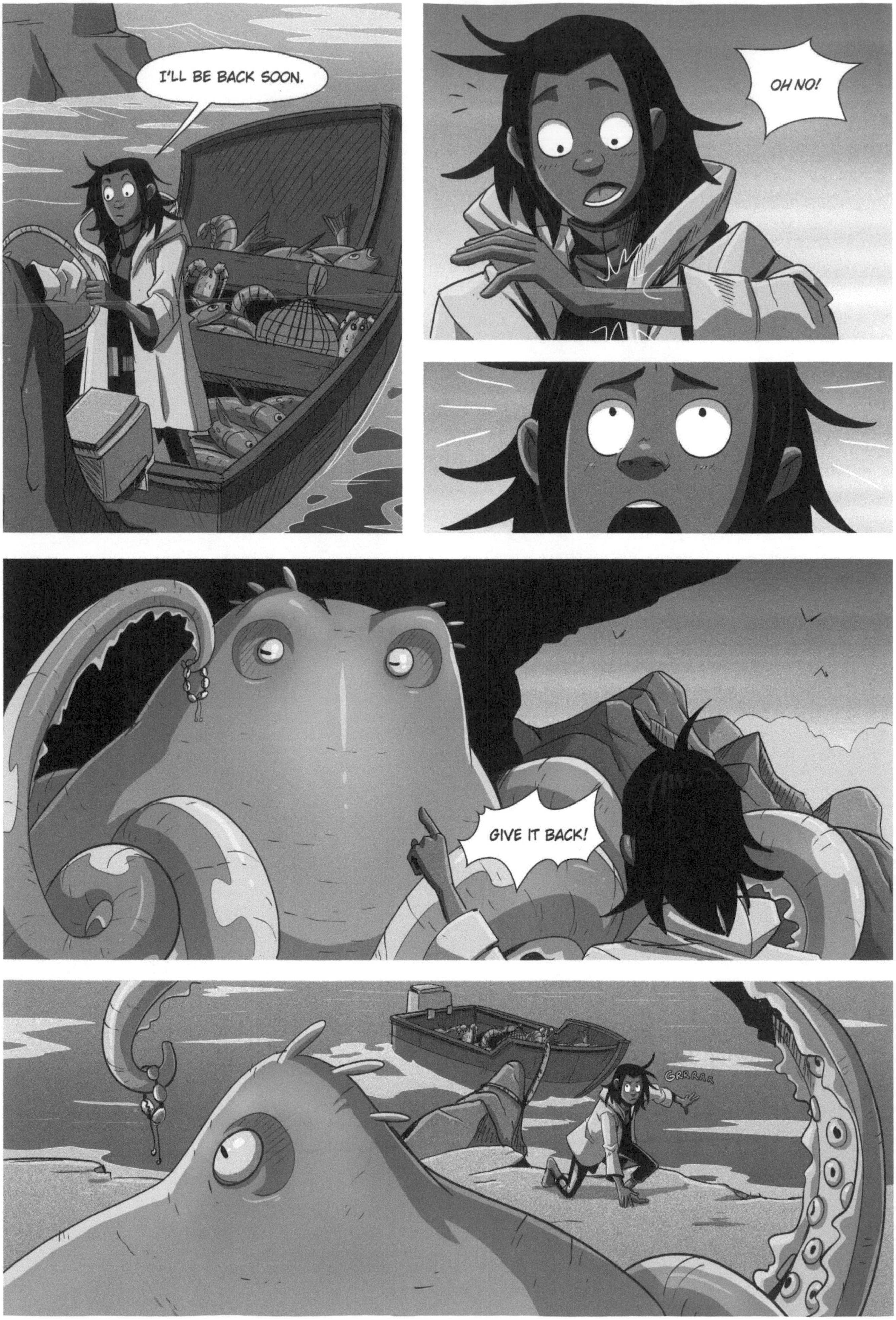
I'LL BE BACK SOON.
OH NO!
GIVE IT BACK!
GRRRRRR

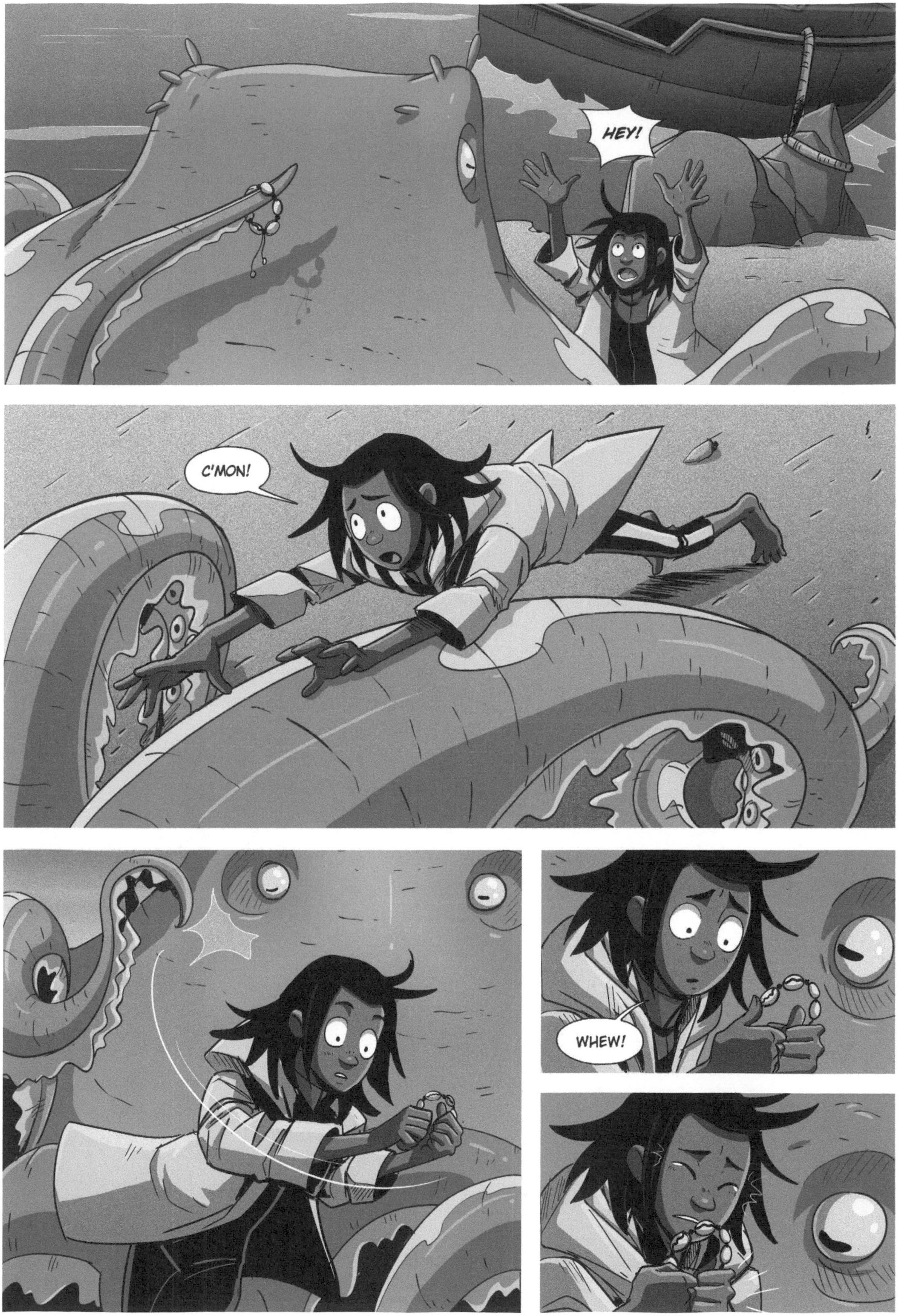
HEY!
C'MON!
WHEW!

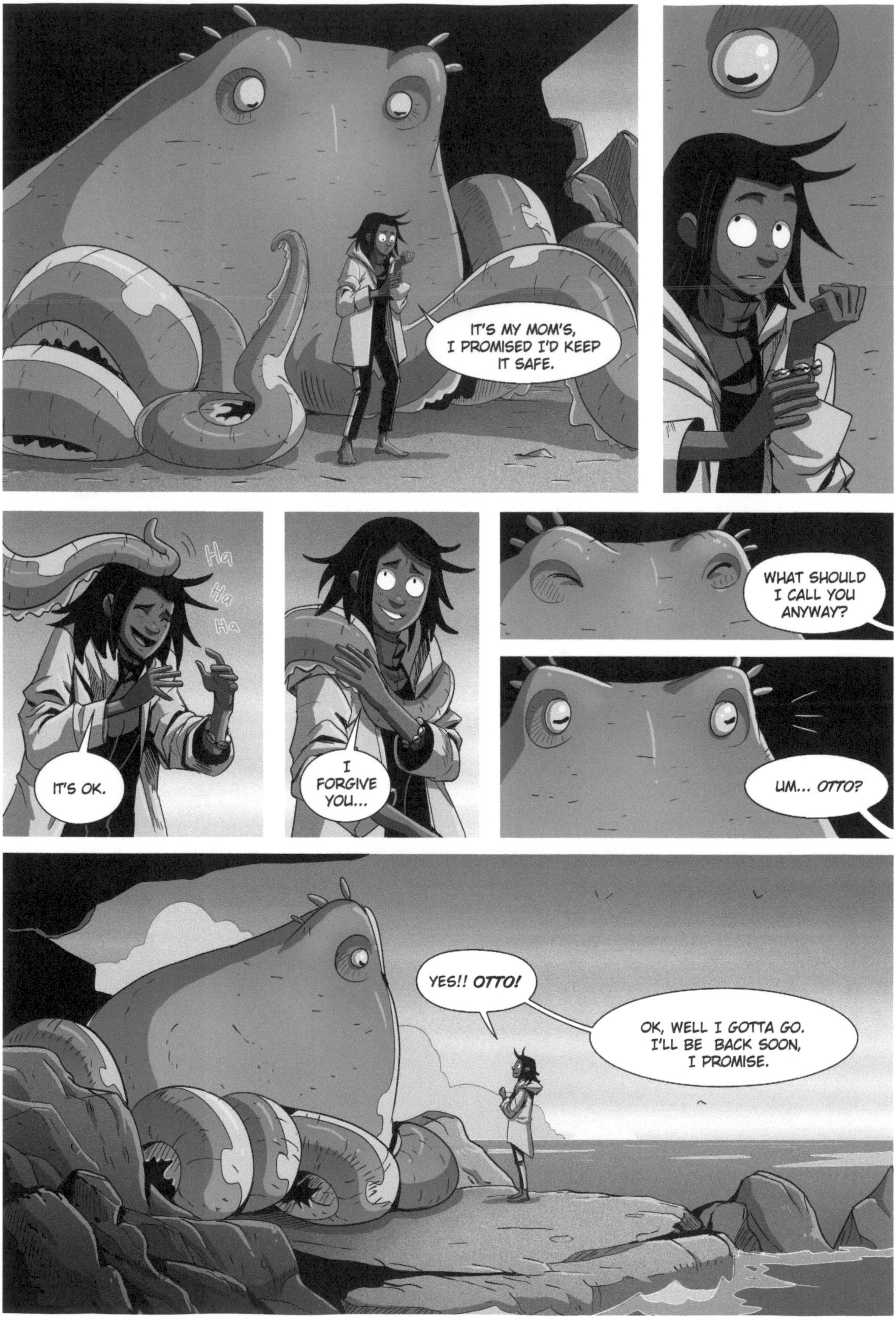
IT'S MY MOM'S, I PROMISED I'D KEEP IT SAFE.
Ha Ha Ha
IT'S OK.
I FORGIVE YOU...
WHAT SHOULD I CALL YOU ANYWAY?
UM... OTTO?
YES!! OTTO!
OK, WELL I GOTTA GO. I'LL BE BACK SOON, I PROMISE.

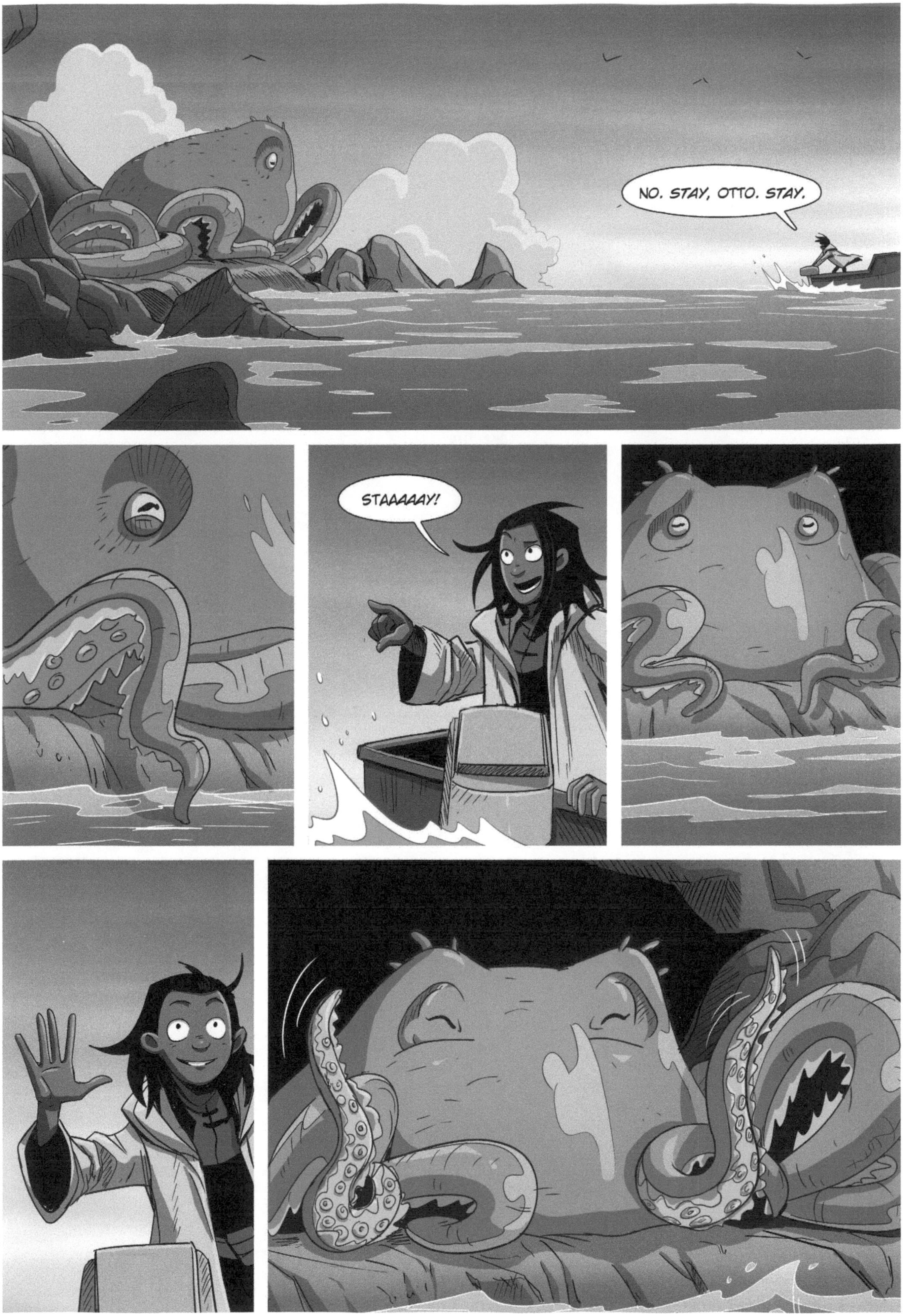
NO. STAY, OTTO. STAY.
STAAAAAY!

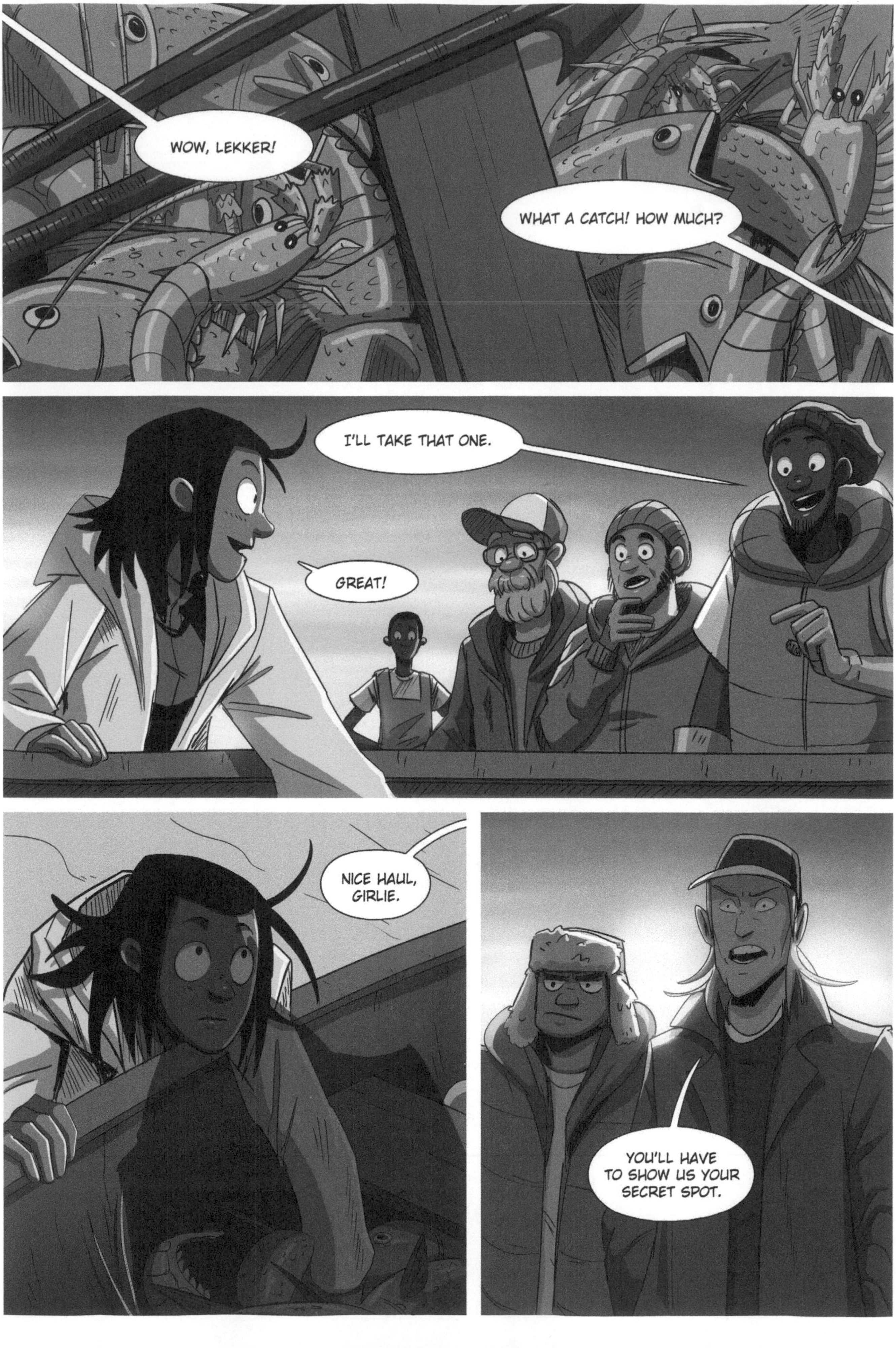
WOW, LEKKER!
WHAT A CATCH! HOW MUCH?
I'LL TAKE THAT ONE.
GREAT!
NICE HAUL, GIRLIE.
YOU'LL HAVE TO SHOW US YOUR SECRET SPOT.

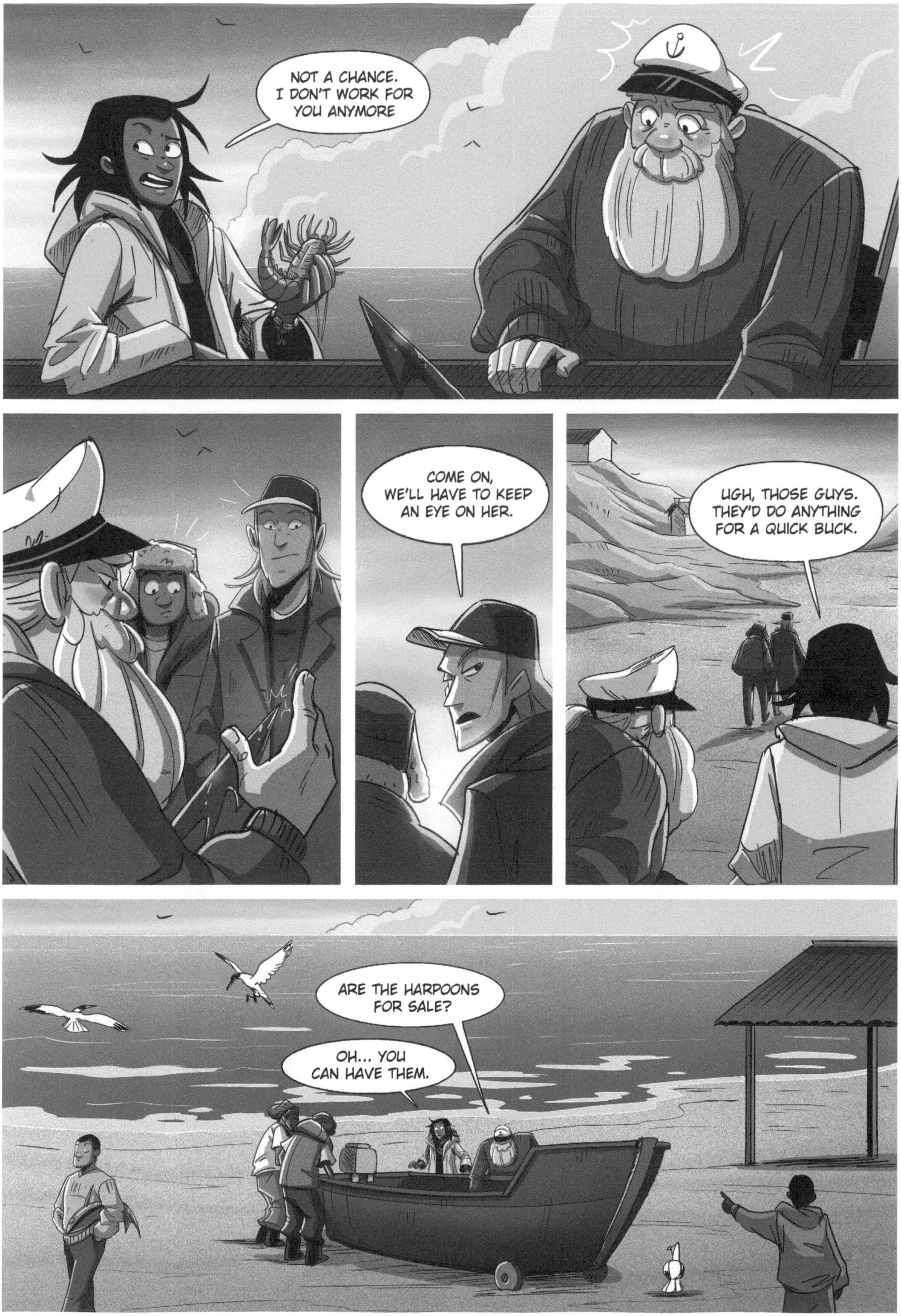
NOT A CHANCE. I DON'T WORK FOR YOU ANYMORE
COME ON, WE'LL HAVE TO KEEP AN EYE ON HER.
UGH, THOSE GUYS. THEY'D DO ANYTHING FOR A QUICK BUCK.
ARE THE HARPOONS FOR SALE?
OH... YOU CAN HAVE THEM.

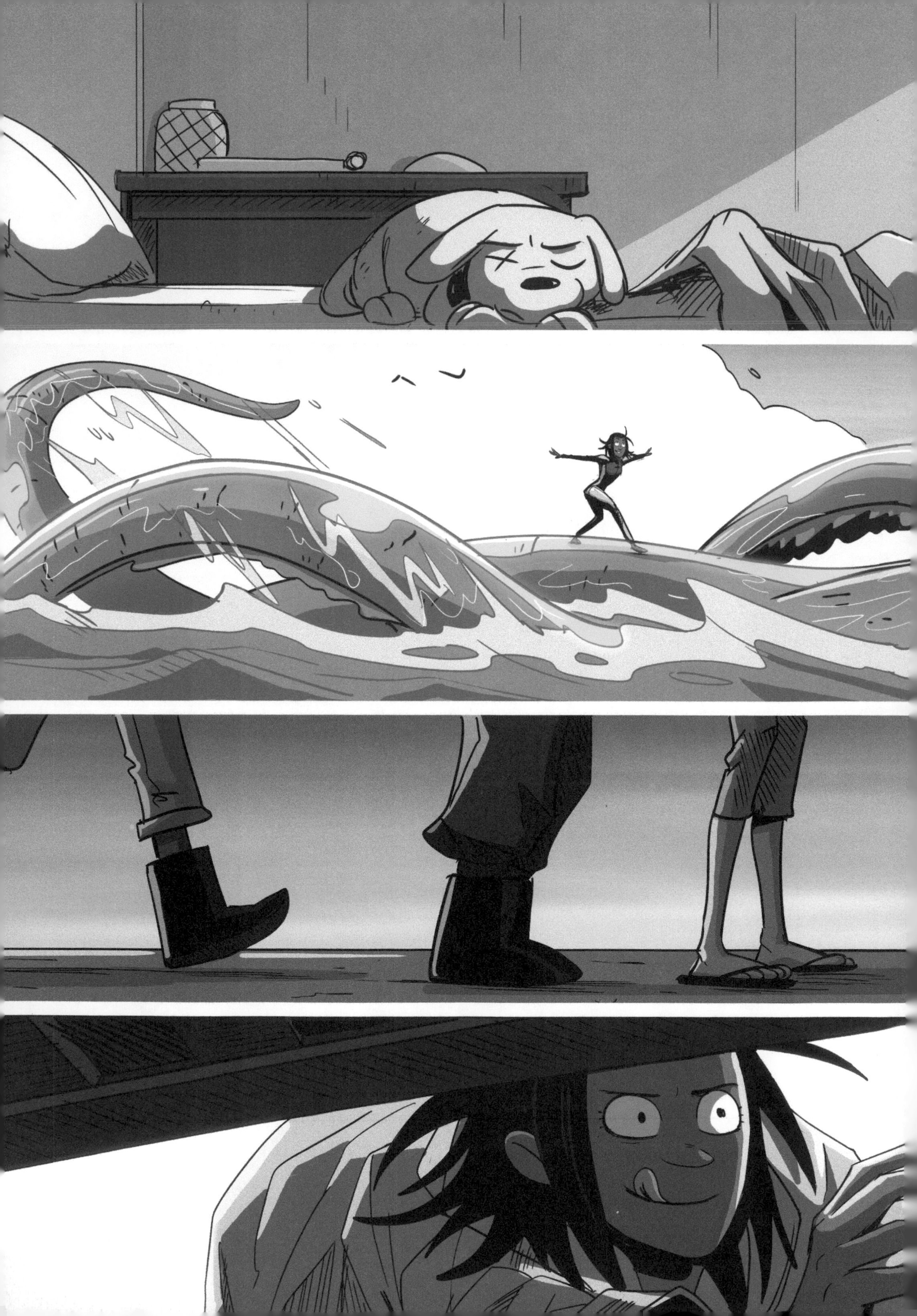

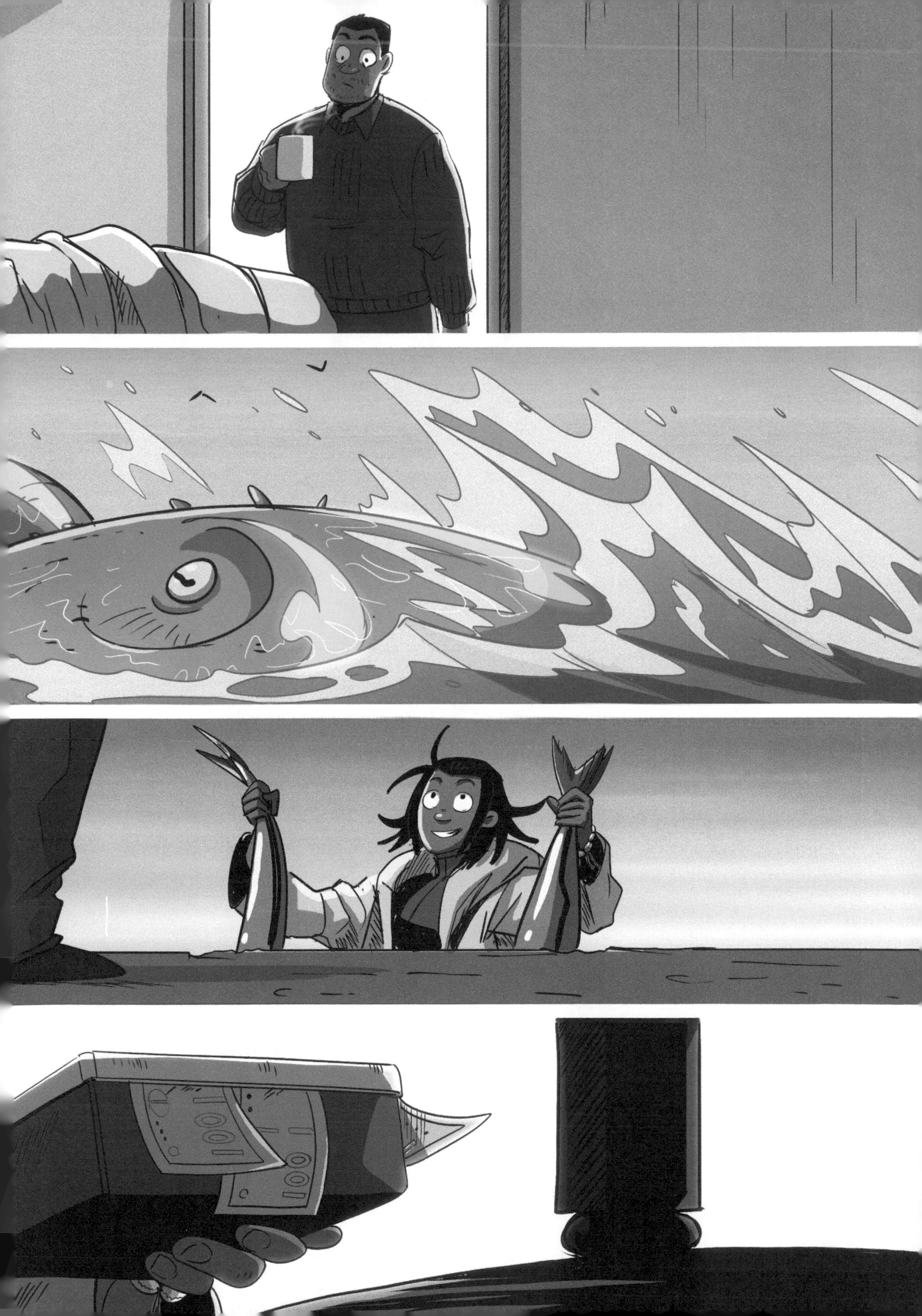

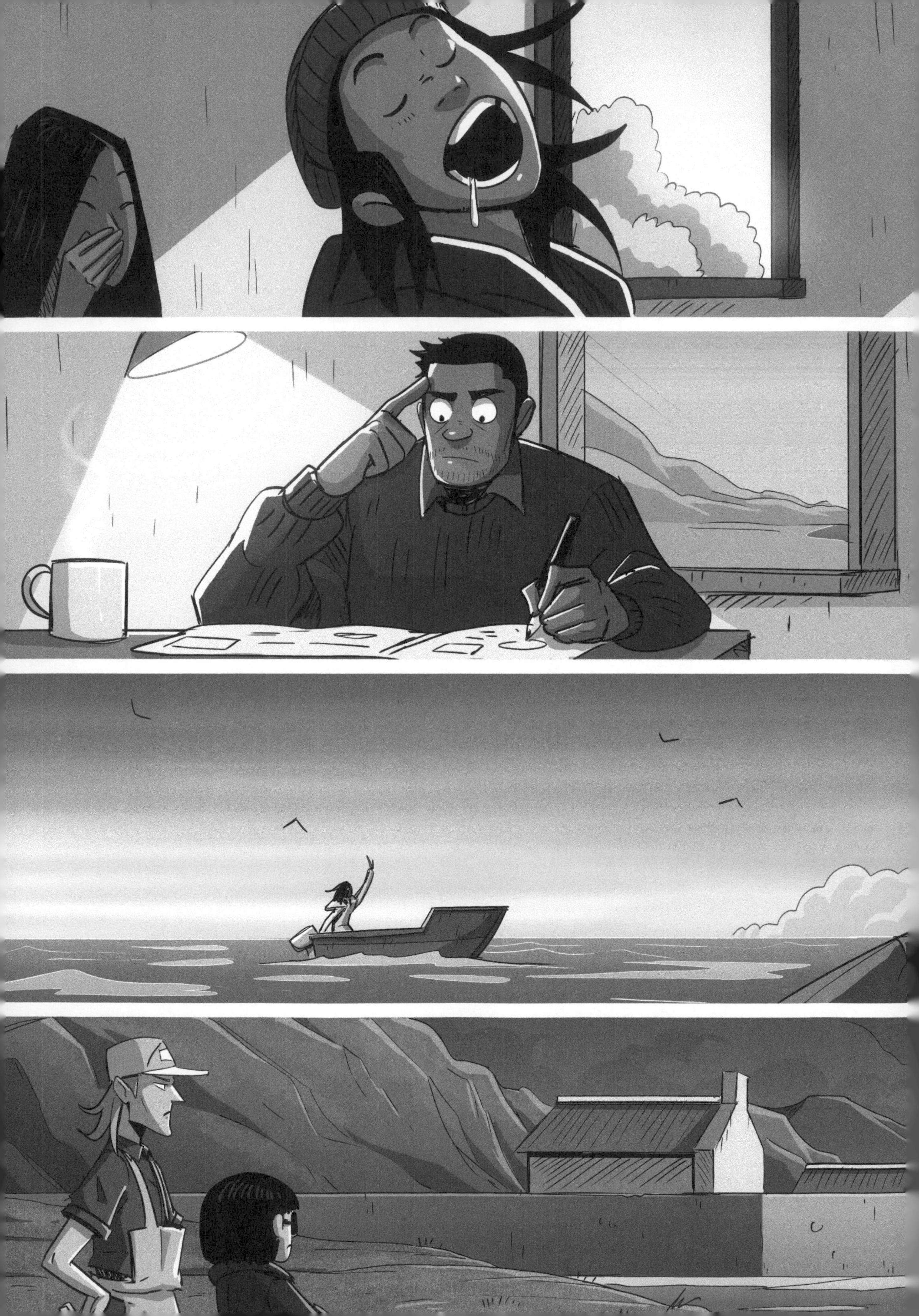

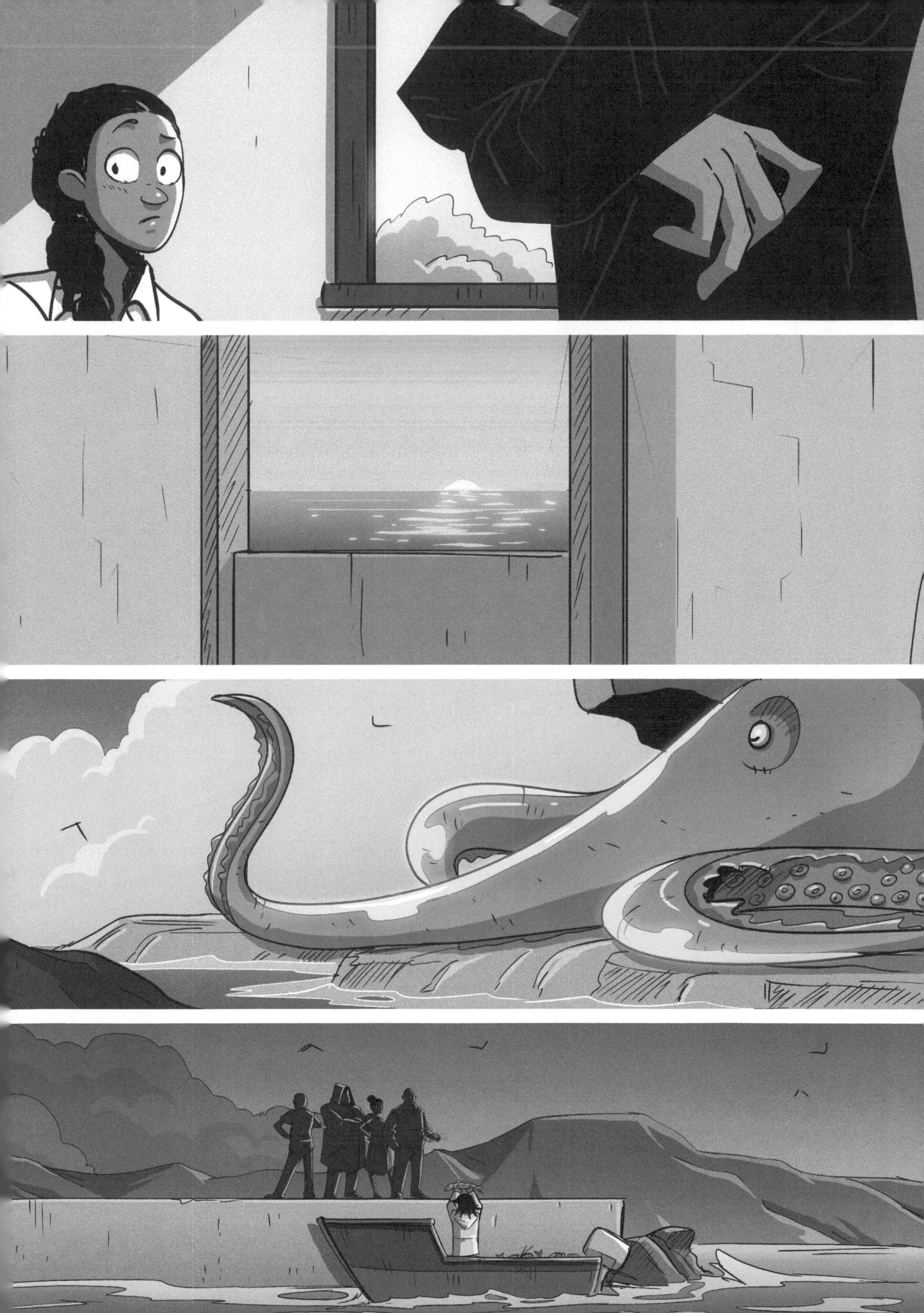

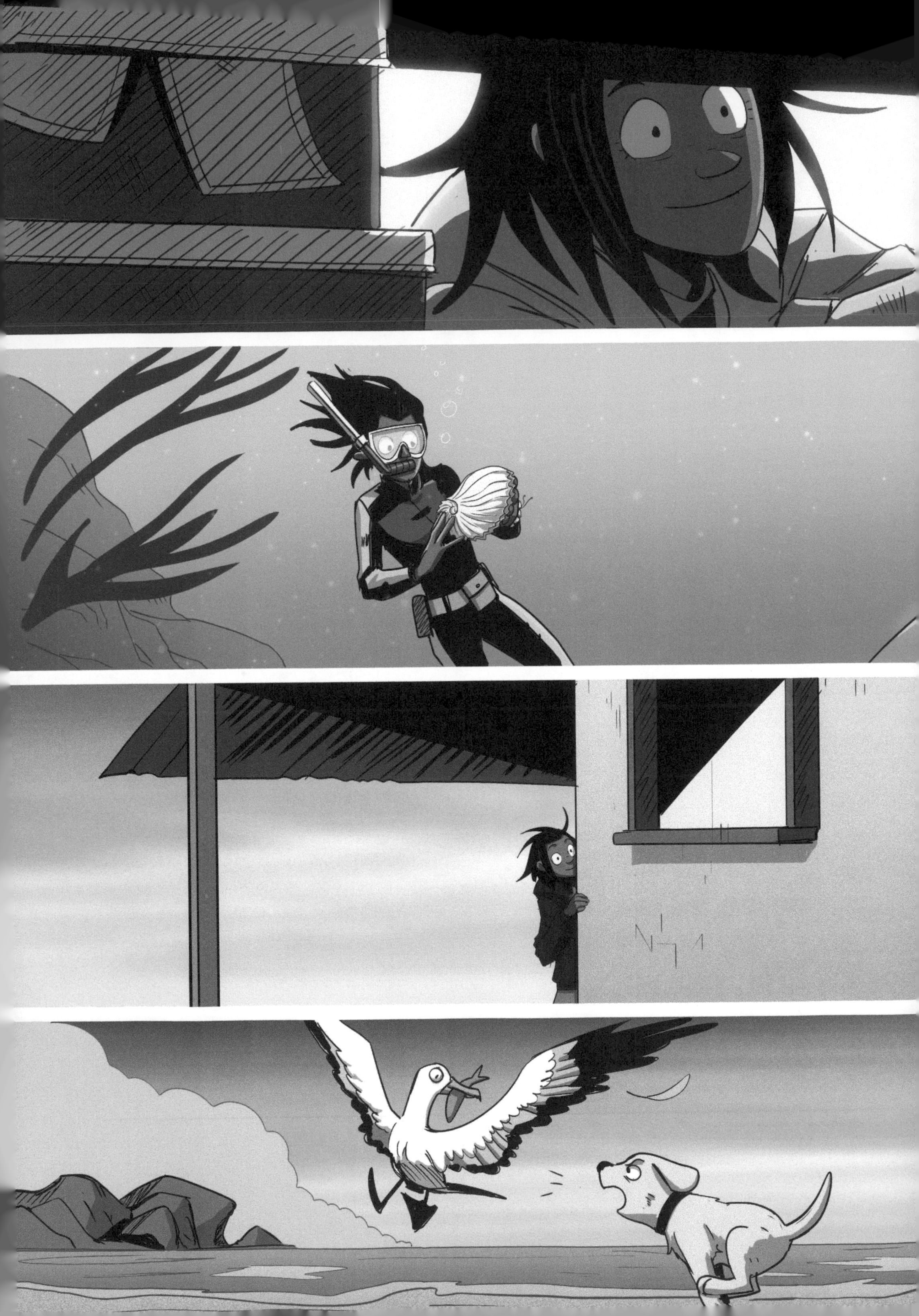

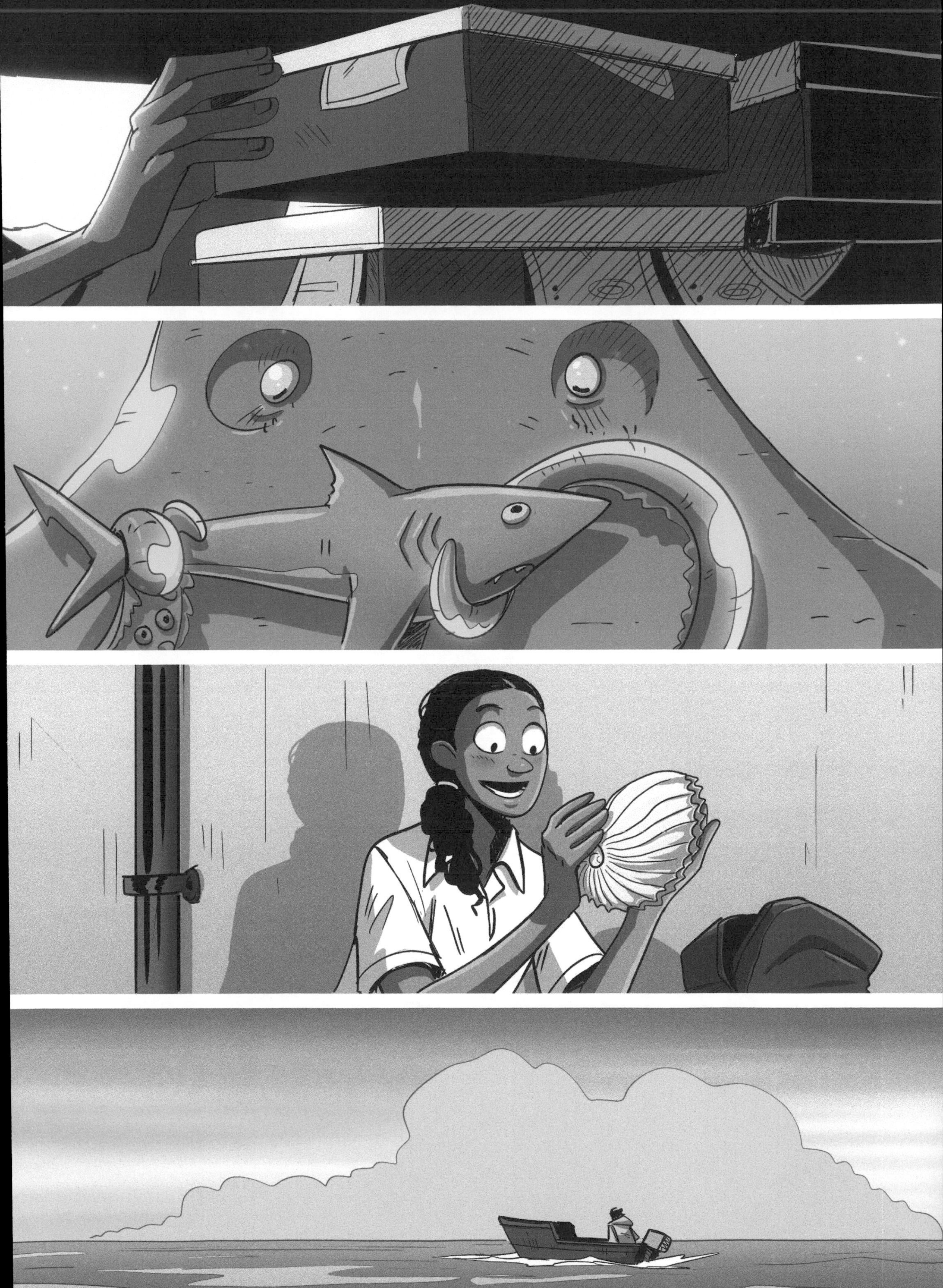

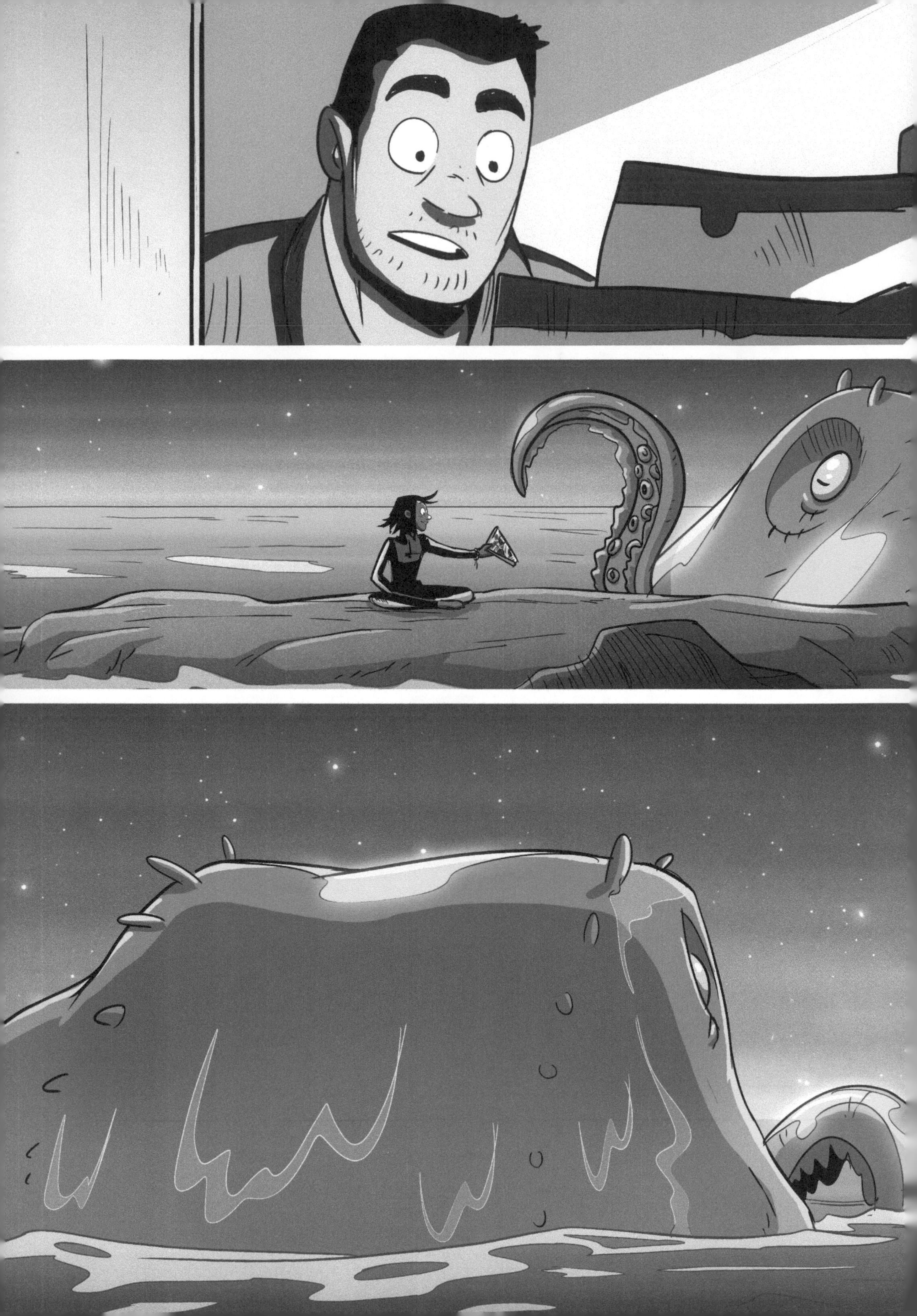

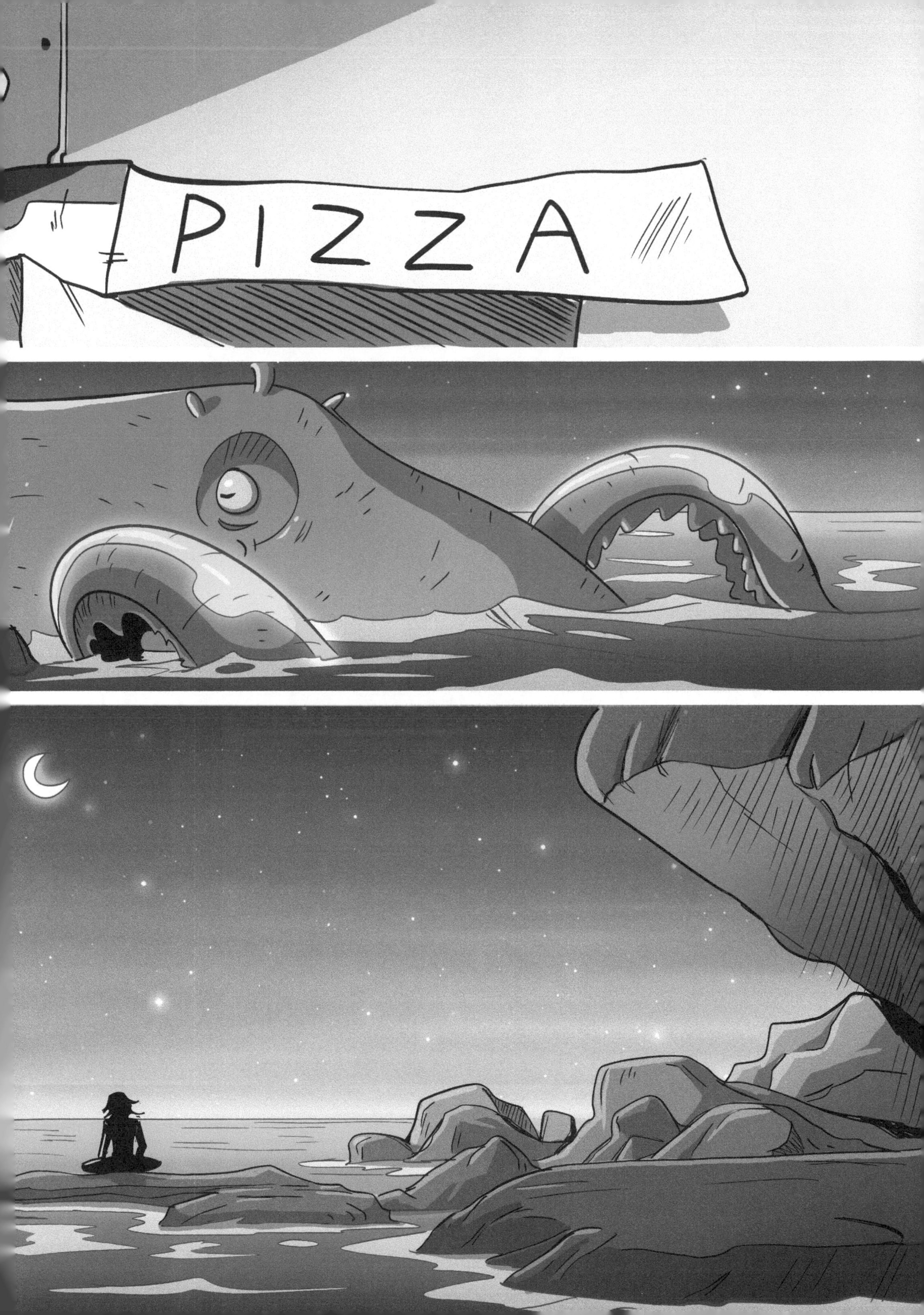
PIZZA

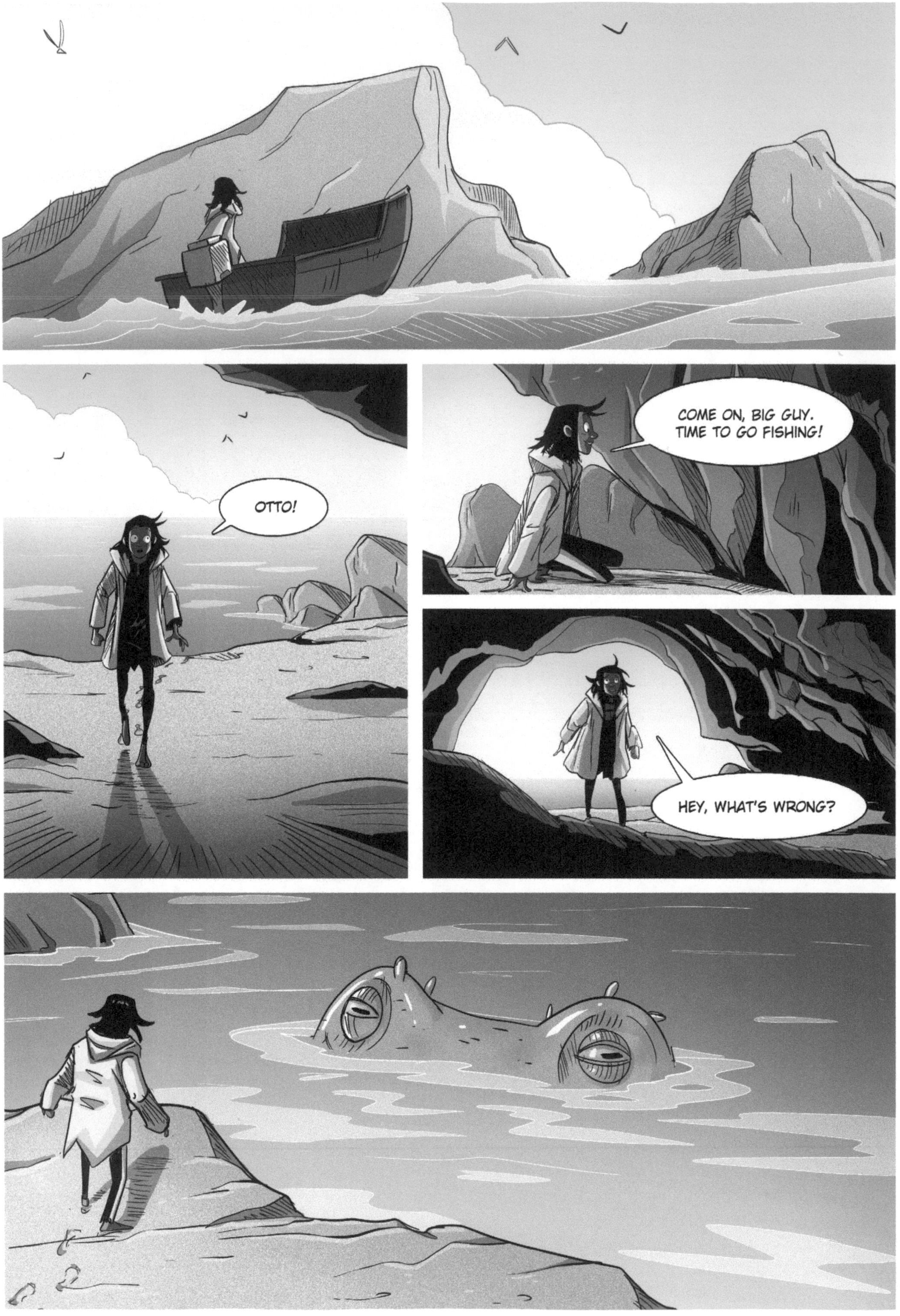
OTTO!
COME ON, BIG GUY. TIME TO GO FISHING!
HEY, WHAT'S WRONG?

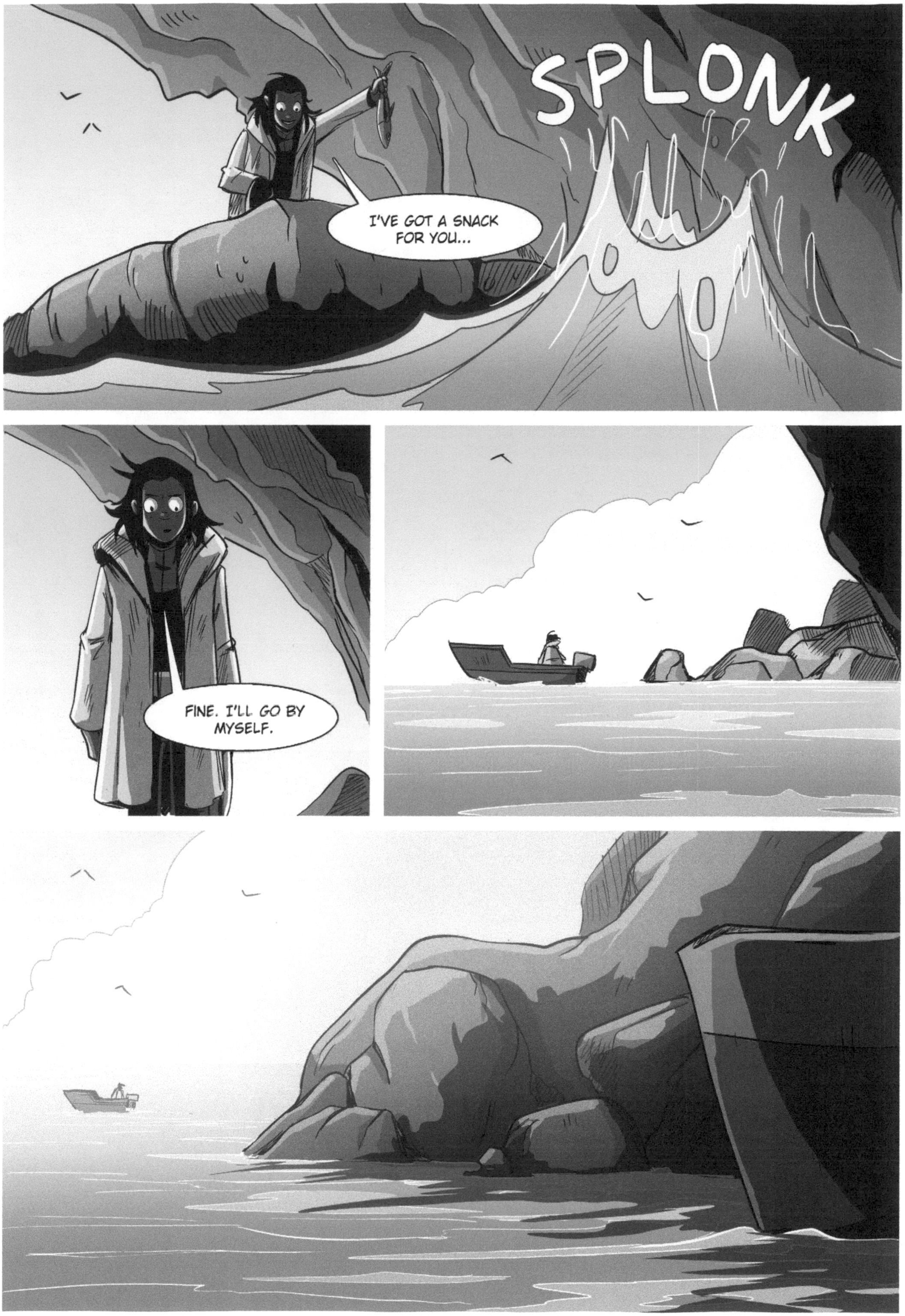
SPLONK
I'VE GOT A SNACK FOR YOU...
FINE. I'LL GO BY MYSELF.

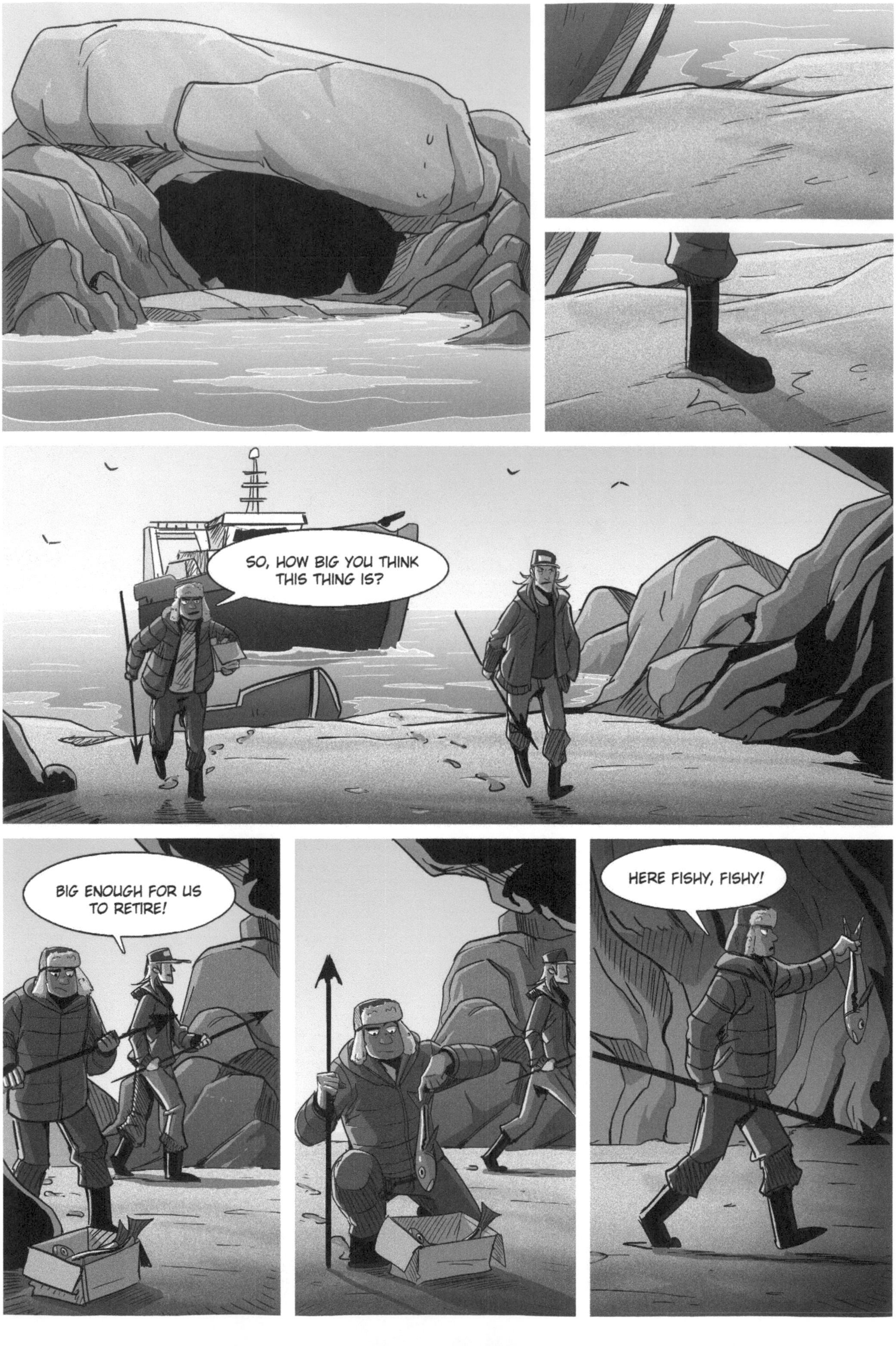
SO, HOW BIG YOU THINK THIS THING IS?
BIG ENOUGH FOR US TO RETIRE!
HERE FISHY, FISHY!

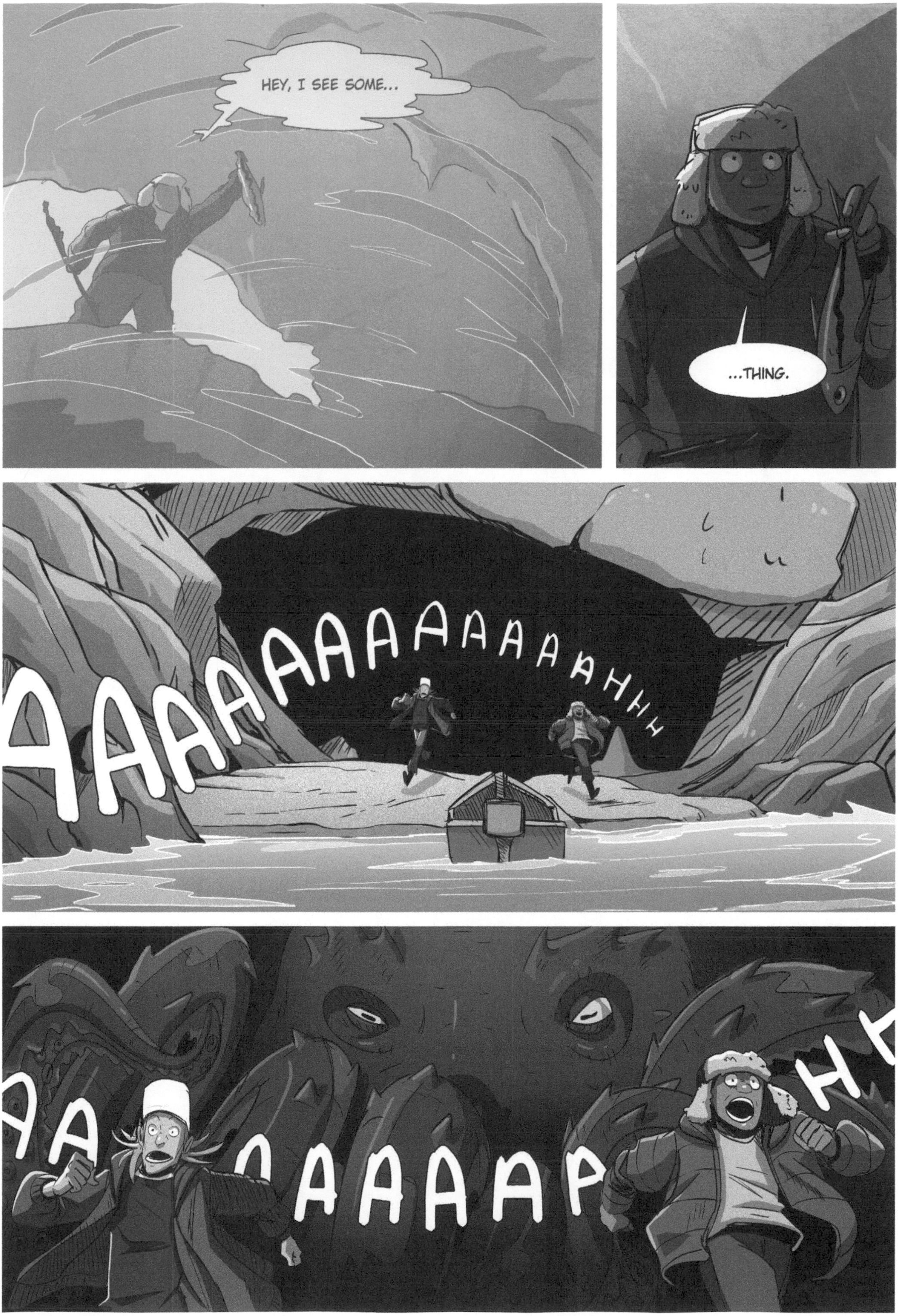
HEY, I SEE SOME...
...THING.
AAAAAAAAAAAAAHHHH
AAAAAAAAH

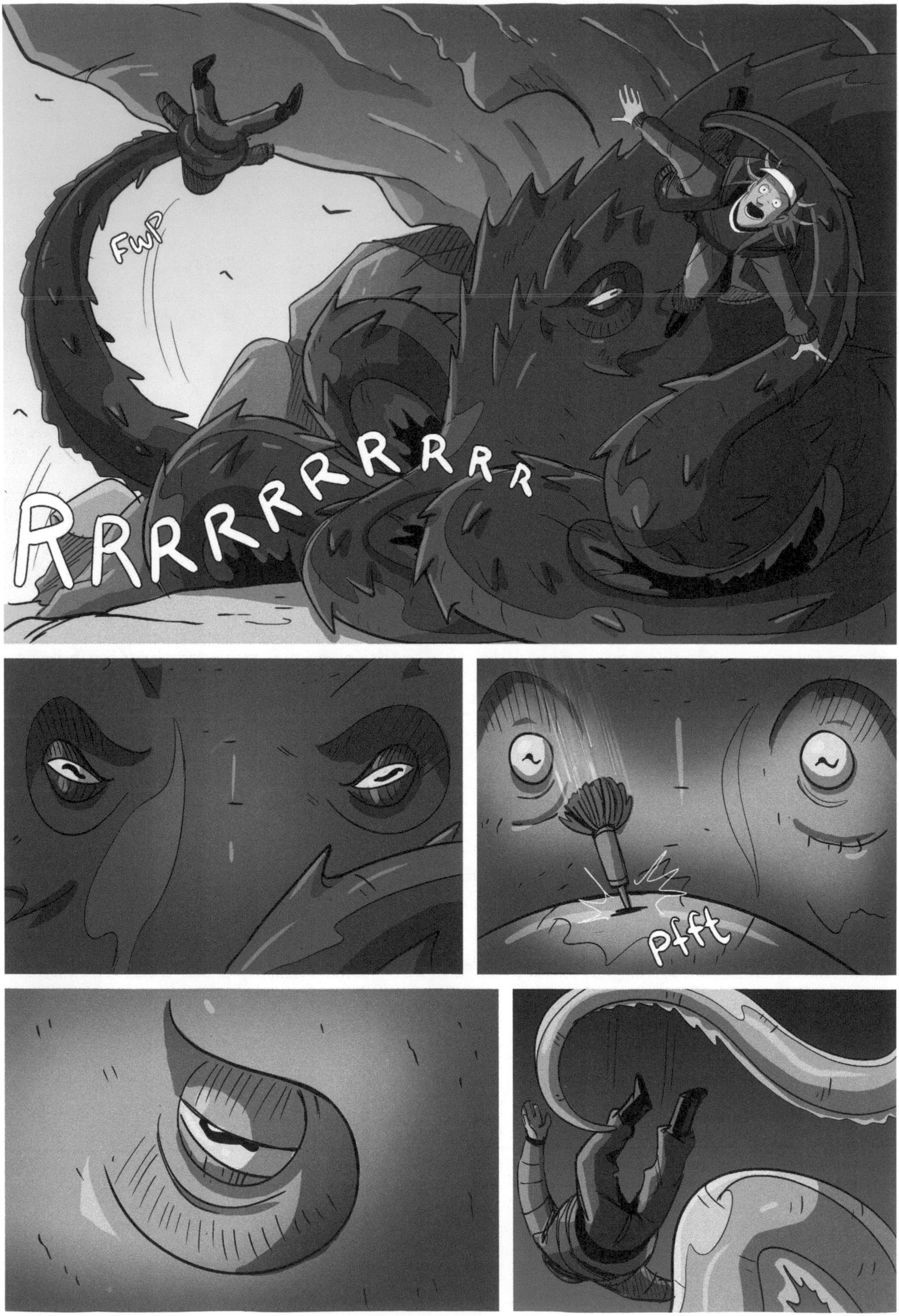
FWP
RRRRRRRRRR
pfft

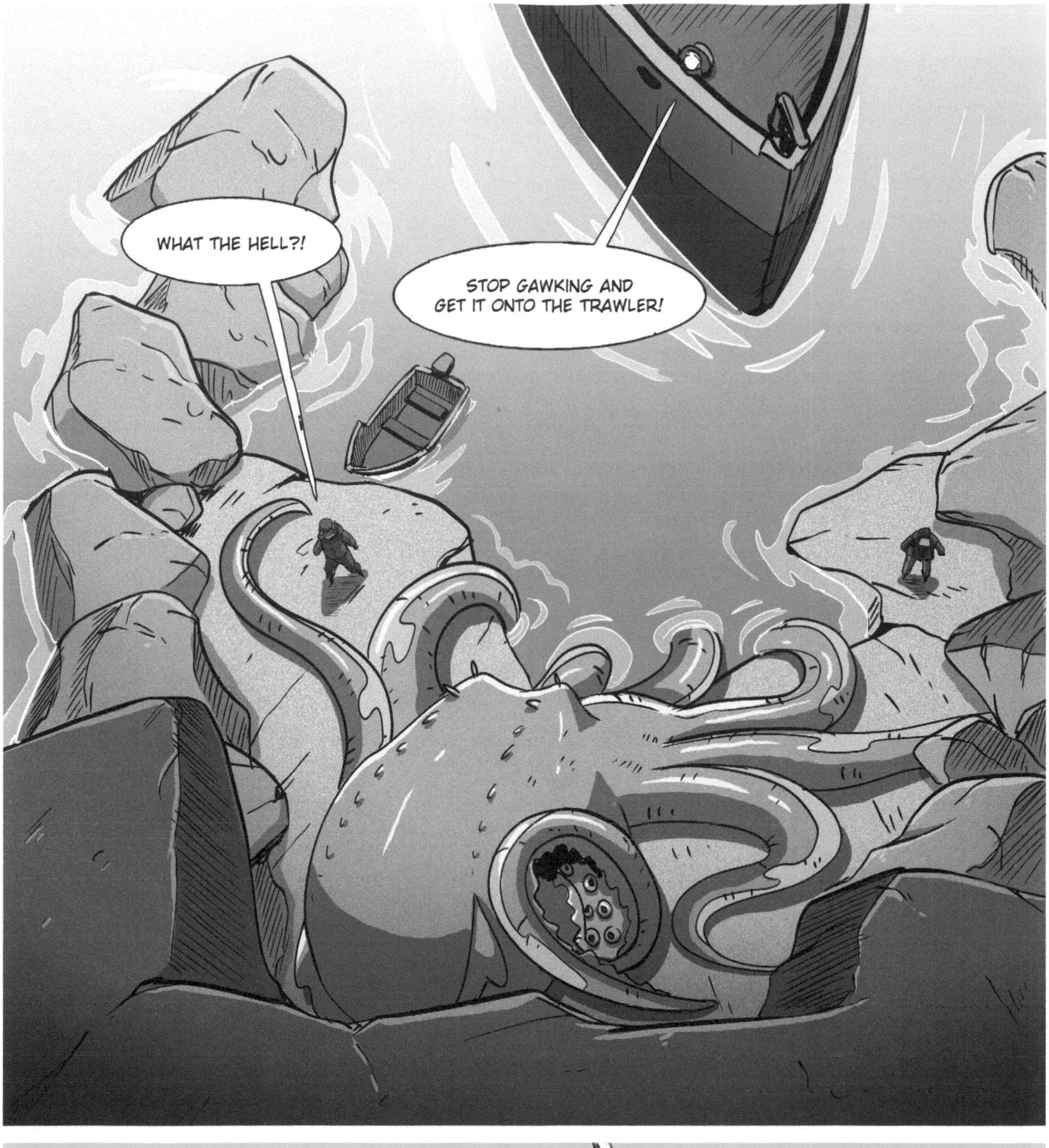
WHAT THE HELL?!
STOP GAWKING AND GET IT ONTO THE TRAWLER!

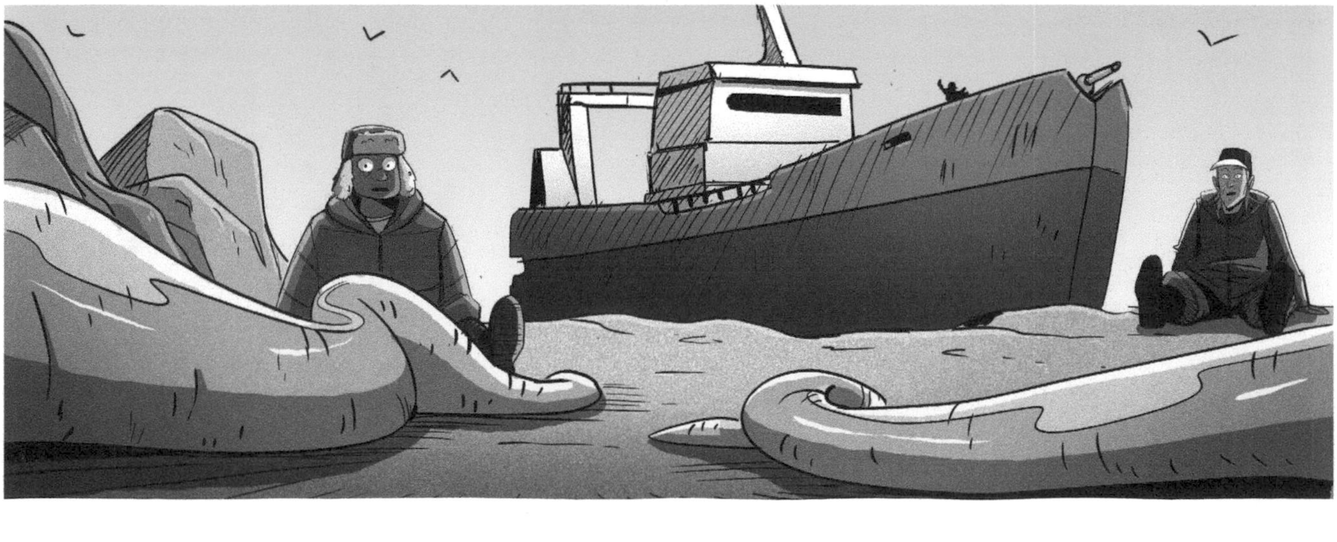

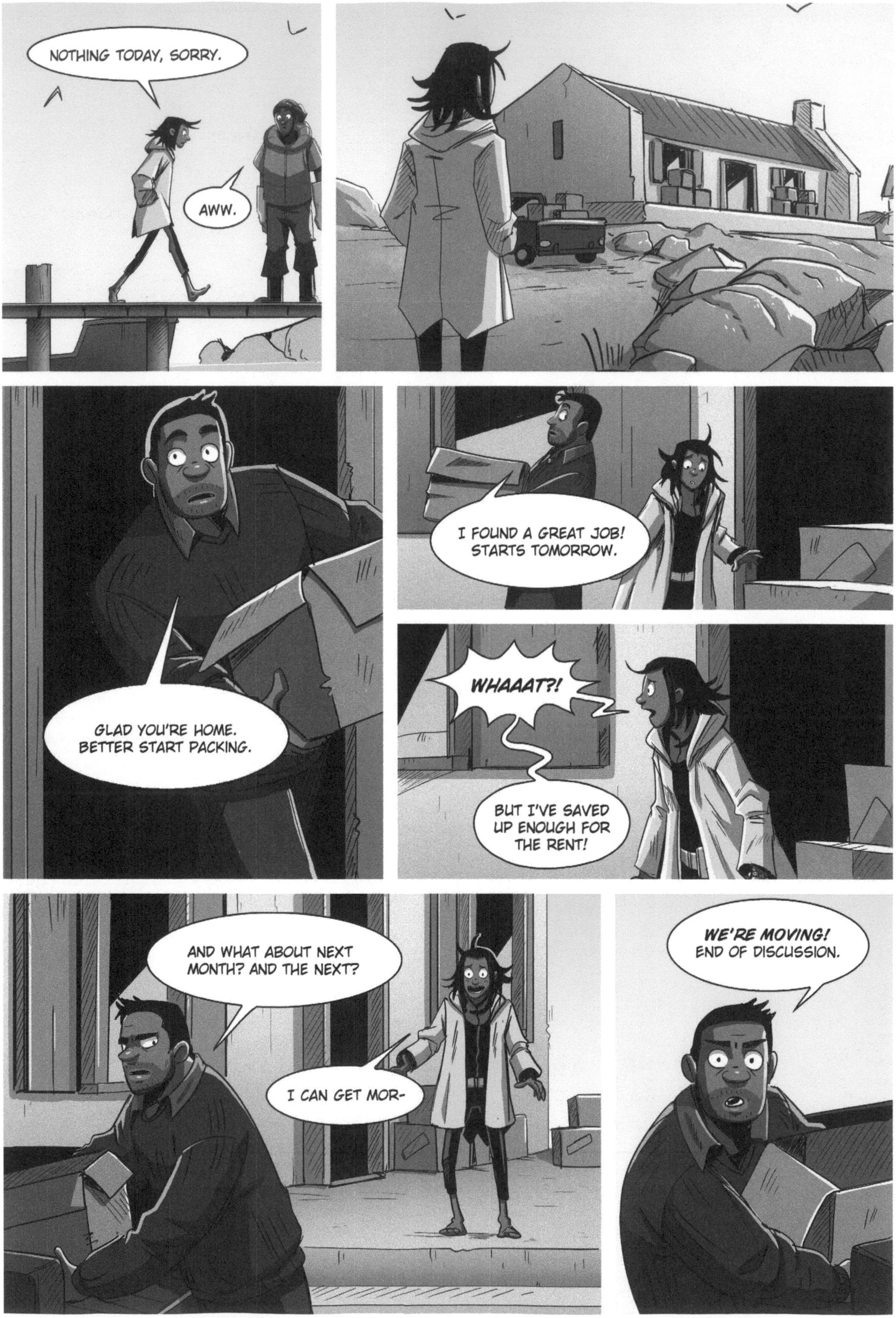
NOTHING TODAY, SORRY.
AWW.
GLAD YOU'RE HOME. BETTER START PACKING.
I FOUND A GREAT JOB! STARTS TOMORROW.
WHAAAT?!
BUT I'VE SAVED UP ENOUGH FOR THE RENT!
AND WHAT ABOUT NEXT MONTH? AND THE NEXT?
I CAN GET MOR-
WE'RE MOVING! END OF DISCUSSION.

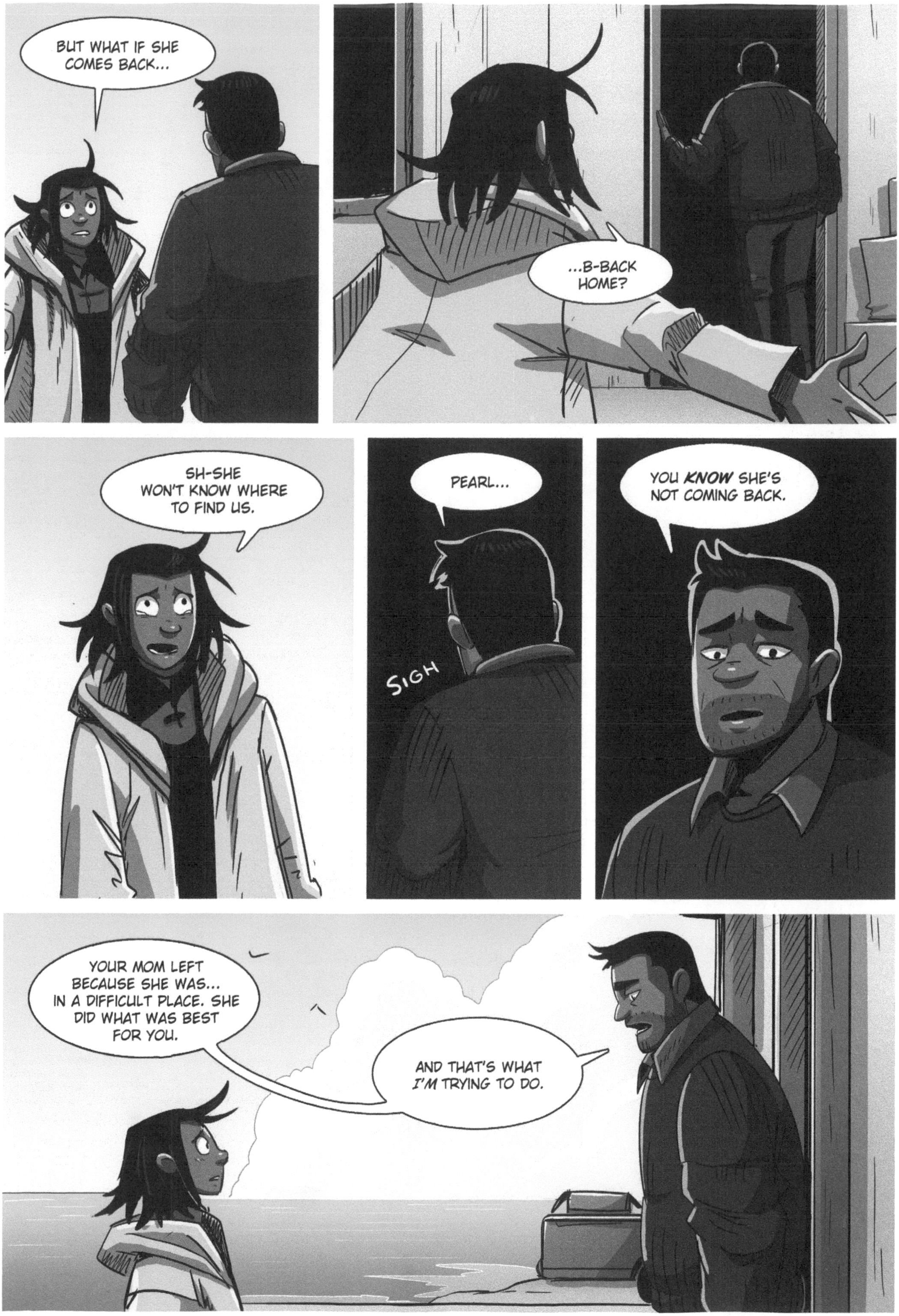
BUT WHAT IF SHE COMES BACK...
...B-BACK HOME?
SH-SHE WON'T KNOW WHERE TO FIND US.
PEARL...
SIGH
YOU KNOW SHE'S NOT COMING BACK.
YOUR MOM LEFT BECAUSE SHE WAS... IN A DIFFICULT PLACE. SHE DID WHAT WAS BEST FOR YOU.
AND THAT'S WHAT I'M TRYING TO DO.

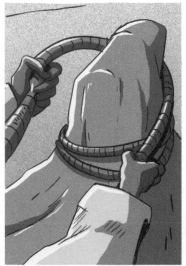

OTTO!

OTTO?

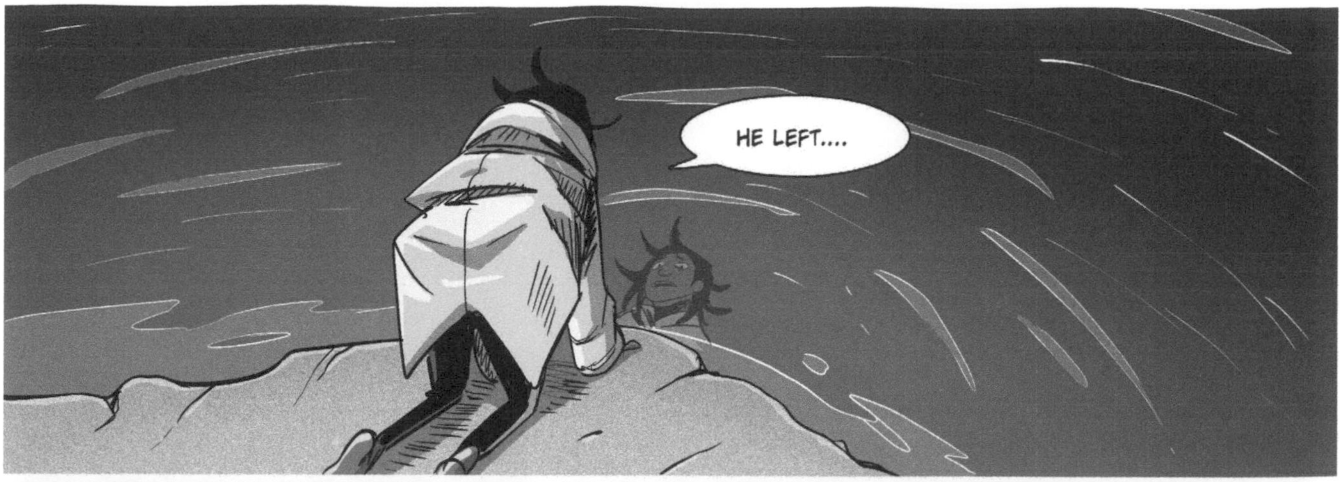
HE LEFT....

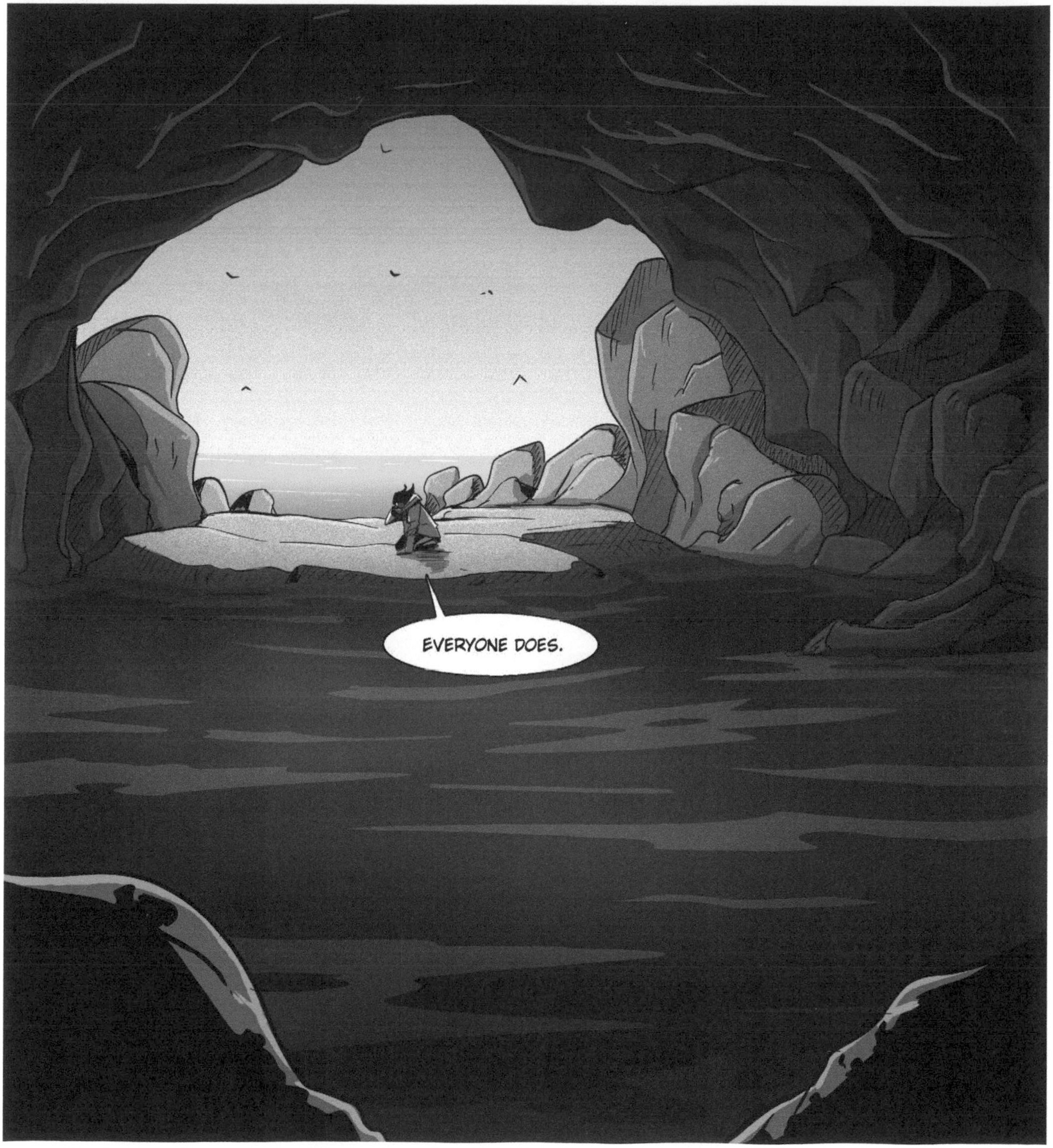
EVERYONE DOES.

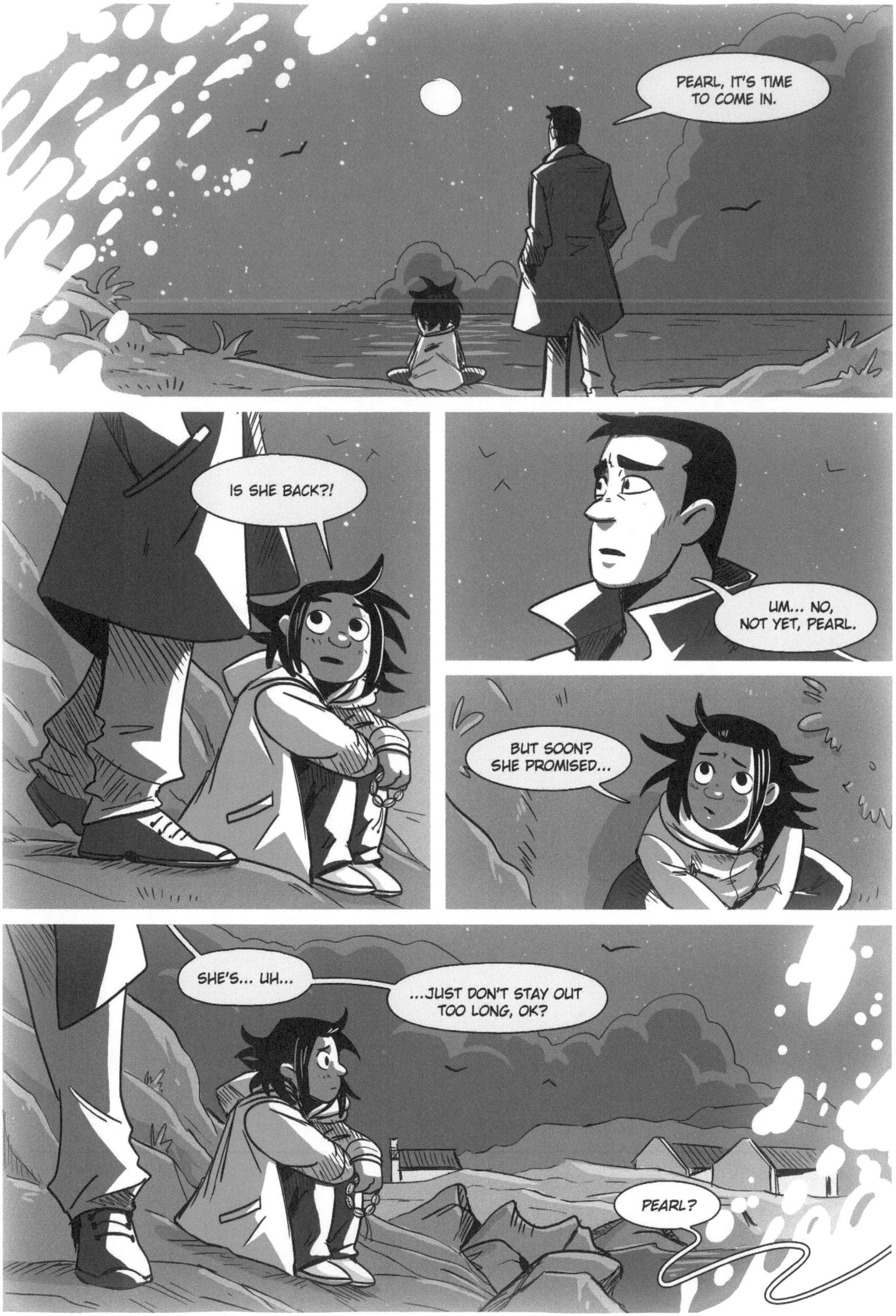
PEARL, IT'S TIME TO COME IN.
IS SHE BACK?!
UM... NO, NOT YET, PEARL.
BUT SOON? SHE PROMISED...
SHE'S... UH...
...JUST DON'T STAY OUT TOO LONG, OK?
PEARL?

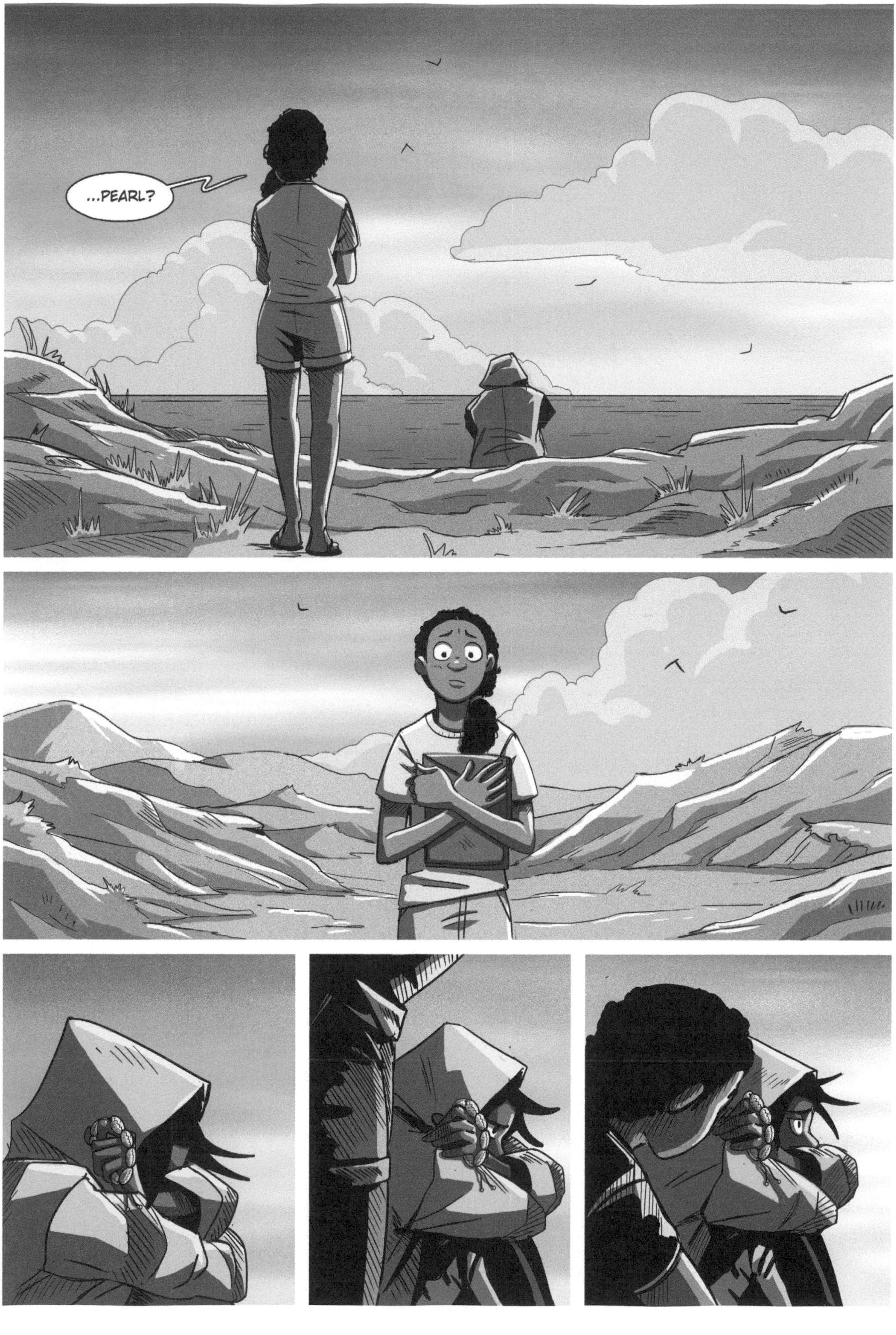
...PEARL?

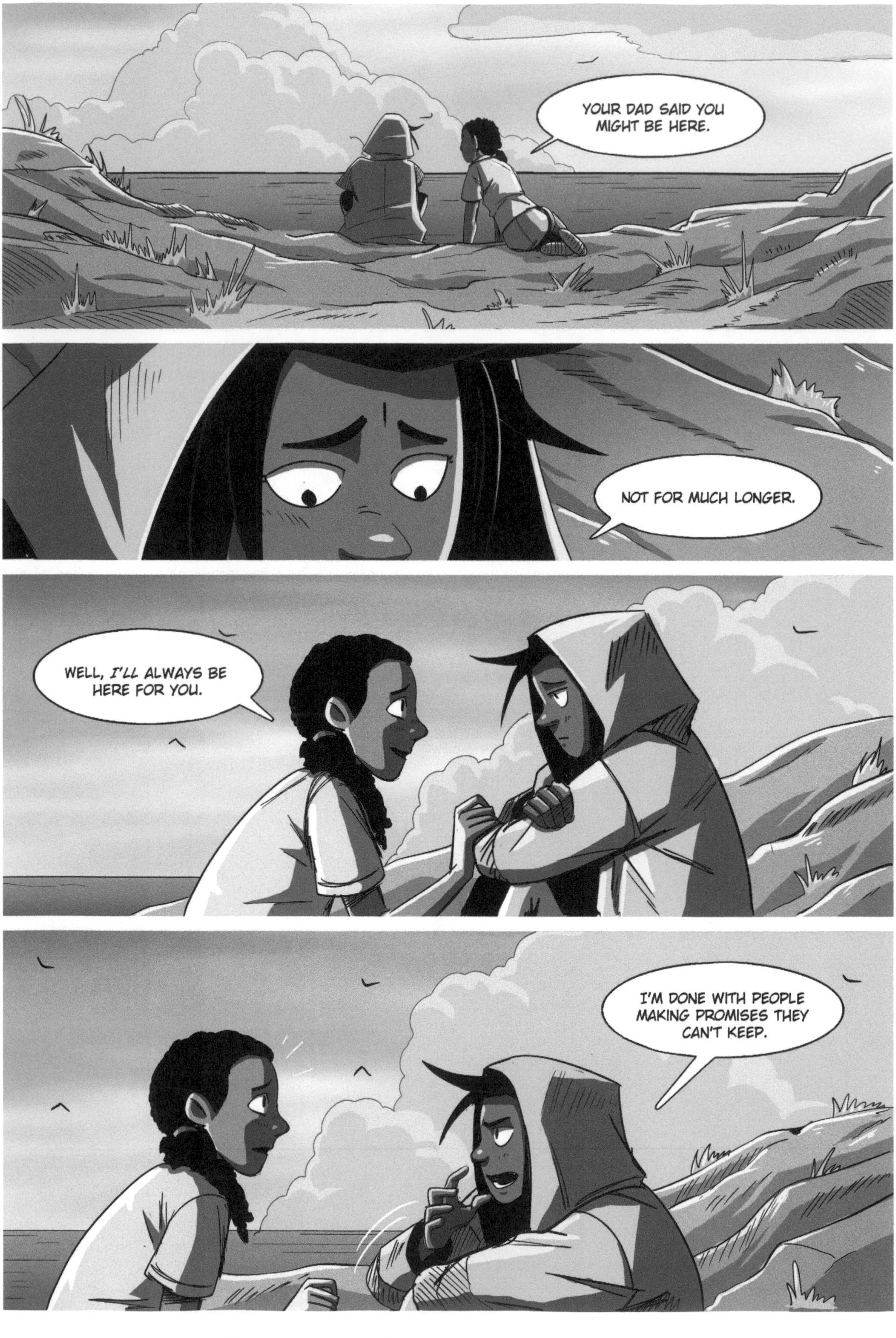
YOUR DAD SAID YOU MIGHT BE HERE.
NOT FOR MUCH LONGER.
WELL, I'LL ALWAYS BE HERE FOR YOU.
I'M DONE WITH PEOPLE MAKING PROMISES THEY CAN'T KEEP.

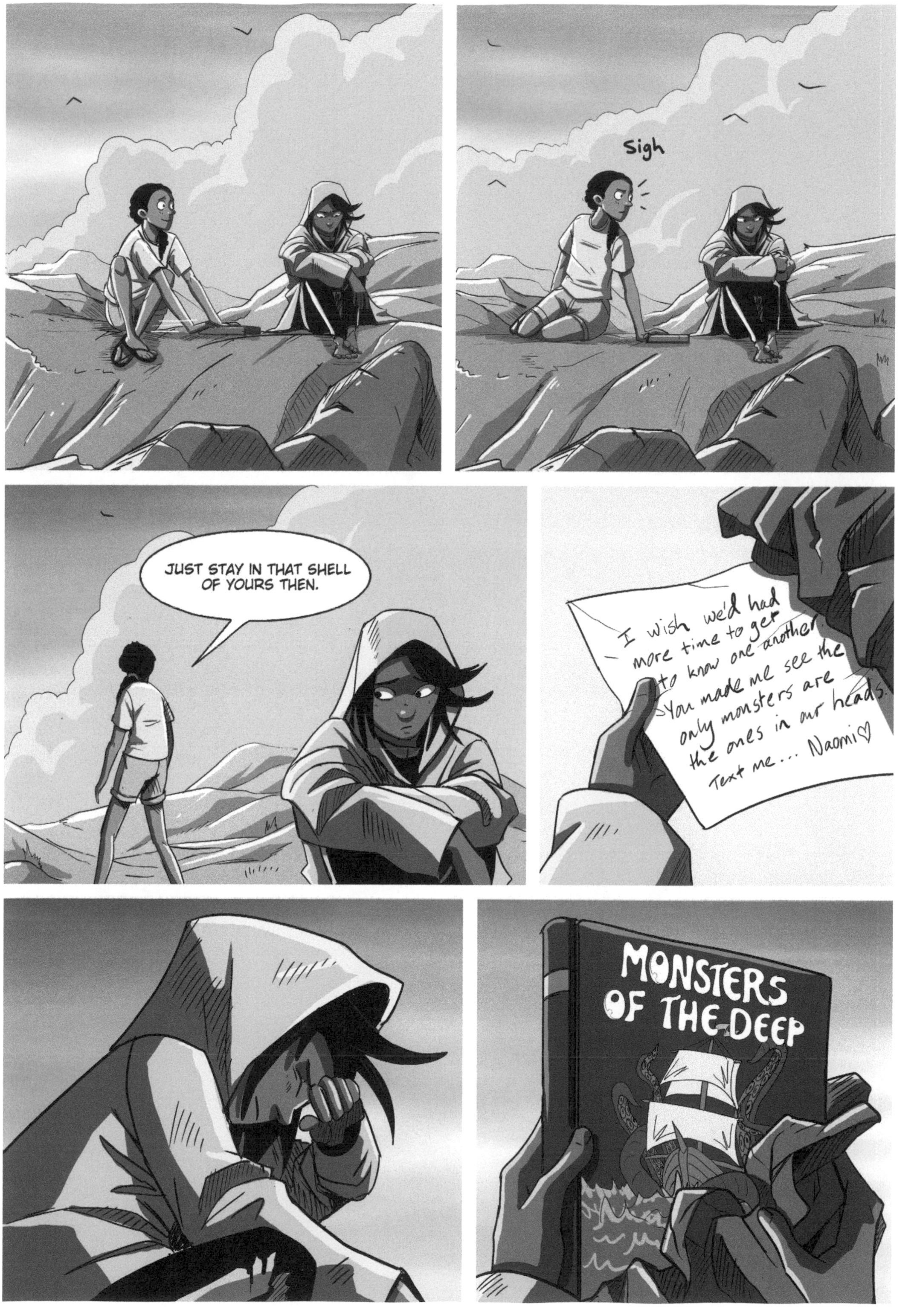
Sigh
JUST STAY IN THAT SHELL OF YOURS THEN.
I wish we'd had more time to get to know one another. You made me see the only monsters are the ones in our heads. Text me... Naomi♡
MONSTERS OF THE DEEP

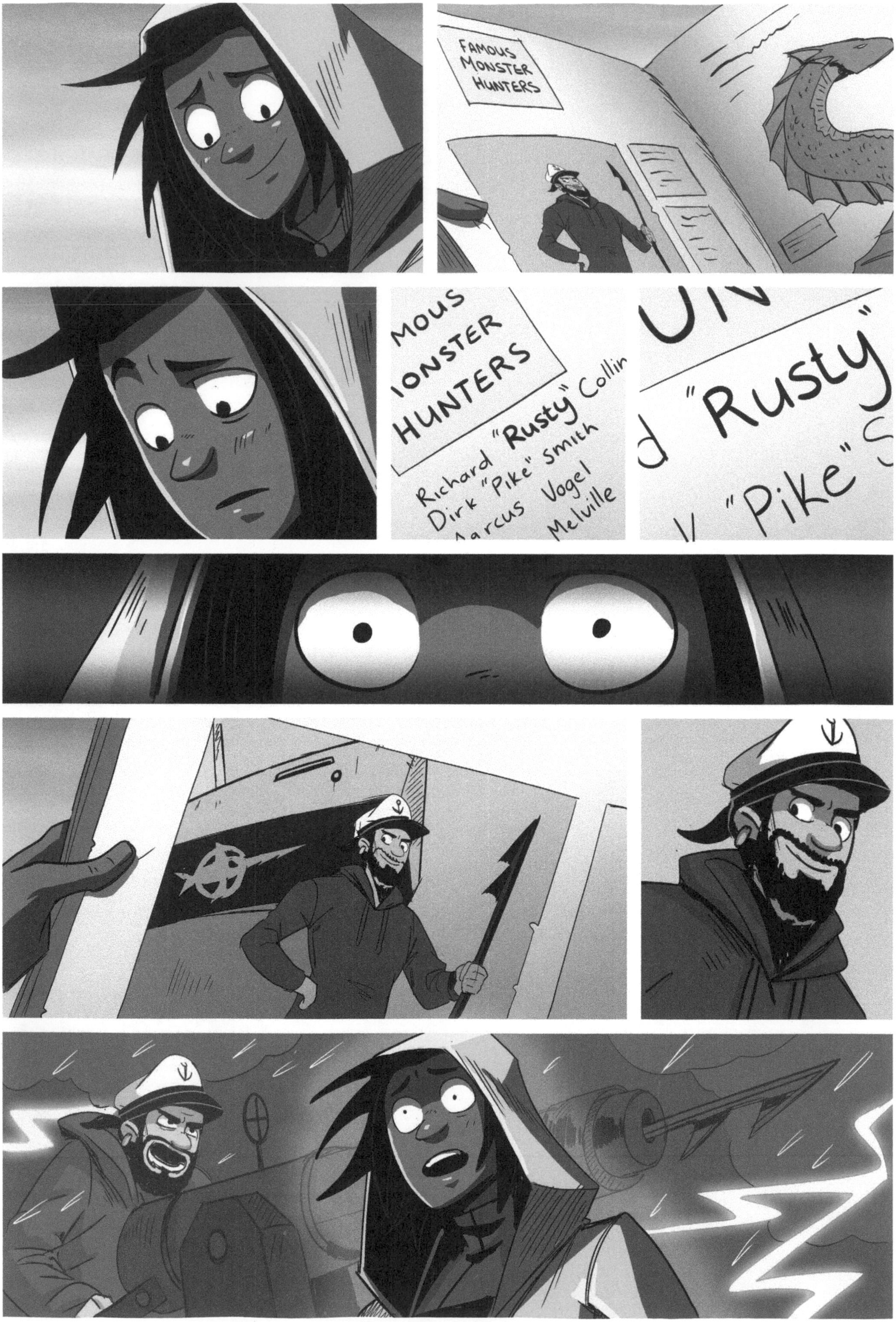
FAMOUS MONSTER HUNTERS
MOUS
IONSTER
HUNTERS
Richard "Rusty" Collin
Dirk "Pike" Smith
Vogel
Melville
"Rusty"
"Pike"

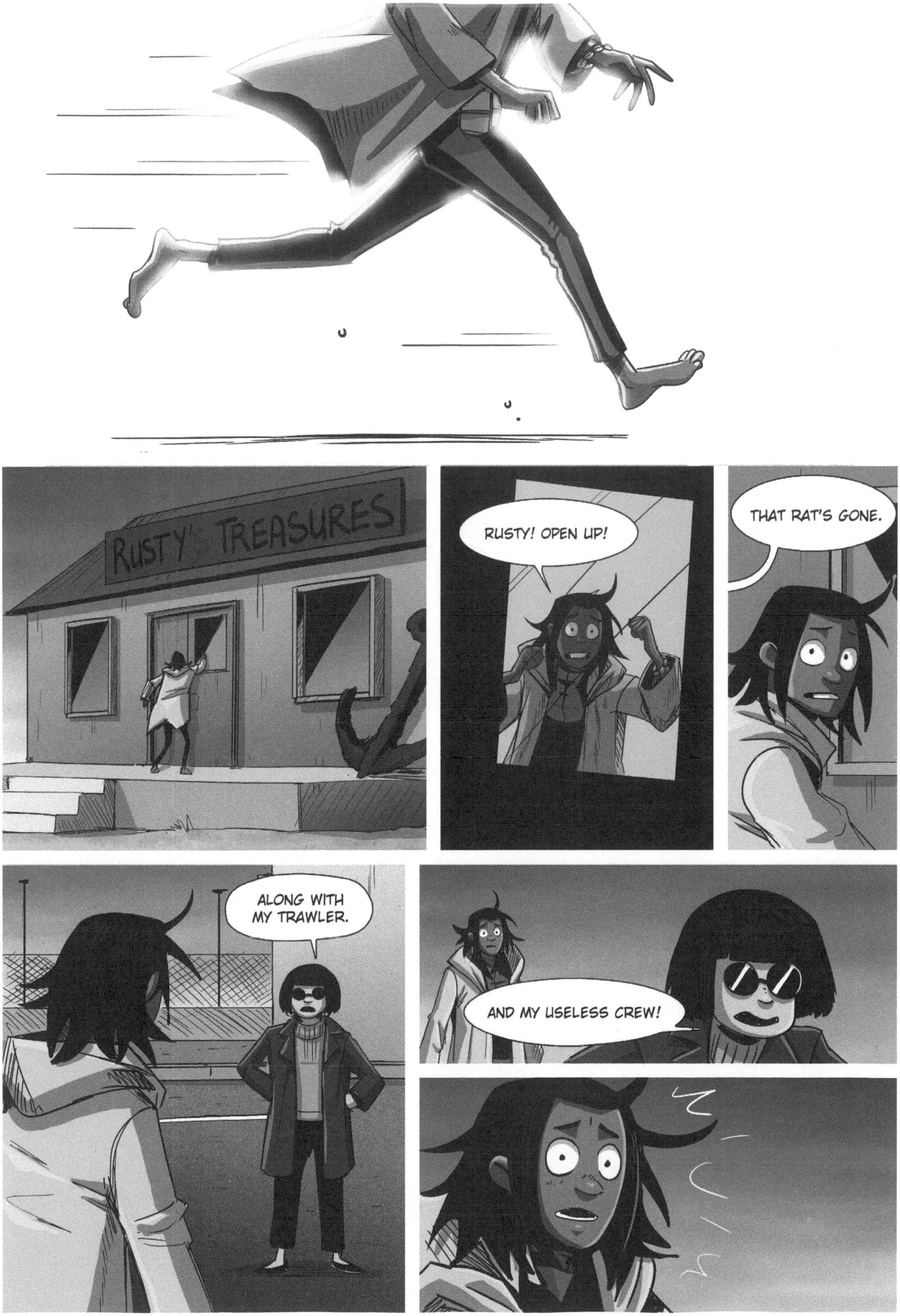
RUSTY'S TREASURES
RUSTY! OPEN UP!
THAT RAT'S GONE.
ALONG WITH MY TRAWLER.
AND MY USELESS CREW!

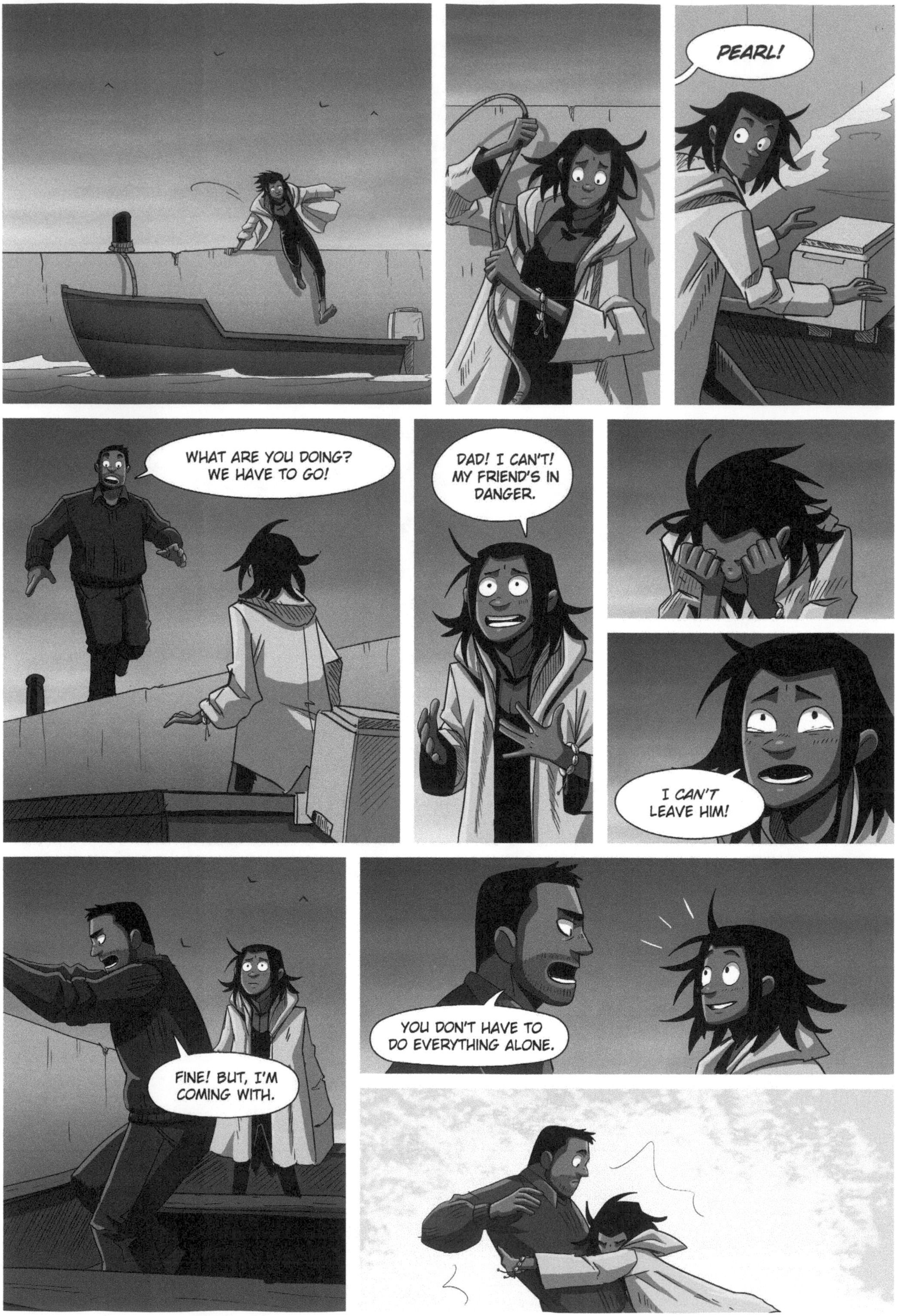
PEARL!
WHAT ARE YOU DOING? WE HAVE TO GO!
DAD! I CAN'T! MY FRIEND'S IN DANGER.
I CAN'T LEAVE HIM!
FINE! BUT, I'M COMING WITH.
YOU DON'T HAVE TO DO EVERYTHING ALONE.

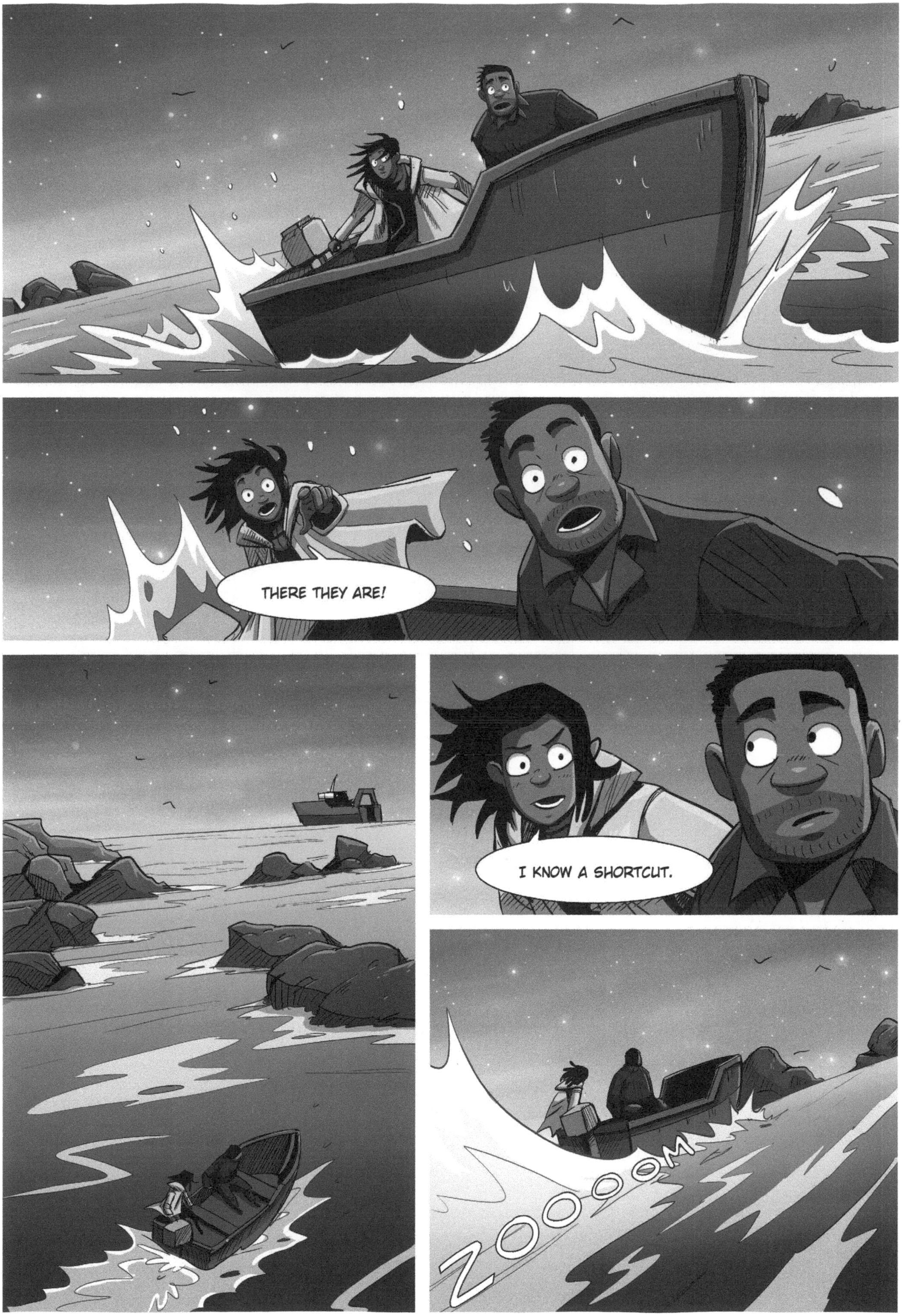
THERE THEY ARE!
I KNOW A SHORTCUT.
ZOOOOOM

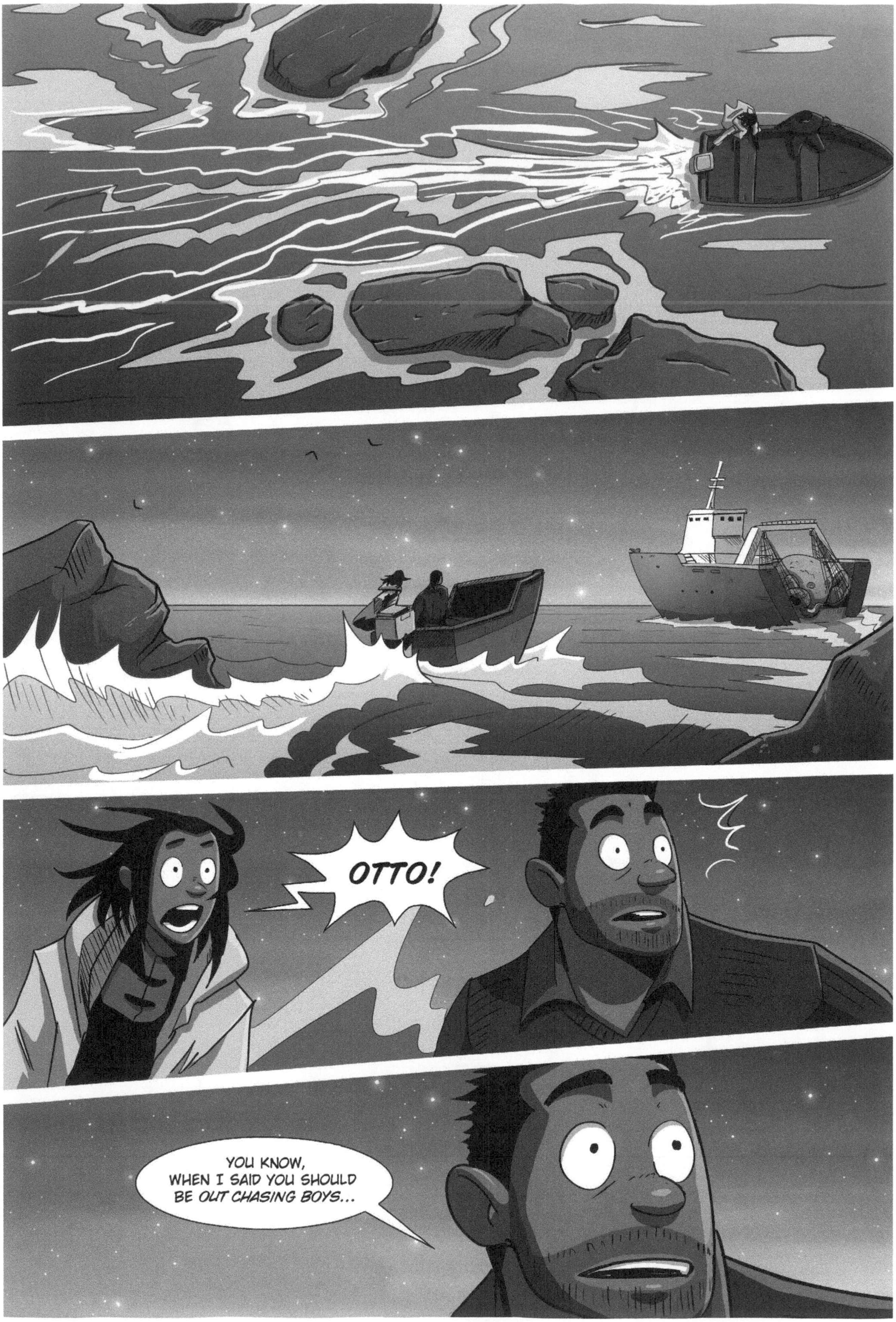
OTTO!
YOU KNOW, WHEN I SAID YOU SHOULD BE *OUT CHASING BOYS*...

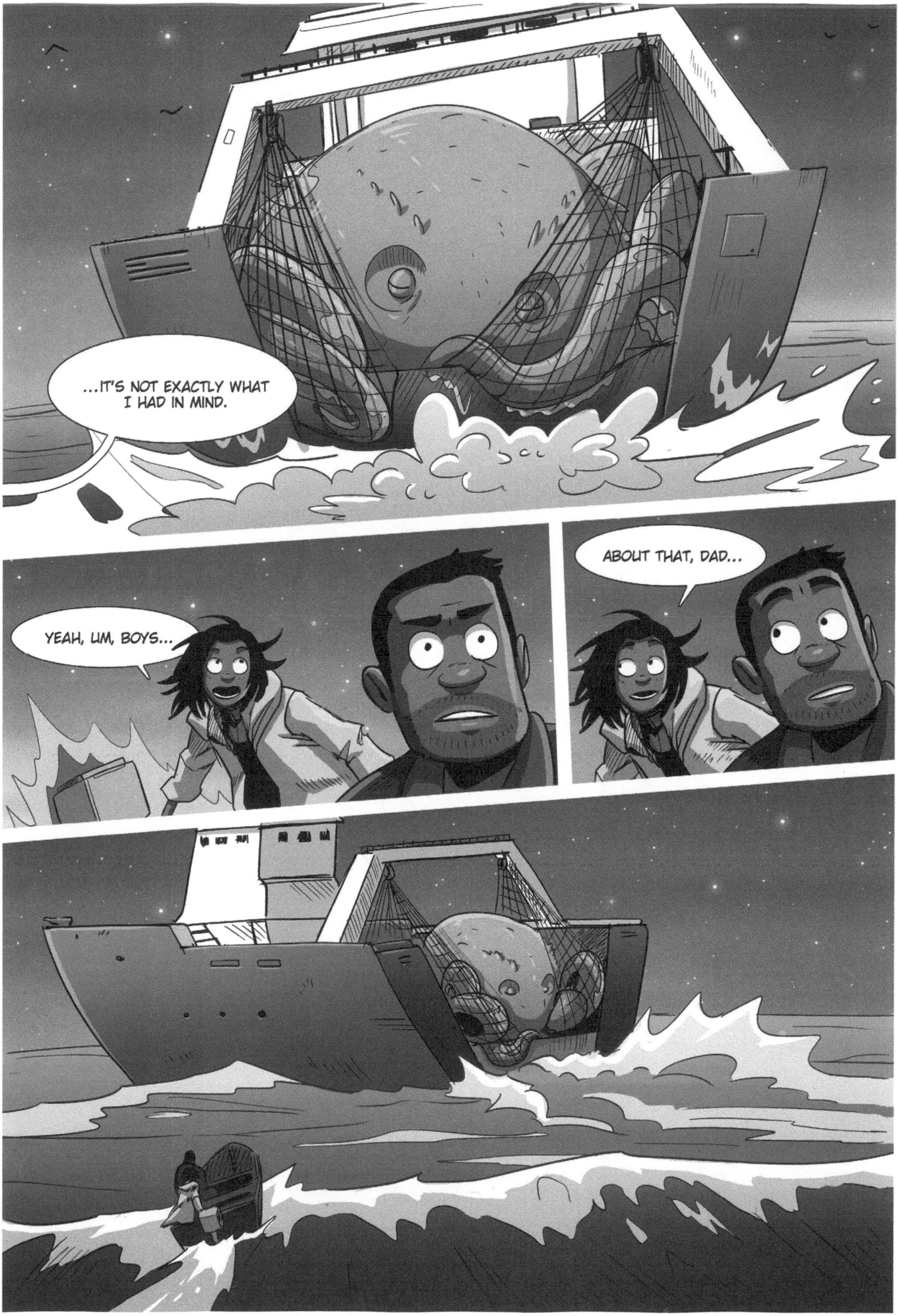
...IT'S NOT EXACTLY WHAT I HAD IN MIND.
YEAH, UM, BOYS...
ABOUT THAT, DAD...

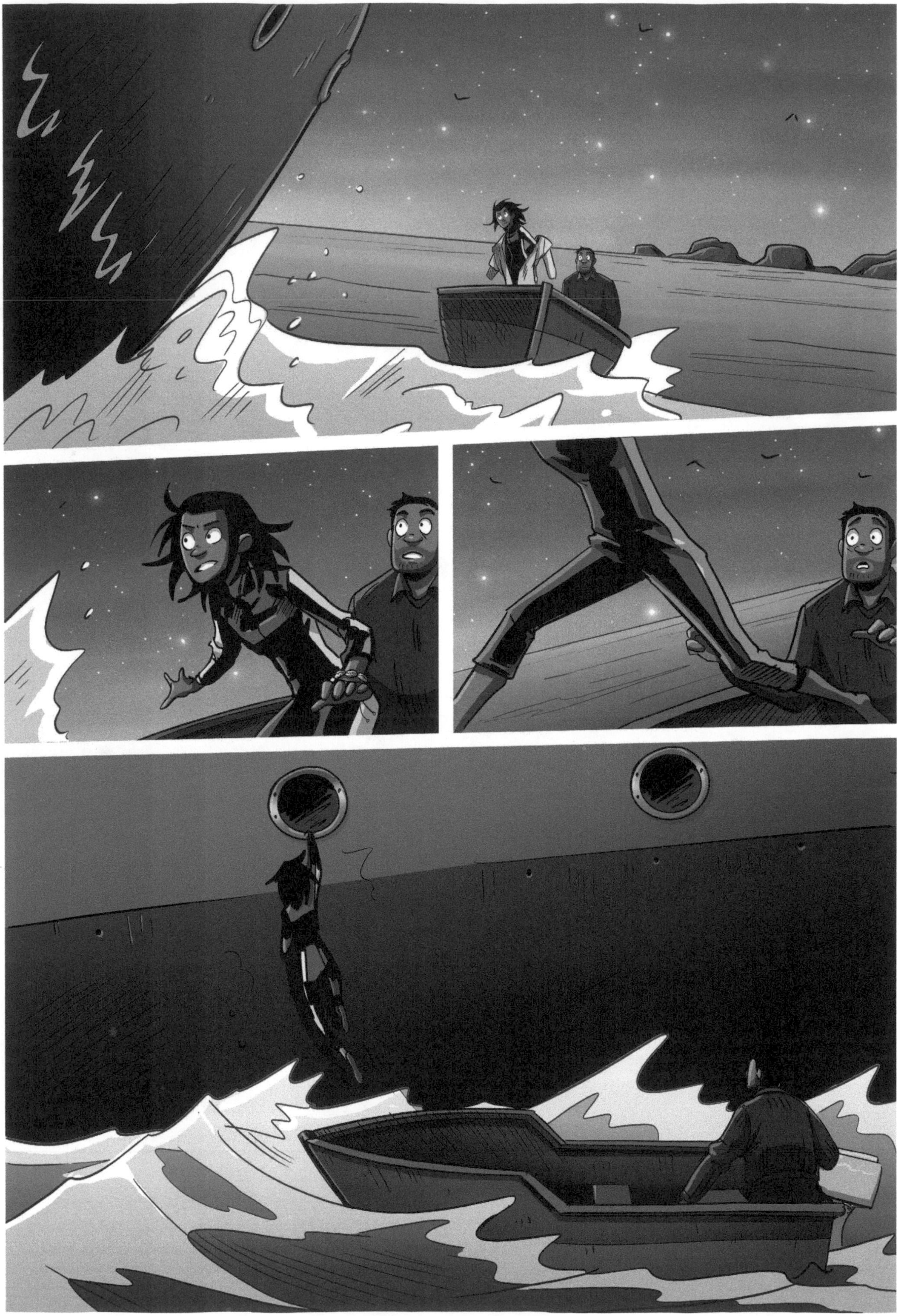

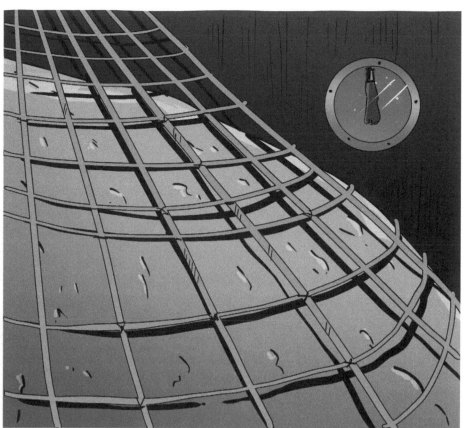

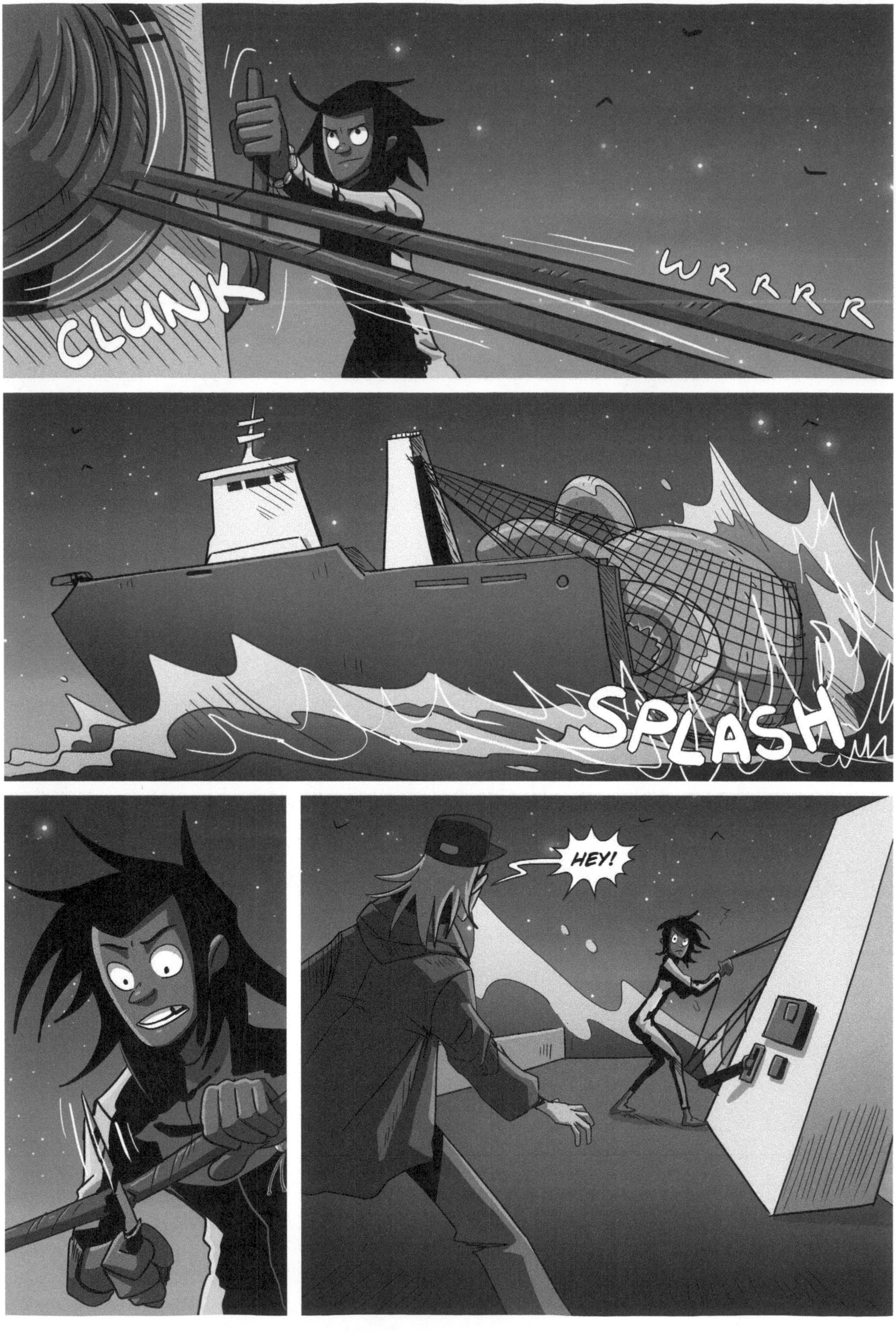
CLUNK
WRRRRR
SPLASH
HEY!

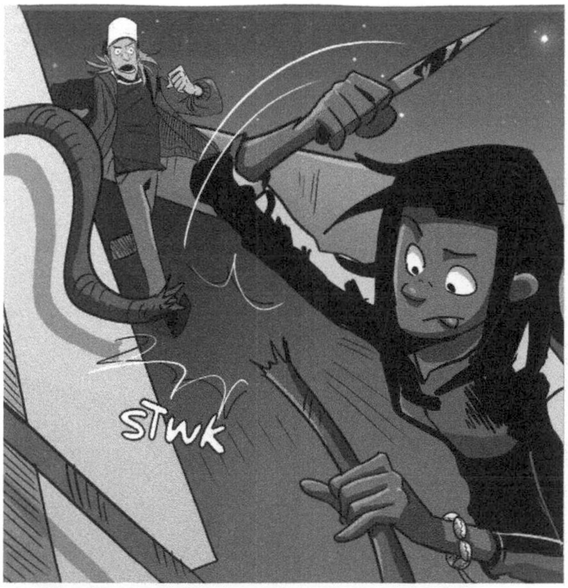
STWK

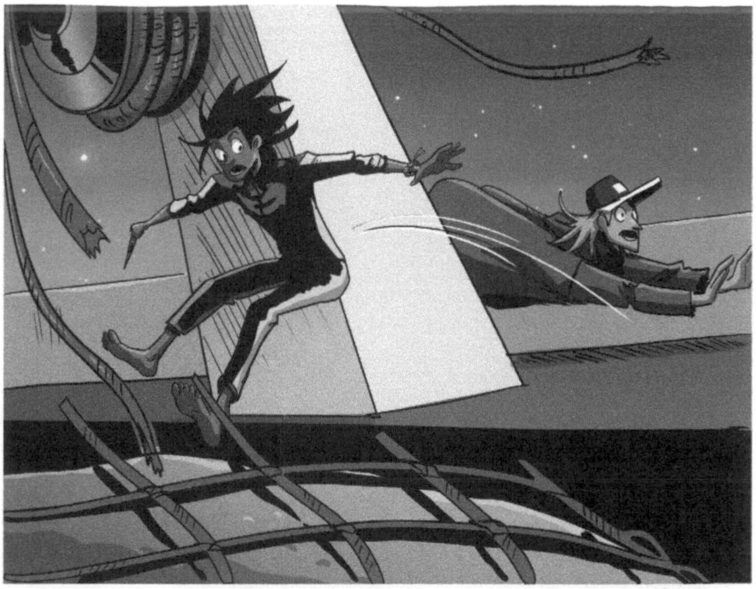

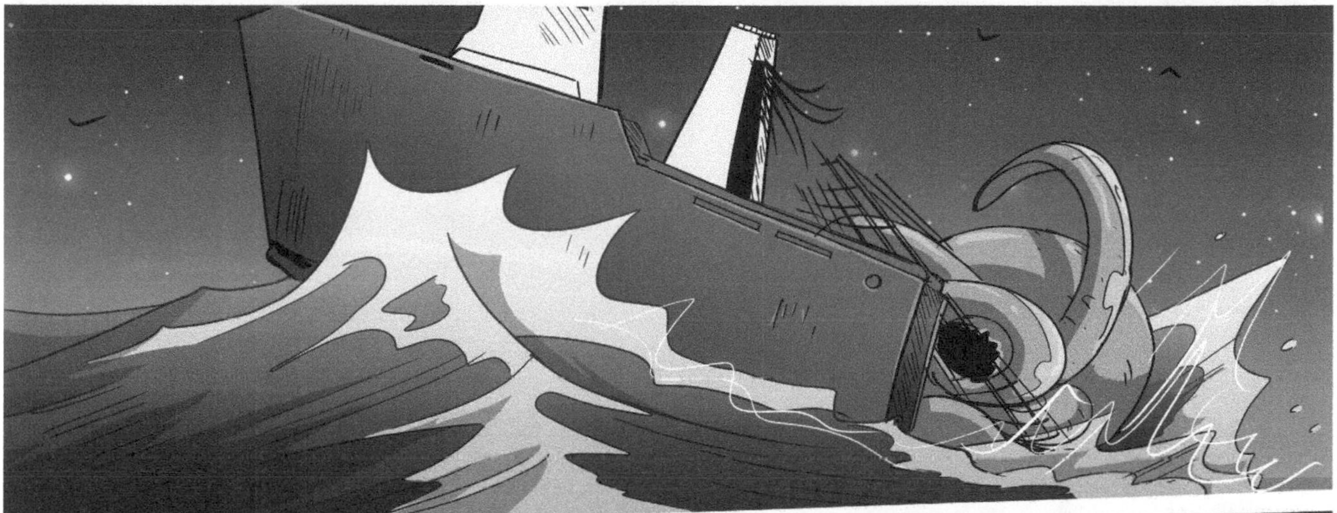

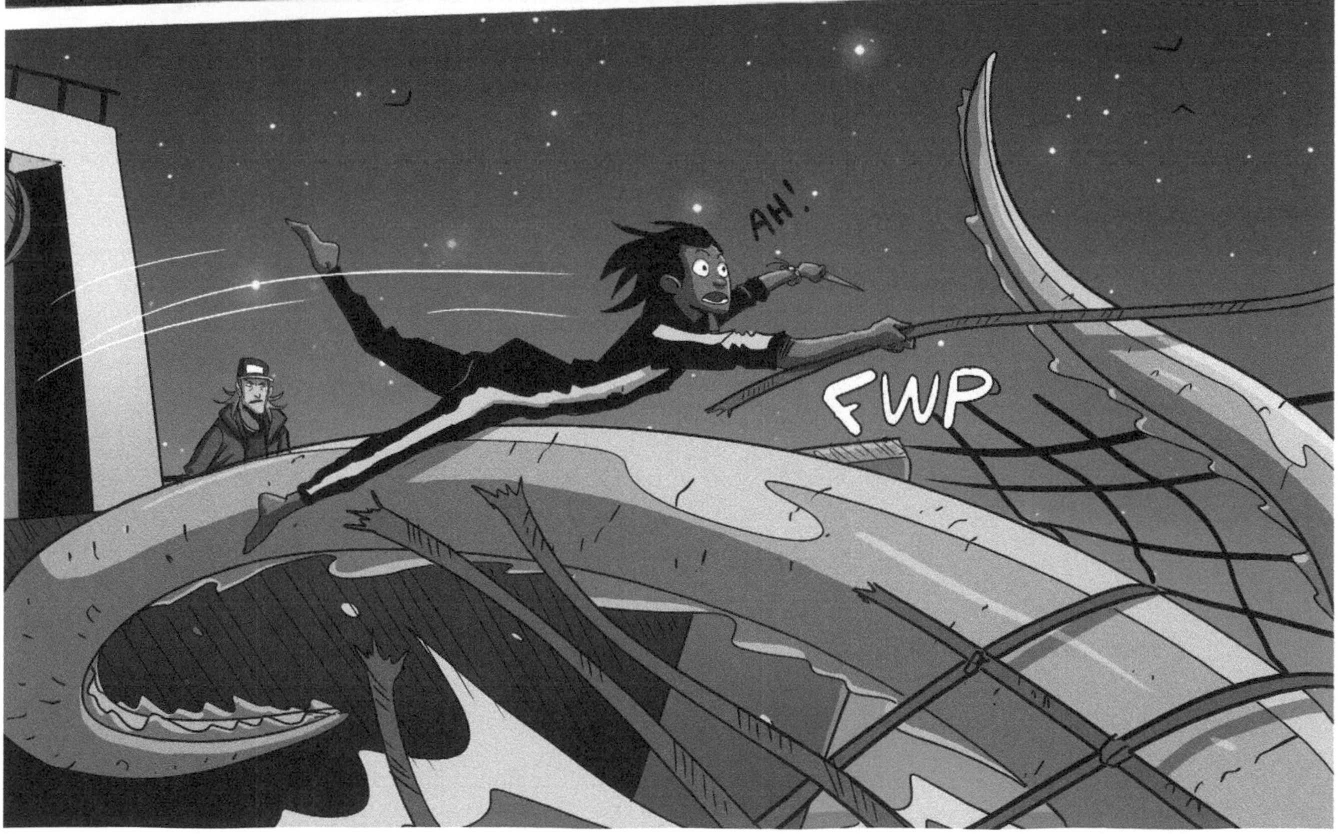
AH!
FWP

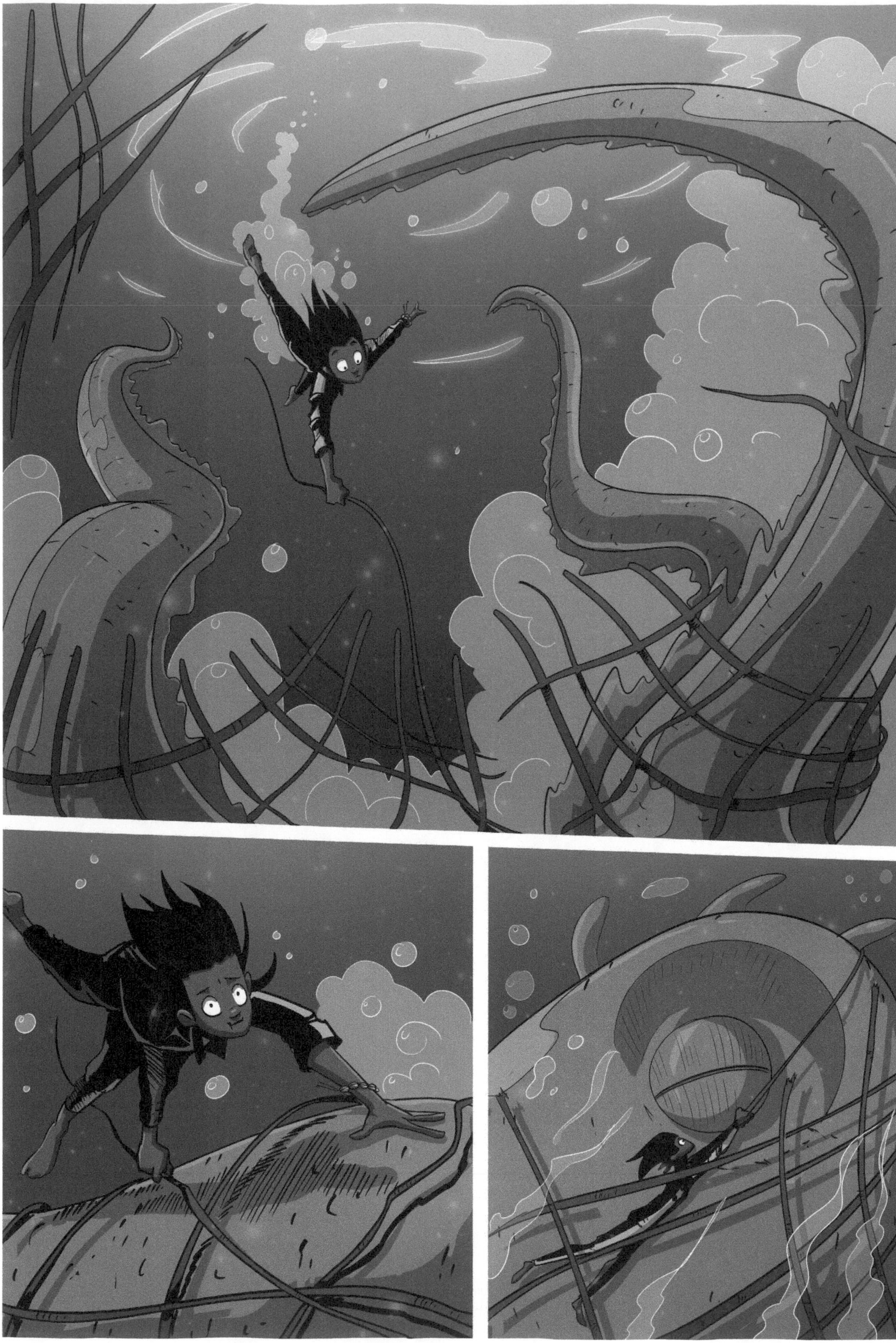

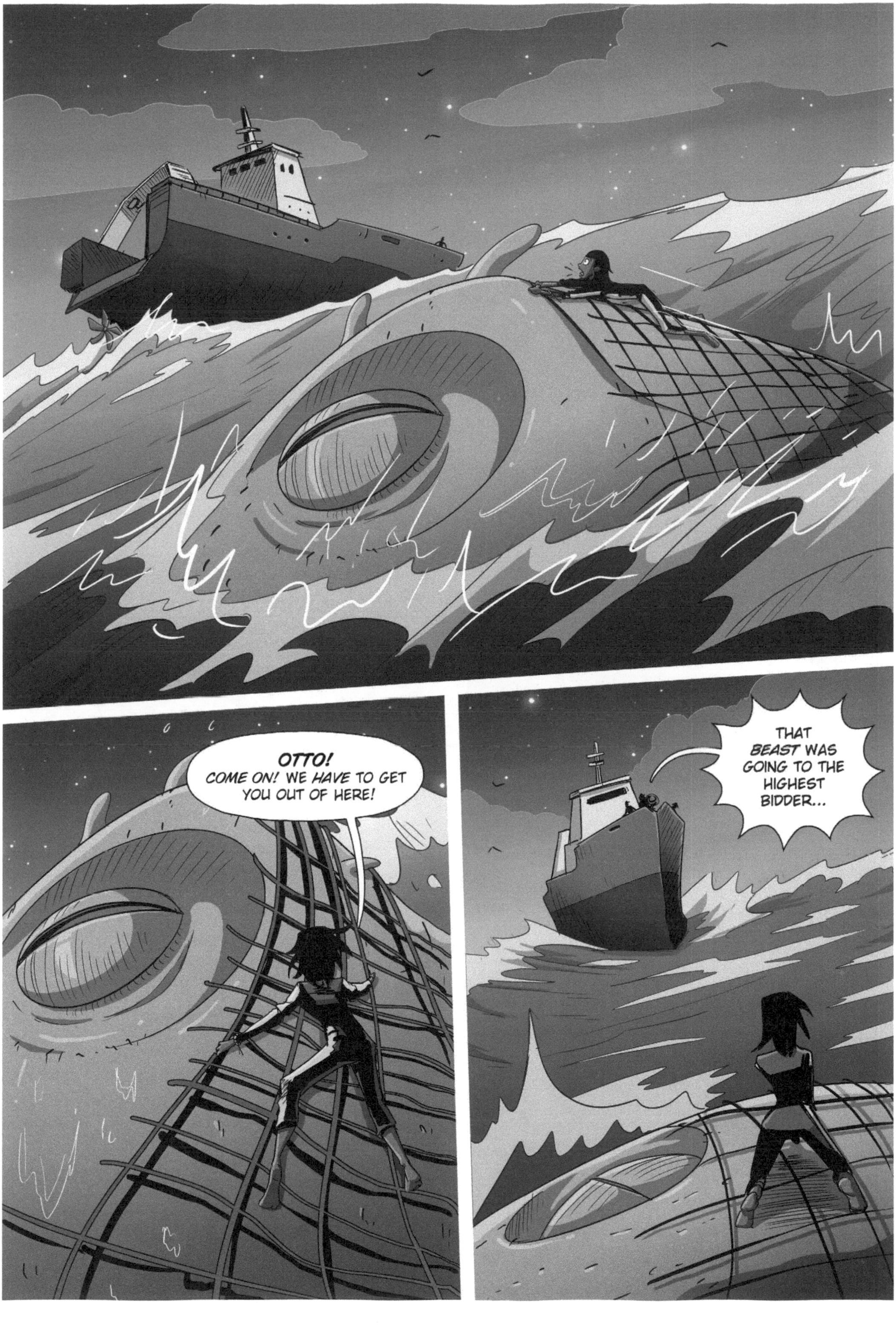
OTTO!
COME ON! WE HAVE TO GET YOU OUT OF HERE!
THAT BEAST WAS GOING TO THE HIGHEST BIDDER...

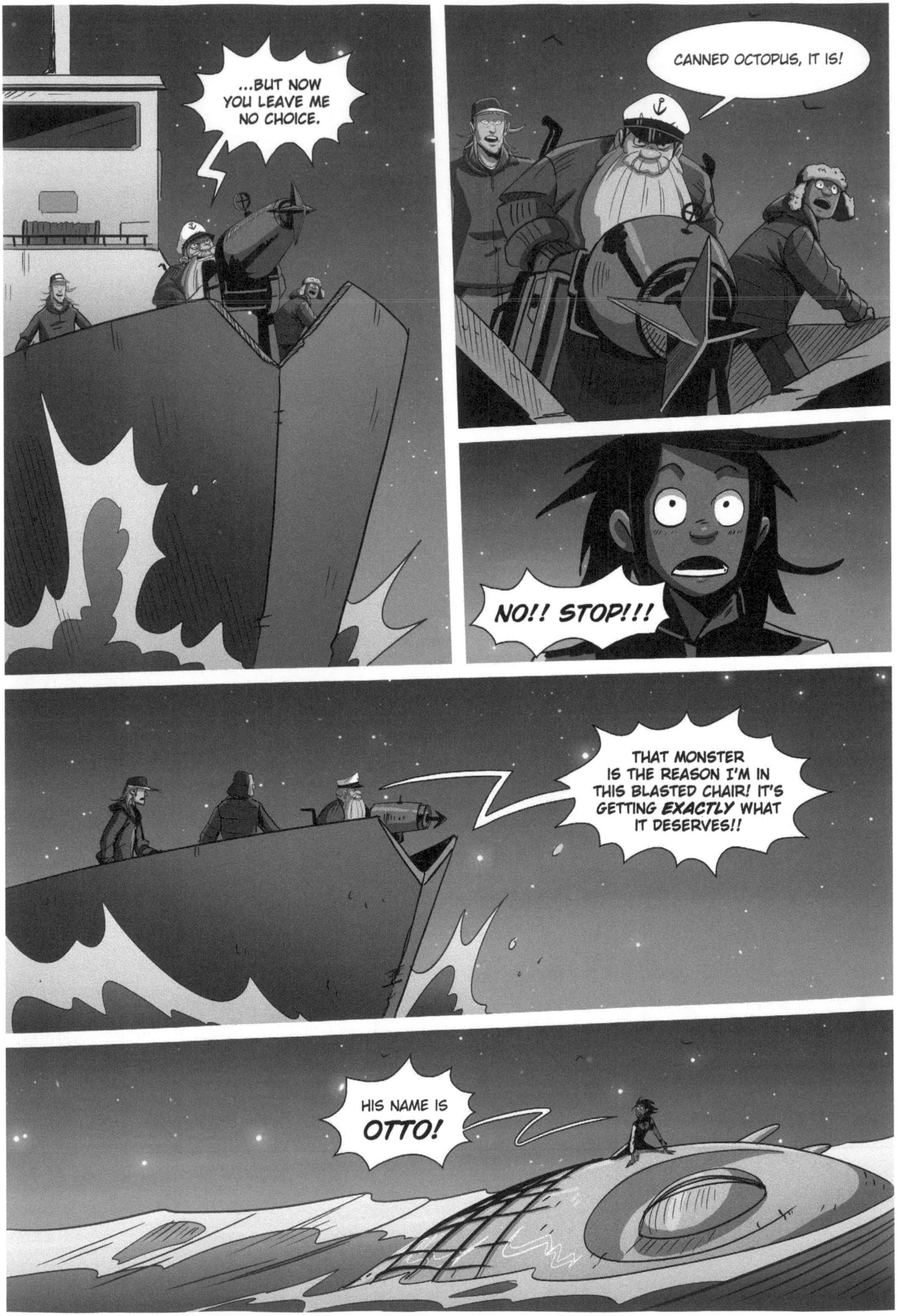
...BUT NOW YOU LEAVE ME NO CHOICE.
CANNED OCTOPUS, IT IS!
NO!! STOP!!!
THAT MONSTER IS THE REASON I'M IN THIS BLASTED CHAIR! IT'S GETTING *EXACTLY* WHAT IT DESERVES!!
HIS NAME IS *OTTO!*

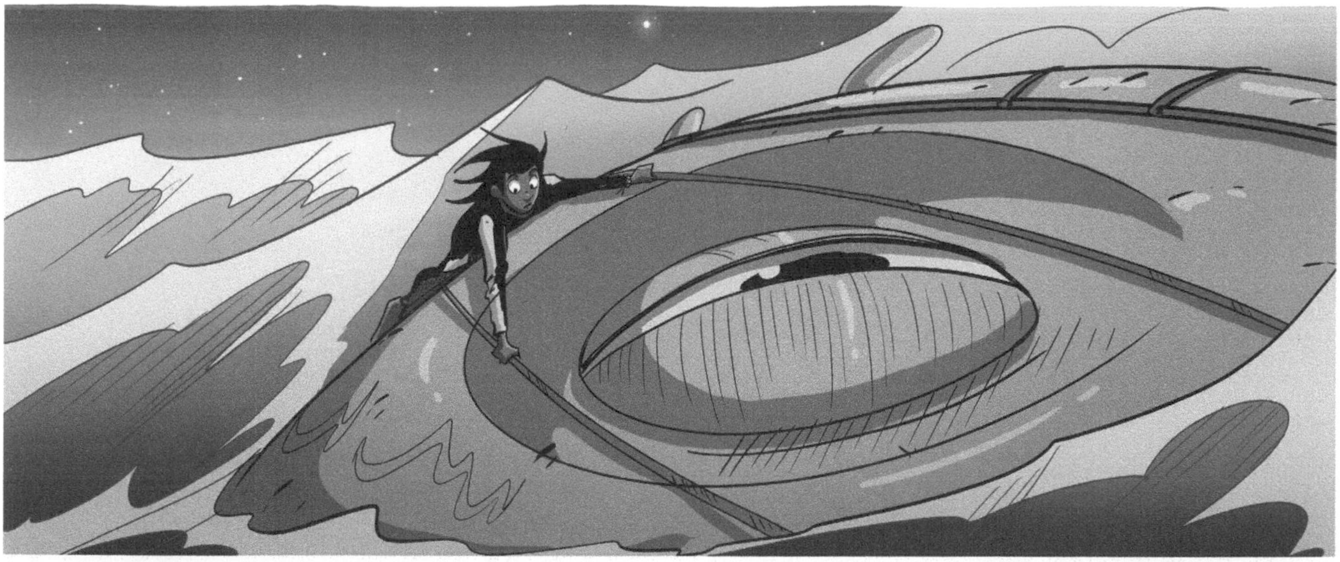

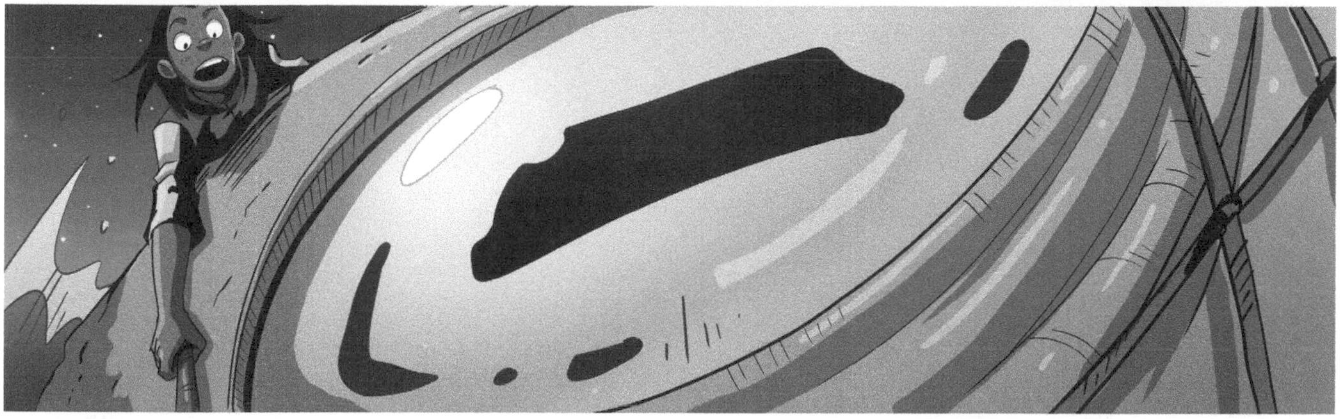

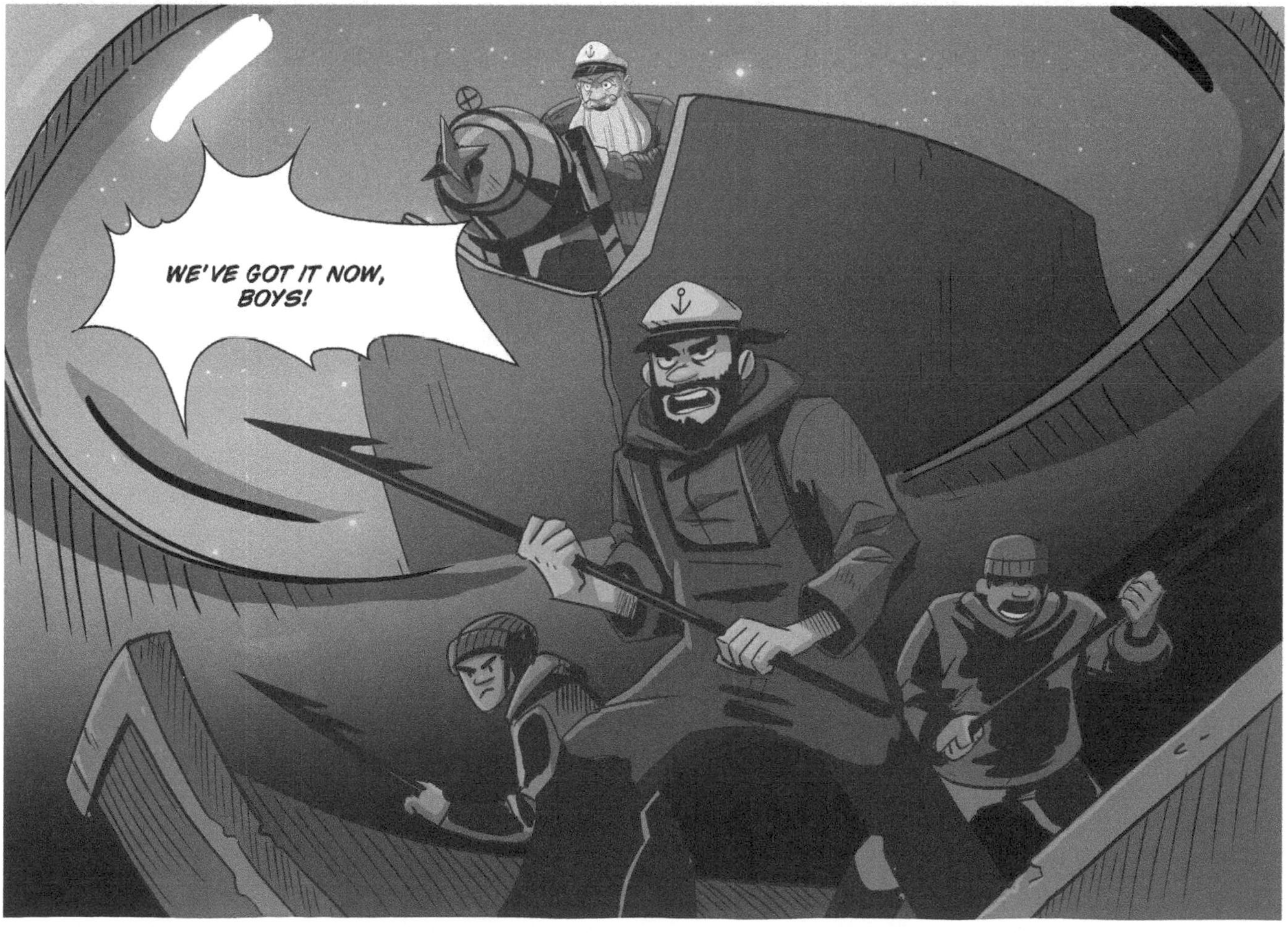
WE'VE GOT IT NOW, BOYS!

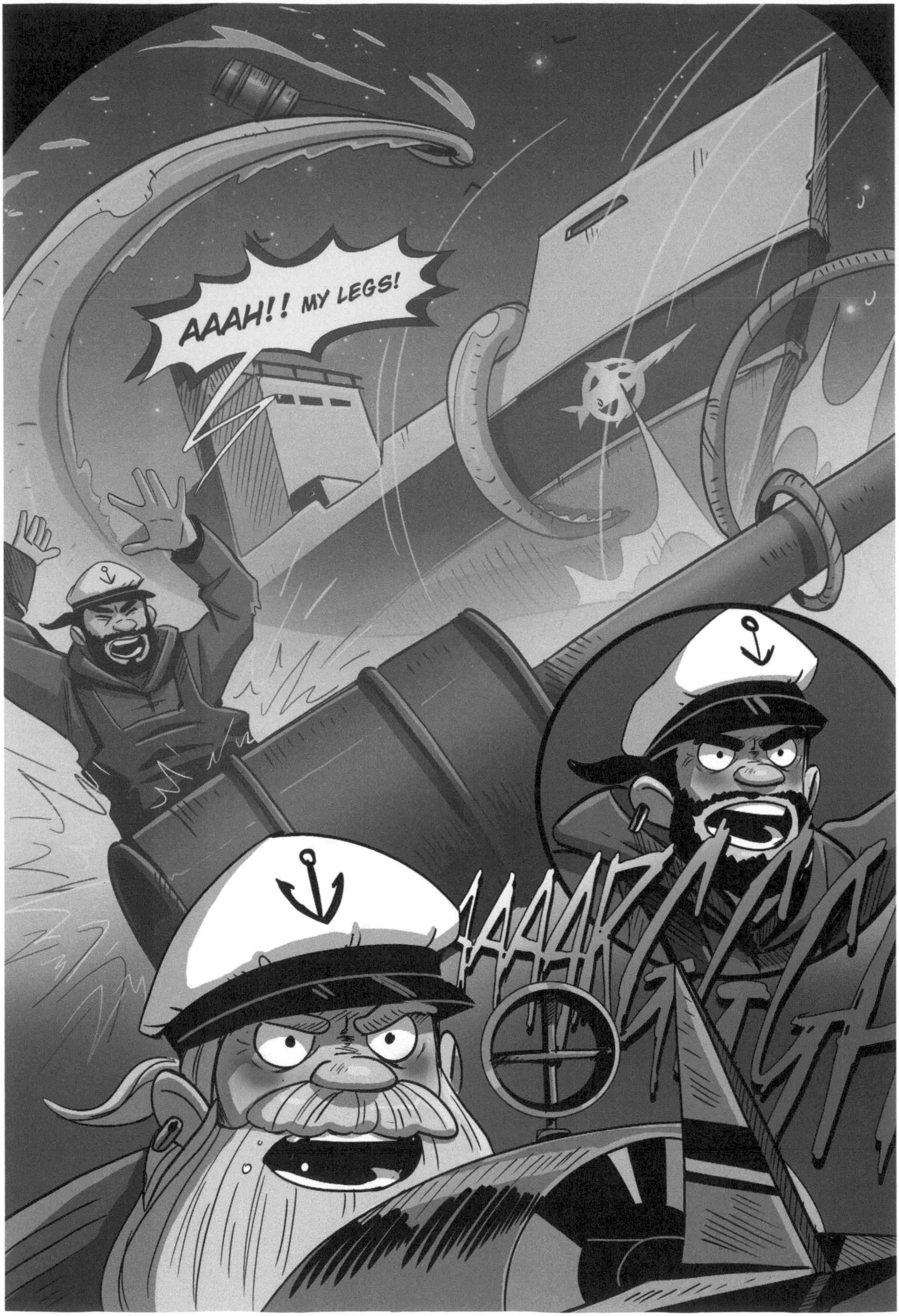
AAAH!! MY LEGS!

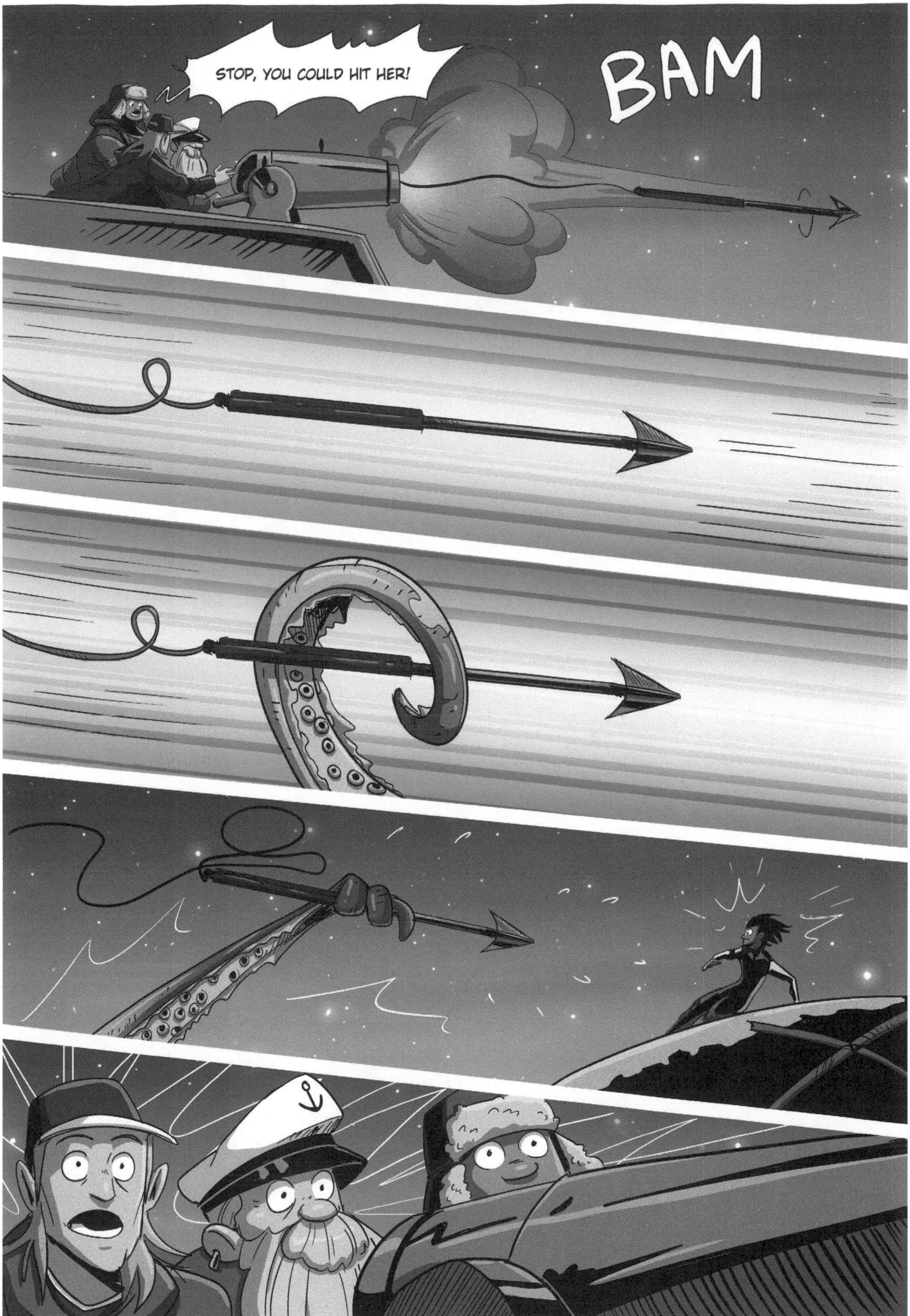
STOP, YOU COULD HIT HER!
BAM

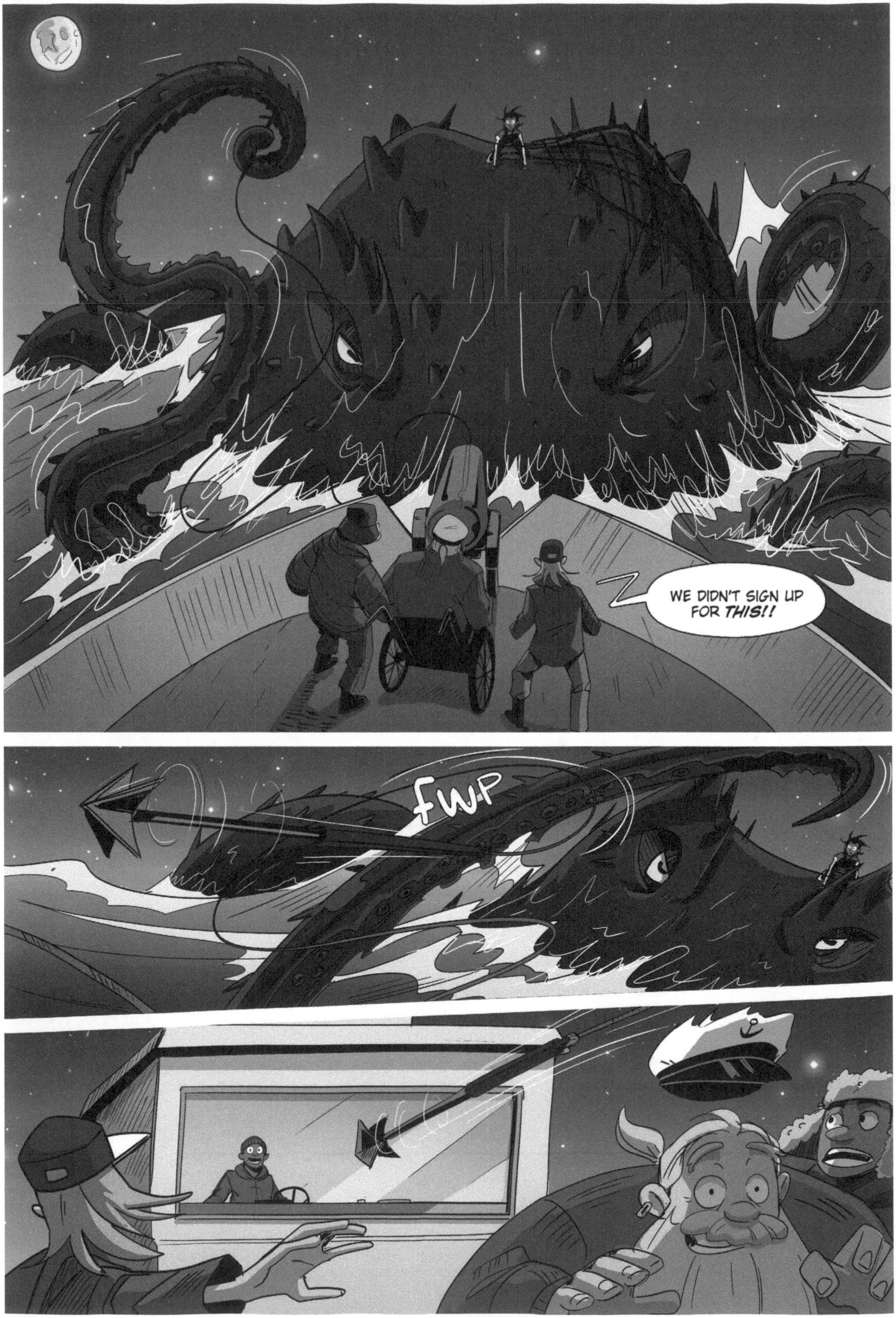
WE DIDN'T SIGN UP FOR *THIS!!*
FWP

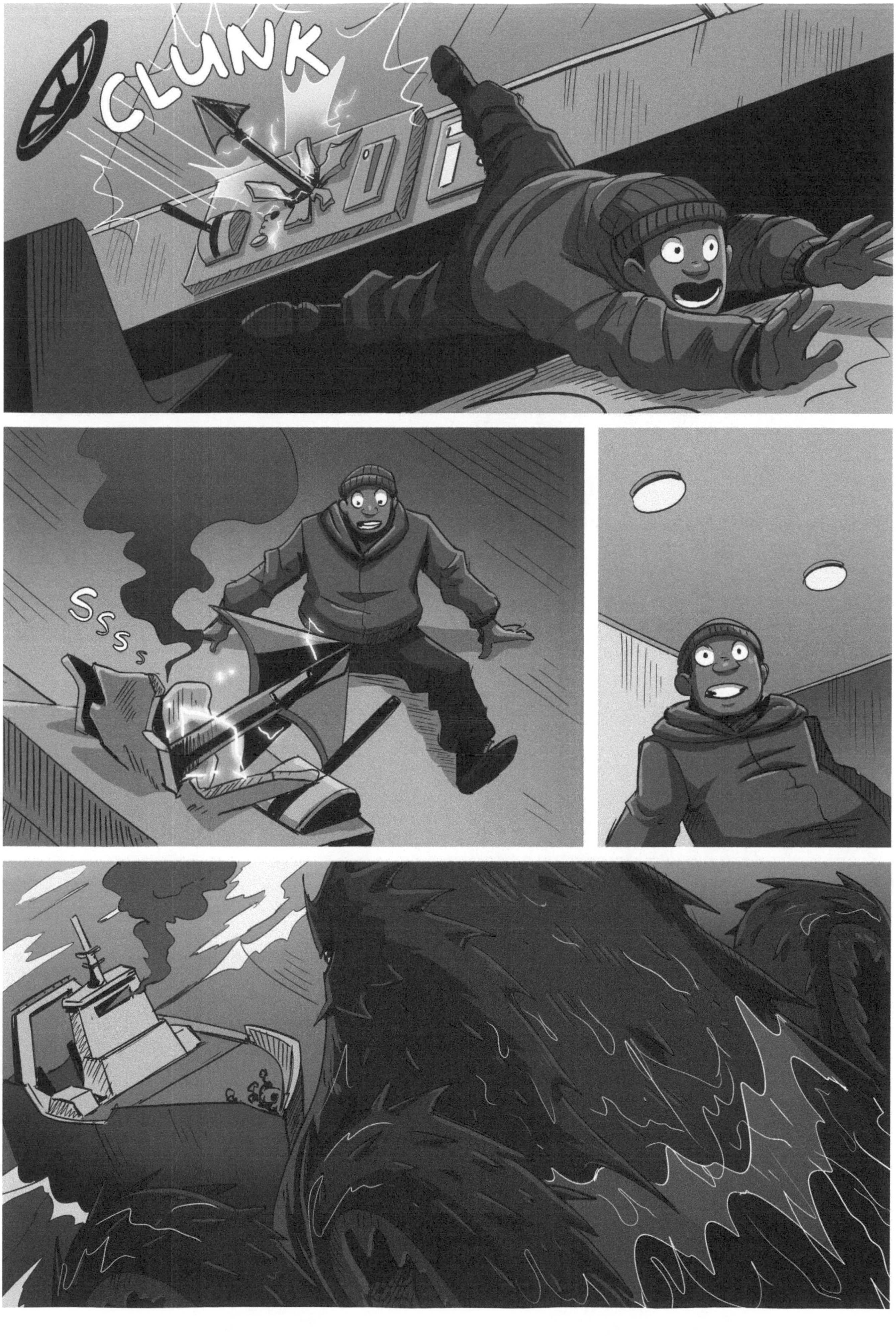
CLUNK
Ssss

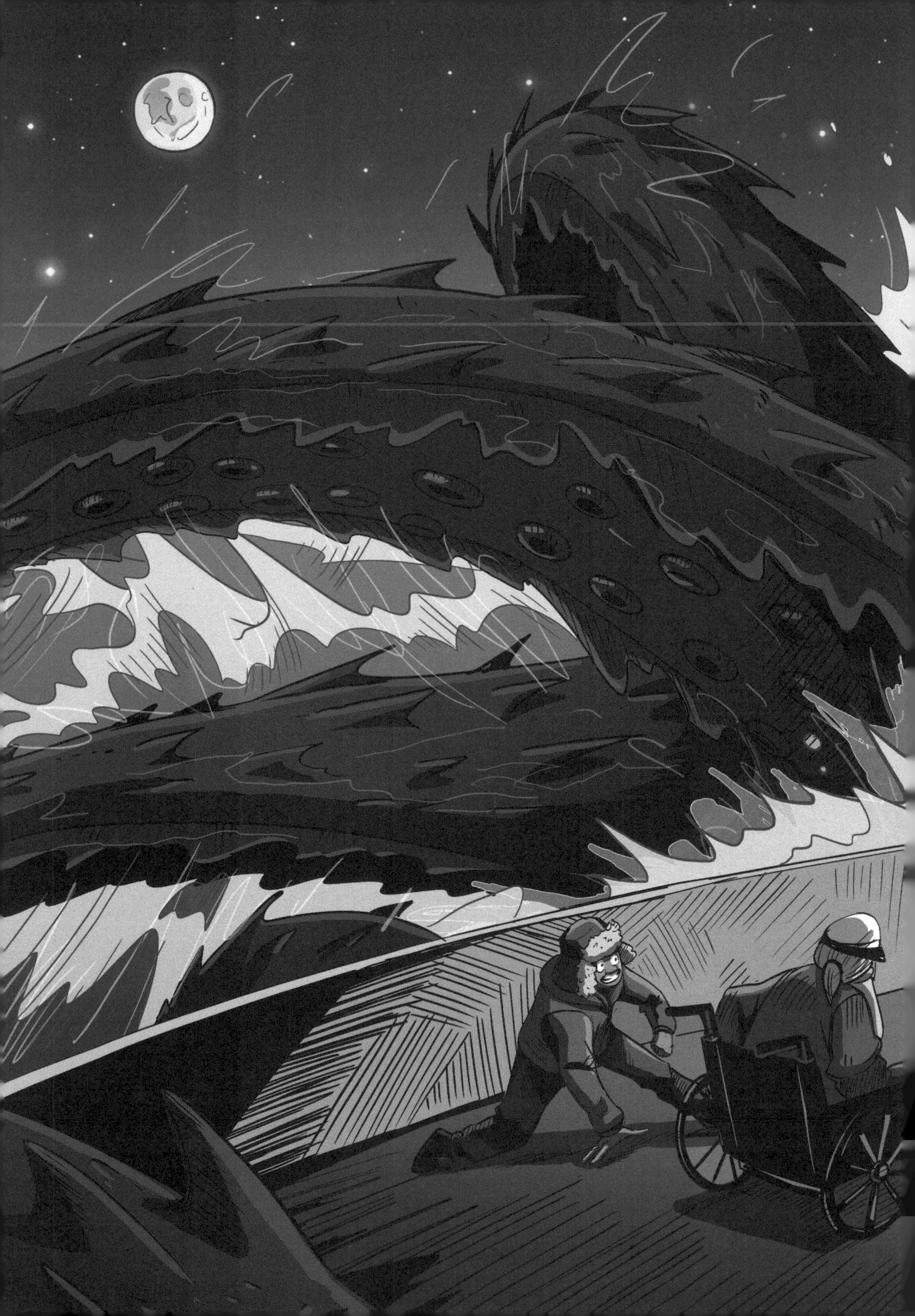

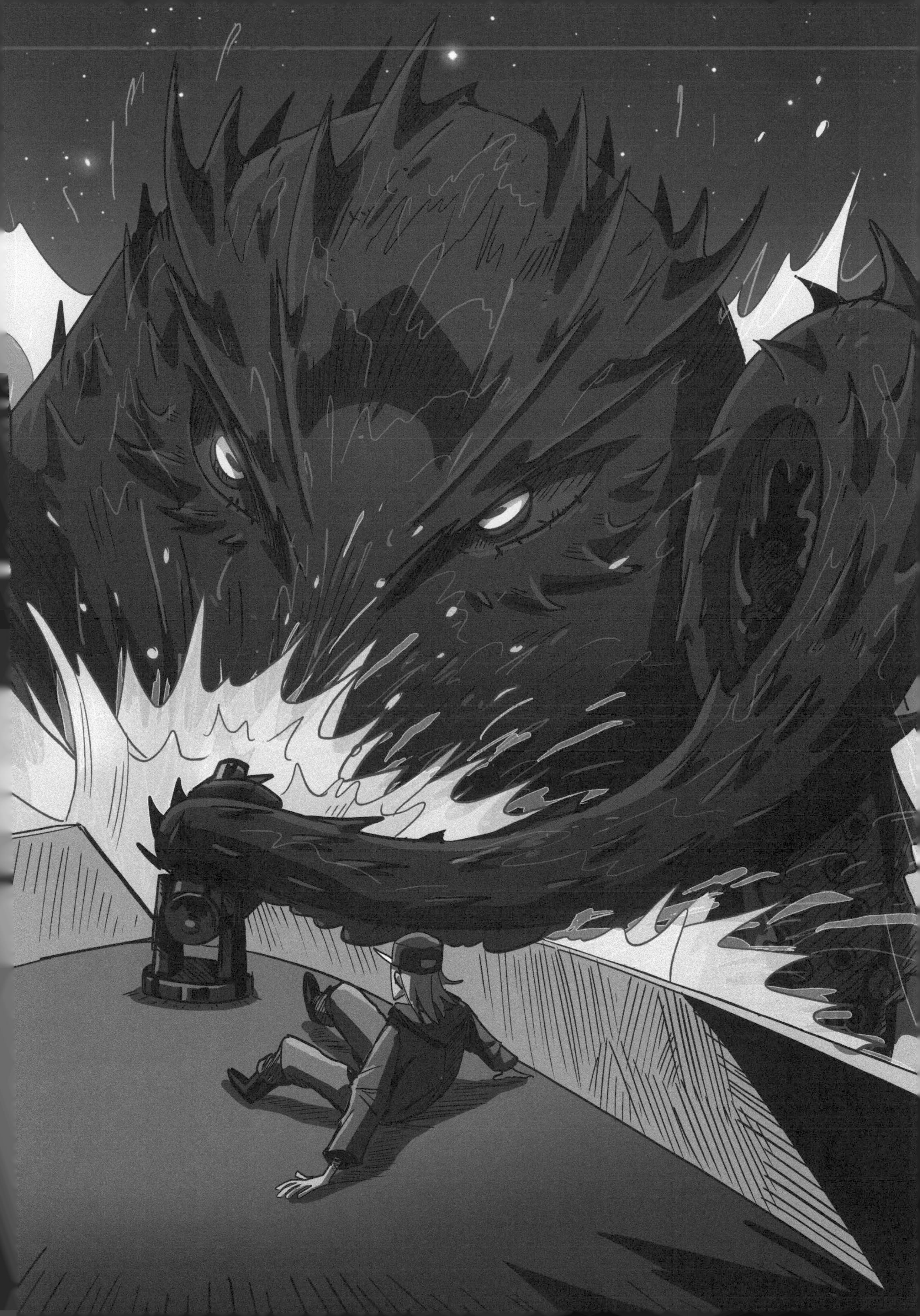

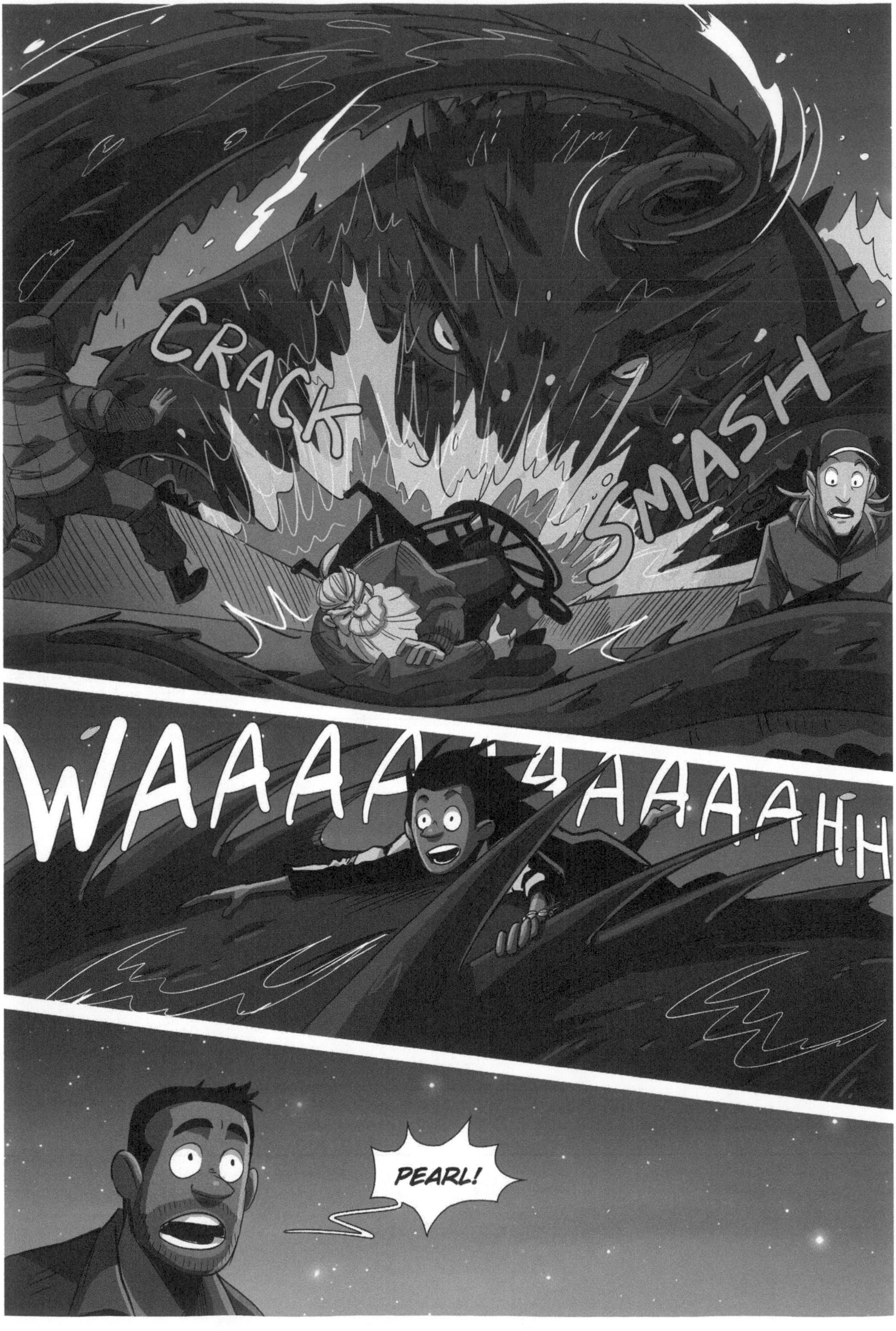
CRACK
SMASH
WAAAAAAAAAAAHH
PEARL!

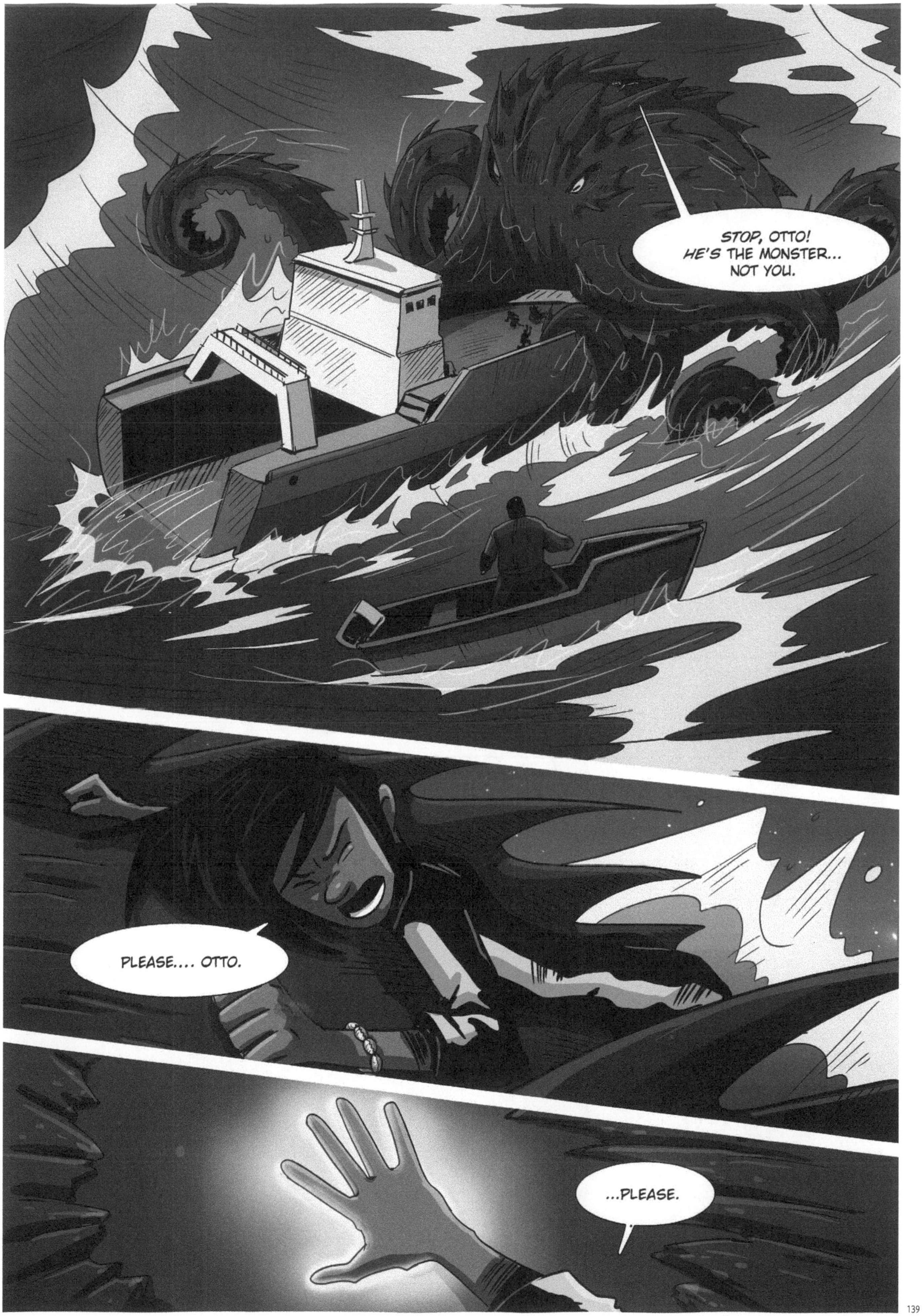
STOP, OTTO!
HE'S THE MONSTER...
NOT YOU.
PLEASE.... OTTO.
...PLEASE.

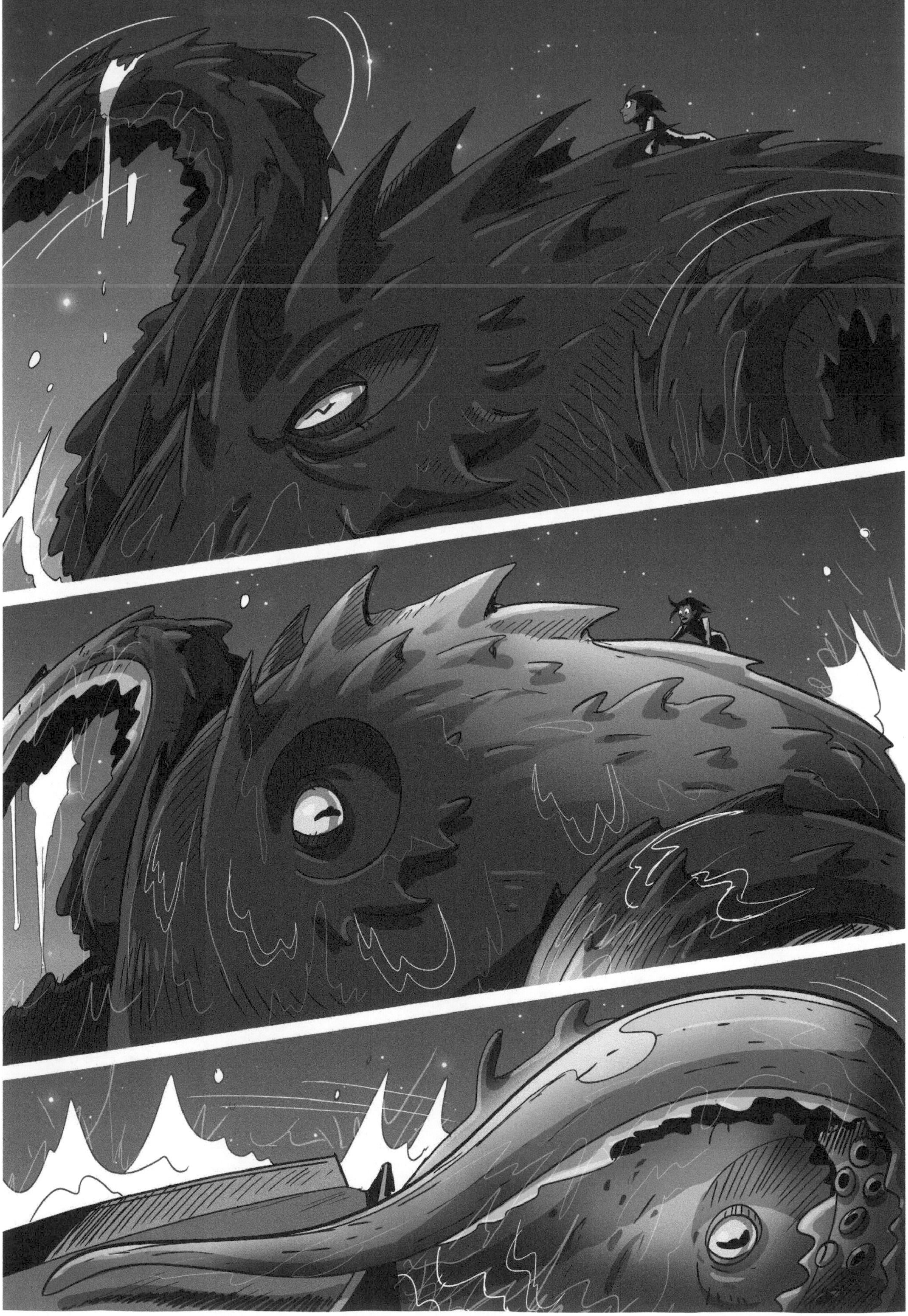

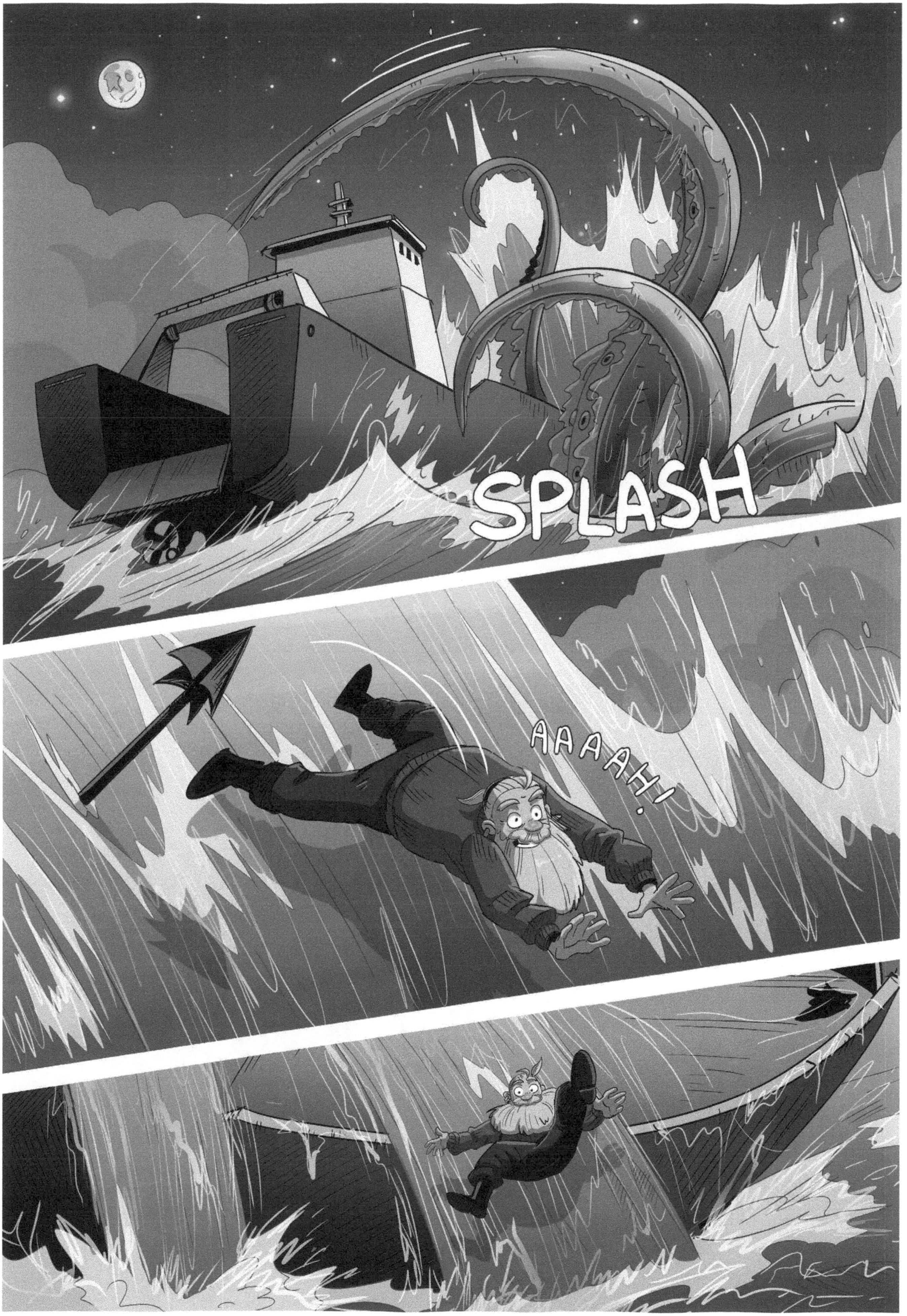
SPLASH
AAAAH!

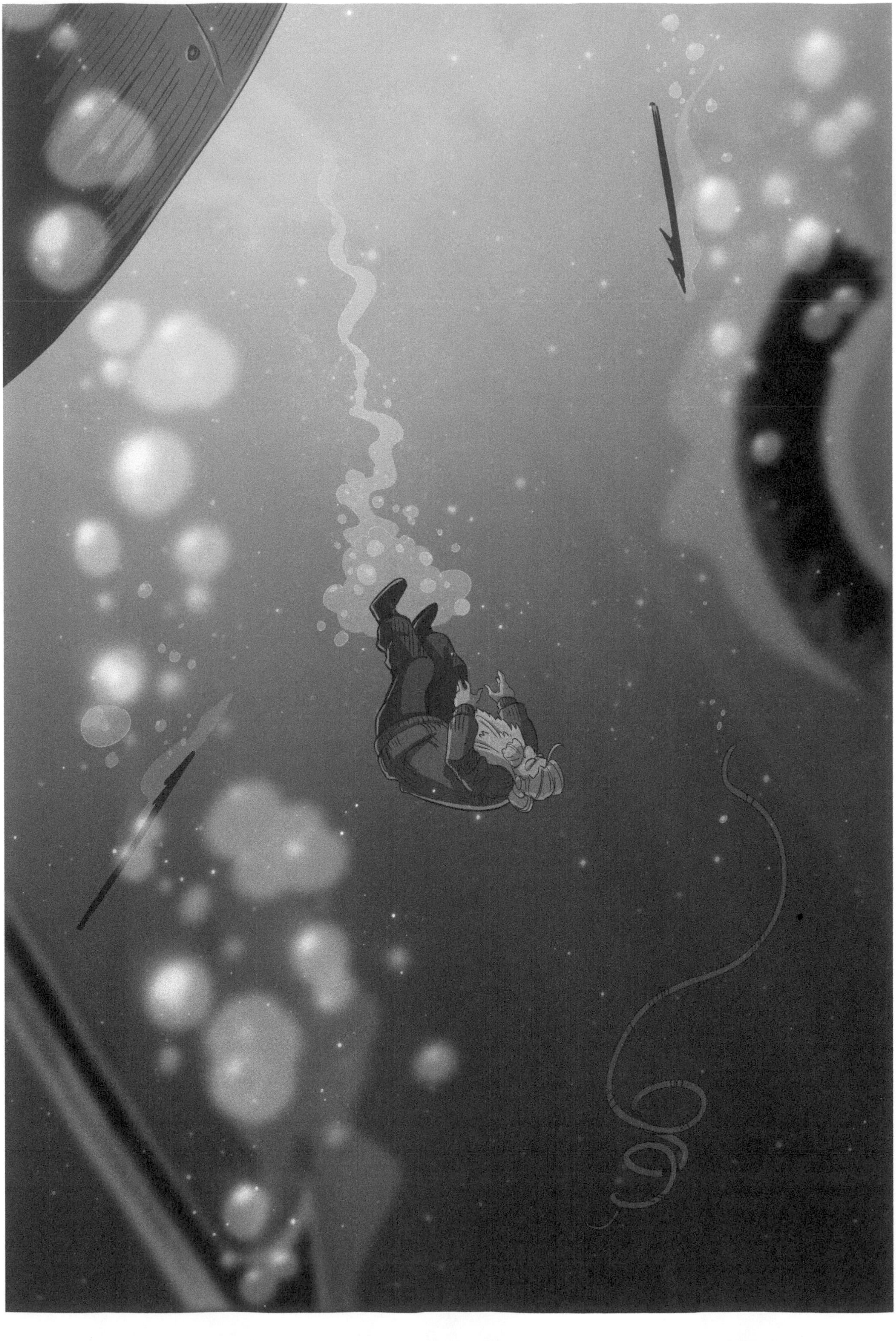

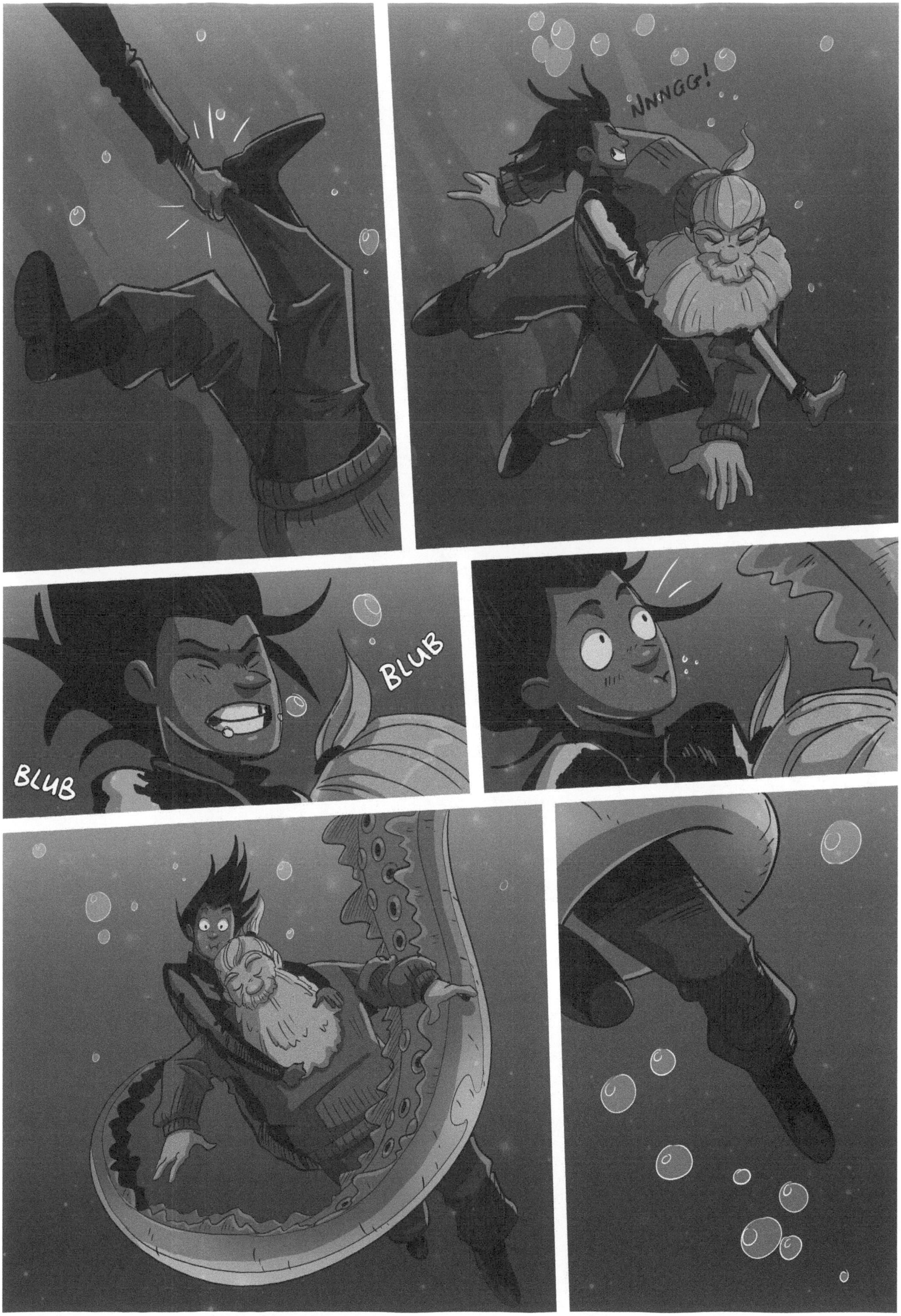
NNNGG!
BLUB
BLUB

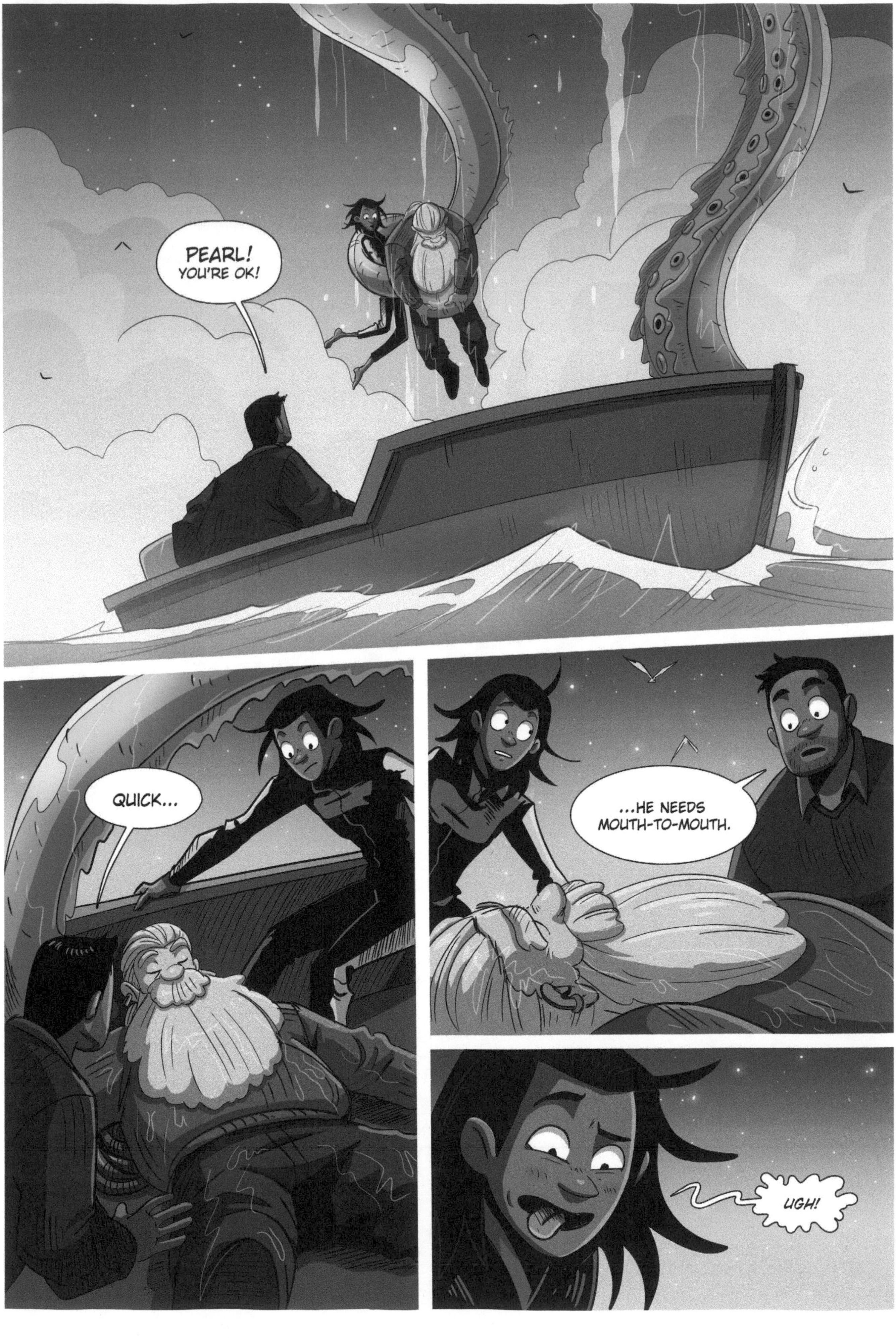
PEARL! YOU'RE OK!
QUICK...
...HE NEEDS MOUTH-TO-MOUTH.
UGH!

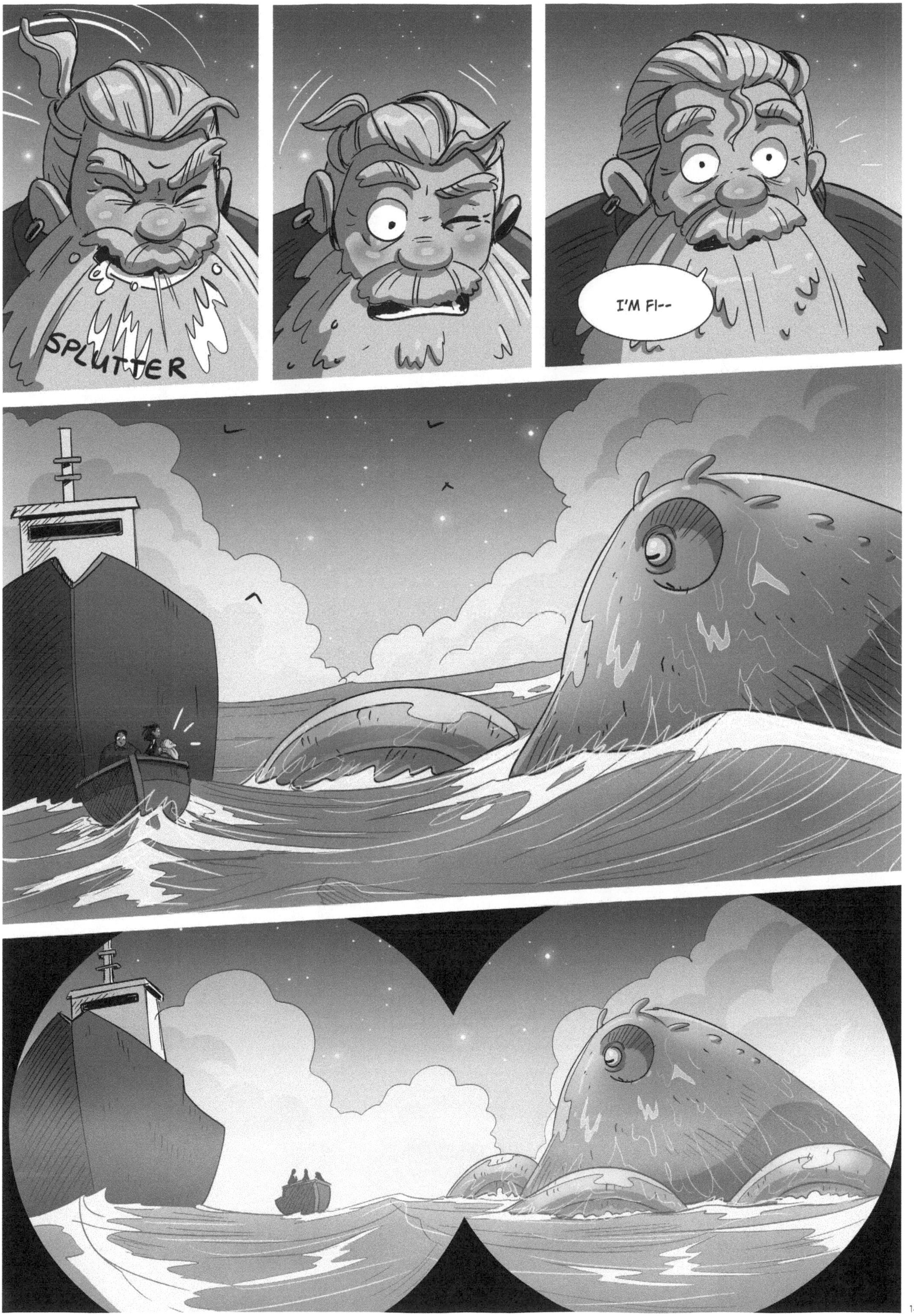
SPLUTTER
I'M FI--

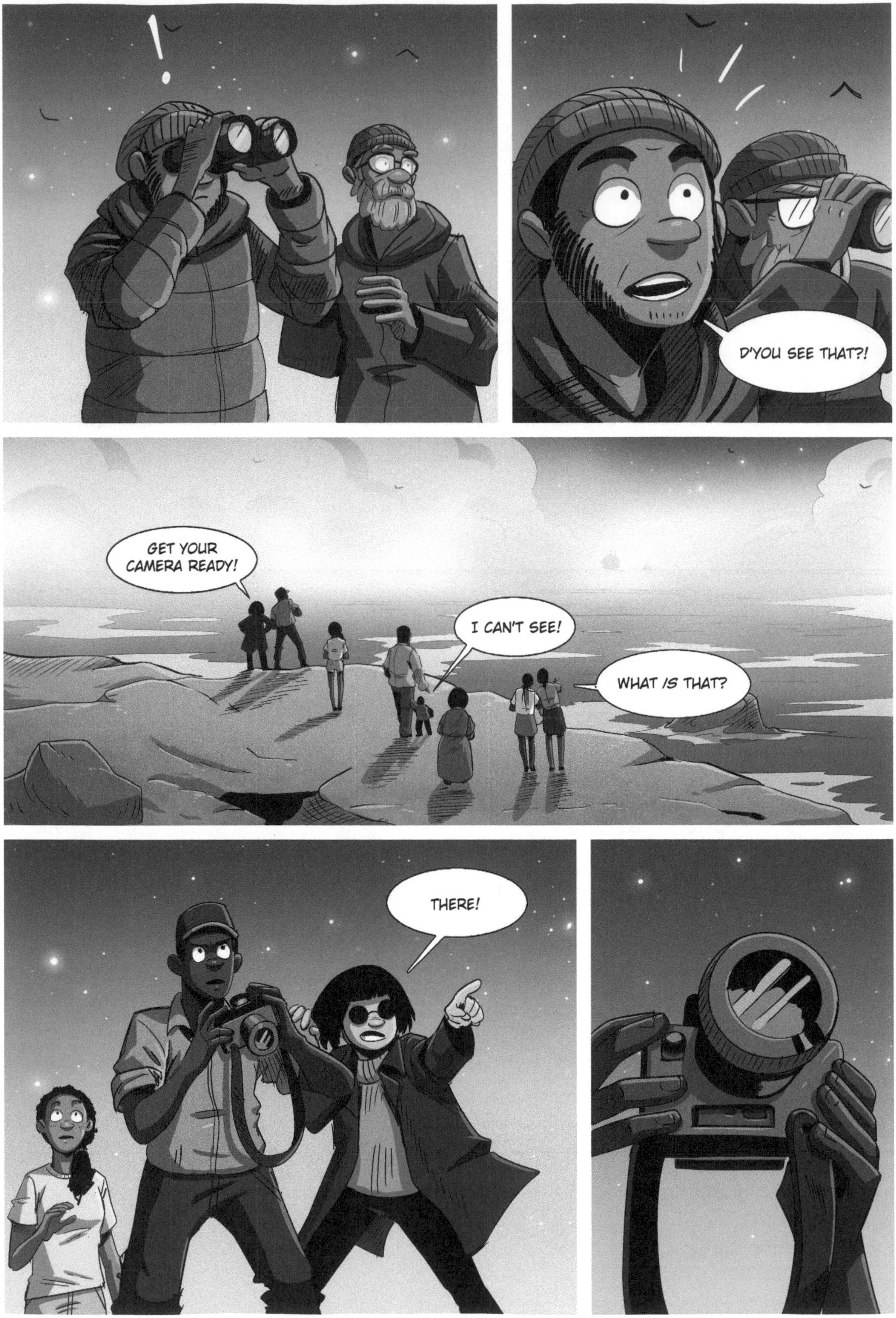
!
D'YOU SEE THAT?!
GET YOUR CAMERA READY!
I CAN'T SEE!
WHAT IS THAT?
THERE!

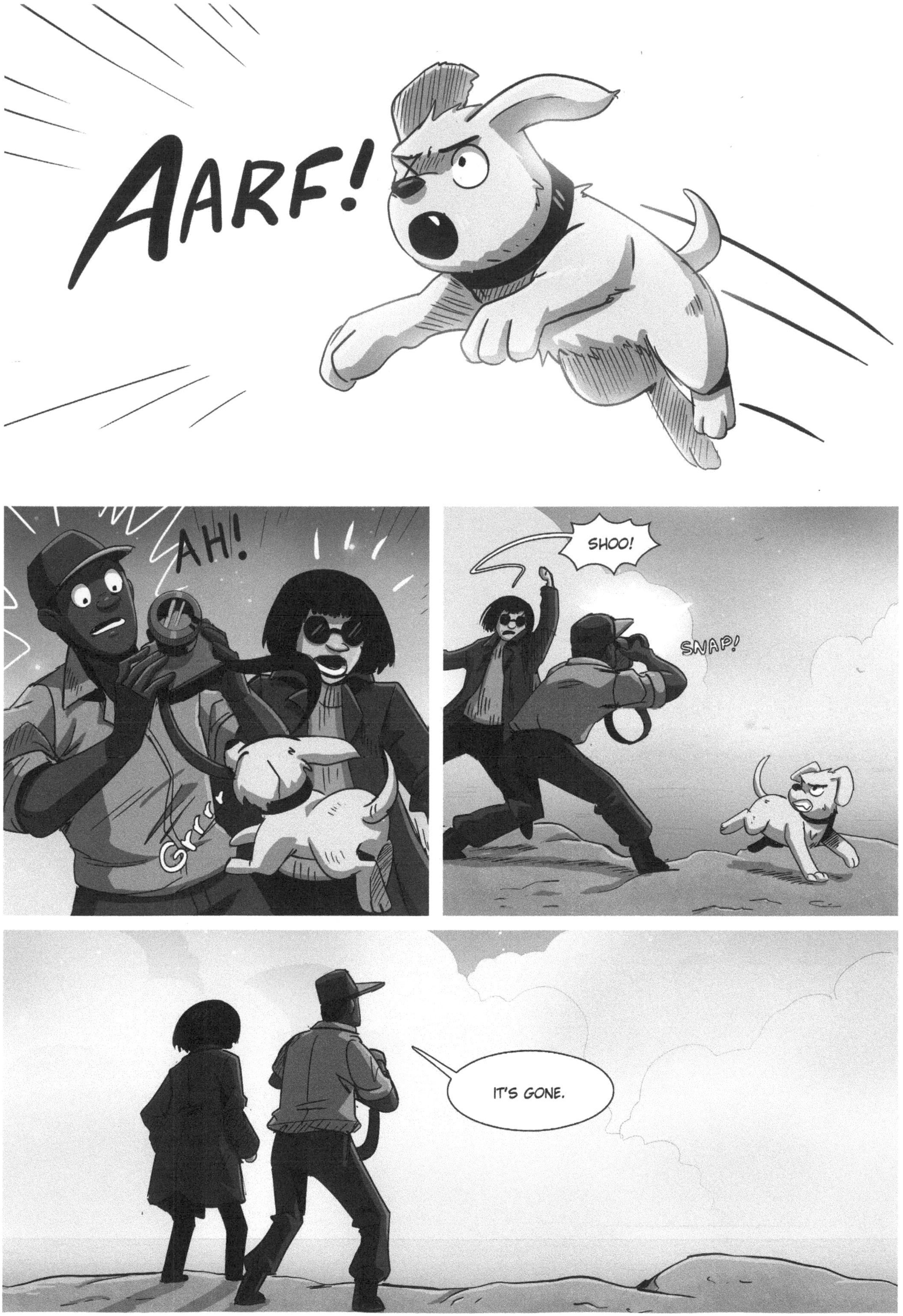
AARF!
AH!
Grrr
SHOO!
SNAP!
IT'S GONE.

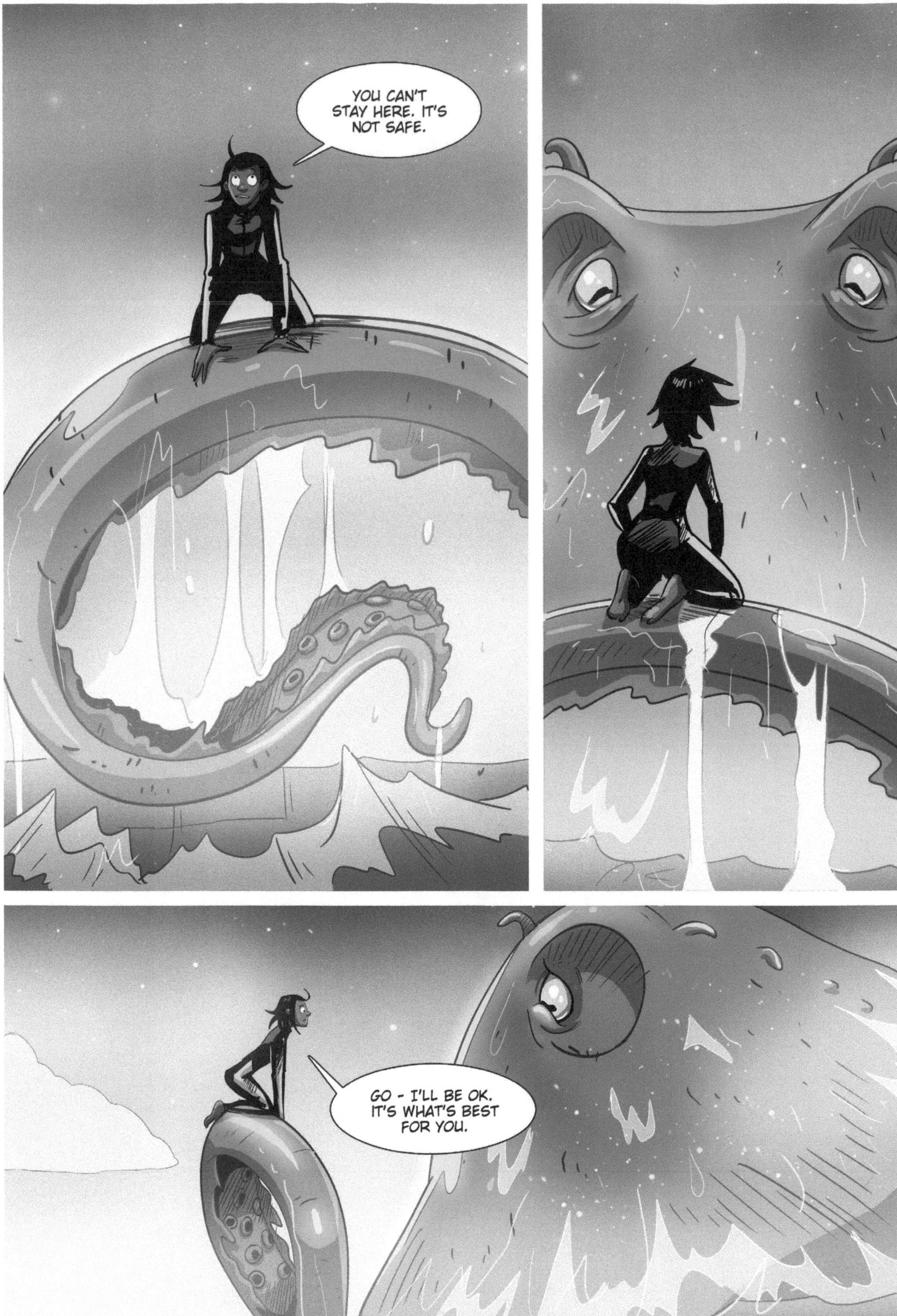

YOU CAN'T STAY HERE. IT'S NOT SAFE.
GO - I'LL BE OK. IT'S WHAT'S BEST FOR YOU.

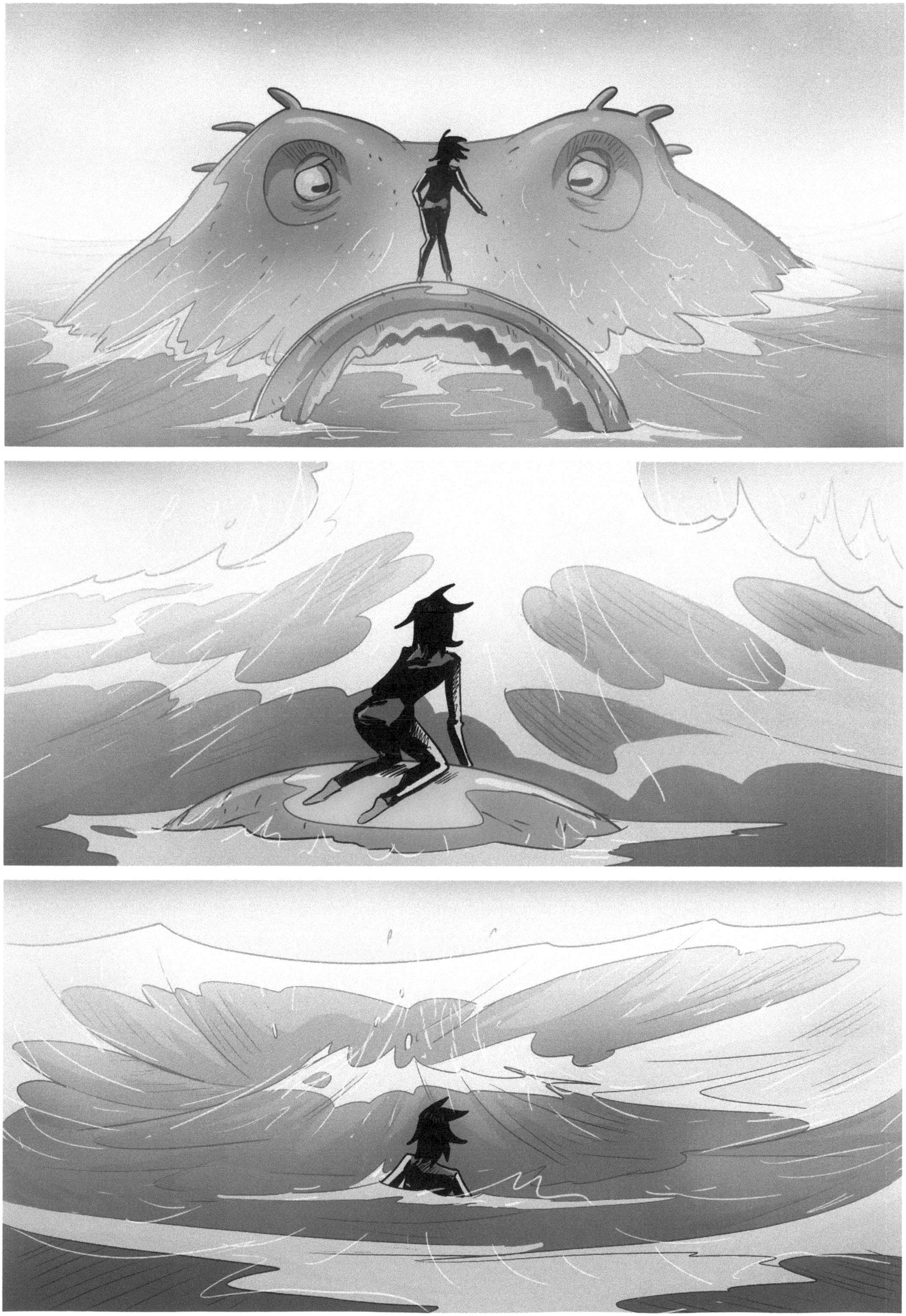

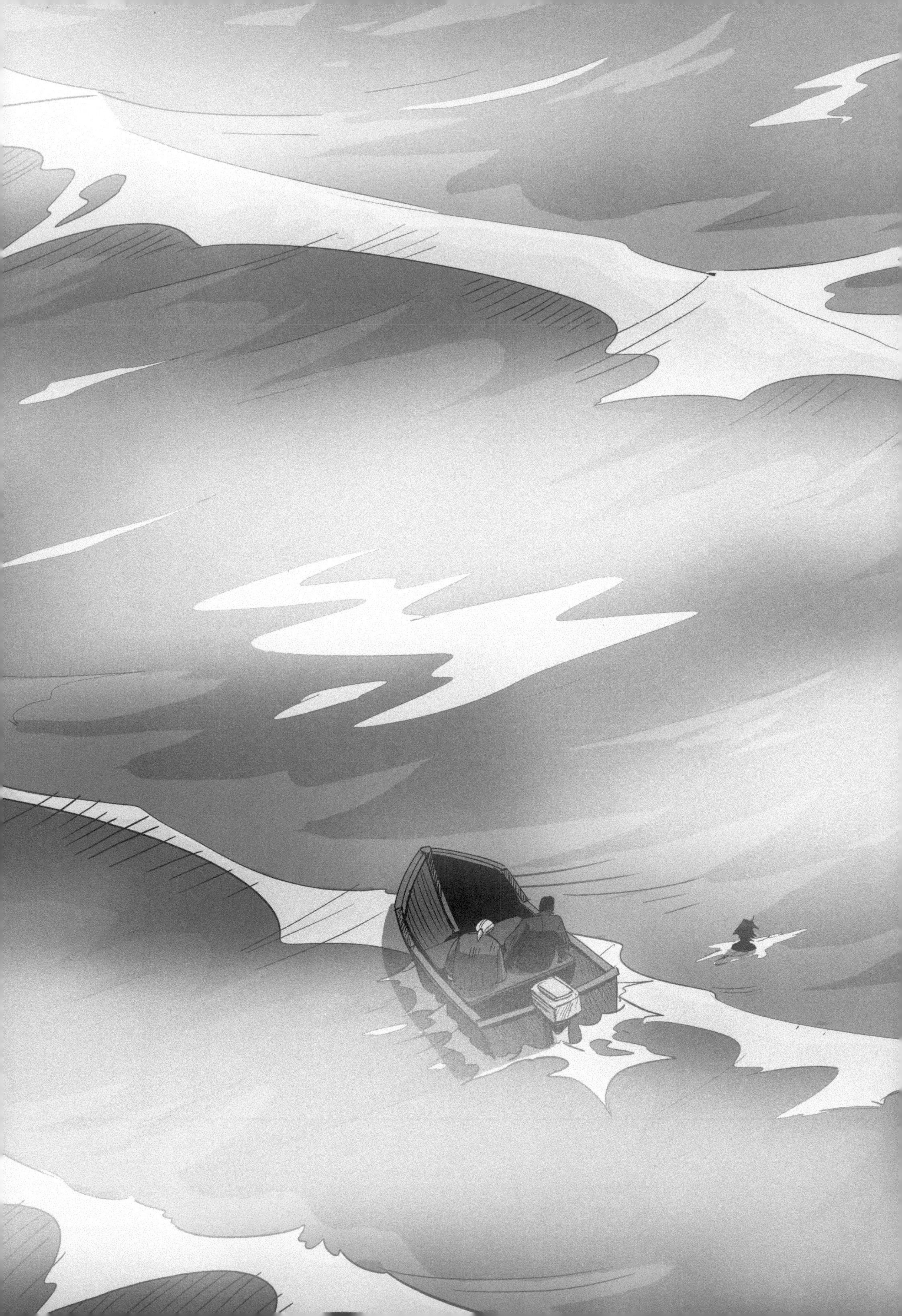

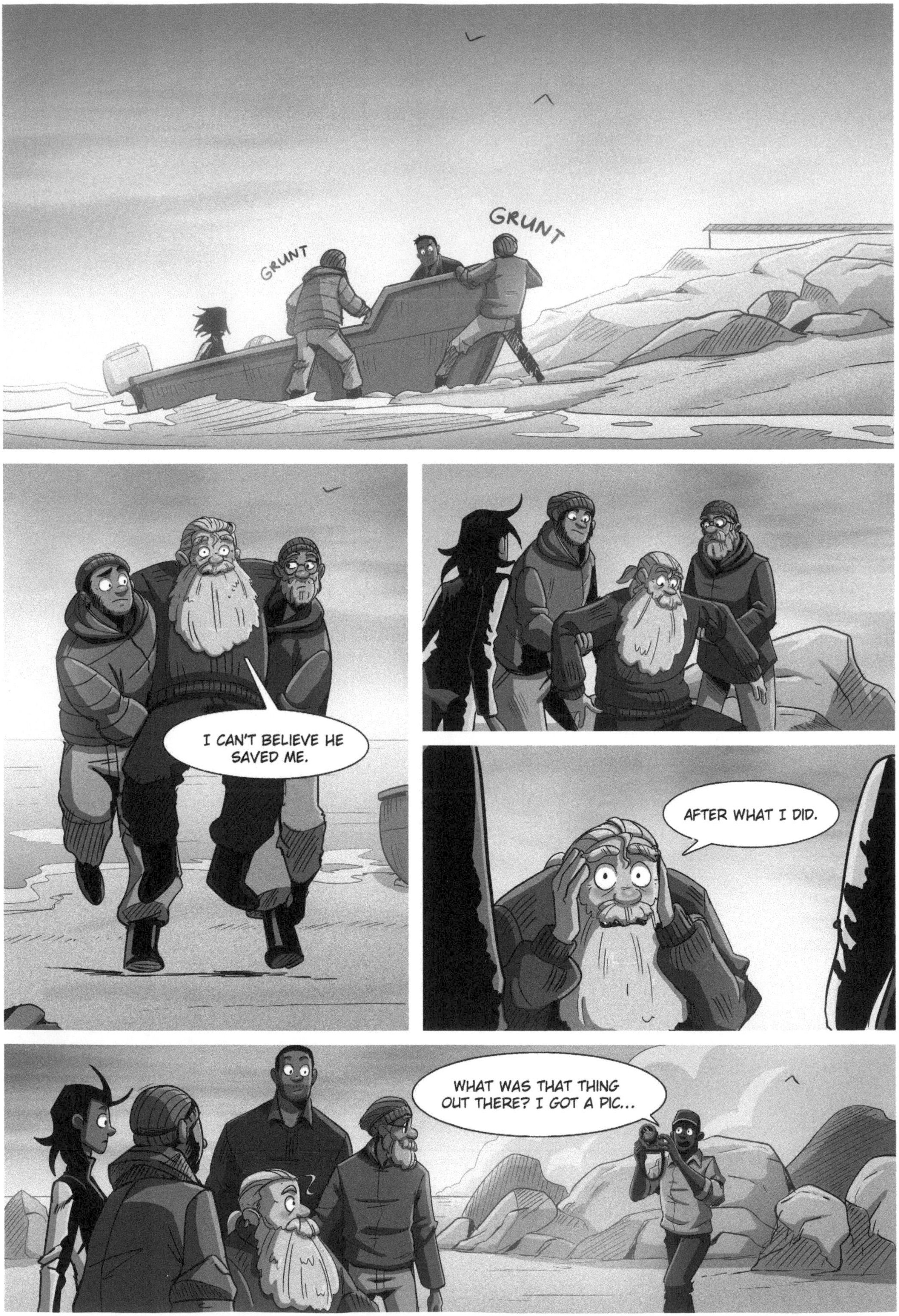
GRUNT
GRUNT
I CAN'T BELIEVE HE SAVED ME.
AFTER WHAT I DID.
WHAT WAS THAT THING OUT THERE? I GOT A PIC...

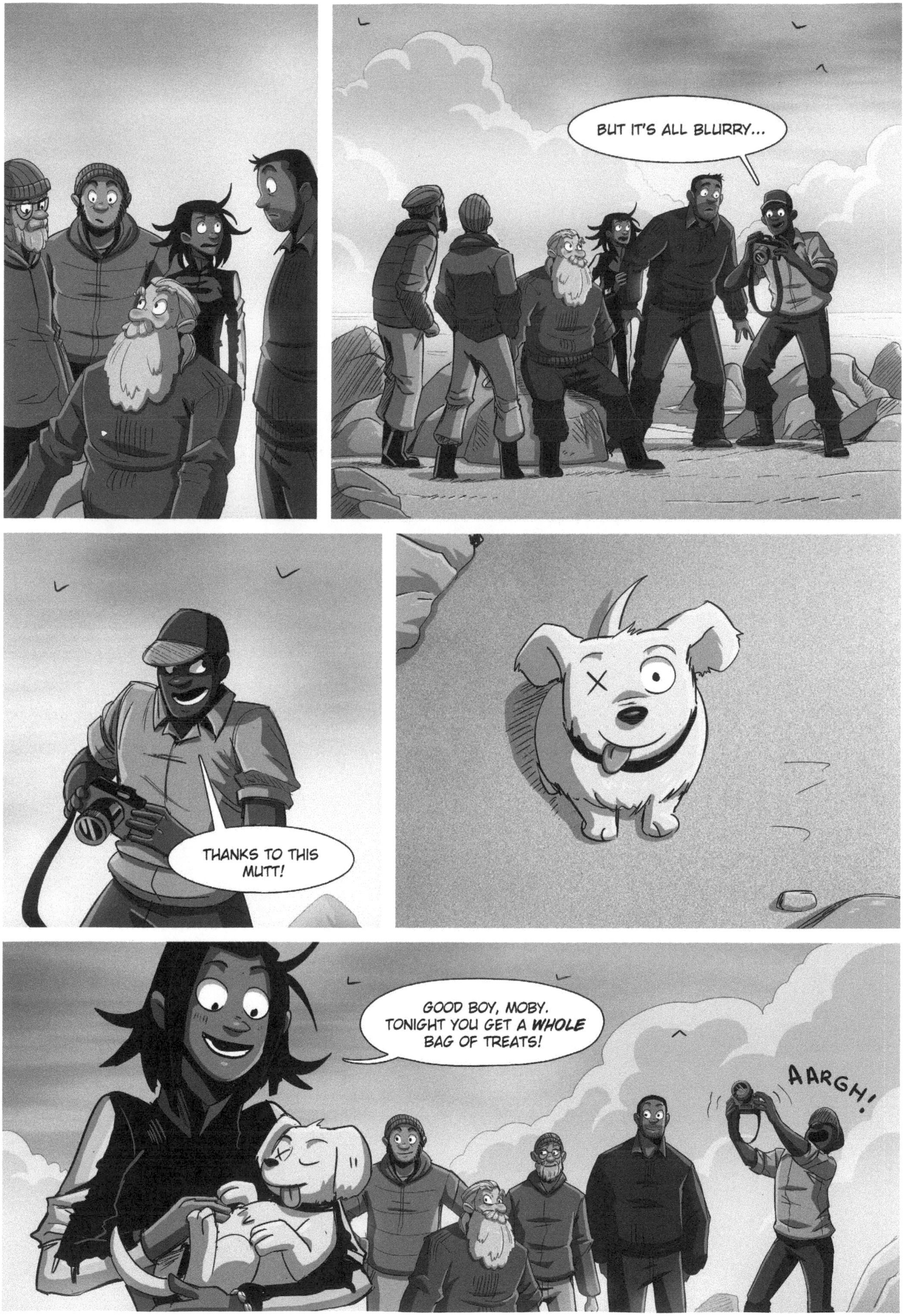
BUT IT'S ALL BLURRY...
THANKS TO THIS MUTT!
GOOD BOY, MOBY. TONIGHT YOU GET A *WHOLE* BAG OF TREATS!
AARGH!

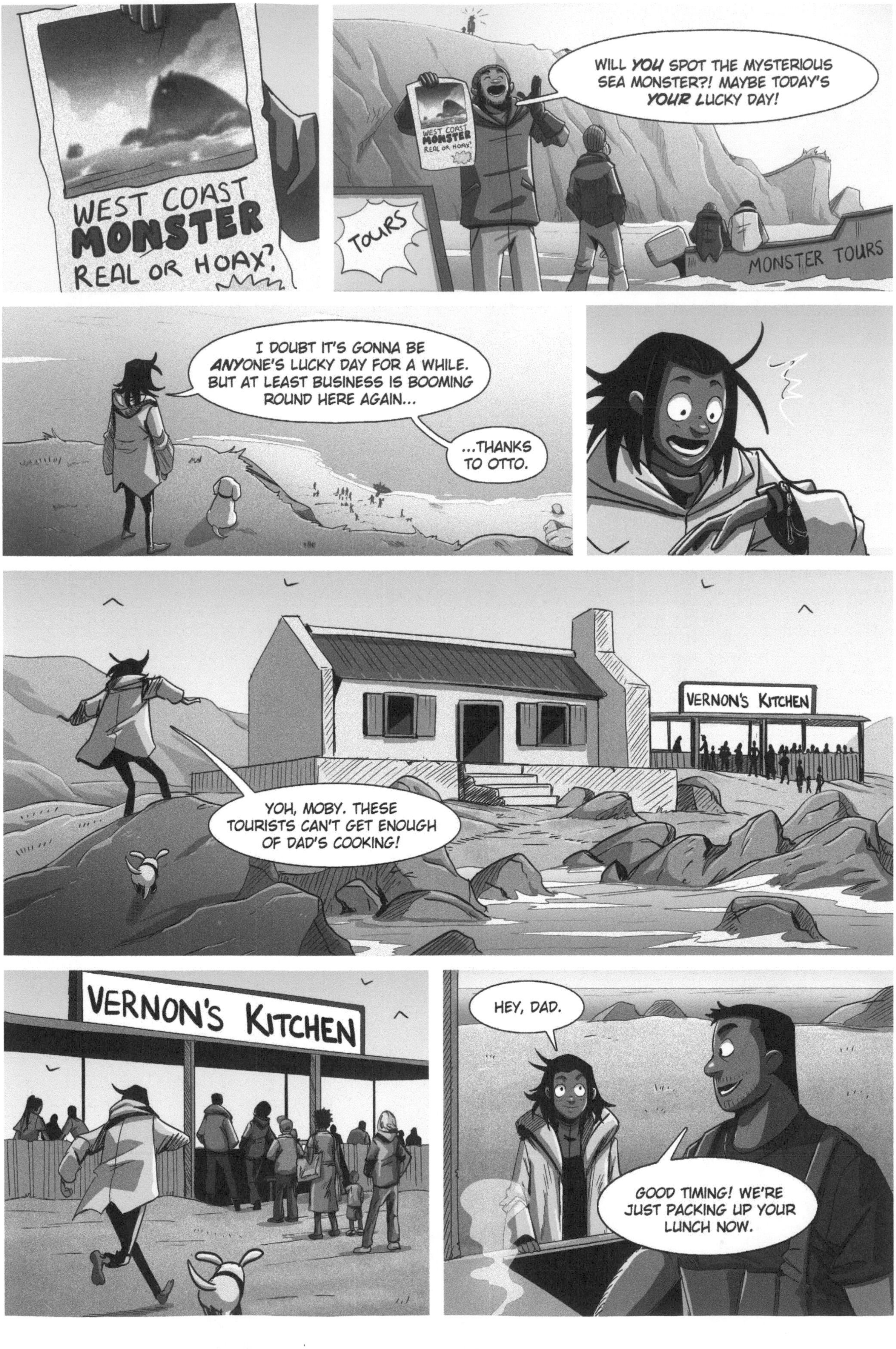
WEST COAST MONSTER REAL OR HOAX?
WILL YOU SPOT THE MYSTERIOUS SEA MONSTER?! MAYBE TODAY'S YOUR LUCKY DAY!
TOURS
MONSTER TOURS
I DOUBT IT'S GONNA BE ANYONE'S LUCKY DAY FOR A WHILE. BUT AT LEAST BUSINESS IS BOOMING ROUND HERE AGAIN...
...THANKS TO OTTO.
VERNON'S KITCHEN
YOH, MOBY. THESE TOURISTS CAN'T GET ENOUGH OF DAD'S COOKING!
VERNON'S KITCHEN
HEY, DAD.
GOOD TIMING! WE'RE JUST PACKING UP YOUR LUNCH NOW.

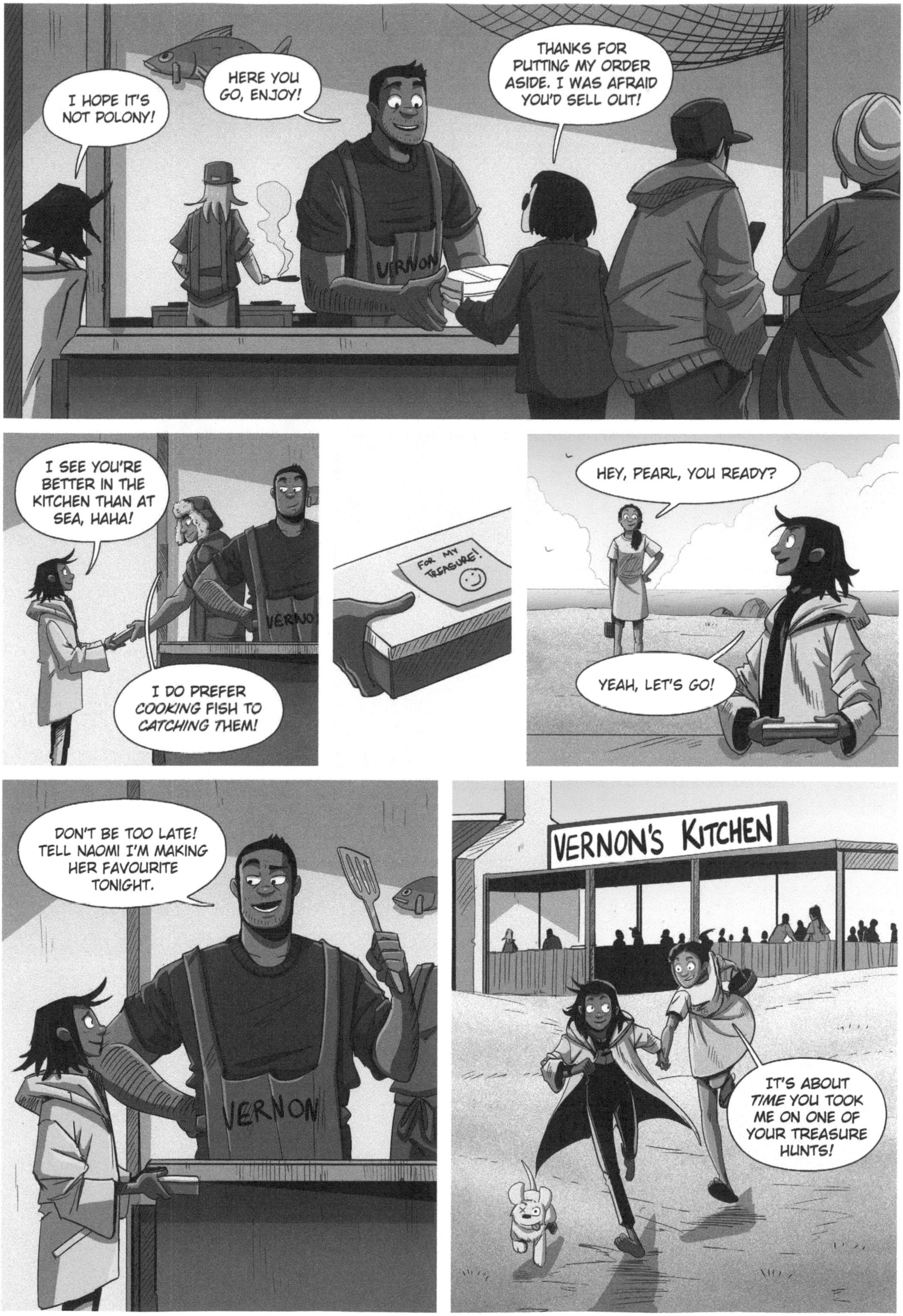
I HOPE IT'S NOT POLONY!
HERE YOU GO, ENJOY!
THANKS FOR PUTTING MY ORDER ASIDE. I WAS AFRAID YOU'D SELL OUT!
VERNON
I SEE YOU'RE BETTER IN THE KITCHEN THAN AT SEA, HAHA!
I DO PREFER *COOKING* FISH TO *CATCHING THEM!*
VERNON
FOR MY TREASURE!
HEY, PEARL, YOU READY?
YEAH, LET'S GO!
DON'T BE TOO LATE! TELL NAOMI I'M MAKING HER FAVOURITE TONIGHT.
VERNON
VERNON'S KITCHEN
IT'S ABOUT *TIME* YOU TOOK ME ON ONE OF YOUR TREASURE HUNTS!

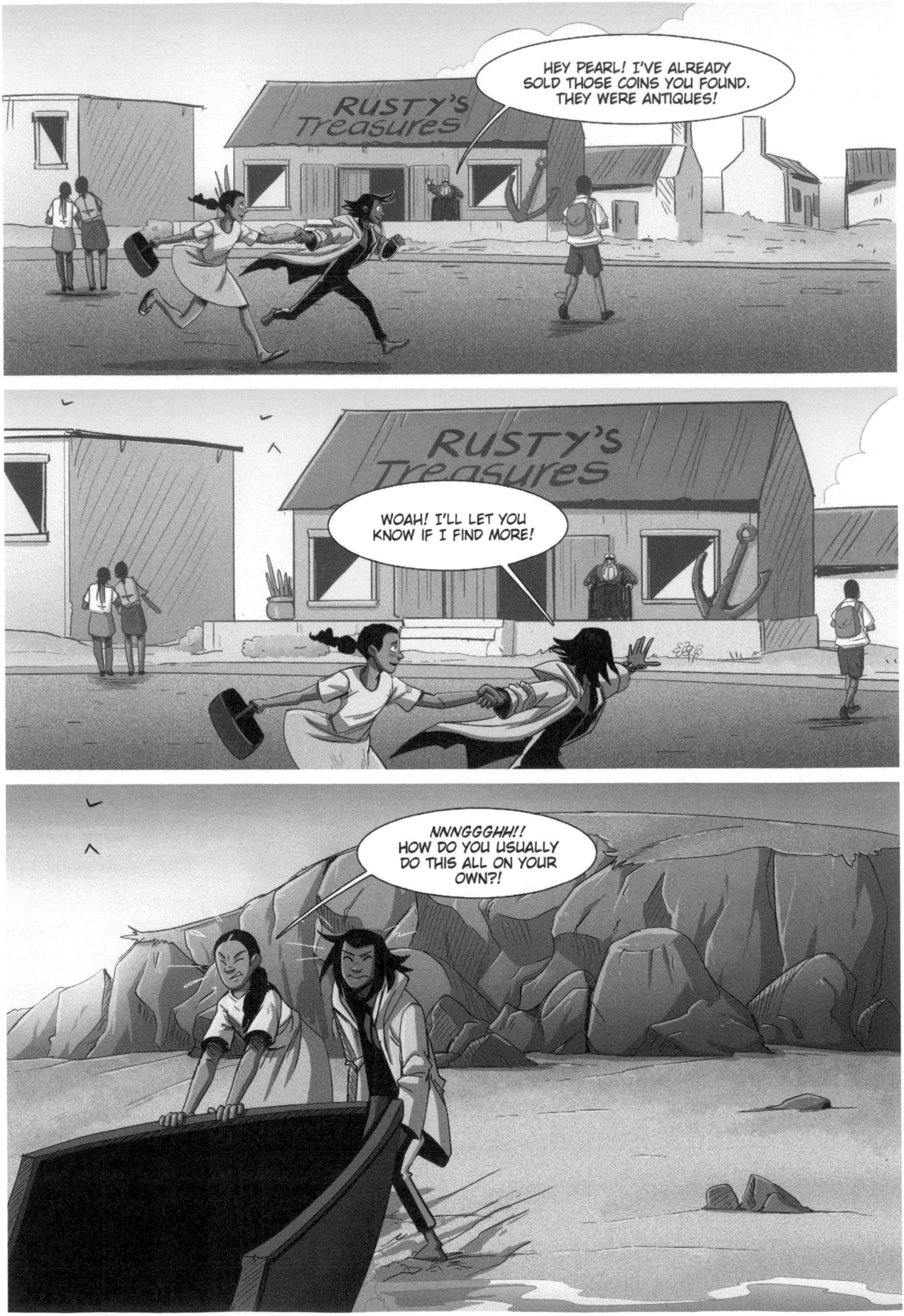
RUSTY'S Treasures
HEY PEARL! I'VE ALREADY SOLD THOSE COINS YOU FOUND. THEY WERE ANTIQUES!
RUSTY'S Treasures
WOAH! I'LL LET YOU KNOW IF I FIND MORE!
NNNGGGHH!! HOW DO YOU USUALLY DO THIS ALL ON YOUR OWN?!

WOOOOOo.

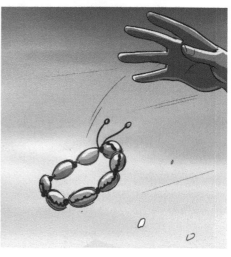

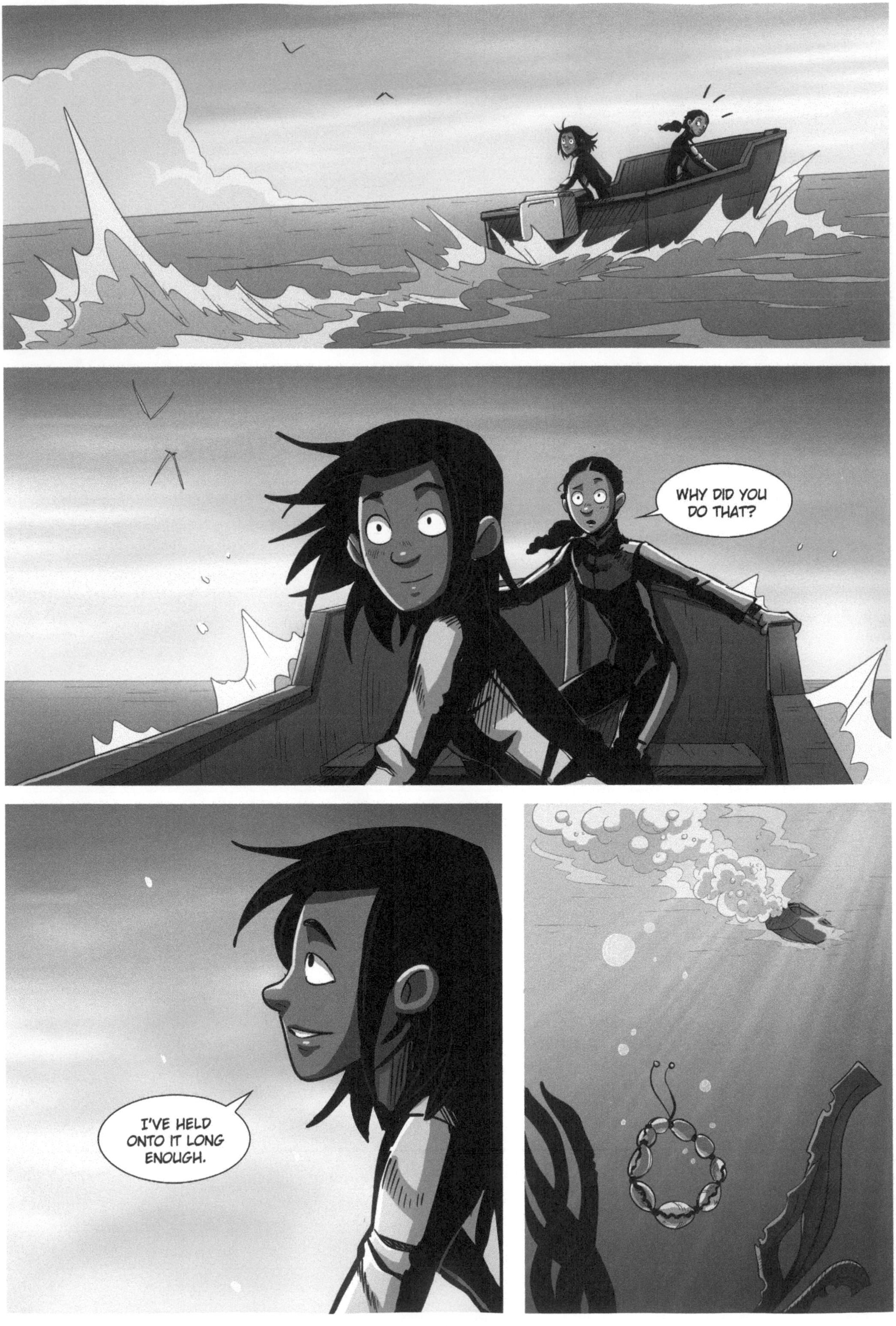
WHY DID YOU DO THAT?
I'VE HELD ONTO IT LONG ENOUGH.

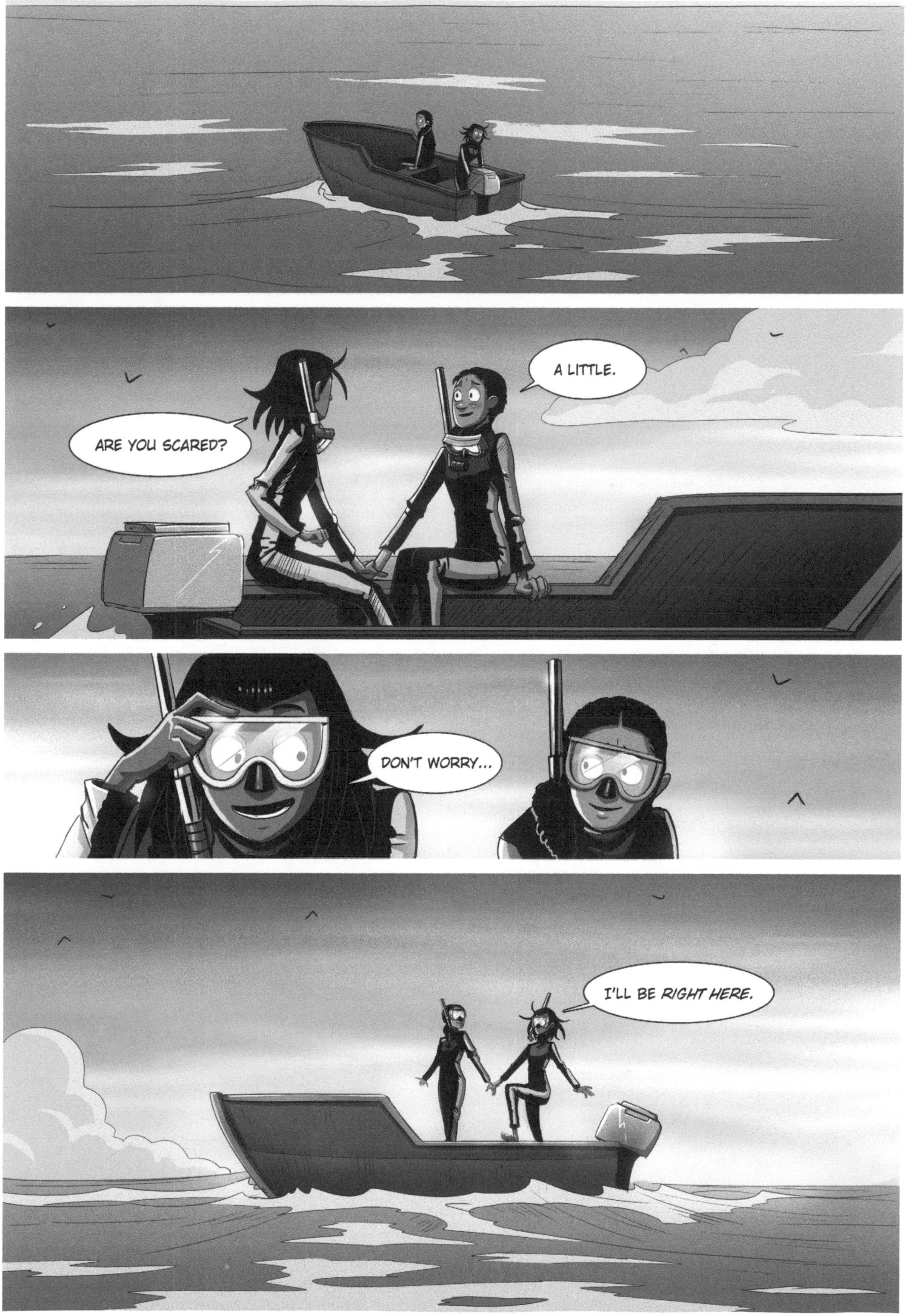
ARE YOU SCARED?
A LITTLE.
DON'T WORRY...
I'LL BE RIGHT HERE.

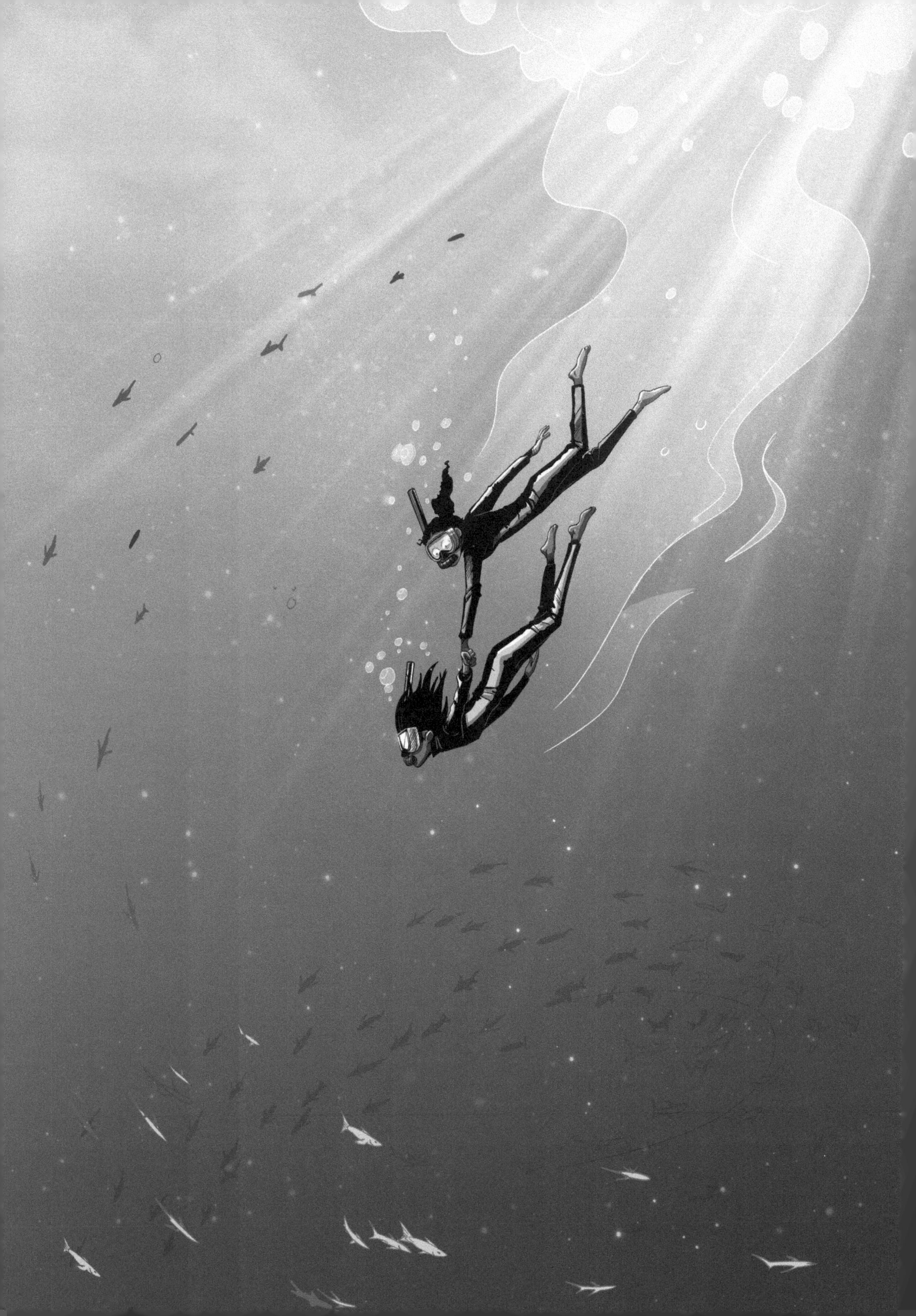

THE
END

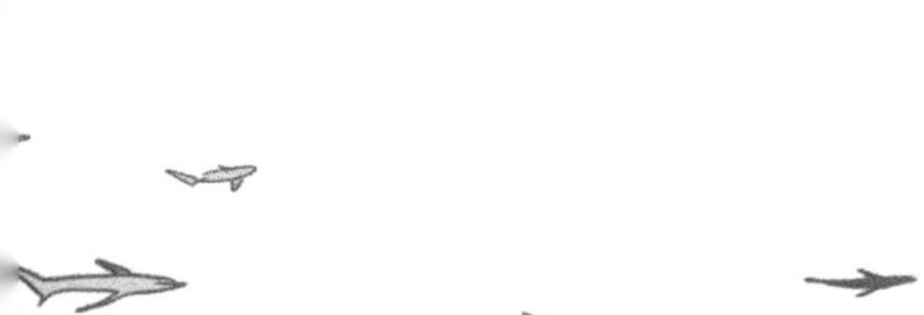

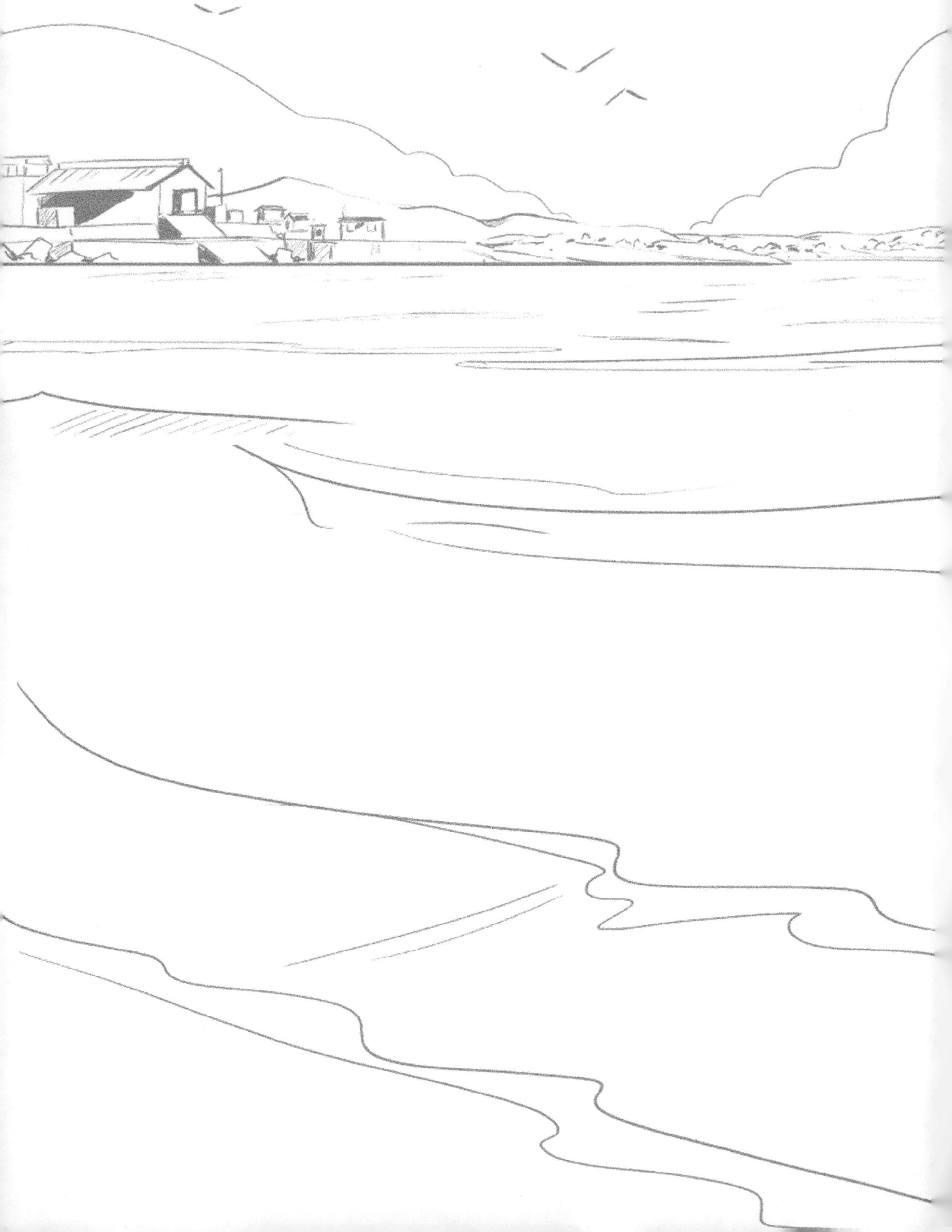

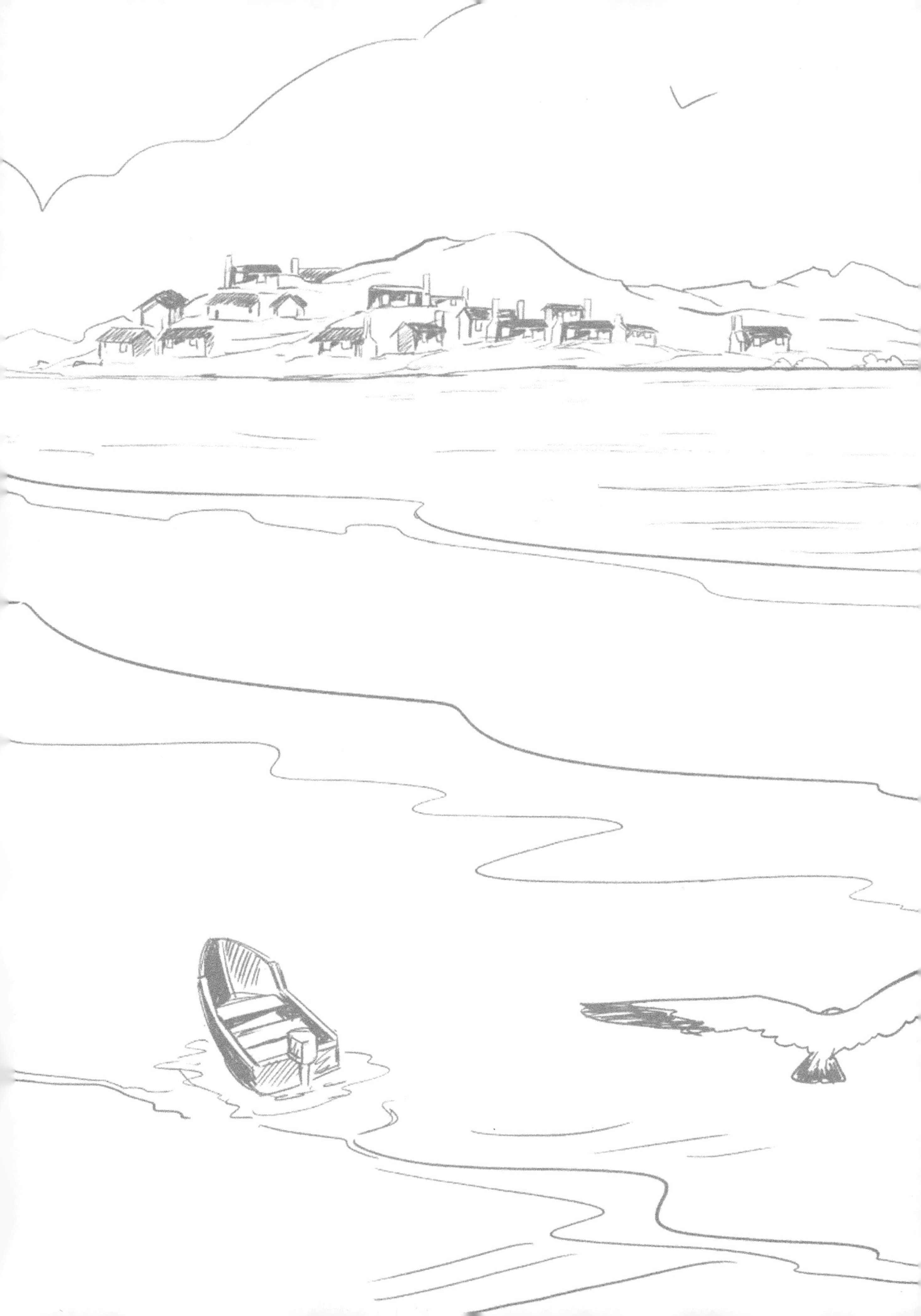

The award-winning creative team behind *Pearl of the Sea*

Anthony Silverston is partner and Head of Development at Triggerfish Animation Studios where he oversees a slate of projects including *Kizazi Moto: Generation Fire* with Disney+, *Mama K's Team 4* with Netflix, and *Kiya* with Disney, eOne and Frogbox, and a number of feature films and TV series. In 2015, he oversaw the Story Lab, which developed 4 feature films and 4 TV series chosen from a continent-wide search that drew almost 1400 entries. He directed and co-wrote the feature film *Khumba* and has written on *Seal Team* and *Zambezia*. Silverston was also producer of the short films *Troll Girl* and *Belly Flop* which screened at over 135 festivals and won 14 awards.

Raffaella Delle Donne has over fifteen years of experience in the animation industry developing and creating content for Disney, eOne, Wekids, Snipple Animation, Netflix, Baobab Studios and Triggerfish Animation Studios. She was the TV Development Executive for the Triggerfish Studios/Disney Storylab that incubated *Mama K's Team 4* and co-wrote the award-winning features *Adventures in Zambezia* and Khumba. Raffaella is currently a writer and Executive Creative Consultant on *Kiya and the Kimoja Heroes*, a new preschool show slated for release on Disney.

Willem Samuel is a visual artist working in animation and comic books. His comic work has featured in zines internationally, including the cult series *Bitterkomix* and the award-winning online anthology *Aces Weekly*. Previously, Willem Art Directed the pan-African comic *Supa Strikas*, which was adapted into an animated series. More recently he served as Head of Story on the animated feature *Seal Team* as well as creating concept art for the Warhammer+ streaming series, *Hammer & Bolter*.